D0115854

Influence

Influence

SARA SHEPARD AND
LILIA BUCKINGHAM

DELACORTE PRESS

This is a work of fiction. Names, characters, places, and incidents either are the product of the author's imagination or are used fictitiously. Any resemblance to actual persons, living or dead, events, or locales is entirely coincidental.

 Published in the United States by Delacorte Press, an imprint of Random House Children's Books, a division of Penguin Random House LLC, New York.

Delacorte Press is a registered trademark and the colophon is a trademark of Penguin Random House LLC.

Visit us on the Web! GetUnderlined.com

Educators and librarians, for a variety of teaching tools, visit us at RHTeachersLibrarians.com

Library of Congress Cataloging-in-Publication Data
Names: Shepard, Sara, author. | Buckingham, Lilia, author.
Title: Influence / Sara Shepard and Lilia Buckingham.
Description: First edition. | New York : Delacorte Press, [2021] | Summary: After her family moves to Los Angeles, Delilah Rollins, already a minor Internet celebrity, plunges into the competitive and glamorous world of social media influencers, but can cosmetics and good lighting conceal cheating, manipulation, blackmail, and murder?
Identifiers: LCCN 2019017480 | ISBN 978-0-593-12153-5 (hc) |
ISBN 978-0-593-12155-9 (ebook) | ISBN 978-0-593-18154-6 (intl. pbk.)
Subjects: | CYAC: Internet personalities—Fiction. | Social media—Fiction. | Fame—Fiction. | Murder—Fiction. | Los Angeles (Calif.)—Fiction.
Classification: LCC PZ7.S54324 In 2021 | DDC [Fic]—dc23

The text of this book is set in 11-point Freight Text.
Interior design by Ken Crossland

Printed in the United States of America
10 9 8 7 6 5 4 3 2 1
First Edition

Influence

PROLOGUE

What happened at Gratitude was not in my plans.

You see, in my world, we planned things very carefully. Everything we did, every move, every smile, every word out of our mouths—it was crafted. We showed you only what we wanted you to see. And, okay, a few things leaked recently that surprised you. But it was fine. I don't know about everyone else, but *I* had my life under control.

Or did I?

Gratitude Prom took place on a clear, warm evening in late June, and it started perfectly. All of you watched the stories and the live feeds and the update videos of me as I got ready (after having everything already done professionally off camera, of course). I posted updates as I piled into the limo that had been secured for free in exchange for a simple mention online. I posted more updates as I paraded down the red carpet. You, my dear fans, circulated my pictures all over the world as I posed with "friends." You shared and re-shared, you posted and re-posted, you made fan edits and comments. You gossiped. Sometimes you were even nasty about me. But I pretended not to notice. I stayed on message, on-brand.

But as I headed to the after-party, which took place in the lavish apartment complex where many of us lived, I started to feel . . . nervous. I told myself to get a grip. Everything was going to be okay in the end—I had it covered. But so many people were angry with me. So many were *disappointed.* Some of you were over me, or thought I didn't deserve to be where I was and *what* I was: famous. And maybe I was right to worry, because look what happened at the end of the night. I barely remembered those blurry, messy hours. The arguments. The betrayal. The pain. The sheer surprise of it all. I barely remembered screaming, and then storming off, and then spinning, and then yelling, and then closing my eyes.

And then . . . *nothing.*

But here's the thing: Don't hate me for filling up your feeds. Don't hate me for the brands I convinced you to buy, the movies I goaded you to see. Don't resent me for the gossip I dropped, breadcrumb-like, for you to devour, obsess over, *believe.* I was what you needed. I was your guiding light, people. That was why they called me an influencer—I had influence over millions of you. But that perfect little world you thought you were witnessing? It was mostly lies. My smiles and sweetness, my big hugs and happy hashtags: it was all a juicy, duplicitous trick for you to share and discuss and gobble up. And those lies were what destroyed me, plain and simple.

But maybe you don't want to hear that. Maybe you'd rather believe I was exactly who you saw on your screens: a girl who was beautiful, unflappable, and untouchable.

And, most importantly, still alive.

One month earlier

DELILAH

Delilah Rollins was going to a very, very important party.

She sat in the back of her family's nondescript SUV—as though her mom, Bethany, was an Uber driver and she was the passenger—biting her nails in excitement and terror. Her mom clutched the steering wheel and fitfully murmured about the chaos of LA traffic, a city the family was brand-new to as of six days earlier, when they'd moved there from Minneapolis. To say they were having culture shock was a major understatement.

"So tell me again what this thing is?" Bethany asked warily, cursing under her breath as another driver cut her off.

Delilah shifted. "It's for Wellness Beauty. It should be great. A lot of influencers and celebrities will be there, there will be tons of photo ops, free stuff . . ."

Delilah's sister, Ava, who was also sitting in the backseat, turned, eyes gleaming. "Ooh, can you get me an eyeshadow palette?"

Bethany frowned. "You're too young for makeup, Ava."

Ava pouted. "Fourteen isn't too young!"

Bethany ignored this, glancing at Delilah again in the rearview mirror. "Who invited you?"

Delilah felt the same thrill that she had when she'd first gotten the invitation. *Only one of the most famous people on the planet invited me, actually.* But she couldn't tell her mom that. It might freak her out. Her mom was wary of famous people, especially *influencers.* "Just some people I know online," she said casually.

"In other words, *strangers.*" Bethany shook her head. "Maybe I should come in with you."

"No!" Delilah begged. "You can't! I'll be fine!"

The argument was curtailed because Delilah's mom had to make a scary merge onto an eight-lane highway. Delilah swallowed hard, then looked at her phone. On the screen was pretty much the most amazing thing that had ever happened to Delilah in her life: a direct Instagram message from @LuluJasmine, aka Jasmine Walters-Diaz, aka Lulu C from *That's Hot!*, Delilah's favorite dance show on Lemonade, which was the Netflix for tweens and teens. Delilah had the message memorized: *Hey, Delilah! I'm a huge fan, and I live in LA, too! I'd love to invite you to a party for Wellness Beauty on Tuesday afternoon at the Evensong Hotel on the Strip! Let me know if you can make it!*

She still wasn't sure it was real.

Twenty million people followed Jasmine's account on Instagram. The posts where Jasmine wore the rainbow skirt and lace leotard, the iconic outfit Lulu C was known for, practically broke the internet. Delilah had no idea how Jasmine found *her* page. Could it really have been from her *Hey, I just moved to LA and*

I'm freaking out! she'd put on her Story a few days back? Delilah was suspicious of Jasmine's message, but her account had the "I'm verified and you're not" blue checkmark . . . so maybe it was true.

As if on cue, Delilah's friend Busy, the only person Delilah *did* tell about her brand-new, über-delicate, maybe-celebrity-friendship, texted. *YOU HAVE TO TELL ME EVERYTHING ABOUT JASMINE,* she wrote. *She's going to replace me as your BFF because I'll be marooned in France on a digital diet.* Busy's family was leaving for a five-week European vacation tomorrow, and her parents had decided that Busy and her younger brother, Brock, would be leaving their phones at home. Which sounded like a particularly torturous circle of hell.

You're going to forget all about me! a new bubble from Busy read.

Oh stop, Delilah wrote back. *No one can replace you.*

She was just as heartbroken as Busy was that a) Busy wouldn't be able to talk all summer, and b) they now no longer lived in the same city, thanks to Delilah's father's internal transfer at his environmental sustainability firm. Delilah and Busy had been friends since first grade, when they both carried matching One Direction backpacks. Busy introduced her to Instagram. They explored Snapchat together. They filmed videos on YouTube about how to make fluffy slime and how to apply Technicolor hair dye without it getting on the carpet. They did normal, non-internet things, too: volleyball tournaments, nights out for pizza, sleepovers, avoiding their pesky little siblings . . . but they weren't as *good* at those things. As time went on, Delilah and Busy became masters at creating stylized, online versions of themselves—kids sought them out for advice on how to craft posts or light pictures or curate daily stories.

And then, just this past March, it happened. Delilah's account went from a meager few thousand followers to hundreds of thousands. And from there, things just . . . *exploded.* Hence Jasmine's DM . . . maybe. Hence Delilah's jittery feeling like she was on the precipice of something . . . *huge.*

Soon, they pulled up to a concrete-colored hotel building flanked by guitar stores. Delilah had a very limited knowledge of Los Angeles, but she was pretty sure this wasn't the coolest part of the Sunset Strip. Her mother wrinkled her nose as though the music shops were drug dens.

"Electric guitars are very high-end!" Delilah chirped brightly.

"I think it looks awesome!" Ava piped up. "You're so lucky, Lila."

Delilah glanced at her sister. Ava was small for her age; today, she was wearing a striped romper from Gap Kids. But her booties were fashionable, as was her black leather crossbody. Back in Minneapolis, Ava hung out with a sweet, well-behaved crowd of girls, but the first day they arrived in California, Delilah received a follow request on her Instagram from @AvaBLove, and there was a tiny thumbnail image of Ava's face as the profile picture.

Bethany pulled into a parking spot and shifted into park. "I'm staying here, by the way. You can go in by yourself, but if you don't send me an A-OK text every thirty minutes, I will assume someone is trying to abduct you into either child slavery or a rock band."

"What about me?" Ava piped up. "Can I peek inside?"

"*You're* not going anywhere. I'm conflicted enough about this as it is." Bethany pointed to Delilah. "Have you tested your glucose recently?"

"God, Mom, *yes.*" Delilah had been given a diagnosis of Type 1 diabetes when she was nine—in other words, a zillion years ago, so she had the whole regular-testing-and-insulin-shots down cold. "I have all my stuff." She patted her bag full of supplies. "Don't worry."

"I always worry!" Bethany cried.

Delilah darted out of the car, but then she circled back, leaned through her mom's open window, and gave her mom and sister a grateful smile. "Love you guys."

There were butterflies in her stomach as she entered the Evensong Hotel. The lobby smelled like peppermint gum. To the left was a sign announcing the Wellness Beauty party in the event space. Two polished, pretty girls in low-cut sweaters Delilah would be grounded for wearing sat behind a long table, checking names off a guest list. Delilah felt a pull in her chest when they eyed her. *You're out of your league.*

Then she peered into the event itself. It buzzed with influencers and photo ops and who's-whos. Online stars Delilah recognized smushed together for pictures. A famous beauty influencer was speaking onstage to a group of adoring fans. Every time someone new walked into the room, heads turned to see if it was someone they should know.

Oh God. This felt like too much. Maybe she should—

"Excuse me?" A tall, skinny girl with long, fake eyelashes looked at Delilah. "Did I just see you on *Ellen*?"

"*Jimmy Fallon,* actually," Delilah admitted, astonished someone was speaking to her. "Last month."

"Right, I remember you." The skinny girl smiled. "What's your handle again?"

"Lila D," Delilah answered. Fake Eyelashes looked blank, so she added: "Puppy Girl."

Fake Eyelashes brightened, then tugged another girl's sleeve. "Gigi, it's *Puppy Girl*! You know, the one who rescued that adorable golden retriever puppy from that fire?"

And suddenly, people were swarming around Delilah. *Just like that.* It was astonishing how one video could change your life. For Delilah, it was a shaky clip Busy shot of Delilah running into a neighbor's burning shed and coming out, moments later, with a golden retriever puppy in her arms. The whole thing was a foolish, split-second decision—her mother grounded her for it, actually, because what idiot besides a firefighter *runs into a burning building*?

But then the video caught on. Went viral. Delilah was suddenly a hero. The clip appeared on a local news show and then, two days later, the *Today* show. Delilah received a flood of new followers and endless phone calls for interviews and, finally, she was asked to make a guest appearance on *Jimmy Fallon*—yes, *the* Jimmy Fallon. During the taping, Fallon kept calling Delilah "the Animal Angel."

"Delilah?" another voice rang out.

Delilah swung around. A gorgeous, dark-haired girl with blown-out hair and a colorful dress hurried up to her. Delilah tried not to gasp. Was that really *Jasmine*? In person?

"So happy you made it!" Jasmine cried in her signature husky Lulu C voice, throwing her arms around Delilah's shoulders. "I am such a big fan!"

"Me too," Delilah spluttered. She felt people watching. It made her feel important . . . but also really, *really* humble.

Jasmine gestured to a willowy girl with caramel skin and gorgeous, flowing red hair next to her. "I want to introduce you to—"

"—Fiona Jacobs," Delilah gushed, starstruck. "I watch your *Sizzle or Drizzle* videos all the time!" She couldn't wait to tell Busy. The two of them binged on Fiona Jacobs's award-show fashion critiques like the episodes were cherry Twizzlers. They loved how *normal* Fiona seemed, despite her otherworldly beauty. And today, Fiona lived up to that: she was dressed more casually than Jasmine, in almost weekend/athleisure attire, but the skinny jeans she had on seemed cut specifically for her body, and her T-shirt fit differently than Delilah's rotating cast of tees from Old Navy, which stretched out after the first wash. Jasmine and Fiona were both carrying identical, U-shaped handbags in buttery beiges and grays. They had to be a name brand—but *what* name? Delilah doubted they were Kate Spade or Rebecca Minkoff, the "it" bags at her old high school. These bags looked like Kate Spade's worldlier cousins.

"Your posts are so cute," Fiona told Delilah. "Whenever I need my puppy fix, I'm like, *Lila D's my jam.* And that puppy rescue! That was, like, amazing."

"I cried," Jasmine volunteered. "After I watched it, I cradled my own puppy and was like, *Oh my God, I will keep you safe* forever."

"Were you scared, running into that shed like that?" Fiona's eyes went wide.

Delilah fiddled with a string on her jumpsuit. "Yeah, of course.

But I had no choice, you know?" After the puppy rescue, people assumed she was really brave, when the reality was she barely had the confidence to speak up in class.

"Well, listen." Jasmine touched Delilah's shoulder. "Consider me and Fiona your welcoming committee. Anything you need, we're here to help."

"We love normal, grounded people on social," Fiona added. "And we try to be, too!"

Jasmine nudged her. "You're *so* not normal. You're lost without a personal assistant!"

"Oh my God, it's been *four days,*" Fiona moaned dramatically. "And I'm losing my mind." She looked at Delilah. "Do you know a good personal assistant?"

"Ha!" Delilah laughed. She wasn't really sure what a personal assistant *did.* "So where do you go to school?" Maybe they'd be going to the same place. She was pretty sure Fiona was under eighteen.

It took Fiona a moment to process Delilah's question. "Oh, I don't go to normal school anymore. I do online." She giggled bemusedly. "Are you planning to go to regular school? Five days a week and all that?"

Delilah felt her cheeks flush. "Uh . . . yeah? My parents enrolled me somewhere called Ventura Prep."

Jasmine gave her a knowing look. "Let's see if that actually happens by the time fall rolls around."

She was about to say something else when the sound of clicking heels echoed across the marble floors. The ions in the lobby rearranged as a new group stalked past. All faces turned to view the passing crowd—and who was at its center, a tall girl with glowing skin; bouncy, white-blond hair; and a curvy, flawless body. The dress she wore had cutouts just below the boobs and along her thighs, leaving little to the imagination.

The girl's gaze flitted to Jasmine and Fiona. "Hey, guys," she said in a blasé voice.

Jasmine's and Fiona's smiles didn't reach their eyes. "Hi, Scarlet."

Her identity came to Delilah like a bolt: *Scarlet Leigh,* aka @ScarletLetter. Delilah didn't stalk Scarlet Leigh's account religiously, but she was practically a Kardashian. She was on every Sexiest Girl Alive list, she'd received sponsorship deals for everything ranging from a small-batch whiskey maker to an airline that likely gave her free tickets to fly anywhere on their roster as long as she featured them in a post. Delilah even heard a rumor that Scarlet was auditioning for a comedy pilot.

Scarlet breezed into the ballroom. Jasmine turned to Fiona, making a face. "You okay, Fee?"

"I'm fine," Fiona mumbled. "Scarlet and I aren't, like, enemies or whatever."

"In what universe?" Jasmine whispered. "That girl has it in for you! And it's not even your fault!"

"What's not your fault?" Delilah asked, feeling lost.

Fiona tapped her perfectly done acrylic nails on her phone three times. It seemed to be an unconscious habit. "Scarlet and I both went to Harvard-Westlake in tenth grade . . . and she claims I stole her boyfriend away."

"That girl hates losing," Jasmine muttered. Then her phone beeped. She glanced at it, then squeezed Delilah's arm. "Listen, I have to run. I have a shoot in thirty minutes."

"You're . . . leaving?" Delilah hated the desperate tone of her voice.

"Yeah, but let's hang out soon. And you should totally check out the stuff inside!" Jasmine gestured to the ballroom. "There's awesome merch. And get your pictures with some other influencers! That's the whole point of these things. Pics build your following."

"It's a lot of fun," Fiona said—she had to leave, too. "Let me get your number. Let's keep in touch. Any questions, *please* text me. Okay?" And the girls were gone.

Delilah was suddenly alone in the bustling Evensong lobby. The conversation she'd just had was overwhelming. Did she really just chat with Jasmine Walters-Diaz and Fiona Jacobs? Days ago, she was sitting on Busy's carpet, making vision boards about being a famous influencer . . . and now she was in the middle of that world?

She peered into the big ballroom of famous people and felt massive stage fright. She couldn't do this alone. She wanted to hide in a booth at the restaurant next to the lobby, order fries and a Coke, and scroll on her phone until an hour passed and she could find her mom.

Which was exactly what she did.

It felt like heaven to sink down into a booth. She gave the waiter a huge smile when he came around to take her order. "Would you like the wine list?" he asked, barely looking at her.

"Um, *what*?" Did he not notice how young she was? "I—I mean . . . no. I'll have . . ."

"*I* think she needs a purple punch."

Delilah turned sharply to the right. On the other side of the banquette, half-concealed in shadows, was a guy with pale green eyes and soft, floppy chestnut hair. He sat up and smiled. There was a dimple on his left cheek, and his front tooth was rakishly, almost intentionally crooked, like he had it fixed to slant that way.

Delilah shot to her feet. "Oh my gosh. I didn't see you there. I-I'll move."

"It's cool. I don't mind sharing the booth."

"Oh." Was he an influencer? He was certainly cute enough. Or maybe an agent? She'd heard a lot of influencers had those.

She glanced toward the lobby. "I'm only here for a second. I just got . . . hungry." It was a lame thing to say, considering the ballroom was likely full of snacks.

A new batch of screams rose up from the lobby; it seemed another internet celebrity had arrived. The guy broke his gaze for a beat, then turned back to her, his grin even wider. "Is this your first one of these?" he asked.

She ducked her head. "Is it that obvious?"

"That's not a bad thing." He leaned back. "What sort of world are we living in where random people are über-famous? People who just . . . make videos, or take photos, or are . . . *a personality*?" He gave her a baffled smile. "What's happened to humanity?"

Delilah chuckled. "You sound like my mom."

He pointed at her. "You're *lucky* she's like that. Most influencer parents are the ones steering the plane. Total Momagers."

"So I guess you aren't on social, then?"

"Oh no, I am." He held up his hands in surrender. "Guilty as charged. YouTube."

Delilah's mouth dropped. She didn't follow guys on YouTube in the same way she followed girls. Watching a guy online didn't feel very intimate. She'd rather get to know one in person.

A drink appeared. She'd forgotten that this guy had ordered her a purple punch. She sniffed it, trying to determine whether it contained alcohol, but she only smelled blueberries.

The guy crossed his arms. "I'm probably supposed to know who you are, too, right?"

"Oh, I'm no one," Delilah said quickly.

"I doubt that." A coy look came over his features. "I know. How about you *guess* what my deal might be online. And I'll guess yours."

It felt like a trick question. Delilah worried she'd say something to offend him. Some sort of niche he absolutely, categorically hated. Or maybe she shouldn't overthink it. Maybe she could just be silly, the way she used to be with guys back home.

The guy's hair was carefully tousled. His T-shirt pulled against his chest and abs but wasn't skintight. Someone might pass him on the street and think nothing of him, only to turn back and think, *Wait, that guy was gorgeous.*

She cleared her throat, going for silly. "Tide Pods. You've gotten famous by eating Tide Pods." She smacked her forehead. "I can't *believe* I didn't recognize you."

He burst out laughing. "Hit the nail on the head! I love eating Tide Pods, girl! Give me more of that toxic grittiness!" He pretended to pop one in his mouth, chew, and then gag and spit it out. Delilah applauded his acting skills—and maybe *this* was why she didn't watch guys online, because they all seemed to do stupid things like eat laundry detergent or put their dogs' shock collars on their necks.

He crossed his arms. "My turn."

She felt his eyes wash over her, first looking at her hair and then her body. His gaze wasn't predatory, but it was interested. Her heart thudded. *Please don't guess Puppy Girl.* Delilah didn't want to be thought of as *just* Puppy Girl. She posted about animal activism and safe pet ownership, and adopting pets versus buying from puppy mills. And she wanted to post about other issues, too. Body acceptance. Anti-bullying. Diabetes awareness. She wanted to inspire. It was a huge reason why the move to LA felt so exciting. Maybe she could break into this universe for real—and help people.

"My Little Pony," he decided. "You adore My Little Pony toys, and you make videos that act out their adventures. You have over twenty-one million followers on YouTube. Your favorite pony to be is Fluttershy, because she's shy but really damn cute."

Delilah's mouth dropped. "Look at *you* dropping My Little Pony knowledge."

"I've got a little sister who's into the show. And maybe I watch it sometimes, too. You know there's a whole subset of us guys who watch it, right? *Bronies?*"

"I definitely need to have you on my channel. You can be my special Brony guest, if you play your cards right . . ." She trailed off. "What's your name?"

"Jack," he answered. "For real. And yours?"

"Delilah."

"Delilah," he repeated. "Pretty."

Chills traveled up her arms. He hitched forward until their knees touched. He was so close she could see the gold flecks in his eyes. *Oh my God,* she thought. *Are we going to kiss?*

There was a noise behind them, and Jack bolted up. No one was there, but he seemed unruffled. He checked the time on his phone. "Man. I have to be somewhere." He reached into his pocket and dropped a few twenties on the table. "I'm sorry to cut this short."

"Oh . . . can I follow you . . . I mean . . . on YouTube . . . not . . . ?" Delilah heard her voice wobble. *Mortifying.*

"Definitely." He blinked his long lashes. "I'll find you, okay? I promise."

He hurried out the revolving door to the street. Maybe he was just a guest at the hotel? Maybe he was on YouTube but had a teensy account?

But then she heard whispers. *"Did you see who that just was?"* And *"I wish I'd gotten a picture."* A girl chased him out the revolving door. "Jack Dono! Love you!"

The guy Delilah had been talking to saluted the girl. It felt like someone had poured a bucket of cold water over Delilah's head. *Jack Dono*? As in *the* comedy YouTuber? Busy adored him. He mostly filmed silly pranks, like driving his parents' beat-up Honda into a big pond in his backyard, or rigging a giant chariot for his two Greater Swiss Mountain Dogs to pull him on in the snow. . . .

He was the most famous guy around.

Except there was something else Delilah was pretty sure she should've known about him. Over the years, Jack's posts changed. Many were still a mix of adrenaline sports goofs, but they were also about his girlfriend. There was a whole fan base about their ship. Rabid fans created accounts re-posting adorable photos of them, images of what their babies might look like, and any scrap of couple gossip they could find. They even had a ship nickname. It was . . .

Delilah gasped. It was *Jacklet.* Jack plus Scarlet, aka Scarlet Leigh from Scarlet Letter—the intimidating girl Delilah had seen in the lobby. They were the most famous ship around.

She needed to get out of here.

Ducking her head, she ran into the lobby and out the front door. "Whoa, that was quick," Bethany said as Delilah threw herself into the backseat and exclaimed, as though she'd just robbed a bank, "Drive, drive, drive!"

Thank goodness she did. Because just as they pulled out of the lot, Delilah's phone began to buzz. *Breaking news.* She noticed Jack's name. And the caption: *IS JACKLET OVER?*—and a blurry picture of Jack sitting on a very familiar banquette . . . smiling at someone across from him. The girl's face wasn't pictured, but Delilah knew exactly who it was.

Her.

JASMINE

Jasmine Walters-Diaz settled into the back of a Cadillac Escalade and rolled up the windows, cutting the fluorescent California sunlight to a thin, anemic glare. It didn't quite block out the image of the people lingering on the curb, though, so she blew her fans one last kiss. An admirer with a T-shirt with Jasmine's face on it and a pin that said she was from Utah looked like she was about to faint.

"Jazz."

Fingers snapped in Jasmine's face. Jasmine's twenty-three-year-old sister, Ruby, sat across from her with an iPad in her lap. "Let's run through your itinerary for the afternoon."

Jasmine shut her eyes. "We already did that at the salon."

"Yeah, but you hadn't had your cold brew yet. Let's do it again, just to make sure."

A soft brush touched her cheek from the left. That was Angie, Jasmine's makeup artist. Sometimes Jasmine had her hairstylist,

Carina, in the car as well, but she'd just had a blowout, so lucky Carina had the day off.

As Angie brushed Jasmine's cheeks with highlighter, Ruby began to recite. "We're going to the shoot with Nike for your rainbow line."

Jasmine glanced down at her outfit. As usual, she was dolled up in a rainbow-themed dress and high white heels, with big, blown-out hair. It had been her look for eight years, since she was eleven and played Lulu C on *That's Hot!* on Lemonade. *Surprise, more rainbows,* she thought sarcastically. Anyone who wanted to do a capsule fashion or makeup or hair accessories line with Jasmine never deviated from the rainbow idea. If she were known for playing Batman, maybe they'd always go with a black, leathery theme. People didn't like thinking outside the box, apparently. Though to be fair, it was a box that had changed her family's life for the better.

"Then it looks like you're free from three until four, but I'd use it to catch up on your video content and replying to some of your DMs. Unless you'd like Sasha to do it?"

"That's okay." Sasha was Jasmine's assistant, and though she was great at impersonating Jasmine in DMs, Jasmine felt bad fooling her fans into thinking they were talking to her when really it was someone else.

"And then you have to approve designs for your label—they're in already, which is awesome. After that, we have to swing by the Brandy Melville flagship because we haven't been giving them very much love. I'd also really like to stop by Children's Hospital and get a few key photos with some of the kids in treatment because I think that really humanizes your page."

"And it's nice to see the kids," Jasmine added as Angie swiped mascara over her lashes.

Ruby paused from tapping her phone. "Huh?"

Jasmine didn't bother repeating. One of her favorite things to do—besides lying around her bedroom and reading, or checking her own *private* social media accounts, which she only shared with a select few—was spend time at Children's Hospital. Years ago, she'd lost her best friend, Lucy, to leukemia; she'd been barely there for Lucy because she was in the middle of filming *That's Hot!* The kids she now visited in the cancer ward didn't jostle her for a photo or shame her for designing ugly clothes. They were just happy someone was chilling with them.

"But it looks like your evening is free." Ruby's brow wrinkled. "Well, there's always the party at the Pier—they'd be thrilled if you came. Or—aha. There's that thing Cosabella is sponsoring . . ." But then she seemed to second-guess this. "Actually, never mind. Über-sexy lingerie might freak out some of your sponsors."

Jasmine peered at the huge billboards whipping past. Famous faces were frozen in all kinds of expressions—joy, anger, intensity, longing. "I could just do my own thing tonight. I could call Fiona, we could order smoothies . . ."

Ruby stopped her. "You're under contract with Kreation. Snap a photo. They'll love it."

Jasmine rolled her eyes. "Sure. Whatever." Sometimes, Ruby didn't just manage, she *micromanaged.* Then again, Jasmine never thought having such a big web presence would be so much work. Back when she was just on TV, things weren't like this.

It was a trade-off. If she wanted to do what she loved—

acting—then she had to embrace everything that came with it. Like today: there were three changes of wardrobe in her trunk. The outfits depended on where Jasmine was in the city, and who she thought might photograph her, and what she wanted to wear for her Instagram and Snapchat Stories at a particular time of day. Jasmine had people who styled these looks—and usually, yes, they were quite colorful, to keep with the Lulu C brand—but Jasmine wanted to be involved just a little, because if she left it to the professionals, they'd totally overdo the Lulu, and Jasmine would look ridiculous.

All of a sudden, Ruby's eyes bugged at something on her screen. "I can't believe it."

She turned her phone for Jasmine to see. An unknown Instagram account showed a blurry succession of images at the restaurant within the Evensong Hotel. A couple sat at a banquette, the guy's face visible, the girl just a mass of dark hair and a crossed leg. As the shots progressed, the guy laughed, then gazed at her lovingly, and then he leaned over like he was about to kiss her.

"That's Jack Dono!" Ruby exclaimed.

"Scarlet's Jack?" Jasmine squinted. That girl definitely wasn't Scarlet Leigh.

"People are going to *freak*." Ruby's eyes gleamed; she adored scandal. "You should comment. Side with the shippers. You're Team Jacklet, right?"

"It's their business. I'm staying out of it."

Ruby pouted. "You need to put more relationship stuff on your pages, Jazz. You realize that's the number one thing searched about you on Google? *Jasmine Walters-Diaz relationship.* People want Jasmine to date."

"You mean they want Lulu C to date." In her fandom's dreams, they wanted Jasmine to marry Luke Lording—aka Archer, her old costar on *That's Hot!* "Archer" was in "Lulu's" dance company. All the six seasons of the show were about Archer pursuing pure-as-the-driven-snow Lulu, and Lulu doing something flirtatious but, in the end, telling Archer she was waiting for marriage to even go to first base. Only in the series finale did they kiss. The fandom lost its mind.

But in real life? Well, if Luke were on his deathbed in a cancer ward, Jasmine would totally stop by and chill with him. But otherwise, they didn't have that much in common.

Jasmine and her crew were pulling up to Nike now. People lingered on the sidewalk, gawking at who might be inside the big car with the tinted windows. When Jasmine stepped out, the crowd became galvanized. "Jasmine!" they yelled, lifting their phones to capture Jasmine's picture. "Lulu C!" just as many of them called.

Jasmine didn't bother correcting them that Lulu C was a work of fiction. It wouldn't matter. To everyone in the universe, Jasmine and Lulu C were one and the same.

After four hours posing with sneakers, Jasmine was finally home, walking through the front doors of the Dove, a sunny, pretty condo building on Vine in Hollywood. Jasmine had bought the condo the moment she turned eighteen; she liked it for its beautiful views from the rooftop deck, its walkability to all her favorite shops and grocery stores, and its brand-newness, everything shiny and dust-free and not showing the rot that most of LA worked so feverishly to hide. The zero-edge pool on the sundeck was often empty. There was a dog run for her miniature poodle, Cosmo, and then a dog wash if his paws got dirty. Jasmine's penthouse felt like home the moment she walked in—way more like home than where she grew up. But, well, that was another reason why she chose the place: it wasn't far from where her family lived. She didn't want to fight crosstown traffic every time they needed her.

Not long after Jasmine moved in, Fiona Jacobs, an influencer friend she'd grown close to, had her parents cosign a purchase for a condo on a lower floor. Fiona wasn't yet eighteen—so technically, she couldn't live there on her own—but she was there often enough, doing shoots, filming content. More influencers migrated there, too. It was as if they were all trying to re-create the ultimate dorm life—a life, ironically, most of them chose not to experience. It was the kind of herd mentality that was so prevalent in this world—when one person was doing something that looked amazing in photos, the community followed suit, even if it meant completely uprooting one's life. Still, the light inside the apartments was great for flat-lays and outfit-of-the-day shots, for baking videos and quick clips showing how to do the perfect ab crunch. It was also only a few blocks from the YouTube and Instagram offices. Building services hired artists to regularly repaint the murals downstairs, and each apartment had a different unique structure—which provided opportunities for content.

So it was great for networking, anyway. It was also why fans of Jasmine and others saw all their favorite social stars posing together on Instagram so often. They literally lived on top of one another.

Jasmine took the elevator up to the twenty-seventh floor and greeted Cosmo at her front door. "Okay, okay," she cried, gently nudging the little dog away from her calves. "I'm so sorry, baby, but I'm not staying long."

Cosmo followed Jasmine to her bedroom, where she stripped off her rainbow everything, plunged into her closet, and perused the 90 percent of clothes she couldn't wear for public appearances. These items were made of rich leathers, sexy silks, clingy denim; their colors were dark and moody, which suited her olive skin, light brown eyes, and sleek, dark hair. Her collection of colorful shoes, many of which had absolutely no wear on the soles, stood at attention on shelves. They were like her private art collection—most were way too sexy for Lulu C's innocent feet.

She grabbed a pair of stiletto sling-backs, a pair of skinny leather leggings, a black, cropped T-shirt, and a long cashmere duster, which was essential. When she was done, she stared at herself in the mirror. Her face looked more angular without all the bright colors against her skin.

Cosmo danced around her as she selected a new handbag and located the Amazon box that had come in the mail. Inside was a black, bejeweled satin mask. She lifted it out and slid it over her eyes. Now she *really* looked like someone else.

She used her second phone to call an Uber. Ruby didn't know she owned this second device; she used it to log on to her private social accounts. Jasmine wished she could leave her real phone at home, but that would raise all sorts of red flags if Ruby tried to reach her in an emergency and couldn't track down where she was.

The Uber arrived quickly. Jasmine climbed into a red Toyota Prius, said a terse hello to the driver, and then begrudgingly glanced at why her "official" cell phone was binging even more incessantly than usual. The screen was full of notifications from Ruby, DMs from fans, and a snap from Fiona about the "Mystery Girl" Jack Dono had been spotted with. *Scarlet is going to be pissed,* Fiona had texted.

Jasmine started to type *Serves her right* but then erased it. It was bad karma to relish someone else's scandal, even if it *was* Scarlet Leigh. Scarlet had always been one of *those* girls, though. She'd always had something against Jasmine, acting aloof and snobbish whenever they were in the same room—which was often, because they turned up at the same events and both lived at the Dove. Jasmine knew Scarlet was just jealous—with the help of her mother, Scarlet had been fighting very hard to be someone since middle school, and she'd certainly achieved that. But she and Jasmine were in different leagues.

Do you think the drama's even real? she typed instead. *Scarlet wouldn't leave anything to chance.*

Fiona sent a Snap back. *So you think she planned it?*

Maybe, Jasmine wrote. People like Scarlet made up gossip for their fans all the time. It was great for impressions stats.

She clicked on Scarlet's YouTube page, half expecting Scarlet to have already posted a vlog about how she and Jack were still "strong together." There was no such post yet, but it had to be coming.

The sun set over the hills, draping the city in a moody, lilac haze. The Uber whisked past neon lights and valet lines and snaked up a side street in the hills. They pulled up in front of a small compound nestled at the mouth of the canyon. The driver glanced at Jasmine in the rearview mirror for the millionth time.

Finally, he cleared his throat. "I'm sorry, but my little sister?" he finally blurted out. "She used to love your show. Could you . . ."

He thrust a piece of paper at Jasmine. Jasmine figured he'd want a selfie, but maybe it was better this way: she didn't need digital, time-stamped evidence that she was at this party. She scribbled her name. The guy looked like he was going to explode with happiness.

It was only after the Uber's taillights disappeared that Jasmine slid the mask over her eyes. The only thing that gave away that a party was taking place at this nondescript building was the bouncer at the door. Jasmine held up her second phone to show him a QR code she'd received. The bouncer scanned it, and she was in.

Inside was a bank of lockers along the wall. Jasmine selected an empty one and placed her phones on the shelf. No phones or posting at this party. She started down the dark hallway. Sexy votive candles pointed toward a main room. Her heart jumped in her chest. She'd been here only once before, but it still felt giddily unfamiliar.

The room opened into a cavernous space full of plants, chandeliers, banquettes, a dance floor, and a lot of bodies. Everyone wore a mask. Some turned to her, but it wasn't because she was famous. Here, she was anonymous.

She loved it.

She sat down at the bar and ordered a vodka soda from a bartender in a bird mask. Normally, she couldn't be seen having more than a half glass of champagne in public—and that was only for something *really big,* like an awards party. At this party, though, she liked something a little stronger to loosen her up.

The DJ switched to a K-pop song, and the crowd migrated to the dance floor. Who were they? People like Jasmine, who wanted to escape the public eye? Or just normal people sick of the superficiality of LA? Jasmine knew there weren't any weirdos here—all guests had to interview with the promoter before being allowed access. When Jasmine passed the promoter her lawyer's standard nondisclosure agreement across the table, he barely glanced at the thing, just whipped off his signature at the bottom.

She sucked down her drink and slid off the stool, then sashayed toward the middle of the circle, moving to the jumpy beat. One could argue that Jasmine could drink and dance in the privacy of her living room, but she *wanted* to be out in the world. Nobody was faking it in here. No one was pretending to be someone they weren't . . . because in here, they were *no one.*

Jasmine swayed, pop-and-locked, and even threw in some choreography moves she'd had to perfect on *That's Hot!* Halfway into the second song, she felt eyes on her back. She turned slowly, paranoia creeping down her spine. It wasn't a *crime* to be spotted here, but . . .

A girl in a mask and dark hoodie was watching her from the edge of the dance floor. At least Jasmine *thought* it was a girl—her cloaklike hood covered most of her face. Jasmine turned away, but before she knew it, the girl was *next* to her. The smell of caramel wafted from her skin. Her movements were graceful and intoxicating. There was something familiar about her body language. Was she here last time?

Her heart started to beat faster. She moved closer to the stranger, her arm grazing her waist. The girl's hand touched Jasmine's hip in return. Jasmine could barely breathe. This was one of those fantasies she'd fully allowed herself to indulge in because it didn't seem possible. And yet here she was, living it.

As they danced, Jasmine felt for the shape of the girl's body under her layers of fabric. The girl shuddered—from desire? Discomfort? Jasmine stepped back, not wanting to make her uncomfortable. But quickly, the girl pulled her closer. She touched the sides of Jasmine's face. Jasmine slid her hand on the back of the girl's neck. This felt delicious—and naughty. But what would Lulu C do if she saw? Even more disconcerting—what would *Ruby* do?

"Come," the girl murmured in Jasmine's ear. They found a dark banquette. Jasmine's stomach felt like it was on the downhill of a roller coaster. The girl edged closer still, cupping Jasmine's chin. Jasmine could only see the outline of her face under her mask, but it didn't matter that she didn't know what the girl looked like. She was enchanted by her essence. She wanted to do this. She wanted to see what this . . . *experience* . . . was like.

Their lips touched. A whoosh swept through Jasmine's core. The girl's mouth tasted like chocolate. Jasmine reached into the girl's hood, touching her ears, her long hair. The girl kissed Jasmine's neck until Jasmine's body felt split open. *Yes,* she thought. Her instincts about herself were correct. Everything she'd repressed, everything she'd always wondered—*this* was what she craved.

She pulled back, breathing hard. The girl peered at her from under her mask, her dark eyes seemingly looking into Jasmine's soul. Jasmine gripped the girl's hands hard. She wanted to kiss her again. She never wanted this night to end.

"Jasmine?" said a voice.

Her head snapped up. Bodies swirled. The music thudded. Then a bright flash assaulted her—*a camera*! Spots formed in front of Jasmine's eyes. The crowd scattered. Someone yelled, "Phone!" A bouncer ran in, tackling the offending person. The crowd shifted, and the music ground on. Another bouncer peered at Jasmine, his brow knitted in concern.

"Miss?" he asked. "Are you all right?"

Jasmine realized she was balled in the booth with her hands over her head. Her heart was thudding for different reasons now. What had just happened?

"I'm fine," she answered shakily, uncurling her legs. Then she turned for the girl she'd just been kissing to see if she was okay, too.

But the girl was gone.

FIONA

Fiona Jacobs really wanted another mint. She felt the tin's outline through her bag; it would be so easy to reach in there and pop one into her mouth. But the Voice told her no. *You've already had five mints today. There's five grams of sugar in each. Twenty-five grams of sugar is already too much for someone like you.*

She folded her hands in her lap. A new thought stabbed her: *Did you brush your teeth today?* She was *pretty* sure. Certainly she didn't come here with bad breath. And she *always* brushed her freaking teeth. Sometimes twice. Sometimes three times, because she didn't do it right the first two times—she didn't brush the top and bottom for exactly ninety seconds, or she forgot to brush her tongue while reciting "Twinkle, Twinkle" in her head.

See, this was why she needed a personal assistant. So someone could remind her to brush her teeth. So someone could track it in an app. Fiona's personal assistant had quit exactly three days ago, and already, she felt on the verge of a breakdown.

Her gaze fell to her phone. It was ten a.m. on the dot. According to her Instagram analytics, ten a.m. was when she received the most likes and impressions on Instagram, and was therefore the best time to put up a post. *You should be adding content right now,* screamed the Voice. *You need to be showing up every single day, girl. You need to be increasing engagement by asking your followers more questions. And you need to* comment *on people's pages, not just heart them, because you know how fickle those fans are. You're terrible at this. You're getting nowhere. You're—*

"Fiona Jacobs?"

A short woman with a smooth blowout peered around the door. She held a clipboard under her arm, and Fiona was pretty sure the shade of lipstick she was wearing was Urban Decay's Scorched. Urban Decay was one of Fiona's sponsors.

Fiona rose to her full height—almost six-one in wedge heels—and started across the room. The other girls stared. They were all prettier than her. Thinner. More glamorous, with better skin. They were looking at her flyaways. They could probably smell her breath because she forgot to brush her teeth. She *needed* a mint. After she crossed the room, it hit her: Did she take exactly twenty-five steps? Did she count correctly? She *thought* so, but . . .

"Hi!" Fiona said brightly to the group inside the smaller room. It was twenty-five steps. She was almost positive. She needed to stop thinking about it.

Besides the assistant who called her name, there was the casting agent, Derek; the producer, Bette; and Mona, the network executive. Everyone spoke at once. They all shook Fiona's hand, which skeeved her out, because she really wasn't into touching strangers. Also: Could they feel how rough her fingers were? She'd forgotten to put lotion on that morning. *How could you have forgotten to put on lotion?*

"Thank you so much for having me," Fiona said, pulling her hands away quickly.

"Are you kidding?" Mona gushed. "We should be thanking *you*!"

They directed Fiona to a folding chair in the middle of the room under a set of hot lights. She made sure to count her steps to get there—eight. Good: an even number. Even numbers were lucky. She crossed her legs so that her pleated midi skirt fanned over her knees. A camera was set up in front of her; Fiona could feel its red eye passing judgment. The Voice was having a field day. *I bet you look fatter than you do on Instagram. Your makeup is caking under your eyes. Your roots are growing out. You should take care of these things. You should be more careful.*

Bette shook her head in wonderment. "God. You're gorgeous."

"The most beautiful thing I've ever seen, basically," Mona murmured.

Fiona's hand fluttered to her throat. "Really? I mean, did you *see* the other girls out there? One is prettier than the next!" She was babbling. She always talked too much when nervous.

Derek glanced at his notes. "Well, clearly millions of other people like your vibe, too. You don't get that many Instagram followers for nothing."

"How *does* one get that many Instagram followers?" Bette asked, cocking her head.

Fiona shrugged. "Well, there are a lot of ways. I did some

really great giveaways at first—of old bags, mostly, but people were still thrilled to get free Hermes and Chanel, even if it's used. And then I styled pieces together that were . . . unusual, I guess? It helps, too, that my aunt has some connections at the fashion magazines—their mentions of my account boosted my numbers for sure. And I'm also really, really into the algorithms. Hashtags, shout-outs, geotagging, getting tagged on bigger accounts and on the Instagram Explore page—it's all about climbing a ladder and getting yourself noticed. Plus I know someone at BuzzFeed, which helped me get more visual. But it's all a science, really."

It felt like she'd been talking for days. She peered at the group, expecting abject boredom if not indignity that she'd wasted their time, but Bette nodded thoughtfully, and Derek and Mona hung on her every word. *Right.* Everyone, probably even George Clooney, wanted to know the secret of how to gain Instagram followers.

"And you grew up in Orange County?" Mona read from the back of Fiona's headshot. "I'm from that area, too. Which high school did you go to?"

Fiona's skin itched. She wanted to scratch, but she'd have to scratch exactly five times—no more, no less—and the casting directors would find that weird. It wasn't like she could tell Mona the real answer to that question. *You need to take that detail off your résumé,* the Voice commanded. *You need to stop saying you're from Orange County.*

"I did online school, actually," she admitted. That wasn't a lie.

"And why acting?" Derek stretched out his legs. "It doesn't sound like you really *need* the job. Just got the acting bug?"

"You could say that." She pointed to her résumé. "Um, you'll see that I was in a few digital series, and then, last year, a guest star on *Riverdale*. I had the best time, and just kind of fell in love!"

Fake. You sound so, so fake.

"You did an episode with Scarlet Leigh, right?" One corner of Derek's mouth twisted mischievously. "What's *she* like?"

"Oh, we weren't in the same episode," Fiona said.

"Yes, but you know each other, don't you?" Mona draped her arms across the back of her chair. "Give me the scoop. Is she a total nightmare? A diva to the nth degree?" She leaned forward. "I'm not supposed to tell you this, but she's up for the part of Kate, too." Then she snorted. Rolled her eyes. The others chuckled.

Fiona forced a smile. It was funny that people thought she and Scarlet were friends. They'd taken a few selfies together and occasionally commented on each other's photos—which looked like friendship. An avid follower of Fiona and Scarlet would know their history, though—and that they definitely, *definitely* weren't close. Not after Fiona stole Scarlet's boyfriend, Chase McGeehan, years ago. But that sort of baggage didn't bleed through to the general fandom.

"Anyway," Bette said. "You've got a great look, Fiona. Especially for the part we're looking for. Did you read the materials about Kate? She's the real trailblazer in her group of friends. Fearless. Beautiful. Saucy. But funny, too."

"Definitely funny," Mona said. "Can you do funny?"

"I *like* funny," Fiona admitted.

"Of course Fiona does funny," Bette said. "Your *Sizzle or Drizzle* shows? You're like a baby Giuliana Rancic!" She leaned forward on her elbows. "I love seeing you rave about such-and-such's gown and roll your eyes when someone looks like a train wreck. It's just . . . gold!"

Fiona tried to smile. In truth, she hated doing the awards episodes. She only did them because one of her sponsors was an advertiser for the SAGs and asked if she would. Then, when the vlog got so much traffic, they pushed her to make it a regular thing on her channel. But Fiona, of all people, shading famous, beautiful people? *Bullying* them? It cut a little too close to the bone. The Voice was always so taunting on the nights she did the Bests and Worsts. *You sound just like* Lana *used to. And look what happened to her. Think about where she is now.*

Bette tapped her pen against her notebook. "Fiona, from what I've seen in your online presence, it seems like your personality *is* Kate. You're meticulous but self-deprecating. You don't settle for second-best. You would be great for this project—so many viewers will already know you, and this will give them a chance to see a fun and different side of you. And, I mean, this pilot is almost guaranteed to go to series. Your account will benefit from that, too."

Everyone nodded. Fiona nodded back. This was the biggest audition of her life. A half-hour scripted comedy called *Like Me.* A fresh storyline about bloggers and influencers—she was *made* for it.

Unless these people saw her cracks. Unless they got too close and realized that she was ruined inside.

Mona handed her a copy of the script with the scene they wanted her to read. Fiona took it even though she had the same copy in her bag. Two copies, actually, just in case. Bette gave her a rundown, even though Fiona had read the breakdown with her agent eight times: "Kate's best friend, Autumn—who's going to be played by this amazing Asian actress who was in this adorable Netflix romance—has just uncovered that her boss is stealing her P90X meals from the communal refrigerator. She's telling Kate about it for the first time. Autumn's only proof is that her boss is getting thinner . . . and Autumn isn't. It's extra complicated because her boss is a guy, and we all know how easy it is for *men* to lose weight." Bette rolled her eyes.

Fiona giggled obligatorily, but something squeezed at her throat. Was Bette hinting that she *knew*? Was she suggesting that she and Fiona were in some sort of kinship, big girls at heart, forever struggling?

Fiona pushed away the thought. Of course Bette didn't know. Fiona was being way too paranoid.

"Whenever you're ready," Derek said, and the team settled back in their chairs.

Fiona closed her eyes and took a few deep, meditative breaths. And that was when the transformation began. All at once, she wasn't Fiona anymore. She wasn't worrying about how many steps she took from her car to the office or whether her bra strap was showing. She wasn't worrying if she forgot to unplug her Vitamix. Her present was gone. Her past, too. She wasn't the girl who used to be on the receiving end of cruel giggles and jeers. She wasn't the girl who once had to make a hard choice about something unthinkably awful on a hot summer night.

Instead, she was a funny, free-spirited girl named Kate who lived in New York City and was ready for big, hilarious escapades. End of story.

The lines flowed out of her like water rippling in a stream.

She noticed the team's charged expressions, the light in their eyes. *This* was why she liked to act. Because when she performed, she could shed herself. It was curative.

"That was great," Derek said at the end. "Can you do it one more time and focus more on the anger than the funny? A little more biting, maybe. A little more justice-for-the-little-guy. Just to see how that plays."

"Of course."

It wasn't as easy this time—anger was always harder, because Fiona needed to channel something that made her angry, and there was really only one thing that did—despite that it had happened years ago. *Lana.*

But she got through it. And when she was done, she looked up again, and everyone was staring, their eyes wide. Her mouth felt dry. *Terrible,* the Voice scolded. *You're a terrible, terrible actress. Just go home.*

"You are *so* Kate," Mona said, her hands clenched at her chest.

"That was just . . . *wonderful,*" Bette seconded.

Derek offered his hand. "I know I shouldn't be saying this and we need to call your agent, but I think we can all say we want YOU for Kate."

"As long as we can work out details with your agent, which I'm sure we can," Bette added.

Fiona gaped. "Wait, *what*?" There had to be some mistake.

But then they exchanged phone numbers. Derek followed her on Instagram. They promised to call Fiona's agent and set up a time to meet so she could do chemistry reads with some of the other actors. They told her not to spill the news yet—the network would handle that—but she could drop hints online.

Fiona's head felt detached from her body. By the time she was at her car on one of the lot's side streets—174 steps—she was shaking. Could she have done it? Could she have freaking *done it*?

She pulled out her phone and opened her front camera. She snapped a few pics of herself smiling, then looking wistfully off into the distance, and a couple shots with a smize—smiling with only her eyes. After about a hundred selfies, she decided she might've gotten *one* good picture. She uploaded the selected shot into Facetune and used the feature that deleted a small pimple on her cheek. She made her eyes just a little bit greener, her teeth a little bit whiter. She triple-checked to make sure her neck didn't look fat, though the Voice reminded her *there's only so much she could do there.* Once she was satisfied, she clicked VSCO for yet another perfect filter . . . and voilà.

She uploaded the picture to Instagram, captioning it, "Just found out some SUPER exciting news. Can't share it quite yet, but I'm just . . . AHHH!"

The comments flooded in instantly, fans telling her how beautiful she was, and how proud of her they were, and oh how they wished they had her life. Moments later, her phone buzzed. It was her boyfriend, Chase. Fiona pressed ANSWER, and Chase's adorable image popped up on FaceTime. "I just saw your post," he said. In the background was the courtyard at Harvard-Westlake School—he was finishing up finals. "Did you get it?"

"I . . . *did*!" Fiona squealed in a bewildered voice. "I'm going to be Kate!"

"Oh my God, babe!" Chase cried. "That's amazing!"

She couldn't stay on the phone with Chase for very long—he

needed to get back to his test. "But I'll see you tonight," he promised. "I can't wait to celebrate!"

Fiona hung up, feeling a warm, tingly thrill. Everything suddenly seemed *right.*

Her phone bleated again, but she turned the device over and started the car—it was probably just someone else who'd seen her post and wanted the scoop. But then her Apple Watch vibrated, too. She looked down at her wrist at an incoming DM from an account she didn't recognize. When Fiona scrolled down the tiny watch face, her vision blurred at a disconcerting, incongruous image: Lana Hedges's oval-shaped face. It was the picture they'd used in Lana's obituary.

Fiona turned off the car and whipped out her phone to get a better look. Her heart was suddenly pounding. Her fingers fumbled on the keypad. She entered her password wrong twice before the thing unlocked. She located the Instagram DM; it was from the number that wasn't even a number, just a few digits and a dash, like the number Verizon texted with when they were sending a bill. And then there was the picture . . . and some words. Reading them, Fiona went boneless.

> I know what you did. So you'd better call ABC and tell them you're not doing Kate after all. Unless you want me to tell everyone the truth.

Transcript of Scarlet Leigh's personal vlog, 6/18 (for her YouTube channel)

Video switches on. Scarlet Leigh speaks into the camera, looking gorgeous with a full face of makeup and blown-out hair. She's standing on a busy street in Beverly Hills, holding a blueberry muffin.

SCARLET

Hey, Scarlet As! I'm coming to you live from outside Café #Blessed, where I'm eating the most incredible vegan muffin I have *ever* tasted. The ingredients are all-natural, there's no GMOs, and you get 100 percent of your Omega-3s in just one 100-calorie treat! I mean, that's a calorie burn of only *ten minutes of hot yoga*!

CORY (O.S.)

What, what!

Scarlet swings the camera around to show her group. We see CORY (21, buff-but-skinny, a head of dyed-blond hair, hoop earring). Next to him is manager CYNTHIA (33, stocky brunette, in a wrap dress), KURT (28, Star Wars tee, cradling a Cavalier King Charles Spaniel), and GINA (late 40s, extremely hot, an older version of Scarlet).

SCARLET (O.S.)

There's my gay husband, Cory, who you also know as my stylist, there's my sweet mama, there's Cynthia, my manager *extraordinaire,* and there's Kurt, my angel doggie nanny, and my widdle baby Peanut!

The dog YIPS. Scarlet swings the camera around on herself again.

SCARLET (CONT'D)

Anyway, here's my OOTD, and . . .

(blinks, seems off-kilter) . . .

and, yeah, um . . .

Suddenly, the camera SHUDDERS. We get a shot of the sidewalk, and then a bad angle of Scarlet leaning over a trash can, THROWING UP. We hear heel clicks; Cynthia grabs Scarlet's phone.

CYNTHIA

You okay, Scar?

Scarlet nods. Wipes her mouth. The camera is all over the place, but Scarlet grabs it and turns it back on herself.

SCARLET

No stress, just the tail end of a stomach bug! I mean, you guys sometimes get the stomach bug, right? *And as Emily Blunt told us in* The Devil Wears Prada, *we're only a stomach bug away from our ideal weight!*

GINA (Scarlet's mom)

Honey, I don't know if people want to see you…

SCARLET

(Grins at camera) I love my mama. Here's my top three reasons: (1) She's my biggest supporter. (2) I love how *dedicated* she is to her children's hospital charity with all her best friends and, of course, to *me*. And (3), how fabulous does Mommy look at 47? I mean, seriously, people.

Scarlet starts to walk toward the restaurant, still talking. We see a valet stand, a patio, a wall full of succulents.

SCARLET

I know a lot of you have questions about Jack and me. You guys are so, *so* sweet to be worried. I mean, sure I'm a little hurt and confused. Jack and I will have a long talk. But innocent till proven guilty, right? And don't worry. We're *solid. I trust my boy.* But I am so grateful for your support. Honestly, it's YOU guys who get me through the bad days!!

CORY

We love you, Scar.

The hostess whisks them to a table. The group winds through a funky dining room and past a long, marble-topped bar. Scarlet's phone is still pointed at her, but off camera, we hear a BUZZ. The camera swings to find Gina hanging back, trying to get Scarlet's attention.

GINA

(murmuring)

Can I talk to you, honey?

SCARLET

About what?

Gina points at the camera.

GINA

Maybe you should turn that off. . . .

Some muffled noises. Then Scarlet appears in the camera.

SCARLET

That's it for today! Thank you so much for watching, and as always, much love.

She blows a kiss and drops the phone into her bag . . . but doesn't turn off the feed. *Oops.* Now all we hear is audio. . . .

SCARLET

What, Mom?

GINA

I just wanted to see how you were feeling about not getting the part in *Like Me*.

SCARLET

It's . . . fine.

GINA

I know Fiona Jacobs brings up old wounds. . . .

SCARLET

I told you. It's *fine*. I've got it covered.

GINA

What does that mean?

But suddenly . . . we hear footsteps, an *ahem*. And here's a new voice . . .

GIRL'S VOICE

Um, excuse me?

SCARLET

(snippy)

Uh, yes? We're not ready to order yet.

GIRL'S VOICE

Oh, I'm not . . . I don't work . . . Oh my God. Oh my God, it's really *you*. (Overwhelmed) I was just watching your live right now and I was like I *think* she's in this restaurant but I wasn't really sure and oh my God... (She's practically hyperventilating.) My name's Melanie. I am your biggest fan.

SCARLET

(coolly, exhaustedly)

Hi.

MELANIE

Can I get a picture?

SCARLET

I'm in the middle of lunch....

MELANIE

Oh my God. Of course. I totally get it. I'm so, so sorry—I'll... I'll leave you alone.

GINA

(whispering)

Scarlet! Take one picture with the girl!

Scarlet heaves a sigh. We hear rustling.... She's grabbing her phone. The picture comes back up of Scarlet's face as she frowns at the screen—and then an *oh shit* face because she realizes her feed was still recording. She stabs END.

Comments: (3,761)

@ScarMyQueen: First!
@MultiFanScarlet: WTF you DESERVE THAT ROLE!! Love you queen!!
@ScarLeighJackletHeart: Ugh I'd literally sell my soul to hang out with you. ALSO like this comment if you'd help take down Fiona and mystery BITCH
@Jacklet4Ever: guys did she mean to not end the live??? i mean not complaining I love seeing scars personal life but kind of worried??
@uwuscarletleigh: @jacklet4ever, idk maybe it's a glitch insta is whack sometimes but tbh the more scarlet the better!!!

(read 2,309 more)

Posted three minutes later on @ScarletFanMel66: A girl grinning her brains out and Scarlet, dead-eyed, holding up a peace sign. Caption: OMG OMG I'M SHAKING BUT IT'S REALLY HER THE REAL @SCARLETLETTER GUYS YOU HAVE NO IDEA HOW LONG I'VE BEEN WAITING FOR THIS!!! Wow ok I'm literally crying gonna go try to calm down now BYEEE

DELILAH

"Let the traditional Rollins family pancake breakfast begin!" Delilah's mother set down plates of blueberry pancakes with dollops of whipped cream. "I used organic blueberries from the farmers' market and a twelve-dollar mix that contains flax," she added. "But you totally can't taste it."

When Delilah looked up from her phone, her parents were staring at her expectantly, their orange juice glasses raised. "Come on, honey," her father, Will, urged. "For old times' sake!"

Delilah picked up her glass of juice and handed it to her dad. Dad handed his juice to Mom, Mom handed hers to Ava, and Ava gave hers to Delilah. It was a ritual that started a million years ago for God knows why—Ava and Delilah used to habitually switch sippy cups when they were toddlers or something, and they'd continued the tradition. It seemed so dorky now.

"So we're officially signing you up for school today," Will said as he forked pancake into his mouth. "The campus is close to the trail to the Hollywood sign. We could go on a hike afterward." He glanced excitedly at Delilah. "You could get a picture for your page."

Delilah made a face. "I'd never put a picture of the Hollywood sign on my page."

"Why not?" Her mother seemed genuinely confused. "If you're going to say it's too touristy, we still *are* tourists here."

"Yeah, but the worst thing we can do is *act* like tourists," Delilah explained.

Her parents exchanged a look, and Delilah suppressed annoyance. How did they not understand how utterly uncool it would be to post a picture at the cheesiest spot in LA?

"Speaking of school," Delilah said, her heart picking up speed. "What do you guys think of online school?"

Her parents glanced at each other, then burst out laughing. "Worst idea ever," her father joked.

"No *thank* you," her mother said at the same time. "I'm not having you kids underfoot all day. Besides, in online school, do you even *learn*?"

Delilah hung her head. As she'd expected. She loved her parents, but they didn't get it. Did they have any idea how her fandom was exploding and what that meant? Ever since having her picture taken with Jasmine and Fiona at the Evensong Hotel a few days before, her account had swelled in numbers. A few small brands had even reached out to ask if she'd do sponsored posts for teensy amounts of money. A photographer named Patrick sent her a DM, too, asking if she would be interested in him taking pictures of her. Delilah reached out to Jasmine about that one—was it a scam?—but Jasmine assured her that Patrick was the best of the best. *Instagram photographers love to shoot up-and-comers,* she added. *It gets them exposure, and you get gorgeous pictures out of it. You should do it!*

Yeah, right. Like her mom would *ever* allow that.

Her gaze dropped to her phone again, thinking of her *other* problem. It had been on her mind since yesterday, when she and Jack Dono had that strange, woozy almost-kiss and images of them started circulating.

And the comments started rolling in, too.

Mystery Bitch, someone with a Jacklet ship account called @ScarletArmy had posted, attaching the blurry picture of Jack leaning toward Delilah. The image earned 986 likes and 102 comments, all of which condemned Jack Dono for merely speaking to another girl.

"Lila?"

She clicked on another post from a Jacklet fan showing the same blurry photo of Jack at the restaurant. Thank God the photographer hadn't been able to capture Delilah's face. But what if someone *else* had taken a photo that hadn't leaked yet—one that clearly identified her?

"Lila?"

Delilah had an online presence, too. Her fandom was nothing compared to Jacklet's, but her picture could be reverse-image searched . . .

"Delilah."

Her family stared. Bethany set down her fork. "Hand over your phone, please."

“What? No!” Delilah pressed her phone to her chest.

“Hand it over,” her father said gruffly. “The phone can wait until we’re done eating.”

I’m not hungry, Delilah wanted to snap.

After scarfing down breakfast, she recovered her phone and stormed upstairs. She could hear her parents murmuring about her in the kitchen. She knew she was being moody, but this Jacklet problem felt like life or death.

She flopped onto her bed. A moment later, there was a knock on the door. Ava poked her open, freckly face inside. “Hey.”

“Hey,” Delilah mumbled without inflection. “What’s up?”

Her sister had her hands shoved into her pockets. She was wearing a fitted sweatshirt and Delilah’s hand-me-down terrycloth shorts. And, because of their mom’s no-makeup-until-fifteen rule, she looked fresh-faced and innocent. “So, um, I wanted to talk about Jack Dono.”

That got her attention. Delilah sat bolt upright. *“What?”*

Ava looked cowed. “I, um, had to use the bathroom while we were waiting for you at Wellness. Mom let me run into the hotel for a *second.* I saw you in the restaurant . . . talking to him. Faith loves him.”

“Who’s Faith?” Delilah wracked her brain. No one from Minneapolis was named Faith.

“Oh. This girl. I met her online, actually, but she only lives a few streets away.” Ava shrugged. “We’ve been chatting a lot.”

“Did you tell *her* about this?” Delilah was mortified.

“No. Totally not. But she knows a lot about Scarlet. And about Jack.” Her throat wobbled as she swallowed. “The fans are saying terrible things about you, Delilah. All those Scarlet supporters—they're *evil.*"

Delilah scoffed. "Don't read that stuff. It's not worth your time."

"Some of them say they want to *kill* you."

A flicker of fear rippled down her spine. "They don't know that *I'm* the girl, and I intend to keep it that way. Anyway, fans make threats like that all the time. It's no big."

"But what if they figure it out? Maybe we should tell someone. Like Mom."

Delilah clamped her hand on her sister's arm. "Don't. She'll blow this out of proportion. It's . . . *normal,* okay? It'll blow over." Of all the people, Delilah didn't want her impressionable little sister to know about her Jack gaffe. She hadn't even been able to tell stuck-in-France-without-a-phone Busy about it yet.

"Faith also told me some gossip about Scarlet," Ava continued. "She's kind of . . . ruthless."

Delilah eyed her warily. "How do you know about Scarlet?"

"I just . . . do. There was this girl last year, ChloeDIY? She did a fashion vlog, some beauty stuff—had a pretty good following . . ."

"I remember her," Delilah said faintly. It was so weird to be having a conversation with her little sister about influencers.

"So I guess Scarlet blew off Chloe at this event? And Chloe ranted about it in a vlog? She talked about how Scarlet isn't that pretty, and that she has a terrible attitude, and that her mom's supposedly a raging maniac bitch and her best friend secretly despises her and how it's weird that she takes her dog *and* her dog nanny everywhere."

"Scarlet has a dog . . . *nanny*?" Delilah asked. "How do you *know* this stuff?"

"I told you—Faith. And watch Scarlet's vlogs—the nanny is all over them. Anyway, Scarlet found out about Chloe's video. And she got mad. So she started spreading terrible rumors about her. People turned on Chloe. She lost hundreds of thousands of subscribers, and hasn't posted since. I've heard she's sworn off the internet *entirely*. Just because of Scarlet!"

A cold, sick feeling washed down Delilah's back. "And this was just because this Chloe person said that she was *jealous*?"

Ava's eyes got wide. "I don't want her to hurt you."

Delilah was starting to feel clammy, but she tried not to show it. "Stop reading up on people. It's all probably just hype, anyway. I've got it covered, okay?"

She shot her sister a confident smile. After a beat, Ava shrugged and turned for the hall. Only once she was gone did Delilah collapse on her bed, panic clamping down. Her life here hadn't even begun yet, and it might already be ruined.

FIONA

Fiona perched at a large table with Chase; her mom, Dr. Rebecca Jacobs; and Martie, the writer of a blog called *Chocolates and Faux Fur.* The blog was a lifestyle/design/culture mashup that attracted the millennial/Gen Z audience Fiona was looking to capture as a brand-new actress on *Like Me.* Today's interview was because the network was about to announce Fiona's upcoming role as Kate, and they wanted to generate some pre-buzz. Fiona was speaking exclusively to this blog, and then she was going to be a guest on a wildly successful YouTuber's channel, where they'd bake ugly, lumpy cookies and chat—that was the YouTuber's thing. Tomorrow, she was scheduled to do an interview with *Variety*, the *Hollywood Reporter*, and *Vanity Fair.*

But maybe she shouldn't be doing promo at all.

They were on the outdoor terrace at Soho House in West Hollywood. A waitress had just set down a kale salad at Fiona's place. She eyed her mother's avocado toast enviously, wishing she'd ordered that instead. *No, it's only kale for you,* teased the Voice.

One, two, three taps of her napkin to her lips. Should she wash her hands again? She needed to count to twenty until she took a bite, too—or . . . or what? Something terrible would happen, obviously. Or had something terrible *already* happened? She felt her knee jiggling so wildly it verged on banging the underside of the table. Chase put his hand on her thigh to steady her. He was so good at calming her down.

"Anyway," Martie said after swallowing a bite of veggie burger. "I love how down-to-earth you both are as a couple. So many young influencers hook up with other influencers and actors—it's great that you're dating someone not in the public eye, Fiona."

"Well, just because Chase isn't in the public eye doesn't mean he's not awesome." Fiona leaned into Chase's shoulder.

Martie looked intrigued. "Are you thinking of starting a career on social, too, Chase?"

Chase opened his mouth, about to answer, but Fiona cut him off. "Oh, no *way*. He sees what I go through, don't you, babe? It's not for the faint of heart."

"That's for sure!" Fiona's mom jumped in.

Dr. Jacobs, who taught archaeology at UCLA, was still in her professor "uniform": chinos, a button-down, and a blazer. Her blond hair was tied back into a ponytail, and her glasses were perched a little too far at the end of her nose, but she seemed oblivious to her lack of fashion sense, even though they were at one of the poshest private clubs in the city. Still, Fiona was glad her mom had taken the time out of her schedule to come. She'd love it if her dad was here, too, but he worked at a hospital on the other side of town, where he delivered babies. Actually, Chase's mom was also an ob-gyn, which made for some weird dinner conversation when the families got together.

"This makes me sound old, but the things these kids share online—and how *mature* they are . . . it's something," Dr. Jacobs went on. "They're worlds ahead of what I was doing at their age."

"But you're proud of what she's accomplished, right?" Martie asked.

"Of course." Fiona's mom took a bite of toast. "I've always taught her to think for herself. When I was growing up, my mother always told me I should be a schoolteacher, not an archaeologist. That's a man's job. But I did it. And I'm going to let my kids do whatever they want, too." Then she offered a sheepish smile. "Anyway. This interview isn't about me." She sat back as if to say, *The floor is yours, Fiona.*

"I just got done with junior year at Harvard-Westlake," Chase volunteered, getting them back on track. "I'm hoping to go to UC Santa Barbara next year."

"I'm so happy he'll be close," Fiona said, leaning on his shoulder.

Martie pushed her recording device closer. "You went to Harvard-Westlake for a while, too—right, Fiona? Before online school?" Fiona nodded. "That's where you guys met?"

"That's right," Fiona said carefully, hoping the blogger wasn't going to get into the gossip about her and Scarlet Leigh. Scarlet and Chase had only been dating for a few weeks before Chase and Fiona met. Still, Scarlet didn't take being broken up with lightly . . . and she was the type who held grudges forever.

"Where were you before Harvard-Westlake?" Martie asked. "Another private school in LA?"

"Oh. Uh, no." Fiona dissected a large piece of kale. "We were in Orange County."

"Laguna Hills," Fiona's mom specified.

"Were you on social then?" Martie flipped through her notes. In moments, she was going to notice that Fiona's accounts started three years ago; odd for a person her generation. Most girls her age started Instagramming practically as soon as they could type their own captions.

"Um, no." Fiona could feel her nails digging into her palm. "I was an awkward tween. Overweight, unhappy, not confident . . ."

Martie looked shocked. "You?"

"She was lovely," Fiona's mom interjected. "Smart . . . driven . . . but it's Orange County. People can be so superficial—and cruel. Especially girls."

"I was bullied," Fiona admitted. "It was tough." *You deserved it,* teased the Voice.

Martie's eyes crinkled with sympathy. "God, I'm so sorry."

Fiona lifted her napkin again. *Tap, tap, tap:* three times to her lips. She knew Martie wanted her to talk more about this. Maybe about how Lana Hedges, her bully, used to call Fiona "Weeble Wobble," referring to the kids' toys of bulbous, legless, fat little people and animals. How Lana spread a rumor that Fiona wasn't fat but actually pregnant with Janitor Carl's baby—which was especially cruel because Janitor Carl was in his mid-fifties, cranky, and rumored to be a neo-Nazi. How, many times over the course of the school year, Fiona would open her locker and find red-painted tampons—she could smell the acrylic paint—spilling out.

Lana teased others, too, but Fiona didn't want to associate with those girls—it would make what Lana was doing even more real. She regretted this now—maybe if she had banded with those other victims, they could have done something as a group. Told someone. Made a difference. But she kept her distance from the others. Until Zoey, anyway.

"Things were getting out of hand," Fiona's mom jumped in. "So we got her out of there. Put her in online school to finish eighth grade . . ."

"And my family moved to LA," Fiona rushed on. "And after that . . . I don't know. Something happened over the summer. I started eating better. Exercising. I started taking care of myself, you know?" *No, you didn't,* teased the Voice. *What actually happened is that you developed rituals. Stopped eating. Exercised nonstop.*

But she kept smiling. "Then I did a stand-up comedy act for a party my parents threw, and everyone *loved* it."

"It was amazing!" Dr. Jacobs agreed. "I don't know where she gets it from!"

"In August of that year, I started my YouTube channel—beauty, fashion, with a funny edge. But I did it for me, you know? Not for followers. Just to try some things out, to figure out who I was."

"That's when we met." Chase set down his fork. "I didn't even know she had a channel. I didn't see how pretty she was, either—I mean, it *helped,* but that's not what I was focusing on. I just thought she was incredible as a *person.* Funny, cool, charming, and deep." He leans forward. "I'd been dating someone else who was also successful and funny and had a big personality like Fiona's, but she had no soul. I liked that Fiona seemed complicated." He inhaled. "I was picked on in elementary as well. I had this stomach flu in fourth grade, and it led to this epic, gross incident of not being able to hold everything in before I got to the school bathroom . . ." He shuddered. "No one would let it go. I was mortified."

Fiona patted his hand. This was one of the first real conversations she and Chase had ever had: how the both of them—attractive, smart, interesting people—endured brutal teasing when they were younger. It bound them together. Well, that and their love for 1980s movies, shopping at thrift stores, and donning full-body wetsuits and going into the ocean in Santa Monica in the dead of winter.

Fiona wasn't sure what she'd do without Chase. He understood her in ways no one else did—she'd even told him a little about her rituals and the Voice. But she hadn't told him *everything.* No one knew everything. Except . . .

Her mind flashed back to the strange DM. Could someone know? *How?*

"And this girl who picked on you?" Martie said spookily, as if reading Fiona's mind. "Has she reached out to comment on what a success you are these days? I'd imagine you'd feel pretty triumphant."

Fiona exchanged a look with her mother. "Actually, there was an . . . accident," Rebecca said quietly, setting down her last bite of toast. "The girl is no longer with us."

"Oh my God!" Martie's hand flew to her mouth. "How awful!"

Fiona's heart pounded. Her secret felt like it was only barely hidden, just one onionskin layer down.

Not much later, Fiona's mother said she had to get back to work. Fiona was grateful to leave. She shook Martie's hand and thanked her for the feature. She counted her steps as she walked out of the trendy Soho House dining room. She did an extra shuffle so that it was eighty-eight steps, an even number, instead of eighty-seven.

But in the parking lot, Chase seemed reluctant to head to his car. "Was everything okay back there? You seemed a little . . ."

"A little what?" Fiona snapped, sounding more on edge than she intended.

Chase shrugged. "I don't know, guarded, maybe."

"I wasn't guarded." Her voice rose an octave. "And anyway, you have to be guarded with those people. If you tell them too much, they'll twist your words into scandal."

"Yeah, but *you* don't have any scandals." Chase bumped her hip playfully.

Fiona's mind screamed, but she tried to keep her breathing regular. "Yeah, but . . ."

Chase shot her an uncertain look, then shrugged and gave her a quick kiss. Fiona's heart thudded as he climbed into his car to head home. *Guarded?* Did the interviewer think that, too?

All at once, her throat felt tight. She looked around, certain someone was spying on her. Someone knew about Lana. Fiona was convinced, suddenly, that the DM she'd received was legit. Someone was going to ruin her. Unless . . .

She pulled out her phone and stared miserably at the screen. *Unless.* Some sacrifices had to be made. And with that, she scrolled through her list of contacts and dialed her agent's number.

JASMINE

On Saturday, Jasmine headed out on her regular visit to her parents' house in the Valley. As she swung into her car—a Tesla sedan, which she'd bought for herself after an ad campaign with Claire's, in which she was bedecked in Lulu C rainbows to advertise the jewelry store's new "Lulu C" earrings line—she called up her texts on the car's giant touch screen. Usually, she made a concerted effort not to smartphone-and-drive, but her phone had been pinging all morning, and she needed to assess the damage.

The damage. Last night. The aftermath wasn't *so* bad, actually. There were shots of Jasmine in the dark club, but not much could be deduced. She was in a mask. The person she was with *might* be a girl . . . but it might be a guy. Mostly, her fans were just intrigued. *Why is LuluJasmine wearing a mask? Is that a long-haired boy she's kissing? Maybe a famous rock star?*

She'd scoured the comments, desperate to see if anyone recognized the girl. Nothing had surfaced yet . . . and that killed her. Jasmine couldn't stop thinking about that kiss. The girl's lips touching hers. That feeling of, *Yes, this is right.* Why hadn't she asked the girl's name? This morning, she'd even called the party's promoter, begging him for a guest list of who was there last night. The guy just laughed. "Privacy is the reason we throw these parties," he reminded her. "If I give you a list of names, it ruins everything."

But she needed to find this girl. They had such a connection. She couldn't just let her go.

She merged onto the highway, pressing the button for a new Spotify playlist. Then she noticed Ruby's name on the list of incoming texts. Ruby had sent sixteen texts since the story broke. Jasmine had meant to call Ruby this morning, but her head was throbbing from the stress, and she wasn't in the mood. In fact, she decided to turn off the GPS tracking on her phone so Ruby wouldn't know where she was. Just for the morning. Just until she could screw her head on straight.

She hated avoiding her sister, though. Back in the day, when Jasmine was just starting out and Ruby was more of a personal assistant/part-time college student than Jasmine's 24/7 manager, they would drive to see their parents together. *Strength in numbers,* they joked. They would make bets: How many times would Mom complain of a mystery ailment? How many times would Dad disappear outside, saying he was "checking on the plants," to sneak a cigarette? Would their grandmother be *nice* to them this visit, or would she be as cantankerous as ever, doting only on her French bulldog, Mr. Snuffleupagus?

But ever since Jasmine's career hit the next level, she and Ruby had felt less and less like sisters and more like diva and adversary. The only way to preserve their family bond was to sever that relationship . . . but how could Jasmine fire her sister? "Never mix family and business," a director had told her once on the set of *That's Hot!* Jasmine wished she'd listened.

It took only a half hour to get to her parents' neighborhood. Every time she gazed upon their imposing, sand-colored ranch, with its orange trees and a beautiful front-yard waterfall, the same thought always gonged in her head: *Wish I'd grown up here!* Not that Jasmine's childhood home was bad . . . it was just on a much smaller scale.

Jasmine struggled to open the front door, but it was locked. When she rang the bell, a woman in a gray dress and an apron answered. "*¿Sí?*" she said brightly.

"Uh, hi . . . ," Jasmine said slowly. "I'm Jasmine, Miranda's daughter?"

"Oh! Yes! The famous one!" The woman opened the door wider. "I'm Esperanza! Your mother hired me to keep the house! Live in!"

Live in? Jasmine thought as she shrugged off her jacket. How much did *that* cost?

"That's you!" Esperanza hooted, pointing to a giant portrait in the foyer.

Jasmine felt her cheeks go pink. The painting was of her from her first year on *That's Hot!* Her parents hung it in their foyer "in homage." Jasmine found it creepy that her parents probably pointed it out to everyone who came through this house—friends, distant relations, repairmen, the massage therapist who did house calls . . .

She walked through a series of rooms nobody ever used; they

were decorated in a fussy, gilded French style like this was the palace of Versailles. She found her parents sitting by the back-yard pool. Her mother was reading *Star* and lying on the back-massager chair the pool guy had dragged out here a few months ago; she claimed it was the only thing that worked on her bad back. Jasmine's father, Raymond, quickly stubbed out a cigarette when he saw Jasmine coming. Too late.

"Daddy, *still*?" Jasmine said sharply.

"It was just a drag." Her father showed off a Nicorette patch. "See? I'm trying!"

"You know how that kills your asthma." His asthma was why he was on permanent disability from the United States Postal Service, where, before Jasmine's rise as Lulu, he was a mail carrier.

She waved to her grandmother, Anita, who was nestled in a cabana with Snuffie. Anita's piercing cocoa-colored eyes glared out from a sea of wrinkles. The expression she made at seeing Jasmine was one someone usually makes when they've accidentally swallowed a gnat. "Hello, Abuela," Jasmine said loudly, because her grandmother was hard of hearing. Anita sniffed and returned to stroking her dog's head.

Her mother closed her magazine and, as Jasmine leaned down, kissed Jasmine's cheek. Her father, after expelling a couple of nasty-sounding coughs, said it was great to see her, and did she see the new built-in grill on the deck? Jasmine peered at the shiny, state-of-the-art outdoor kitchen, suppressing a tug of dread. "Boy, you really went all out," she mused in an even voice.

"Every home needs an outdoor kitchen," Miranda said airily. "We used the same kitchen designer as Jennifer Aniston!"

Jasmine shifted her weight. *She* grew up without an outdoor kitchen, and she was fine.

Still, look at her parents! They were sitting together, in the sun! They both looked so contented and at peace! Even Grandma wasn't cursing the universe! Oh, how Jasmine's family had struggled when she was growing up. First, there were the are-we-going-to-have-enough-money-to-pay-the-rent arguments. Then came the health problems that sidelined her father from work. Then Anita had to move in because they couldn't afford a nursing home anymore. Miranda juggled three jobs to make ends meet, barely seeing Jasmine and Ruby.

It was Ruby who took Jasmine to the walk-on audition for Lulu C, totally on a whim. Dance had always been something Jasmine loved—and something her parents scrimped to pay for—and when she saw the open call, she'd thought, *Why not?* She never thought she'd get it. In fact, when she'd walked into that room of pretty, blond, pale-skinned girls in their dance tights with their professional headshots, she'd walked right out again. But Ruby had grabbed her arm. "The character you're reading for, Lulu? She isn't those girls. She doesn't come from where they come from. She's scrappy. An outsider. But *sweet.* They're not going to get it. *You* are."

Jasmine had no idea where Ruby's faith in her came from, but she went back into that casting room. And she booked the part. Even better, her brand-new agent outlined the terms of her contract—with the money she'd earn, she'd be able to help her family.

As soon as that first check came in, things began to change. Her parents' fighting stopped. The crying ceased. Jasmine's mom slept full nights again—she quit all three jobs. As Jasmine's stardom grew, as she was offered movies and deals and built her social media base, she gave her family more and more—cars, new appliances, trips, a new house. She loved providing for them. She loved seeing them happy and stress-free. But the problem was that she wasn't just giving them gifts. She was *supporting* them—*still* supporting them. Jasmine's gentle nudges for them to save the money she gave them seemed to fall on deaf ears. They kept buying outdoor kitchens and hiring live-in housekeepers. Her father had recently leased a Range Rover. Where was it going to end? And the worst part was that the money that supported them was money Jasmine made from her merchandise deals based on the Lulu C brand. So did that mean she had to remain demure, silly, rainbow-bright Lulu C forever to keep her family afloat?

"You have some explaining to do."

Jasmine turned. Ruby was marching through the sliding glass door, past the brand-new outdoor kitchen—the plastic on the appliances hadn't even been removed yet—and straight to Jasmine. Following her were Jasmine's hair and makeup people and Kim, Jasmine's agent.

"H-how did you know I was here?" Jasmine asked, cowering a little.

"I called Mom, and she said she saw your car pull up. Of course, this was *after* I called all over LA looking for you because you decided to turn off your GPS and ignore my texts. Why is that, do you think?" Ruby's eyes blazed. "Perhaps because you did something last night? What am I even *looking* at here?"

"What did you do?" Miranda rose to her feet with remarkable agility for someone with back problems. Ruby thrust her phone in their mother's face. On the screen was the image of Jasmine kissing the person in the mask. Miranda frowned. Cocked her head. "Were you at a costume party, baby?"

"Yes, *please* explain this." Ruby's tone was condescending. "You were supposed to be home drinking smoothies. I called Kreation Juice and told them there would be content from you last night. They were expecting it. Instead, they get these pictures of you out and about doing God knows what!"

"But your face is so pretty!" Miranda looked confused. "Why would you cover it with a mask?"

"And those *clothes.*" Kim stepped forward. "I've received calls from the Lemonade execs asking what's going on. You sort of look like . . . a spider woman."

"A dominatrix," Ruby clarified.

"No I don't!" Jasmine cried. "I had on leather pants and a black top, that's hardly a dominatrix! Have you ever been to New York? It's what *everyone* wears!"

Jasmine's mother pouted. "You look much prettier in colors, baby. Lots of colors."

Jasmine shut her eyes before the volcano in her head erupted. "It was just this party. Everyone had to wear masks. No one knew who anyone was. It sounded fun."

"Was it sponsored by anyone?" Ruby asked. "Did a website invite you? An influencer?"

"It had nothing to do with social. That's why I wanted to *go.*"

Everyone's eyes were on her. It was clear no one understood what had just come out of her mouth. She touched the edge of the ivy plant that spiraled around the chaises. She remembered paying the landscaping bill for when these plants were put in. It was over twenty thousand dollars.

"I needed a break," she said. "I didn't think anybody would recognize me."

"Well, someone did," Kim sighed. "Someone always sees you. You know this! People are *always* watching! So what about this person you kissed? Is it a guy? A girl?"

"Of course it's a guy," Ruby snapped before Jasmine could speak. Jasmine felt her heart break. Because even though this was the twenty-first century, and even though Ruby supported LGBTQ+ rights, God forbid Jasmine kissed a *girl*.

"Did you kiss him, or did he kiss you?" Ruby demanded.

"I . . ." Jasmine wanted to tell the truth—about everything. But everyone was bearing down on her so viciously. "He kissed me."

"Okay, Jazz. Okay." Kim inhaled. "I get you want to hook up. Of course you do, you're young! But we have to play this right. We have to get the right *person* for your brand. You can't just go hooking up with anybody, you know?"

"Wait." Jasmine frowned. "You're saying I can't choose a significant other myself?"

Kim made leveling motions with her hands as if to say, *Settle down*. "Of course you can. Preferably, your fandom would love it if he were in your same sort of sphere—like the way Jack Dono and Scarlet Leigh are. But he doesn't have to be. But . . . well, we want to control how the world finds out Jasmine Walters-Diaz is a sexual being. Keep in mind, a huge contingent is really pulling for you and Luke Lording to get together. Archer and Lulu, just like on the show! That isn't possible by any chance, is it?"

Jasmine pressed her hands over her eyes. *This* again? "I'm not dating Luke."

"Okay! And that's fine. But let's just take this slowly. And when you find someone, we'll roll out your new boyfriend in a carefully crafted plan. In a way your fans will have no choice but to accept. We'll make them adore whoever he is."

Kim smiled happily like everything she'd just said was totally rational. But it was like Jasmine's feelings, her desires, were some sort of product campaign or marketing initiative. *Roll out a new boyfriend? Carefully crafted plan?*

She lifted her head, a lump in her throat. She needed to set them straight. Except the words felt jammed in her mouth. The truth wouldn't come. She felt like such a coward.

"We've done damage control already." Ruby collapsed into a chaise and started tapping on her phone. "We said you were rehearsing a scene for a role in a film you can't reveal yet. A film that involves people in masks."

Jasmine snickered. "What, like *Phantom of the Opera*?"

Ruby ignored her. "It minimizes the kiss. Everyone will assume it's for a movie, it doesn't mean anything. Got it?"

Jasmine's throat felt like it was stuffed with cotton. She glanced around at everyone on the patio: her stylist, her hairdresser, her agent. As far as she knew, *she* was their biggest client. And then there was Ruby, her brow furrowed, her eyes sharp, her lips pursed. Ruby's livelihood depended on Jasmine. Jasmine's parents hinged forward, too—her dad looking like he was dying for a smoke, Miranda's eyes wide and worried. As much as Jasmine wanted to snap her fingers and pivot her life, as much as she wanted to say, *You know what? That kiss DID matter. I can't stop thinking about it . . .* , she knew she couldn't. A pivot would affect so many other people.

"Okay," she said softly. "I got it."

"Good." Ruby snapped her fingers. "Now, let's get you ready for the day."

The hair and makeup team rushed forward, and in moments, Jasmine was being fluffed, plucked, and powdered. "It's actually not a bad idea to come out here, Jazz," Ruby murmured. "The lighting is awesome for an update post. And your fans love when you check in with the fam."

"Uh-huh," Jasmine said wearily, realizing she had to do an update post and lie about that kiss *right now.* What if the girl saw it? She was out there, somewhere. What if this broke her heart?

After the touch-ups, Ruby set up Jasmine's phone and started recording. And like a lightbulb flashing on, Jasmine felt the corners of her mouth automatically lift into a smile. "Hey, guys!" she chirped, bright-eyed, positive, and cheerful. There was no sign she was having the biggest existential crisis of her life. No sign she felt totally lost.

That was because she was a good influencer. She never let anybody see what was really inside.

Transcript of Scarlet Leigh's personal vlog, 6/20 (for her YouTube channel)

Video switches on. SCARLET and JACK DONO sit on a black leather couch, all business. Scarlet is in serious-looking glasses and an oversize (but still cool) sweatshirt. Jack's in a hoodie, slumped. They both look at each other at the same time.

SCARLET

You wanna start?

JACK

No, you go ahead. Or…

SCARLET

Okay, I'll… are you sure?

JACK

Yeah. Go.

Scarlet looks at the camera.

SCARLET

Hey, guys. It's us. Jacklet.

She pauses for a moment to let this sink in.

SCARLET (CONT'D)

This is a different format for me, but I want to talk to you about something really important—you've probably been talking about it or maybe heard about it, and I've been so upset—I mean, yesterday I was literally sobbing all day. And to be honest, when Jack called me, I wasn't sure if I wanted to do this video. I mean, I just felt so *hurt*. But I love this guy.

She reaches over to touch Jack's hand.

SCARLET (CONT'D)

I love him, despite everything. I wasn't kidding when I said our bond was strong. So that's why I'm here, and we're both talking to you, because we're a team. We're a ship, and you ship us, and we love you all so much. Don't we, Jack?

JACK

We totally do.

Hangs his head. Takes a breath. Scarlet waits for him.

JACK (CONT'D)

Look, guys, I'm really sorry. Those pictures you saw of me—talking to someone—look, I'm not going to say that it was taken out of context or people got it wrong. I... I betrayed Scarlet. But I care about her so, so much . . . and I care about you guys, too. I'm so, so sorry for letting you down. We know how much you support us. You've made us what we are.

SCARLET

And we are what we are because we're showing you our love, together. We're trying to keep it real. This is *real love,* people. It's messy. And sometimes, we get in over our heads with things.

Reaches down, grabs her dog onto her lap.

SCARLET (CONT'D)

I know how you guys like these, so we're going to do a couple's gift exchange. We both got each other a little something to, like, show each other how much we care. (Looks at Jack.) You wanna go first?

JACK

Sure . . .

He bends down out of the shot to reach for a box. Suddenly, a BEEP off camera. Scarlet frowns off to the left.

SCARLET

(whispering)

Mom! Turn that off!

GINA

Scar. Holy shit.

Jack pops back up with a beautifully wrapped box from XIV Karats. But Scarlet is looking at her mom.

SCARLET

What is it?

GINA

It's Mona. From ABC. I don't know why, but they want to talk to you.... Oh, wait. Wait. Now she's *calling*.

SCARLET

What? What?

A phone comes into view on-screen. Scarlet presses the button for the speaker. Jack sits quietly, Scarlet's present in his lap.

SCARLET

Hello? Mona?

MONA

(Through the phone)

Scarlet! How are you?

SCARLET

(Eyes darting)

I'm... fine.

MONA

So listen. I rounded up the team here, and we've all talked, and we'd absolutely love for you to play Kate in the *Like Me* pilot. What do you think?

Scarlet looks flabbergasted. Jack stares at her with wide eyes like *what, what?*

SCARLET

W-what about Fiona Jacobs?

MONA

Well, look, we've all talked, and we want *you*.

SCARLET

I was told Fiona got the role. Is this some kind of joke? Is Fiona okay?

MONA

Absolutely not a joke, and Fiona's fine as far as we know. But hey, if you don't want it—I totally get it.

SCARLET

No! I want it! Oh my God. I want it.

She presses the phone to her palm and mouths to her mom.

SCARLET (CONT'D)

(in a whisper)

THEY'RE OFFERING ME KATE!

There's a GASP offscreen.

SCARLET (CONT'D)

This is a total dream come true. (She hands the phone back to her mom, turns to Jack.) So... I just got the role as Kate.

JACK

Holy shit, babe!

Scarlet stands. Starts gathering her things.

SCARLET

I need to talk to my agent, I need to get into my role, this is amazing.

Just as she's walking offstage... Jack proffers the present.

JACK

Babe? Scar? Gift exchange?

But Scarlet doesn't answer. Jack stares dead-eyed into the camera. And then the screen goes black.

Comments: (3,876)

@LeighLove: First!
@MultiFanScarlet: ok I literally called it I knew they'd change their minds!

@ScarLeighJackletHeart: take that Fiona!!! Scarlet proves once again she is sUPERIOR
@TinyTee: Scar can you do another post about what Jack got for you? I literally get butterflies when I watch you open presents.
@RiotAct91: Um, can we talk what this vid is really about—APOLOGY? Guys, you don't have to apologize to us. Everyone knows people make mistakes. And anyway Jack it's not your fault it's that MYSTERY BITCH'S, she should be removed for trying to break up Jacklet and ruin the world's cutest ship. Who agrees??
@marniemarine18: still waiting for someone to expose Mystery Bitch. @IGteaV got any updates??
@MizzGuava55404: Hey can you guys please stop talking about the Mystery Girl like you want to hurt her? She's a real person you know. Probably with feelings and a family. these comments probably hurt her.
@LAGirlz7766: Who are you, MizzGuava? Maybe YOU are Mystery Girl? Get off this account. Literal trash

DELILAH

A few days later, Delilah sat in the backseat once again as her mother shuttled her to another invite-only event. And once again, her mother was swearing at the traffic on the highway. "You could just let me Uber!" Delilah reminded her.

Bethany shook her head. "I don't feel comfortable with that."

"Everyone else does it."

Her mother's eyes narrowed. "Don't use that line on me." She signaled to move into the left lane, letting out an *eep* when a motorcyclist zoomed up the shoulder.

Ava was in the car, too, with Faith, the brand-new friend who seemed to know oodles of gossip about Scarlet Leigh. Faith was tall, gangly, also fourteen, and had such fair coloring that her eyelashes were nearly invisible. Faith glanced surreptitiously at Delilah with what seemed like awe and then whispered something in Ava's ear. "Faith says you look cute today," Ava reported.

"Thanks." Delilah was wearing skinny jeans, a fitted black

sweater, and new leopard-print boots her mother had bought her for her upcoming birthday. She glanced around her sister to smile at Faith. "You can tell me yourself, you know."

Faith giggled in answer. Delilah felt both celebrity-special and big-sister annoyed. Then she stretched out her feet to admire her new shoes. "These boots are awesome," she said, hoping it would help to show some appreciation before her big ask. "I might wear them for a meeting this photographer wants to have with me."

Bethany frowned. "Photographer?"

"His name's Patrick. Apparently, he's great . . . and he wants to shoot me. Maybe with another influencer. It's sort of what you do, in the business."

Bethany chuckled. "I'm not leaving you alone with a male photographer, Delilah. I'm not that stupid."

"But it's important for me to do photo shoots if I want more . . ." Delilah stopped before she could say "followers." She and her mom often argued over that term. Bethany said it sounded very pied piper, and, as she put it, "You shouldn't be caught up in how many people like you when they haven't even met you."

". . . if I want more visibility," Delilah decided to say instead.

Bethany looked unimpressed. "Explain."

The hills flaunting the Hollywood sign passed. In the lane next to theirs, Delilah noticed an honest-to-God Rolls-Royce. Her mother's gaze felt like a spotlight, seeking out all the cracks and flaws in Delilah's logic. "Maybe I want to become a creative person in LA someday. Like a writer. Or an actress."

Bethany raised an eyebrow. "Since when do you want to be an actress?"

Delilah opened her mouth but then shut it again. Faith cleared her throat. "Delilah would be an awesome actress."

"Totally," Ava echoed.

"You've never expressed an interest in acting." Bethany's eyes were playful. This was a joke to her. "It's always been volleyball, or pets, or cooking. A celebrity chef I could see, but—"

"Forget it," Delilah interrupted sourly, turning away. This felt even more humiliating with Ava and Faith in the car. The only way to remain the cool, idolized big sister, after all, was to get everything you wanted.

The Real Real event was packed with influencers posing for photos, giving interviews, and perusing the goods. People Delilah recognized as YouTubers, influencers, and actors lined up on the left side of the red carpet, fidgeting with their hair and reapplying lip gloss while waiting to get their pictures taken. A Musically star that Ava liked snapped at her publicist, while one of the stars of a new Freeform spinoff walked the carpet. *Whoa,* Delilah thought, once again feeling overwhelmed.

She stood in the back of the line before a middle-aged woman with a clipboard approached her. "Delilah?" She didn't wait for her to respond. "I'm Karen. I run marketing. Jasmine said you were with her." At that, Karen gestured for Delilah to follow and pushed to the front of the line, hustling Delilah onto the carpet with a thumbs-up.

Cameras flashed. Some people called out her name. Thrust into the spotlight, Delilah tried to smile brightly—tried to remember all the ways to pose. She was hyperaware of the fact that she had very little makeup on. And was her hair *too* curled? And God, those lights were bright. . . .

As Delilah walked into the party, she got the same jolt of nerves as she had at the Wellness event, though today a few people turned to her with interest. "Lila D, right?" a girl with large blue eyes in a black jumpsuit and block-heel booties asked. "I love your page."

"Oh my gosh, really?" Delilah cried, astonished.

"Actually, here." The young woman pressed a card into Delilah's hands. "I'm a jewelry designer. I'd love for you to check out my stuff. Give me a call!"

"O-okay," Delilah stammered, staring at the little card in her hand. *Adina's Jewels.* She was pretty sure she'd seen this stuff sold on Shopbop. Was this her first potential sponsor?

"Delilah!" a voice called.

Jasmine stood across the room, surrounded by a cluster of adoring fans taking photo after photo of her. Once Delilah reached her, Jasmine gave her a huge hug. "You're a lifesaver. Everyone keeps asking me about this movie I'm doing, and I'm tired of answering questions."

"You're doing a movie? Congratulations!" Delilah was surprised. When did *that* happen?

"No, I'm *not* doing a movie—my manager made it up for confusing reasons. . . . It's a long story." Jasmine rolled her eyes. "I'll tell you later. Remind me to tell you about Fiona later, too."

"Why? Is Fiona okay?" Delilah asked.

Jasmine made a face that seemed to say she wasn't sure. "She sent me this really cryptic Snapchat saying she was offered a role in a big sitcom . . . but she's turning it down."

"You're kidding! *Why?*"

Jasmine checked over her shoulder as the crowd pushed closer. "Fiona has . . . issues," she said in a low voice. "But I didn't think that would matter. Anyway, we can't talk about it now. Come join me for some pics, 'kay?"

Jasmine pulled Delilah into a group of fans. To Delilah's delight, quite a few of them knew who she was. She and Jasmine posed for photo after photo—Delilah copied some of Jasmine's gestures, as the girl was a pro. As Jasmine signed a few autographs, a teenage girl sidled up to Delilah's left. "You're so lucky to know Jasmine," she murmured in the sort of low voice one might use to pass someone a secret message. "What's it like to be famous?"

"Oh, I'm not famous." Delilah wanted to laugh.

The girl looked at Delilah almost hungrily. She had thin hips, fringe-y bangs, and sort of a Mayim Bialik vibe—except shorter and stockier and in more makeup. She was also wearing a T-shirt with Scarlet Leigh's face screen-printed across the chest. Beneath the photo, in swirling, splashy letters, was the handle *ScarletOrDie89*.

The girl noticed Delilah staring. "That's my account!"

"You're a Scarlet fan?" Delilah asked shakily.

"Totally." She grinned excitedly. "Are you friends with her? Do you know if she's coming? Someone said they already saw Jack, so I bet she is!"

"I don't really know her," Delilah heard herself saying, though her brain buzzed at something else the girl had said. *Jack* was here?

She tried not to search the room for him. She should probably just leave. What if he somehow gave away she was the Mystery

Girl? Or worse, what if he pretended not to know her? She didn't know which outcome was worse.

The crowd thickened. More fans pulled Jasmine in for pictures. Delilah stepped around a table of gently used Gucci handbags, searching for an exit. People kept smiling at her. That über-fan in the Scarlet shirt was now perched by a rack of dresses, trying to chat up another influencer.

Finally, a side door. Delilah ducked out. The air was cool outside, and the sky had become gloomy. It matched her mood. She leaned against the storefront, taking deep breaths, trying to get her bearings back to the Beverly Center, where she and her mom had arranged to meet.

"Hey."

Delilah saw Jack's reflection in the store window before she saw Jack himself. He looked even better than he had at the restaurant at Wellness. It took her a moment to realize he was smiling at *her*. And now walking *toward* her.

"Go back inside," she blurted out. Her voice was both wounded and panicked.

"Can I talk to you?" Jack asked. "Please?"

Cars rushed down Melrose. Everything felt way too exposed. "Not *here,*" Delilah said, the fear rising.

Jack nodded, then hurried around the corner, motioning for her to follow. She reluctantly trailed after him to the front of a nondescript apartment building across from a Lululemon store. There was a truck in front of the apartment building unloading boxes; they came to a stop behind it, as it served decent cover. The sidewalk was empty.

"There," Jack said. "Does this work?"

He looked like he found all of this amusing. "Excuse me for being worried, but I'd rather not have anyone speculating that I'm your Mystery Girl," Delilah grumbled, feeling a zing of annoyance. "I doubt your fans would like it, either."

Jack cocked his head. "I don't do *everything* for my fans." He bit his lip. "Look, I wanted to check in on you before—as soon as all of that happened. But I was afraid you'd see my Finsta account and think it was a joke."

Delilah made a small huffing sound. She probably *would* have thought Jake's super-secret Finsta account was a joke.

"I'm fine." Delilah studied the tinted windows in the building across the street. What if someone was inside, staring out? "You didn't have to check up on me."

"Yeah, but I've thought about you a lot."

The tenderness in Jack's voice ruffled her resolve. She turned away, arms crossed tightly over her chest. "You're with Scarlet. You posted a big apology. You love each other. Which—great. Good for you."

She hadn't meant to sound so upset. She wanted to be cool, collected, standoffish, unbothered. It shouldn't hurt that Jack already had a girlfriend. There were tons of guys to meet in this city.

But she'd liked meeting *him*.

"That video . . ." Jack stared into the sky. "It's a lie. Scarlet and I aren't really together. I mean, we were, at first. And our fans loved it. They loved the posts about us as a couple. They loved our pictures popping up in *Us* and on TMZ. Both our followings grew. But we haven't talked in months. I doubt she wants to be with me any more than I want to be with her."

Delilah frowned. "You're staying together for your followers?"

"Yeah. It's my dad's idea. And Scarlet's team's, obviously. Those people plan my whole life, and I hate it. I used to make my own decisions. But now . . ."

His voice cracked. Did he expect her to feel sorry for him? And yet, despite everything, she felt a tiny bit flattered he was telling her all this.

"My team—especially my dad—tells me that if I break up with Scarlet, my career will take a hit. It's why I made that video. What you didn't see is Scarlet and I barely speaking before we got on camera—well, except for Scarlet giving me hell for being photographed with you."

Delilah's heart stopped. "She knows it's *me*?"

"No way. I didn't tell her a thing. I know how vengeful she can get." He stepped closer to Delilah. She got a faint whiff of something spicy on his skin. "I don't want to be with her anymore. I want something that's real."

She wasn't sure how to interpret that. Was he saying he wanted *her*? But he didn't even know her! Still, she allowed herself to indulge in the fantasy for a split second. How amazing would it be to grab his hand and run off with him? Spend the whole day with him—talking, laughing, getting to know who he was?

But all those nasty comments rushed back. All the negative consequences. Dread streaked through her veins. Delilah took a big step backward. "I have to go," she blurted out. And then she turned around and ran.

JASMINE

"Cut!" a voice called from the dark set.

A bell rang, and Jasmine's smile faded. Angie the makeup artist rushed onto the stage and started touching up Jasmine's foundation. The show's hairstylist, whose name Jasmine had forgotten—which was unlike her, as she was usually chatty with the stylists—hurried over with a flat iron. Jasmine smelled the warm, nutty scent of coffee and sensed that Ruby was nearby, too—probably about to give notes.

"Doing good," Ruby appraised. Right on schedule.

Jasmine opened her eyes. While she was in an older take on her rainbow dress, white lace stockings, and huge hair, Ruby looked über-comfortable in leggings, Vans, and a fitted UCLA T-shirt. "But you seem . . . *down.*"

"I'm not down," Jasmine argued. "I just don't like lying."

Ruby's eyes darted to Annalise, the host of *Saw It on the Gram,* a web-based entertainment show that had loose ties to *Young*

Hollywood. Jasmine was doing an interview with her at their studios in Venice Beach to discuss "all things Jasmine and Lulu," including the latest damage control, as Ruby put it—their spin on those photos of Jasmine sharing a kiss with the anonymous someone at the party. The party line was that she was shooting a new movie. *You can't even tell us if it's a movie for the Lemonade franchise?* Annalise pushed. *The fans would lose their minds if you were doing a* That's Hot! *movie!*

But Jasmine kept mum. Her silence would stir up unnecessary speculation, but then it would blow over soon enough. A few months later, eagle-eyed fans might question whatever happened to Jasmine's mystery movie, but in Hollywood, movies fell apart all the time.

But Jasmine couldn't stop thinking about the girl. What if she was as dazzled with Jasmine as Jasmine was with her? What if she was searching for a way to get through to Jasmine *right now*? How could a person just disappear into thin air? Every bleat of her phone, every buzz of a text—she was sure it was *her*, reaching out, revealing her identity, indicating that she wanted to take things further.

But still nothing.

"Ready to go again?" the director, a petite woman in glasses with hip-length blond hair, asked Jasmine and the host. Annalise gave a thumbs-up. Jasmine's smile was a little weaker. In moments, the camera was rolling again.

Annalise turned to Jasmine. "Let's move on. Everybody's talking about potential Jasmine ships. Are you seeing anybody? Maybe having one of those online-only relationships?"

Jasmine flashed a bright movie-star smile. "I'm not a fan of having relationships where your only communication is through DMs. For me, it's about getting to know the person . . . *physically.*"

"Ooh." Annalise's eyes twinkled. "So is there someone you've been physical with?"

Jasmine's mind flashed back to those stolen kisses. Did she dare dangle a carrot? "There might be someone." She turned toward the camera. "You know who you are."

Offstage, Ruby inhaled sharply. Annalise leaned forward, intrigued. "I know you like your privacy, but can you give us a little hint? Is it Luke?"

"No, it's not Luke." Jasmine suppressed the urge to roll her eyes.

Annalise seemed to get a bolt of brilliance, and her whole body straightened. "Oh my God. It's Jack Dono, isn't it? Is that *you* in that picture?"

"What?" Jasmine blinked, caught off guard. The lights were so hot all of a sudden. "Absolutely not. I don't break up ships."

There was a naughty twinkle in Annalise's eye. "If you *say* so . . ."

"I *do* say so," Jasmine snapped. "That's a really idiotic assumption to make."

"Jasmine!" Ruby sounded horrified.

But this just seemed to rile Annalise up more. "Whoa! What's that line from *Hamlet*? 'The lady doth protest too much, methinks'?"

"I'm not protesting!" Jasmine cried. And then the interview ended. It was a horrible note to go out on.

As soon as the director yelled cut, Ruby marched onstage, her expression contrite. "Annalise, I am so, *so* sorry."

"It's cool," Annalise said mildly, dropping her weird fake smile. She gave Jasmine a chilly sidelong glance before she retreated to her dressing room.

Ruby turned to Jasmine. "What's wrong with you?"

Jasmine lifted her hair off her neck. "I had to shut her down! I don't want people thinking I'm with Jack Dono!"

"They won't think that. They're only going to be thinking about how bitchy you've become."

Jasmine scoffed. "She asked me an inappropriate question. I wasn't bitchy at all."

She started toward the exit, but Ruby caught her arm. "Where are you going? You still have the shoot."

"What shoot?" Jasmine's heart sank. She was really hoping to get a few hours in at the beach, since they were all the way out here.

"For *Young Hollywood*! You forgot?" Ruby guided her toward the stage. "What's wrong with you today? I feel like a mother chasing after a toddler!"

"I already *have* a mother for that." But then Jasmine felt a stab of sadness. Her mother was Ruby's mother, too. They shared so much history. They used to be allies.

Years ago, before Jasmine was anybody, when she was just doing community theater and the occasional audition and lots of dance classes, Ruby had her own interests. She was on the art track in high school, taking painting and sculpting, hanging out with kids in bands and skaters and surfers. Jasmine went to Ruby's sophomore art show; Ruby's paintings were big, swirling tornadoes of color, dramatic and evocative. One of them hung in Jasmine's bedroom, actually. There was another in their parents' house, but it was pushed to a back room, in the darkness. Jasmine would rather it hung in the spot where her *That's Hot!* portrait was in the foyer.

"Do you ever paint anymore?" Jasmine asked suddenly.

Ruby's eyes boggled. "Are you on drugs?"

Did Ruby even apply to college? Jasmine was fourteen when Ruby was a senior; back then, Jasmine was so focused on her new career that she didn't pay attention. She was pretty sure Ruby moved straight into the role of being Jasmine's manager. It was good timing, their mother said—Jasmine's first manager, a man named Adam, was sketchy and slick, and tried to push Jasmine into too much too fast. *But Ruby understands you. This will be a great learning experience for her.*

But all of a sudden, Ruby's *learning experience* was such a responsibility.

A door at the back of the soundstage opened, and Jasmine noticed a woman she'd met from *Young Hollywood* coming toward them, her tall form eerily backlit by the klieg lights.

Then time seemed to slow down, turning to taffy. Jasmine stepped away from her sister. Without saying a word, she bolted out the studio door in the opposite direction. She couldn't do a shoot right now. She couldn't fake-smile and pose. If they made her, she might explode.

The daylight startled her, and for a moment, her eyes couldn't focus. The funky Venice Beach storefronts and murals were so bright they hurt her eyes. Letting out a moan, she turned to the left and started to run, her shoes clacking on the sidewalk.

Passersby gazed at her in alarm. They could have been shouting her name. They could have been taking pictures of her. But it was like she was moving through a cattle chute, seeing only ahead.

Neon lights blinked at the next block, catching her eye. *Tattoos,* read a sign above the door. The entire building was painted black, which intrigued her—it was the opposite of her garish rainbow outfit. She lunged for the door and pushed inside.

The room smelled like weed. The artwork on the front wall was of large-eyed women with big, exaggerated lips, grinning skulls, a black widow spider giving a peace sign. At the back of the room, a large bearded man was lying bare-chested on a table while a tough-looking girl with waist-long dreadlocks leaned over his upper thigh, tattoo machine in hand.

"Help you?"

An African American woman with a huge afro sat at a counter Jasmine hadn't noticed. She blinked at Jasmine impassively, like she didn't think Jasmine was anything special. There was something alluring about her, though. Her rawness, her honesty—she seemed so utterly *herself.*

"Me?" Jasmine cried ludicrously.

"Yeah. You. You have an appointment?" Then the woman looked Jasmine up and down, her lips curling into a smirk. "Who are you, Rainbow Brite?"

The artist working on the man at the back let out a guffaw. "Are you even eighteen?"

"Nah," the dude getting inked chimed in. "She looks like she's about twelve."

Jasmine peered down at her rainbow dress. They weren't wrong. Then she turned to the window, reality snapping back.

Lulu C had just run down the streets of Venice Beach and burst into a tattoo parlor. Had she lost her mind?

"I have to go," she blurted out, whirling around and pushing against the door.

Back out in the sun, she heaved a deep breath. Down the block, she spied Ruby in front of the studio, her hand shielding her eyes. Jasmine was about to slink back to her sister when a shadow across the street snagged her attention. Someone was ducking behind a parked BMW.

Cars swished past. Jasmine adjusted her bright, ridiculous dress, feeling like a beacon easily viewed from space. She watched as the figure, still hunched, moved away from the BMW and hurried into a store that sold cowboy boots. She saw a swish of blond waves. The sharp point of a jaw. Was that . . . ? It *couldn't* be.

Inside the boots store, the figure stood straighter. And . . . it *was.* Scarlet Leigh was in that boots store. Was Scarlet Leigh . . . *spying* on her?

That wasn't good.

FIONA

"So all of us were watching the game during our free period, and there was like one minute left, right? And if Arsenal won, they'd make it to the semifinals. So in the last minute of stoppage time, Mesut Özil makes this insane pass, and they score. They win the game, and now four boys on the soccer team owe me fifty bucks." Chase grabbed a fry from Fiona's plate. They were having dinner at Craig's, a trendy bistro in LA. So trendy, actually, it was named one of the best places in the city to see celebrities. Being "seen" was something Fiona definitely didn't need right now, but Chase seemed so excited to eat here that she didn't have the heart to cancel the reservation.

"And my dad got us tickets to the semifinals!" Chase continued enthusiastically. "Can you believe?"

"Mm-hmm." Fiona tried to smile, but she couldn't stop surreptitiously scanning the room. Was that four-top across the room whispering about her? She shrank down in her seat just a little.

"Fee?"

"Yeah?" She jolted back, giving Chase another jagged smile.

Chase sat back in his chair, his brow crinkling. "You looking for someone?"

"Me? No." Fiona speared a bite of organic salmon and began counting the number of times she chewed. "Why would you think that?"

Chase tapped his fork against his plate. "Your eyes haven't left that doorway."

Fiona brushed a piece of hair out of his eyes. She wanted this date to be normal and chill, but she'd never been a person who could hide her emotions. Of course Chase could sense something was wrong.

"Excuse me, are you Fiona Jacobs?"

A slight, slender guy with perfectly coiffed hair and a fitted navy jacket fidgeted nervously above her. He held his cell phone in one hand, but the screen was facing toward him, as though there was something on it he didn't want Fiona to see.

"I'm so sorry to bother you," he said in a rush, "but I just wanted to say I read about you on *Deadline.* And whatever you're going through . . . you're in my thoughts."

Fiona's face burned. "Thanks."

The guy bowed and then receded. Fiona stared down at her meal, suddenly not hungry. Forks clinked. Across the room, someone bellowed, "You are *kidding* me." She could feel Chase staring, but she couldn't muster up the courage to make eye contact.

"'Whatever you're going through'?" he repeated. "Wanna explain?"

"It's nothing," Fiona said quickly. But this was Chase. She couldn't keep this from him any longer.

She sighed and took a long sip of water. "I turned down the part of Kate. It probably just hit *Deadline*."

Chase blinked. "Wait, *what?* Why?"

"It didn't feel right."

"But you were so excited!"

She pushed the wilted greens around her plate. "I decided that it was too much."

One breath. Two breaths. She could do this. She could tell Chase what she'd told her mom: that she wasn't sure if she could handle the role because of her OCD. Playing that card was the easiest, after all. After they'd moved to LA, after Fiona's rapid weight loss and constant need to exercise, her mother had obviously noticed the counting and rituals. "We'll manage this," her mother had assured her. "There's great medicine. And we'll get you the best therapist money can buy. It's nothing for you to be ashamed of."

But Fiona had known even before she'd gone to a therapist or taken medications that no medical plan would work. Her behaviors had arisen purely and completely from the guilt and shame in what she'd done to Lana. After all, they hadn't existed *before* Lana—not even when Lana's teasing was at its worst. Had it never happened, perhaps Fiona would still suffer with minor obsessions and compulsions now, but it probably wouldn't be nearly this bad.

But now someone knew the root of her problems. Someone

was going to crack her secret wide open. And, okay, they didn't give *specifics* of what they knew . . . but they knew Fiona had a secret, and Fiona wasn't taking any chances. Which was why she'd turned down Kate.

"I mean, I'll support you no matter what," Chase said in a voice so tender Fiona feared her heart might shatter. "But . . . it's just so sudden. Did something bring it on? Some . . . *comment,* or something? People can be so cruel. . . ."

Fiona shook her head. "Nothing like that."

Chase stared miserably at his food. "Do you just want to go? We don't have to stay here. I can pay the bill. . . ."

Fiona nodded, and soon, they were heading out of the restaurant.

"Want to drive somewhere? Laurel Canyon or something?" Chase asked.

Fiona bit her lip to keep from crying. "I just want to go home. I'm staying at the Dove tonight—my mom is staying with me there. I can get an Uber, since it's in the opposite direction from you." She opened the app on her phone.

Chase slowed his pace, uncertainty on his face. "You're sure there's nothing you're not telling me about this Kate thing?"

"Yes, I'm sure," she answered, feeling more miserable by the second.

"Whatever it is, we'll get through it together."

The hot prickle of tears behind her eyes made the neon lights blur up and down the street. "I know," she whispered. But was that really true? If Chase knew who she *really* was, what she was capable of, would he be so forgiving?

The Uber came quickly. After a gloomy goodbye with Chase,

Fiona climbed into the car and leaned her head against the leather seat. Her phone vibrated against her hip. Now that the Kate story had broken, new comments greeted her left and right: *RU okay?* wrote a fan. *U look tired.* There was a paparazzo shot of her hurrying into the spa earlier today, her hair disheveled, her face pale, the corners of her mouth turned down in a frown. It had been years since such an unfiltered photo of her had appeared online. The fact that people were passing it around the internet, sharing and re-sharing, made her feel itchy; she wished she could take it down.

Then she scrolled back through her Notifications, moving back from earlier today to last night, and then yesterday, when she'd texted her agent saying she was turning ABC down. And then she scrolled back further until she got to her alerts from days ago, just moments after her audition for the pilot. God, she wished she could return to that happiness. There, peppered among the instant fan reactions about the "secret thing" she teased on her feed, was the pretty photo of Lana. It was one of the last photos anyone had taken of her before she died.

Now Fiona stared at Lana's face until her eyes crossed. If only the Zoey thing hadn't happened. Maybe everything would be normal now.

Zoey Marx was a little under five feet tall, and so childlike in a lot of ways; sometimes substitute teachers noticed her in the middle school line at the private girls' school they all attended and said gently, "Elementary is over *there*." But Zoey wasn't bothered. She took eleventh-grade math. She played cello like a virtuoso. And though she didn't have many friends, she seemed self-possessed in a mature, independent way, like she didn't care what people thought.

Why did this bother Lana so much? Because someone was good at something she wasn't? Because someone was okay with themselves and all their non-Lana attributes instead of shriveling up, wormlike, in Lana's presence? Lana turned on Zoey the spring of eighth grade. First, she did silly things: in art class, she put Zoey's art project on the highest shelf so Zoey couldn't reach it. In gym, she moved Zoey's locker to a top one, which would mean Zoey would have to stand precariously on a bench to access it. As Zoey floundered to get to her school uniform in the new gym locker, her post-shower towel slipping from under her arm, Lana and her cronies watched with satisfaction from around the corner, recording the whole thing. It ended up posted on a *Zoey Marx Is Lame* Facebook page the next day.

But Zoey just plugged along with these inconveniences like a Who in Whoville, undaunted that the Grinch had stolen her Christmas decorations. It was unclear if she even saw *Zoey Marx is Lame*, but if she did, she acted like it didn't matter. This only riled Lana up more. She started a rumor that Zoey was cribbing answers for eleventh-grade calculus tests from someone in another class. That got Zoey called into the headmaster's office, where she explained, unfazed, that she wasn't a cheater. Lesser girls would have called out Lana—it was so *obvious* Lana was behind everything. Lesser girls also would have mentioned that on the *Zoey Marx Is Lame* Facebook page, there was a clip of a gym towel slipping from around Zoey's nonexistent chest again and again on a boomerang loop. But Zoey did neither. The principal gave her detention, and she had to take the next calculus test under supervision to make sure she wasn't cheating. And still, Zoey was as cool as a cucumber.

Lana sat in front of Fiona in homeroom, so Fiona saw, firsthand, how annoyed Lana felt that her latest victim wasn't cracking. There were a lot of things Fiona wished she could have changed about her behavior that final day. She should have warned Zoey that Lana wasn't going to give up. She should have told Lana to leave Zoey alone. But here was the truth: Fiona was thrilled when Lana turned around in her desk and looked at Fiona with interest—not like a terrifying bully, but like a peer.

"What do *you* think would get under Zoey Marx's skin?" Lana asked conspiratorially.

Fiona thought for a moment. Horribly, shamefully, she wanted to please Lana. She wanted to make her happy. "Cello," she said. "She likes cello, so . . ."

A devious smile spread across Lana's lips. If Fiona could yank back the suggestion, she would have, because she just knew—*this* would be Zoey's undoing.

And it was.

"Miss?"

The car was stopped at the front of the Dove. "Oh," Fiona said thickly, feeling like she'd emerged from hours of dull, heavy sleep. "Thanks." She grabbed her bag and hurried out.

Her phone beeped just as she was unlocking the front door. She didn't really want to check the screen—she wasn't in the mood to do any more explaining tonight—but the tug of curiosity was too great. Jasmine had sent a text.

Is this true?

Attached was a link to a new article from *Deadline*. Fiona clicked it numbly, figuring it was going to be more news about her downward spiral. But when the page loaded, Scarlet Leigh's headshot filled the screen. *Scarlet Leigh, actress and mega-influencer, signs comedy pilot deal with ABC.*

Fiona's eyes bounced across the words. She noticed familiar names: Mona Greenblatt, Bette Lawson—the very same people she'd screen-tested with the other day. And then a pull quote: "I'm so, *so* excited to be playing Kate," Scarlet said. "Her life seems a lot like mine!"

The realization crystallized in Fiona's mind. *Scarlet Leigh.* Her forever competitor. It made sense. Years ago, Fiona had stolen something of Scarlet's, and now Scarlet had finally found a way to get her revenge. In some ways, it brought Fiona relief—at least she knew who'd sent that cryptic DM now. At least she knew who'd found out her secret.

Except that person was Scarlet. And as all things with Scarlet, Fiona had no way of predicting what Scarlet might do next . . . or how to make sure Scarlet would never, *ever* tell.

Transcript of Scarlet Leigh's personal vlog, 6/22 (for her YouTube channel)

Camera clicks on to show Scarlet's face backlit by a bright California sky. She's in a tight-fitting hoodie and yoga capris and has a Supreme ball cap on her head.

SCARLET

Hey, guys, what's UP! Welcome to Workout Wednesday! So I'm out here with Cory…

Turns the camera to CORY, who's also in athletic gear. He gives a "Woo!" and a thumbs-up.

SCARLET

And we are getting our sweat on at Runyon Canyon! It's bee-*yoo*-teeful out today!

She sweeps the camera around to show the dramatic rocks and the dramatic view of the city.

SCARLET

Anyway, Cory and I are going to take you through a new workout today. You don't need to be on a canyon path to do this—you can be in an airport, in your bedroom…

CORY

…Hiding in the school library during lunch…

SCARLET

(uncertain)

Cory, did you used to hide in the school library during lunch?

CORY

Only every day. (Sighs.) High school was not the most fun for me.

SCARLET

Well, thank God *I* found you.

They laugh, and he gives her a kiss on the cheek.

SCARLET

Anyway, guys, maybe you're just feeling like getting into better shape—for us, we need to get toned so we can bring it to a big event that I'm cohosting next week.

CORY

#Gratitude!

SCARLET

I'm teaming up with Kyle Charlie, the King of Makeup on YouTube, to hold the party this year! I'm *so* excited.

VOICE (O.S.)

Hey! Scarlet Leigh! Heard you're gonna be on a sitcom!

Scarlet smiles and waves, yelling, "That's right!" Then she turns the camera back on herself.

SCARLET

I can't wait to walk you through my get ready with me video—and this year, you guys are going to vote on my dress! The options are amazing.

CORY

Seriously amazing.

Scarlet points the camera at him.

SCARLET

This one turned me down to be my date—he's taking his boyfriend, Cooper, instead. Which I guess is okay because we all know and *adore* Cooper, but still, I'm heartbroken.

CORY

Oh, stop. Everyone wants to see Jacklet, not Corlet.

They walk a few more steps. They're at a steep part of the climb, and they're both starting to huff and puff.

SCARLET

So what do you say we dive into our workout! Cory's gonna take the cam, and I'm going to start us off. Let's get warmed up by jogging the rest of the way up this rise! Just do whatever gets your heart pumping—jumping jacks, jogging in place, burpees... thirty seconds, go!

Scarlet hands Cory the camera. There's a little shakiness, but he aims it at her as she takes off up the hill. We hear Cory groan, but he follows after her.

Scarlet rounds the corner. Cory follows a few paces behind. But when he does, Scarlet is gone. Cory stops.

CORY

Scar?

The camera swings around across the scrub grass and rocks. Hikers pass obliviously. The camera jostles as Cory runs forward and looks around another bend. But Scarlet isn't there, either.

CORY

Scar? Scar! NOT FUNNY!

More running. The trail is empty. This feels kind of creepy. And suddenly, the camera swings around, and Cory gasps. Scarlet is collapsed against the rock face, her face ashen. . . .

Cory lunges for her, video still running.

CORY (CONT'D)

Scar! Holy shit!

There's shuffling as he places the phone on the ground. It's tilted at an angle where we can see. Cory crouches next to Scarlet and holds the sides of her face. Scarlet comes to. . . .

CORY

Did you trip? Did someone hit you?

SCARLET

(croakily)

I . . . I don't know. I just suddenly felt really dizzy. . . .

WOMAN'S VOICE (O.S.)

Is she okay?

Cory throws his body protectively over Scarlet.

CORY

Just went a little too hard on her interval! No biggie!

(Turning back to Scarlet)

Do you need something? A Kind bar?

SCARLET

I can't have a freaking Kind bar, Cor. They're not my sponsor.

CORY

Well, at least you're not brain damaged.

He hands her his water bottle, and she sips. She still looks really, *really* out of it. Cory sits back on his haunches.

CORY (CONT'D)

(in a whisper, but loud enough to hear)

You need to get it together, girl.

SCARLET

Cor, I'm fine.

CORY

Oh yeah? You're not cracking up on me?

SCARLET

Stop it. Of course not.

CORY

Okay. That's good, girl. 'Cause imagine how your *mom* would react.

They both snicker. The color is coming back into Scarlet's cheeks. Then she notices the phone propped up against the rock and grimaces.

SCARLET

Cory, what the hell, it's still *running*?

She lunges for the camera and shuts it off. Black.

Comments: (8,445)

@LoveMeScar: FIRST!

@ScarLeighJackletHeart: Vitamin B-12, Scar! It's a total lifesaver!

@LeighLeighMe92: omg I pass out all the time. We're twins scar!! Love you forever xx

@ILoveScarScar09: GUYS THEORY!! What if Mystery Bitch pushed her or something and is out to get her. We seriously need to figure out who she is. She'll pay for what she did

@MizzGuava55404: Watch the video, guys. No one is behind Scarlet. No one pushed her… unless it's Cory.

@ILoveScarScar09: @MizzGuava55404 Cory is the actual best friend ever he'd NEVER hurt scar

@ScarletFanMel66: Hi Scarlet, remember how we met the other day? It was the most amazing experience of my life. I wish I was at Runyon Canyon this morning. I would have helped you up. Cory seems like he sucks. I love you!

DELILAH

"Whoa," Delilah whispered as she stepped into the airy open-plan rooms in Jasmine's penthouse. The place looked like something out of a magazine. The gourmet kitchen gleamed as if everything was brand-new and unused. Boxes of food containing Jasmine's sponsors, like Blue Apron and Fit Tea and Whey protein powder, were stacked on a back counter against the subway tile. There was a canvas print of Jasmine's dog on the living room wall. A huge chandelier of frothy pink glass bubbles hung from the ceiling.

Mom would love this, Delilah thought. Delilah had finally admitted to her family that she and Jasmine Walters-Diaz—yes, *that* Jasmine Walters-Diaz—were friends, and after Ava and her new bestie, Faith, screamed with excitement, after fifteen long minutes of Delilah's parents grilling her about Jasmine (did she drink? Throw wild parties? Where were her parents? Had she graduated high school? Wasn't she awfully *young* to live alone?), they reluctantly allowed Delilah to come over here tonight to prep for a Snapchat TV event. Perhaps if her mom saw how polished and grown-up Jasmine's condo was, she'd be convinced that Jasmine was a genuinely good, responsible person.

She walked through the living area, admiring the pale pink upholstery, shiny gold fixtures, and a whole accent wall of green potted succulents. "It looks exactly like that studio in LA they rent out for influencer shoots," she told Jasmine, who was following Delilah around, cradling her little dog in her arms.

"You know that's in this building, right?" Jasmine asked.

"No way!" Delilah felt dazzled. She'd peered at so, *so* many shoots from the famous Photo Studio.

"Yeah, but they stole a few of my ideas. The Polaroid wall in there? Totally me first. They have this couch, too." She gestured to a gorgeous pink sectional. "I'm thinking about getting rid of it because everyone thinks I'm shooting in the studio and not in my own home." She glanced over her shoulder. "If you want it, Fee, it's yours! I know how much you covet it, girl!"

"Huh?" Fiona asked distractedly. She was sitting on a high stool in front of a giant Hollywood vanity, her auburn hair falling over her face. Splayed beneath her looked to be the contents of an entire Sephora store: dozens of huge eyeshadow palettes, jars of foundation and primer, and at least fifty Chanel lipsticks, arranged even more beautifully than they would be at the Saks counter. Delilah thought about the '80s retro Caboodle carrier she stored *her* makeup in. She'd considered doing an Instagram Story about her stash . . . but maybe not.

Delilah skipped over to hug Fiona, and though Fiona tried

to smile, her body was stiff, and there was a distracted look in her eyes. Delilah remembered that Jasmine had said Fiona mysteriously turned down the Kate part. They still didn't know quite why.

"How are you?" Delilah asked cautiously.

Fiona listlessly picked up a blush brush. "Okay. Tired."

Jasmine headed over to the makeup corner, too. "I'm so jealous you have your own space," Delilah said to her. "Did your parents give you a hard time about it?"

"Not really, but that's because I put them up in a pretty sweet house of their own." Jasmine's face darkened. "It's the one thing they can't really give me crap about, actually."

"Your parents give you a hard time, too?" Delilah picked up a makeup brush. "Mine are on my case all the time."

"Oh yeah." Jasmine shrugged. "I'm in the doghouse with them right now, actually."

Jasmine leaned into the vanity to apply a second coat of dark red lipstick. Delilah shifted, feeling awkward all over again. This morning, an alert had popped up on her phone about Jasmine: *Is the* That's Hot! *actress pulling a Britney?* Then came some images of Jasmine running like mad down a funky, beachy block and into a tattoo parlor.

Who cares if she gets a tattoo? Delilah had thought—though the article said Jasmine had signed some sort of "morals clause" and her sponsors, including Lemonade, would terminate her contracts if she conducted herself in a manner "unbecoming to her public image."

Was the tattoo shop a cry for help, then? Was Jasmine feeling trapped, just like Jack? A guilty feeling needled Delilah: *Stop thinking about Jack.* But she couldn't. Not just because he'd cornered her the other day, either. Because they'd started talking. A *lot.*

Shortly after Jack found her at Real Real, he reached out on his Finsta. *Hey, it's me. Not a faker,* he wrote. *Hit me back if you want to talk.*

Delilah waited eight hours before she wrote back, telling herself it was all kinds of wrong . . . but then she cracked. *Hi, non-faker,* she replied. *I am also a non-faker.*

Cool, he responded almost immediately. And then: *So what are your thoughts on homemade slime?*

The question was so out there and unexpected that it put Delilah at ease. She wrote back how she felt about homemade slime, asking Jack what his thoughts were on the recent *Avengers* movie. That turned into some pretty serious movie and TV talk—she was delighted to find out that one of Jack's favorite shows was the old, black-and-white *Twilight Zone,* as it was a favorite of hers, too. When boarding an airplane, they both immediately thought about the episode where there was a gremlin on the plane's wing, dismantling the thing in hope of a crash. *It's why I can never sit near a wing,* Jack said. *Me too!* Delilah agreed.

Delilah told him silly stories, like about how she and Busy used to write mystery stories about their families: *The Case of What Happened to the TV Remote, The Mysterious Sound in the Dryer.* And about her dog, Robot, who they'd had put to sleep the previous summer—and that she was dying to get a new puppy. They talked a lot about dogs, actually—which breeds they liked, how their dorky dream vacation was to go to the Westminster

Dog Show in New York City. Sixty-three messages that first day. Seventy-one the next. Delilah's final message to Jack last night was a jumble of letters because she'd sent the DM as she was falling asleep. In fact, as she glanced at her phone screen, a new message from him had come in only a few minutes before. She was dying to look at it, but . . . well. She couldn't. Her new friends might see.

It was just so easy to talk to him . . . but what were they doing, exactly? Did Jack like her . . . or did he just want to be her friend? He and Scarlet had released an apology video, after all. They'd recommitted themselves to one another or whatever. But if Jack was still so into Scarlet, why would he *need* to talk to Delilah? It didn't make sense.

Suddenly, she felt Fiona's gaze on her and jolted in alarm. She hadn't said any of this out *loud*, had she? "What was that?" she asked, wondering if Fiona had said something Delilah missed.

"Um, is that what you're wearing to the party?" Fiona asked carefully.

Delilah peered down. She had on her new leopard booties, her favorite skinny jeans, and a silk black tee. But Jasmine wore a one-shouldered dress and high heels. Fiona had on leather pants, cut-out booties, and a funky crop top that showed off her perfect abs. "Do I look awful?" she asked in a small voice.

"Oh, honey, no," Jasmine said. "But we could make you look even *better*."

"After all," Fiona said, her eyes suddenly twinkling. "There are going to be plenty of cute guys at this thing! We could find you a guy for Gratitude Prom!"

"Gratitude . . . Prom?" Delilah asked slowly. "What's that?"

Jasmine smiled. "Instagram throws it. They're launching a new feature that has something to do with gratitude—an explosion of praying hands when you like something, I think? Anyway, they're holding a dance to celebrate. It's for teen influencers. Last year's was a blast."

"You have to come," Fiona gushed. "There's a make-your-own crown table, In-N-Out sponsors, Charlie Puth performed last year . . ."

"And the messaging is anti-bullying, anti-trolling, kindness, and graciousness," Fiona added. "And going is a great way to gain followers. Good visibility, you can get tons of pictures with people who will help you grow your brand, that sort of thing." She nudged Delilah coyly. "And it's *really* fun to go with a date."

"Yeah," Delilah said shakily. Little did these girls know she'd already *found* someone she wanted to take as a date. The problem was, doing so would set off Instagram World War III.

Forty minutes later, Delilah wore a silky minidress gifted to Jasmine from an up-and-coming designer. Jasmine looped a stack of bracelets around her wrists and put big, shiny earrings in her earlobes. Fiona took over hair and makeup, giving Delilah a dramatic cut crease eye and flat-ironing her hair so that it looked like a long, shiny piece of glass. Neither girl allowed her to see her finished look until they were done, and when they'd spun the makeup chair around, Delilah had gasped. She looked so . . . different.

As Delilah was admiring herself, Jasmine held her phone outstretched, snapping shots of her face and body. "Are you going to post those, Jazz?" Fiona asked. "They're not even filtered."

"Nah, these are just for Ruby for approval," Jasmine said, rolling her eyes. "I'm under lockdown right now, so my team needs to sign off on all my wardrobe decisions."

"Really?" Delilah asked, startled.

Jasmine sighed. "Don't even get me started."

Soon enough, they were pulling up to the valet line at the Beverly Hilton. Delilah heard a peal of screams and turned, startled to see rows and rows of fans behind sawhorses. "Jasmine!" they called. "Fiona!" A bunch of kids squealed excitedly as Chase, who came in a separate Uber, glided up to Fiona and took her arm. And then, astonishingly, the fans turned to Delilah, and some of them called *her* name, too.

Delilah smiled and waved. The fans raised their phones. Then Jasmine pulled on her arm. "Official photos are over here on the step-and-repeat. Just follow my lead, okay?"

A *step-and-repeat*! It was straight out of the Oscars! Delilah peered at the long backdrop bearing the Snapchat logo. Photographers were standing on the other side of the room, their cameras outstretched. People were taking turns posing in front of the wall, turning this way and that, smiling with all their teeth. Delilah recognized a TV actress, and then a semi-famous comedienne, and then a woman who'd apparently won a silver medal in snowboarding at the X Games. The photographers called their names: "Over here! This way!"

Delilah's heart hammered as she got closer to the front of the line. It was one thing to post selfies on Instagram, but this felt official. She so wished Busy were here.

"What is with this freaking *line*?"

A grating voice behind them set off alarms in Delilah's head, and she slowly twisted around. Standing a few people back was a tall, slender, model-beautiful blonde in a long silver dress. Delilah would recognize her face anywhere. *Scarlet Leigh.*

Her heart dropped to her toes. She peeked at the group Scarlet had come with, praying that Jack wasn't among them. She recognized everyone in her group as regulars on Scarlet's vlogs: the cute makeup artist, Cory, who was wearing a burgundy tux; Scarlet's agent, Macy, who looked frumpy next to Scarlet but would be a bombshell anywhere else; and Scarlet's mom, Gina, who nervously touched an understated white-gold necklace twinkling at her throat.

No Jack. Thank God.

But Scarlet's mouth was curved down in an impatient frown. "I mean, does everyone even deserve to *be* in this line? It's not like it's for *every single guest.*" Then her eyes clapped on Delilah's group. "Hey, Jazz. Hey, Fiona," she said drolly. Her gaze sharpened when she noticed Fiona's boyfriend. "*Hi,* Chase."

Chase gave Scarlet an uncomfortable half wave. "Uh, hey." He stepped closer to Fiona, wrapping his arm around her shoulders as if to say, *We might have dated once, but that was a long, long time ago.*

Fiona, strangely, went stiff at the sight of Scarlet. Her face drained of color, and she stepped from the line. "Um, I just have to . . ."

Suddenly, she was running away. "Fiona?" Chase called, heading after her.

"Fiona!" Jasmine called, too, standing on her tiptoes. But

Fiona was lost in the venue by then. Jasmine glanced at Delilah. "What was *that* about?"

"I have no idea," Delilah answered.

"Guess she didn't want to get her picture taken," Scarlet's friend, Cory, simpered behind them, sounding like he was holding in giggles.

"Who's this, Jazz?" To Delilah's horror, Scarlet was now staring directly at her. "Your plus one?"

Jasmine bristled. "No, this is Delilah Rollins. Lila D?"

Scarlet's smirk didn't change. Cory nudged her and whispered, *"Puppy Girl."*

"It's Delilah, actually," Delilah said loudly.

Scarlet's gaze was now on Delilah's waist. "Are you on *drugs*?"

Delilah was puzzled at Scarlet's question until she noticed that her supply of insulin and needles, always on hand, was clearly visible inside the going-out bag Jasmine had loaned her. "Um, no." She quickly snapped the clasp. "I'm diabetic."

Scarlet was already looking elsewhere, having lost interest. Was Delilah *that* unimportant? Was diabetes that boring? Suddenly, she felt so tempted to say, *Guess what? There are over 100 DMs between me and your boyfriend on my phone right now. How do you like* that?

But instantly, this fact filled her with fear, not triumph. Her phone felt so exposed. What if Jack chose to DM her right now—and Scarlet saw? She had to get out of here.

She peered into the crowd. "I'm going to check on Fiona."

Jasmine frowned. "But it's almost our turn for red carpet."

Delilah shrugged. "Rain check." Then she broke from the line. Damn that Scarlet for spoiling her very first major photo op!

She wove through people giving interviews and a group posing in a designated photo area and found Chase standing guard outside the bathrooms. “What’s going on?” she asked him. “Where is she?”

He gestured at the door to the women’s room. “She ran in there. Wouldn’t tell me what’s wrong.” A pained look crossed his face. “I think it was seeing Scarlet. You know she got the part Fiona turned down, right?”

Delilah nodded. It was all over the internet. Scarlet had done a ton of PR for the show already.

“That girl is toxic,” Chase continued with gnashed teeth. “Fiona probably thought Scarlet was going to rub it in her face or something.” And then a hopeless look came over his features. All he wanted to do was fix this. *What a good boyfriend,* Delilah thought.

She squeezed Chase’s arm. “I’ll check on her, okay?”

She headed inside the bathroom. It was moodily lit, exquisitely tiled, and smelled like mint. Delilah snaked around a few girls posing at full-length mirrors opposite low velvet couches. “Fiona?” she called out. “Hello?”

A lone girl at the sinks turned off one of the taps and flounced off. Delilah was about to leave, too, but then she heard a tiny voice coming from around a corner: “I’m back here.”

The room turned a corner at the end of the stalls, opening into yet another set of couches. Fiona was curled up in the corner of the very last one. Even in the dim light, Delilah could see that her cheeks were stained with tears.

She rushed toward her, filled with worry. “What’s going on?”

Fiona’s throat bobbed. She raised a trembling hand to wipe

her eyes. Before she could answer, Jasmine had appeared, too, her heels clacking noisily against the tile. "Honey," she simpered to Fiona, throwing herself on the cushion next to her. "What is it?"

A whimper escaped from Fiona's throat. "I . . ." She took a deep breath. "I just couldn't be around her."

"Scarlet?" Delilah guessed.

After a beat, Jasmine's eyes widened, and then she winced. "Oh my God, honey. I completely spaced about the Kate thing. Of course you didn't want to be near Scarlet right now." But then she frowned. "But, I mean, you were the one who booked the part first—and you turned it down. I hate that Scarlet got cast, but *someone* was going to have to take your place."

Fiona carefully licked her lips. "I only turned down the role because Scarlet blackmailed me."

"*Blackmailed?*" Delilah cried.

"What happened?" Jasmine asked at the same time.

Fiona laid her head against the pillow. "It's such a mess," she said in a low voice. "I got a text from someone saying they had dirt on me and would tell everyone if I didn't turn down the Kate part. Once I realized they cast Scarlet—she must have been their second choice—I put two and two together. She's behind it."

"What does she know about you?" Jasmine gasped. But a look of dread washed across Fiona's face, and Jasmine held up her hand. "Never mind. It's your business. Though you know you can talk to me about it. I'd never say a word."

"I wouldn't, either," Delilah promised.

Fiona nodded ruefully, though she then changed the subject. "I can't even be around her right now. It fills me with panic."

Jasmine grabbed Fiona's tightly coiled fist. "It isn't fair. She can't do this to you."

"Yes, she *can*. She's holding all the cards."

Jasmine clucked her tongue. "Well," she said after a beat, "if it makes you feel any better, I think she's trying to take me down, too."

"What?" Delilah exclaimed. "*You?*"

Jasmine nodded. "This interviewer the other day had this theory that *I* was the girl in the Jack Dono picture. Scarlet might believe the hype."

Delilah felt every muscle tighten. "What!" Fiona exploded. "You wouldn't do that!"

"I know. But Scarlet's following me around anyway. Trying to expose something about me. And . . . she might have something."

"What is it?" Fiona asked, but then caught herself. "Never mind. If it's too personal . . ."

"No, it's okay." Jasmine fiddled with the stack of silver bracelets on her wrist. "It's about the person I was kissing at that party. The one I'm saying was for a movie role. It *wasn't* for a movie. It was a real kiss."

"Really?" Fiona gasped. "Who was it?"

"I'm not sure—that's the problem. We were both wearing masks. But . . . well, it was a girl." She pressed her lips together in a closed-mouth smile. "And it was amazing. Just like I always thought it would be."

Jasmine glanced at both of them with what seemed like a held breath, like she wasn't sure how they'd take what she'd just told them. Delilah wondered if they were the first people she'd ever admitted this to.

She quickly squeezed Jasmine's hand. "That's incredible."

"Totally, Jazz." Fiona gave her a hug. "I'm so happy for you."

"Uh, *don't* be, actually, because I'm pretty sure Lulu C's fan base isn't ready for Lulu C to be kissing girls, so it's not like I can act on it if I want to retain my brand identity." Jasmine shut her eyes. "Anyway, I don't think Scarlet actually *knows*—because if she did, she'd realize I'm not Jack's Mystery Girl and maybe back off. But she senses that I'm hiding *something*. So basically, I've had Scarlet surveillance on me at very weird moments all week."

Fiona made a face. "This is so none of her business!"

"I know, but when has *that* stopped her?" Jasmine shrugged. "And for all I know, if Scarlet did find out what I'm hiding, she might expose it anyway. Just for fun."

"God," Fiona grumbled.

"I know." Jasmine slumped back on the couch, seeming drained.

Delilah vibrated with stress from what she'd just learned. She needed to say something about Jack. She couldn't have Scarlet following Jasmine around, figuring out Scarlet's secret. She should come forward, be the sacrificial lamb.

Except . . . then *she'd* be ruined. There had to be another way.

"I'm so sorry she did that to you, baby," Jasmine sighed as she stroked Fiona's arm. "Is there anything I can do? Maybe we could spread rumors about her on Twitter. Or send gossip to IGteaV?"

"No, no." Fiona shook her head. "She'll know I'm behind it. And then maybe she'll actually tell my secret instead of just holding it over my head."

"Okay, then we could hack her account and send her fans snarky DMs."

Fiona let a small smile play at her lips. "You're just naming things *Scarlet* does. And again, if she figures out it's me . . ."

"I know." Delilah snapped her fingers. "We could find some dirt on her, maybe? Fight fire with fire?" She looked at Jasmine. "Maybe we could get her to back off you, too."

Fiona looked thoughtful. "Do you think Scarlet would let any dirt slip?"

"You could tail her. Put a PI on her. I'll hire him, if you want. My uncle used to be in the business."

The girls stared at her for a moment, and then Jasmine burst out laughing. "Whoa, girl, you had me going for a second. I really thought you were serious."

"Right?" Fiona patted Delilah's knee. "Be grateful you haven't gotten into any trouble yet. People like Scarlet? They always find out."

Delilah nodded, smiling sympathetically until her lips ached. But inside, a doomed refrain echoed over and over: *That's exactly what I'm worried about.*

JASMINE

"A-B-C, easy as 1-2-3!" Jasmine bellowed into a headset microphone as she twirled with a group of Lemonade actors and characters. They were in front of the *Guardians of the Galaxy* ride in the Hollywood Land section of Disneyland's California Adventure, and it was at least eighty degrees out and sticky. A large crowd watched as they spun and sang. Jasmine and a few other *That's Hot!* actors were the main event at this particular performance—the crowd was alerted beforehand, and they were bursting with excitement, teeming to get close. For the song's finale, Jasmine climbed onto a Mickey-themed float and belted out the last refrain, punctuating the end by sticking out a rainbow-clad hip and throwing her multicolored arms into a V.

The crowd cheered. Jasmine grinned like she'd done a perfect-10 gymnastics performance even though she could do this particular dance in her sleep. Still, dance appearances weren't so bad—especially when they took place at Disney. How

could you be grumpy at Disney? And she really *did* love her fans. It wasn't *their* fault she felt pigeonholed as Lulu C.

Afterward, the performers exited to a Disney staff-only area to decompress. Jasmine grabbed a water bottle from a bucket of ice on the table and drank it in nearly one swallow. As she was setting the empty bottle back down, she felt Ruby's arm clamp her bicep.

"What the—?" Jasmine cried.

"C'mere. We need to talk." Ruby started walking, her shoulders hunched almost to her ears. Jasmine pasted on a smile and nodded to a few of her old costars, as well as a Mickey and a Buzz Lightyear, who were no doubt staring underneath those giant character heads.

What could Ruby be mad about? Jasmine thought as Ruby pulled her through a back door and out again into the bright sunlight. Jasmine was trying to be good. She had been wearing her obligatory rainbow everything to every outing. She'd nailed the song just now. She hadn't said one snarky thing in an interview for the Lemonade website earlier today. She'd even sent an email apology to Annalise for being rude in the interview. For her fans, she'd made a video explaining why she was at that tattoo place: she'd wanted to check it out for a friend, certainly not for herself.

Ruby came to a stop on the other side of the *Frozen* ride at a restroom pavilion, where they were still mostly concealed from the general public—though in her bright colors and with her huge hair, Jasmine still might turn some heads. There were little circles of sweat under Ruby's arms, and red blotches on her cheeks.

"So what was so important that you dragged me out of that

luxurious air-conditioning?" Jasmine asked, adding in a nervous laugh. "It's brutal out here!"

"Why was Scarlet Leigh standing on the sidelines like a stalker?" Ruby demanded.

Jasmine blinked, then peered into the thoroughfare, where mobs were meandering past the Disney attractions. "Scarlet's not here. People would have noticed. There would have been a scene. She would have been mobbed."

"She had on a baseball cap and sunglasses. But *I* knew it was her." Ruby put her hands on her hips. "That girl is trouble. Why is she following you?"

"She's got it all wrong," Jasmine murmured.

"What's that supposed to mean?" Ruby asked, hackles up. "What's going on? Is this about Jack Dono?"

Jasmine leaned against the restroom's outer wall. "Of course not. Don't be ridiculous. I'd never date him."

Ruby held up her hands defensively. "How should I know? The way you've been going off the rails, nothing would surprise me."

Jasmine raised an eyebrow. *Going off the rails.* Like a naughty puppy who needed to be crate-trained. That stung. "Ruby, chill, okay? I'm trying to be your perfect Jasmine, and I think I'm doing a good job. And to be honest, it seems like you're the only one who's hot and bothered by every single mistake I make."

"Oh, is that what you think?" Ruby's voice was razor-sharp.

"It's what I know. Lemonade hasn't complained about any of this. I haven't gotten a single call from them. You're over-reacting."

Ruby stepped back almost into a water fountain. "Uh, Lemonade hasn't called you because I saved your butt."

"Oh, please." Jasmine threw up her hands. "You're acting like I set fire to the back lot!"

Ruby's eyes flared. "Lemonade was really pissed at you. *I* dealt with it. So a thank-you would be nice."

"They were pissed at me for what?" Jasmine cocked her head. "You really had to jump through hoops just because I went into a tattoo shop? Because there's a picture of me kissing a person in a hoodie in the dark? Are they *that* sensitive?"

Ruby's eyebrows shot up, but her expression was suddenly . . . strange. "Wait, you really don't know?"

Jasmine's skin prickled. "Know what?"

"I mean, look," Ruby said quietly, her eyes darting. "It doesn't matter anymore. I put an end to it."

"Put an end to *what*?"

"That . . . person." Ruby tripped a little over her words. "That *girl* you kissed at the party. Because I know it's a girl, Jasmine. She wrote this thing about the masked party and the kiss for a Tumblr. And though she didn't, like, specifically say your name—or hers—it's obvious it's you she's talking about. I think she was going to expose you."

A fire ignited in Jasmine's chest. "Wait. She *wrote* about me? She was . . . thinking about it?"

"I was sure you saw this." Ruby looked confused. "I mean, you see *everything*."

"I didn't." She lunged for the phone in Ruby's hand. "Who is she? Where's this post?"

Ruby stepped away and held her phone aloft. "I made her take it down, Jasmine. And I have no idea who she is. She wouldn't say her name, only asked that *you* reach out to her in private. I didn't name who *I* was, either, or who *you* were—the last thing she needs is confirmation—but anyway, I said that if she didn't retract what she wrote, we'd sue."

Jasmine started to shake. "Wait, she asked me to reach out? She wants to talk to me?"

"Well, I'm sure she doesn't *now*," Ruby said matter-of-factly. "I scared the shit out of her. I said she was going to lose everything if she tried to mess with you."

"But . . ." Jasmine could hardly breathe. "But, Ruby, I've been *looking* for her!"

Ruby waved a hand. "Don't. She's trying to trap you. She's doing it for money. She isn't actually *into* you. She probably figured out who you were that night but thought if she lured you in, made you trust her, she could squeeze out more cash. It's classic extortion behavior."

"How do *you* know that's what she's doing?" Jasmine screamed, her heart breaking. "You. Weren't. There!"

Ruby gaped. Inside the pavilion, someone flushed a toilet. The cloying smell of homemade waffle cones from a nearby ice cream stand suddenly wafted into Jasmine's nostrils. "What is your *deal*?" Ruby finally said. "I saved your career and probably your finances. But you're acting like I just committed murder."

And all at once, Jasmine split open. "What if you did commit murder? What if that girl I kissed—and believe me, I *knew* she was a girl—was a relationship that was supposed to happen? A relationship that was destined?"

Ruby reared back, her mouth an O. It looked like she wanted

to laugh—or fight—but then her gaze slid to the right, where an even bigger crowd of people was passing by. "Look, keep your voice down. People are staring."

Jasmine snorted. "You worried my fans will hear? Or Mickey Mouse? Or some Lemonade spy?"

"Jasmine!" Ruby's eyes searched the passersby desperately. A few people had turned. One girl pulled out a phone and snapped Jasmine's picture. God, she was so conspicuous in her rainbow dress.

But suddenly, Jasmine didn't care if people saw. Let *everyone* see! She marched from the restrooms and fell in line with the crowd like she was just another tourist—in head-to-toe rainbow garb. "I kissed that girl, Ruby!" she shouted to her sister. "I *like* kissing girls. That's what I figured out about myself. I've always known, actually. I've just tried to hide it for years because I didn't want to upset anybody. It's not very Lulu C, is it?"

Ruby's smile was wobbly and embarrassed, and her eyes pinged around the slowing, gawking crowd. Some of them nudged one another, trying to figure out what was going on. "You've had a really long day," Ruby said loudly, clearly for the crowd's benefit. "*Way* too much sun."

"Yep, that's probably it!" Jasmine whooped as she passed the animation exhibits and *Disney Junior Dance Party!* show. She didn't know where she was walking, but she just needed to move. "Too much sun! That's probably why I *like kissing girls*!"

A preteen nudged her mom. A different mother clapped a hand over her ten-year-old daughter's ears. *Oh, come on,* Jasmine wanted to snap. *Are you really that much of a puritan?* Something was unfurling inside her. She felt unwieldy, suddenly . . . and also free.

Ruby didn't get it. Maybe she'd never gotten it. It was always about *her* needs: the handsome salary Jasmine paid her, a salary so big that Ruby could afford the payments on a BMW 5 Series and a nice condo in Hollywood. Or their parents' needs: the bills Jasmine paid, the peace she created, the status quo. No one wanted to step back and consider what *Jasmine* wanted. Because that would destroy their perfect little setup, wouldn't it?

Except she couldn't be their perfect little doll anymore. Something about what Ruby had done—hiding that girl's open letter, quashing any possibility for romance, even getting freaking *lawyers* involved, all behind Jasmine's back—seemed unbearably thoughtless. Maybe Jasmine wasn't being logical right now—maybe Ruby really thought she was protecting Jasmine—but in this moment, it felt like Ruby was purposefully putting up a roadblock to Jasmine's happiness.

It was time to change.

"You know what, Ruby?" she said, swirling around to her sister, feeling the tears prick her eyes. "You're fired. Effective immediately."

DELILAH

The next morning, Delilah stood on Hollywood Boulevard in front of Grauman's Chinese Theatre with six thousand other tourists. A band on the sidewalk played a No Doubt cover. People ogled various actors' stars on the sidewalk. A junk shop selling Hollywood snow globes and ugly T-shirts was packed. And Delilah's parents kept wanting to take *pictures* of her.

"Ava, Delilah? Squish in next to Batman!" Delilah's father said, raising his giant SLR camera.

Delilah glanced at the tubby guy in a Batman suit. "Do I *have* to?"

Ava giggled as Batman wrapped an arm around her. Begrudgingly, Delilah got into the shot, too. Thank God she had big sunglasses on. She'd be mortified if someone recognized her. She'd tried to tell her family that no self-respecting native Angelino came to this part of town—it was like New Yorkers *choosing* to go to Times Square, for fun—but her parents didn't listen. "We have to see the Walk of Fame," Delilah's mother insisted. "Come on. Don't be all too-cool-for-school."

And now here Delilah was. But she'd only acquiesced because she had a big ask for her parents. A question that was important, but a question she dreaded.

The girls broke away, Delilah's father paid Batman a ridiculous amount of money for the photo op, and the family started walking again. Delilah didn't get the allure of this street. All of the shops were either filled with tourist crap, weird, sexy clothes more suitable for a Vegas showgirl, or were the standard chains you'd find in malls—the Gap, Sunglass Hut, Buffalo Wild Wings. Finally, after they'd avoided another wave of people dressed as superheroes, she cleared her throat. It was Go Time.

"Mom, I really want to do that photo shoot with Patrick."

Her mother didn't miss a beat. "Not happening."

"What's this now?" Delilah's father asked.

"A photographer offered to shoot me. For my Instagram," Delilah explained. "I mentioned it to Mom already."

"And I said no already," Bethany said.

Her father looked at Delilah blankly. "But your own photos are really good, Delilah. You don't need someone else to do them."

"Especially not some man," Bethany added.

Delilah bit down hard on the inside of her cheek. "But it's an amazing opportunity. You guys can *come,* if you want." Yesterday, after her account had broken into the 900,000-followers mark, she'd received another DM from Patrick. *Really, really interested in working with you,* his note had said. *I have some ideas on how to grow your brand.*

They'd had a long conversation over DM about all the things Patrick's shoots could do for Delilah's career. It wasn't just tailoring her brand for specific ad campaigns with huge companies—he'd thrown out dazzling names he had alliances with, like Target, Adidas, and Delilah's favorite brand of high-end hair products—it was also about growing Delilah as an enterprise. *Have you considered singing? Modeling? Acting? Starting a company? Becoming an activist?* Patrick had written. *Because we can do all that, too. I'm in the business of collaboration. Growing businesses. I see real potential in you.*

Delilah's mouth had watered. It felt like she'd woken up one morning with someone saying, "Here's your dream life, now go live it." How many people were given this opportunity? But she also knew there was a tradeoff. How could she be a brand and also a school student? Of course a traditional plan wouldn't work.

Her family stopped at a crosswalk. Delilah noticed Ava looking at her encouragingly. *Keep pushing!* she mouthed.

But then her mom said, "When we lived in Minneapolis, you weren't begging to do photo shoots with strange people. Just because we live in LA now doesn't mean you need to be different. It also doesn't mean you're suddenly famous."

"Oh, I'm not?" Delilah's heart thudded with adrenaline and annoyance. "You want to make a bet on that?"

Bethany let out a condescending chuckle. "Sure, Delilah. I'll bet."

"So if we go to the Grove right now, you don't think I'd get recognized?" She waved her arm around Hollywood Boulevard. "No one seems very plugged into the social world *here*."

“What’s the Grove?” Delilah’s father asked, in that typical out-of-the-loop dad way.

“It’s this big outdoor mall,” Bethany said quietly, her brow knitting. Delilah could almost see the gears turning. “Do you have friends planted there?” she asked suspiciously. “Is this a setup?”

“I don’t. I swear. But you’re saying, if we go to the Grove right now, nobody will know who I am. Not a single teen or tween girl walking around, *glued* to her phone, *glued* to influencers, will know who I am.”

The light turned green, and a billion tourists crossed the street en masse. Delilah’s mother stayed where she was, letting out a plume of air from her lips. “Kids must see a zillion images online every day. You’re not . . . I don’t know, an actress.”

“So, if we go right now and someone *does* recognize me, then will you understand? Then will you let me do the photo shoot?”

“I mean . . . fine. Sure.” Bethany glanced at Delilah’s dad. “Do you want to come, or do you need to get back to work?”

“I’ll skip this one,” Will decided. “I’ll just take an Uber home.”

Delilah swelled with excitement—she was about to prove her mother wrong. Or course, the Grove was a tiny bit of a cheat. Minor young celebs and internet stars who wanted to make themselves feel better—or boost their confidence—went to the Grove, where the teeming masses of teenagers were seemingly on the hunt for famous faces. The place was crawling with paparazzi, too, trolling for pictures. More than half the time, it was the minor celeb who called the paps herself, trying to make herself feel more famous than she actually was.

Ava leaned over. "Do you want me to call up Faith and get her to go down to the Grove?" she whispered. "She'll totally do it."

Delilah laughed. "That's sweet, but let's play by the rules."

Soon enough, they were pulling into the mall's underground parking garage. When they emerged on the street, Delilah's knees were shaky. The outdoor walkways were mostly empty. The hot sun reflected off the stiff awnings for Barney's New York. Most of the restaurants weren't even open yet. There wasn't even a line at the American Girl Doll store.

Still, Delilah walked around with purpose, trying to figure out if she should go into Apple, Brandy Melville, or perhaps Nordstrom, looking for young, impressionable fans. With every step, her confidence faltered. Maybe her mom was right. Maybe she was fooling herself. *You're walking around an outdoor mall getting worked up because no one recognizes you. Maybe Mom is right. Maybe you* have *lost your way.*

"Excuse me?"

Delilah turned. Standing behind her, See's Candies bags in hand, were four girls a few years younger than she was. Three of them lingered back shyly, but one brazenly approached Delilah, her eyes popped wide.

"You're Lila D, aren't you?" the girl said. All Delilah had to do was give the smallest of nods, and the squeals began. She was suddenly swarmed by the four—and bombarded with questions about puppies, fashion, makeup, and what it was like to know Jasmine Walters-Diaz and Fiona Jacobs. Delilah peeked to her left. Ava's jaw was on the floor, and her mom was blinking hard in disbelief.

"Can we take a selfie? Please, please?" One of the shyer girls from the back burst forward, waving her phone in the air.

"Of course," Delilah said.

She snapped selfies with all of them. When a few more kids trickled in—some of them familiar with her account, too—they also wanted selfies. Even the ones who *didn't* know her wanted selfies. They asked Delilah to follow them, too, which of course she did. They peppered her with questions about how they, too, could become influencers, or Instagram stars, or at least a person who was recognizable at the Grove. Delilah deliberated carefully before answering, aware that her impressionable sister and skeptical mother were listening in. "I think you should just be exactly who you are," she said. "Don't try to fit in a box."

"And saving a puppy from a burning shed wouldn't hurt, either," one of the fans cheered.

The group blew kisses as they left. Delilah turned to her mom and sister, a triumphant grin on her face. Her mother had her arms crossed, but she didn't seem angry. In fact, Bethany finally looked like she understood the power Delilah held.

She even looked proud.

That evening, Delilah attended an event called "Insta Roll." It was at a roller rink in the Valley, among strip malls and dry-looking palm trees. As she walked inside, it was like she'd stepped into an '80s movie. Everyone was in neon colors, and Cyndi Lauper's "Girls Just Wanna Have Fun" was playing over the loudspeakers.

Instagram had partnered with a new YouTube network that produced scripted shows featuring micro and macro influencers to throw this party. Two girls with huge followings were in talks to play the lead on the new show, and rumor had it that the interviews they gave at this party would decide which one of them would get it.

In fact, Delilah spied one of the girls now: Emma Krissy, with her long lashes and glossy dark hair. She looked even prettier in real life than she did in her photos. She stood tall against the wall of the rink, listening to a fan ramble about how much she loved Emma's latest YouTube video. Then Delilah spotted the other girl up for the role: Taylor Singh, who was an eye-pleasing mix of Indian and Irish, per her bio. She perched by the snack bar, chatting up a group of older women, one of whom Delilah recognized as the founder of the YouTube network—she'd read up on her a few days ago.

But despite the smiles, despite the poppy music and the fun colors, the room was thick with competitive tension. Delilah was beginning to notice this was a common theme at these parties—everyone was always looking around to see who they needed to take a selfie with, or who was more famous than they were, or who was making a bigger splash. A lot of people didn't seem like they had actual *fun*.

Delilah waved to a few girls she'd met at Real Real, and then another team of vaguely familiar influencers she'd chatted with online, who probably associated with her because of her connection to Jasmine and Fiona. As for Jasmine and Fiona, she could locate neither girl, which unnerved her. She'd texted both earlier and they'd said they were coming, but she'd also heard some chatter online that Jasmine had fired her sister-manager. Maybe she was dealing with that? And perhaps Fiona was still recovering from turning down the Kate role? Delilah still shuddered at the thought of Scarlet blackmailing Fiona. After Fiona had broken that news, Delilah had promised herself to stop DMing Jack. She was playing with fire.

But then another message from him had popped up: *Favorite dog movie. Go.* And that had led to an hour-long discussion of the merits of *101 Dalmatians* vs. *Air Bud.*

Still. She had to stop talking to him. She *had* to. If Scarlet could hurt Fiona's career for stealing a casual boyfriend years ago, what on earth would Scarlet do to *Delilah*?

Delilah headed over to the window to retrieve some skates—unlike everyone else at this party, she decided that she was going to enjoy herself. She plopped onto a bench and started lacing up the skates, her gaze falling to the crossbody bag she'd brought for the occasion. The zipper was pulled tight, allowing no view of the bag's insides. She'd learned her lesson at that YouTube event when Scarlet Leigh had spied her insulin supplies and thought she was on drugs. *So* rude.

"Are you Delilah?"

She felt a tap on her shoulder. Standing in front of her was the same woman Taylor was just talking to—that YouTube bigwig. Chestnut hair framed her face, and her brown eyes were wide, making her look a little bit like Bambi. She must have been in her forties, but her face was completely free of any wrinkles or blemishes.

The woman extended a hand. "I'm Kerri Block. I run Digi."

"Hi! It's so nice to meet you. This party is amazing, thank you so much for having me." The words rolled off Delilah's tongue. All those years of her mother insisting on manners came in handy.

Kerri smiled. "Of course! All of us at Digi love your Instagram, and we have you in mind for a couple of projects we're working on. Do you have an agent we could get in touch with?"

Delilah's stomach flipped. They were thinking about her for, like, a *show*? "Um, I'm working on the agent thing. I, um, just moved here." God, did that sound *completely* amateur?

Kerri nodded. "Well, if you need any recommendations, I've got loads. And I'm sure they'd all be happy to meet with you."

She winked and walked off. Delilah sucked in a huge breath. Her. On a digital show. Huh.

"Hey!" Two identical girls skated up. Delilah recognized them as Musically stars, and remembered that they'd DMed her once or twice. Their names were Katie and Sadie—but Delilah wasn't sure which was which.

"Hey, girl! What'd Kerri want from you?" one of them asked, her eyes keen.

Delilah faltered. "Well, keep this on the down low, but she said they're interested in me for some of their new stuff."

Something, maybe jealousy, flashed on Sadie . . . no, *Katie's* face. But the other twin squealed and gave her a tight hug. "That's amazing! You are killing the game." Before Delilah could reply, a photographer motioned for the girls to get together. A quick flash went off.

Delilah laced up her skates and started around the rink, meeting more kids she'd previously connected with online. Throughout the rest of the night, whenever a camera turned her way, she smiled brightly, remembering to squash in with acquaintances for pictures. On what felt like her fortieth lap around the rink, she suddenly felt someone staring from across the room.

She swiveled her head just as a figure ducked out of view. Her chest tightened. Was that Scarlet? *Don't be silly,* she told herself. She'd know if Scarlet were here. Scarlet made a scene wherever she went. She took a deep breath and did another lap.

"Look out for that wall," someone called on her next time around.

Delilah turned just in time to see Jack Dono so close behind her that their bodies were almost touching. She let out a yelp and—bam. The front of her skates hit the boards hard. She grabbed the edge of the wall for support, nearly falling over. Jack glided next to her, chuckling.

"You okay?" he asked.

"Fine," Delilah muttered under her breath. "You just surprised me, is all."

"This has got to be the dumbest social event yet. Who roller skates in 2019?" He laughed again. "If it were up to you, I bet we'd be playing pool."

Delilah wanted to smile—in a DM last night, she'd admitted that while her sister loved going to Dave and Buster's for the video games, Delilah was always looking for people to play pool with. It touched her that he remembered—but she also wanted to run. It was weird: she had such an intimate relationship with Jack, but it was all through texts, not face-to-face. Being in the same space with him made her nervous—it would be hard to hide her feelings. Plus, this was insane. At least a hundred gossipy influencers were gliding past, watching them.

Jack seemed to sense her hesitation, so he skated a few feet behind her as she did another lap around the rink. Delilah felt overly aware of all her movements across the concrete. Did Jack think she was a good skater? Was Jack looking at her butt?

Finally, on the second time around, he moved a little closer and murmured, "Don't worry. Scarlet isn't here. But I'd love to talk to you."

"We can't," Delilah said, a knee-jerk reaction.

Jack skated over to one of the exits off the rink, then glanced over his shoulder at her for a millisecond, his look saying, *Please?*

Delilah bit her lip and glanced around the room. No one *seemed* to be paying attention to her, but what if Scarlet had planted spies? Still, the pull to Jack felt magnetic. She wanted to talk to him, too. In person. Up close.

She exited the rink and started in the direction of where Jack had disappeared. But to her surprise, once she'd weaved past the benches and vending machines, she didn't see Jack anywhere. Her phone pinged. It was a new DM from Jack's Finsta. *There's something for you on the last bench.*

Delilah peered at the last bench in the row, but all she saw was a torn corner of a receipt the person at the rental desk gave everyone in exchange for roller skates. She picked it up curiously. Tucked inside the folded paper was a flat, beige card with the words *SLS Hotel* printed on the front. *Hotel?* A key?

Another DM: *This is for the hotel next door. Room 308. I did a promo with them a while ago, so I always get a room for free. I totally understand if you don't want to meet me in a hotel room. I promise I'll be a total gentleman—I just want to talk. I have so much fun talking to you.*

Delilah's mind spun wildly. Was it cool that Jack was insisting he'd be a gentleman—or a teensy bit disappointing? Cool, for sure—chivalrous, respectful—but did that mean he thought of her only as a friend? Maybe he was really lonely. Maybe he *did* just want to talk. But what would her mom think about all of this? According to her watch, she still had an hour before her mom picked her up—if Bethany got here and found Delilah gone, she'd go ballistic. Maybe she shouldn't go. She *definitely* shouldn't go. This felt wrong on a lot of levels.

Except . . .

She crushed the note between her palms and looked around. Skaters whizzed past. Girls clustered together for selfies, offering big grins. At a table off the rink, an art supply company was holding a roller-skate-decorating project, and some of the craftier influencers—Delilah recognized a young woman who was famous for her innovative cupcake designs—were participating with gusto. It still didn't seem like anyone was watching her. . . .

She unlaced her roller skates and exchanged them for her shoes. One of the event's organizers, a perky girl in her twenties who worked for the art supply company, seemed crestfallen when she spotted Delilah sneaking out. "We'll miss you, Dolores!" she said. *Dolores?* That didn't make Delilah feel as bad about leaving.

Out on the street, the SLS Hotel's big neon sign blinked like a beacon, but Delilah didn't go in right away. Instead, she walked down the avenue toward the Whole Foods on the corner. Halfway down the block, she stopped and bent to fix her shoe, glancing behind her. There was no one following. Straightening, she stepped through the automatic doors of Whole Foods and walked the aisles aimlessly, picking up a bag of clementines, considering organic toothpaste. Again and again, she figured she would whirl around and spot a Scarlet spy . . . but it didn't seem like anyone had a clue.

Ten minutes later, she was at the back entrance of the hotel, which was concealed in a maze of hedges. Her legs wobbled as she slid the key Jack gave her onto a keypad. The lock clicked, and a door to a back staircase opened. As she climbed to the third floor, she breathed in the scent of fresh flowers that permeated the stairwell. She pushed open the door to the third floor and came upon not a corridor of doors, as she expected, but a small landing with only a few doors leading to what looked like suites. Across an atrium was the door she was looking for: 308. It was closed. She didn't know what she'd expected—for it to be open? For Jack to be standing in the doorway, arms thrown wide?

Had she been foolish to come?

She took a deep breath and crossed the hall. At 308's door, she knocked so quietly that she doubted Jack would be able to hear. Steeling herself, she knocked again, a little louder. In a moment, the latch clicked, and the door opened a crack. Delilah stood back, feeling foolish and red-faced and panicky. "Hey!" Jack said, sounding relieved. He opened the door wider. "Come in!"

Delilah started into a palace-sized suite of couches, bureaus, and art. Floor-to-ceiling windows offered a view of the city.

Jack stood in front of her, his hands shoved into his pockets. "So, um, hi."

"Hi," Delilah said. "Again." She giggled. God, she was nervous.

"You want to sit?" Jack pointed anxiously to a couch. Then he started babbling. "I have cookies. A whole giant fridge of snacks, actually. You can have anything you want—it's all free, because they sponsor me, but if I were a paying guest? It would be stupidly expensive. Like a twelve-dollar mini pack of Doritos. Twenty-five-dollar gummy bears."

"The gummy bears are twenty-five dollars?" Delilah cried. "Are they made out of gold?"

Jack turned to the little minibar basket and extracted a tiny jar. "This is how many you get." The jar fit neatly into his palm. Brightly colored gummy bears were squished against the glass sides. "It looks like ten bears in there. *Maybe* twelve."

"That's more than two dollars a bear," Delilah joked. "I feel like we need to try them. They must be something very, *very* special."

Jack unscrewed the lid to the gummy bears and offered her one. Delilah's hands were shaking as she plunged her fingers in to select a red bear. *I'm going to remember this forever,* she thought. *Sitting in this massive hotel room, eating gummy bears with Jack Dono.* And yet it felt so easy. So fun. Exactly like their DMs. She began to relax.

She popped the gummy into her mouth and started chewing. Jack looked at her expectantly. "Well? Is it amazing?" he asked.

Delilah nodded slowly. "It tastes like the most incredible gummy product I've ever eaten. In fact, I think it's going to give me magic powers."

"Oh yeah? Like being able to fly?"

"Nah. Nothing quite that powerful. More like entry-level powers." She thought for a moment. "Like . . . the ability to charge your phone with your mind."

"Whoa." Jack looked impressed. "That would come in handy on airplanes. And on long press events." He popped a yellow bear into his mouth. "Yellow bears . . . they make you look good in any lighting situation."

"Nice." She plucked a green one from the jar. "Green bears give your Instagram feed double the amount of cute dog posts."

"Dude, I need more green, then." Jack dug around for another green bear, but then selected a nearly translucent one instead. "These, though? They're bad luck." He smiled mischievously. "You know the puppy-ears filter? Eat one of these, and those ears become your *real* ears. For the rest of your life."

"That sounds cute, actually!" Delilah shrugged. "I wouldn't mind puppy ears!"

"Actually, you'd look really cute with puppy ears," Jack said.

His voice was so earnest that Delilah burst into giggles. He started laughing, too. And suddenly, for reasons she couldn't explain, they were laughing really hard. Maybe because of magic gummy bears. Or maybe because of something else.

And then Jack grabbed Delilah's face and kissed her.

His lips were soft. Warm. They tasted like salt. She could feel Jack's body loosen, and hers did, too. Her hands were in his hair. He was kissing her cheekbone, her earlobe, her neck. Delilah was hit with feelings so exciting and overwhelming that she shuddered.

They pulled back, breathing hard. There was a goofy, bewildered smile on Jack's face. "Wow," he whispered. "*Those* are some magical bears."

"I know." But all at once, Delilah felt a bolt of doom. "Jack . . . we can't do this."

Jack stepped away, palms raised. "I'm so sorry. I told you I'd be a gentleman."

Delilah laughed sadly. "No. That's not what I meant. I . . . *loved* it." She swallowed a lump in her throat. Her lips were still tingling from the kiss. "I'm terrified of someone finding out. Aren't you?"

Jack's eyes softened. He cupped her face in a gesture that was so romantic, such a staple in Delilah's fantasies of how-I'd-like-my-dream-boyfriend-to-touch-me, it almost didn't seem real. "I just . . ." He bit his lip adorably. "Getting to know you, I feel something . . . *real.*"

"I know," Delilah admitted. "But, I mean, this would ruin your career."

"So? I'll get another career. I'm kinda over YouTube anyway."

If only it were that easy! "Yeah, but what about me? People online are so mean. I'll probably get death threats."

"We'll report them to the police." He squeezed her hands. "If you're worried about your following, you shouldn't be. Once everyone gets used to us being together, your profile will sky-rocket. I mean, not that I want *that* to be the reason you want to be with me . . ."

"It wouldn't be," Delilah said quickly. "It isn't."

"I mean, if you also wanted us to go dark on social completely, I'd do that, too." Jack grinned. "It's like, with you, my future is this wide-open book."

Delilah stared at him. She kept thinking that she'd blink and be in the hallway again, things with Jack not even having started, or else she'd be back at the skating rink, or even in her old bed-room in Minneapolis.

Would nothing change if they got together? Could she really believe Jack? She wanted to. Desperately.

“Okay,” she said quietly. “I’m game.”

Jack’s face brightened. He pulled her close and kissed her again. This kiss was deep and excited, and it made Delilah’s heart race. She closed her eyes, bowled over, getting lost in it. . . .

Bam.

They shot apart at the sound of splintering wood. Delilah heard the shouting before she saw an actual person, but the next thing she knew, Jack was on the ground, and a large, dark-haired man was straddling him in some sort of wrestling hold.

“What the hell?” the man screeched. “You seriously can’t keep it in your pants?”

“Dad!” Jack groaned, shoving him off. “Wha—what are you doing here?”

Dad? Delilah recoiled. This was Jack’s *father*?

The man’s head whipped up, and his eyes narrowed into slits when he noticed her standing against the wall. “Are you *her*?” he asked Delilah. “His *Mystery Girl*?” His voice was filled with bile.

“I . . . ,” Delilah squeaked out.

“Leave her alone, Dad,” Jack warned. “This isn’t her fault.”

Jack’s father’s lip curled. “You’re giving up Scarlet for *this*?”

“Hey!” Jack’s voice was dangerous. “Don’t talk about her like that!”

Delilah snatched her purse. “I should go. . . .”

Mr. Dono crossed his arms. “Yes. I think you should.” Then he turned back to his son, glowering. “You *know* the rules. We had an agreement.”

“I don’t like that agreement anymore,” Jack said, puffing out his chest.

"I don't *care* if you don't like it. You agreed to it, and that's final."

Mr. Dono's voice made every cell in Delilah's body cower. And it hit her: Jack wasn't kidding when he told her his dad was controlling. It made her grateful, for a tiny beat, that she had very, very different parents.

She skirted around them, hurrying out the door before the tears could fall. She *knew* this was wrong. But as her hand curled on the doorknob, Jack was behind her, touching her arm. "I'm going to make this right. I'm going to make it so we can be together. Come to Gratitude Prom, okay?"

Delilah searched his face. He was thinking of Gratitude Prom at a time like this?

"Jack, what are you doing?" Mr. Dono shouted from inside the room. "Get away from her."

But Jack's gaze didn't diverge from Delilah's face, his eyes full of longing. "It's in a few days. *Come.*" And then, swiftly, crazily, he yanked a bouquet of flowers from a vase by the door and handed them to her. "Consider this my promposal. I want you to be there. I want to see you. I have a plan, and then we'll be able to be together."

Delilah stared at the flowers, speechless.

"Jack," Mr. Dono said again, lurching forward and grabbing the back of Jack's T-shirt. "What the hell are you doing?"

But Jack stood his ground. He leaned in toward Delilah, whispering four of the most romantic words Delilah had ever heard.

"Meet me there. *Please.*"

Transcript of Scarlet Leigh's personal vlog, 6/27 (for her YouTube channel)

Camera on Scarlet's face. She's in big sunglasses. Her hair is glossy. She's sitting in the driver's seat of her car.

SCARLET

Hey, guys! What's up! I'm checking in because I realize I haven't done a vlog in a while. Have you missed me?

BEEP! A second cell phone pings. Scarlet answers, puts the call on speaker.

SCARLET

Hi, Mama! I'm doing a vlog right now! Say hi to the Scarlet As!

GINA (OVER THE PHONE)

Hi, Scarlet As! Love ya! Listen, honey, I was just checking to see if you were going to make it to that vampire facial. I just got an alert that it's on your calendar.

SCARLET

Of course! That's why I'm doing a vlog!

(turns camera on herself to address her viewers)

Guys. I am about to go to the most amazing facial appointment in the world. It's at Shadi Darden Spa, who I'm going to be teaming up with, and get this—*you* are going to get to witness the whole experience! I don't know about you, but I definitely need some R&R before I head to Gratitude Prom with Jack tomorrow. And this seems like the perfect little treat!

GINA (OVER THE PHONE)

Don't let them into the steam room with you, baby!

SCARLET

Oh, Mama, you're so silly. Listen, I'm in the parking lot right now—I'll call you when I'm done, 'kay?

(turns to fans)

Be right back to you guys when I'm inside, okay!

She hangs up. Moves to press a button on the phone to pause the live stream... except the live stream doesn't pause. When she gets out of the car, she's not in a spa parking lot at all... but in the lot of a busy CVS. She pulls her baseball cap over her eyes. The camera is wobbly as she moves to the automatic double doors and goes inside.

CVS WORKER

Can I help you find anything?

SCARLET

(a little surly)

I'm fine.

She moves up and down the aisles with purpose, every so often glancing over her shoulder like she's worried she's going to see a fan. All of a sudden, she notices her phone. The vlog is still going. There's a muffled groan, followed by what sounds like a curse word.

And then the feed goes dead.

Comments: (1,432)

@ChanelGoddess7623: First!
@myangelscarlet: @ChanelGoddess7623 I was first actually
@LeighIsMe99IO: Guys, what's been up with Scar's vlogs? I think she's been hacked. is someone trying to blackmail her or something?? HACKING IS NOT OKAY!!!
@drawbaby10: Hey guys check out my page for cool drawings of your favorite influencers!
@MultiFanScarlet: Scarlet, are you okay? Why are you in CVS? #Praying4Scarlet
@ScarLeighJackletHeart: She probably just needs some tampons.
@Jacklet4Ever: Ew! She probably just needs a bottled water. And moisturizer. JK Scarlet your skin is goals!
@ILoveScarScar: Guys I think I know who Mystery Bitch is. I'm this close to figuring it out. When I do she is going DOWN. Request my account to see who it is. accepting the first 100 to request.
@FanBoy99K: Why hasn't Scar posted the massage update yet? I wanted to see what the vampire facial was like!
@MultiFanScarlet: Dude, you just wanted to see her naked.

FIONA

At three p.m., as Fiona was about to do a beauty flat-lay, she received a notification: *Scarlet Leigh is doing a live video. Watch it now!*

Her heart juddered. She'd decided to take her friends' advice to heart and beat Scarlet at her own game. It seemed unlikely she'd find gossip about Scarlet that was on par with her secret . . . but perhaps Scarlet was hiding *something.*

All day, amid a busy schedule of visiting with her sponsors, meeting with her manager to brainstorm new content, having a tail-between-her-legs call with her TV agent, who still couldn't comprehend why Fiona had turned down the Kate role, and fending off worried calls from her mother and Chase, Fiona binged Scarlet videos. Scarlet had so much content on her pages. Vlogs. YouTube tutorials. Weird mashups of Scarlet modeling her favorite outfits. She definitely knew Scarlet way better than before. For instance: when Scarlet wasn't thrilled with something her mom said, her left eye started to twitch. Even if Scarlet praised her mom up and down for her suggestion, told the audience how awesome her mom was—she wasn't truly happy.

And Cory? Was he a friend or a frenemy? In some videos, Cory told Scarlet she looked beautiful in gowns that were unequivocally hideous. Did he *want* her to look ugly? Was he *hoping* for a downfall? The rest of Scarlet's posse was odd, too—jumpy, jittery, like they were afraid they were going to be caught doing or saying the wrong thing. But *what*? Were they all just afraid of Scarlet's wrath . . . or was something else in play?

But she hadn't dug up anything real.

And now, a new live vlog. Fiona clicked on it. Scarlet was in mid-sentence, babbling about some sort of massage treatment she was about to try. She was sitting in the front seat of her car, and her hair looked a little greasy—but then, if she was massage-bound, it would get messed up anyway, so maybe she didn't care. Fiona was about to click off when Scarlet told her fans that she'd be "back in a second," which she usually said when she was about to sign off. The camera wobbled. But the video kept rolling.

The hair on the back of Fiona's neck prickled. This was, what, the third time Scarlet's vlogs continued to record after she bid her fans goodbye? Maybe there was something wrong with her device. Perhaps someone was hacking her. If it were Fiona, she would have gotten a new phone by now, called some IT people. Why hadn't Scarlet's team advised her about this? Even weirder, the vlog now showed that Scarlet was getting out of her car and walking toward a CVS. Definitely not a spa.

Then Fiona noticed the Wilshire Boulevard sign in the background of the video. Wait a minute. This was the CVS not far from her condo. Fiona could probably get there in a few minutes. She sprung off the bed. This felt like a lead.

The video was still rolling. Now Scarlet was walking into the pharmacy. The view was mostly of the gray-and-white-tiled floor, but Fiona heard someone, presumably a salesperson, ask, "Can I help you find anything?"

"I'm fine," Scarlet replied. There was an edge to her voice. She *definitely* didn't know the video was still streaming.

Fiona was in her hallway by now, waiting for the elevator. When it dinged, she stepped inside, relieved that she was alone in the car. The walk to the CVS was only a few blocks, but Fiona took it at a run, afraid that she'd miss Scarlet and whatever was going down. *Was* anything going down?

Across the street, Fiona spied a woman walking into a pet groomer; she had her left hand in a large, unwieldy cast. An image popped into her mind, unbidden: Zoey's hand, bandaged up the same sort of way.

Fiona had only seen Zoey once after her tragic accident, at an outdoor mall near their house. Zoey sat in the food court with her mother, trying to eat a bowl of fast-food spaghetti with one hand. The other hand—her left, which fingered the strings on her cello—was curled in her lap, wrapped in a thick, ugly layer of gauze. Fiona had to look away fast, the guilt making her woozy.

If only Lana had just broken Zoey's cello. Instruments could be replaced. But what she'd done instead—rigged the paper cutter in the art room to slice down on Zoey's fingers without anybody, *anybody* knowing she was behind it—was viciously, unthinkably ruinous. Fiona hadn't been in the class when it happened, but the rumor traveled quickly through the school, and hot flames of repulsion and horror and shame rippled through Fiona like a virus. Lana wasn't just a mean girl. She was a monster.

And *Fiona* had given her the idea to do it.

Zoey's joyless expression in the food court had stuck in Fiona's mind for weeks, gathering strength and warping her mind. She knew that if she didn't do something, she'd never forgive herself. And then came the perfect moment: the end-of-school party, which took place in the oceanfront home of a wealthy classmate. Everyone from school was invited, whether you were popular or an outcast. All night, Fiona bided her time, glowering at Lana from afar. She kept noticing Lana sneaking up to the home's rooftop, which was technically off-limits. Usually, her friends went with her, but later in the evening, Lana went up alone.

So Fiona followed her.

Rage crackled through her body—it was so powerful, she thought electricity might shoot from her fingers. But Lana seemed amused by Fiona's fury, which just enraged Fiona even more. "These are people's lives," Fiona bellowed. "You need to stop."

"And what are *you* going to do about it?" Lana teased. "*Nothing.*"

Fiona hadn't realized how close to the roof's edge they'd been. She was unfamiliar with the deck, and she had no idea that a section of it had a very low wall that afforded a breathtaking view of the ocean but probably wasn't safe. There was also a hole in her memory of what exactly happened—she remembered yelling at Lana, and Lana laughing, and then how Fiona had felt afraid. Then she remembered Lana tumbling backward *over* that

wall. Fiona had rushed toward Lana in horror as Lana lost her balance and was suddenly gone. Fiona tilted over the wall and stared down at the dark, sharp rocks not very far below. All she could see was a strip of Lana's strawberry-blond hair and the edge of her bright pink dress. It had all happened so fast. And then it was done.

And then Fiona ran.

The miraculous thing was that no one noticed her rush down the spiral staircase and out of the house. No one could even put her at the party that night—after all, she was sort of a loser back then, and no one was really paying attention. The family who hosted the party didn't have security cameras everywhere, so there was no evidence that Fiona had climbed up to confront Lana on the roof. In fact, the family themselves were blamed for having such a dangerous setup.

When Lana's body was found, smashed against the rocks, her death was deemed an accident. An autopsy found alcohol in her blood, and friends admitted they'd snuck up to the roof to sneak sips from a bottle of red wine. The theory was that Lana was tipsy, walked to the edge, and slipped.

With that, it was done. Fiona got off scot-free. The bully was dead. It should have been a happy ending. But of course it wasn't. She'd *killed* someone. A terrible someone, but still, a person. *She'd killed a person.*

"Fee!"

Fiona whirled around. "Chase?" Her boyfriend was loping toward her. "W-what are you doing here?"

"I was visiting my mom's office." He gestured to the glass building across the street. His mother had her ob-gyn practice in

that office complex; Fiona and Chase always joked that Chase's mom had set up shop there to convenience *them,* since the Dove was just a few blocks away. He looked her up and down. "Where are you off to so fast?"

A horn honked, and Fiona realized they were standing in the middle of the busy crosswalk. She hurried to the other side. When she peeked at her phone screen, Scarlet's vlog had ended. *Shit.* What did she miss?

"I need to go in there." She gestured to the CVS. "Still don't have a personal assistant, so I have to do all my shopping myself!" She tried to laugh, though it came out more like a weird, nervous bleat.

"Cool. I'll go with you." Chase fell in step beside her. "I need razors."

"No!" Sweat prickled on her neck. "I want to go alone."

Chase's brow furrowed. "Why?"

Her mind scattered. What could she say to make him go away? She glanced at Scarlet's page again. The live was over, but Scarlet's car, a matte-black Range Rover, so easily recognizable, was still in the parking lot. Was she still in the store?

Chase's gaze fell to Fiona's phone, and though Fiona tried to hide the screen, it was obvious Chase saw what she was looking at. "Why are you on Scarlet's page?"

Fiona's nerves snapped. "No reason!"

There was an inscrutable expression on his face. "Is this because of the role? What's she saying to you?"

"She's not . . . Don't worry about it." Fiona's head whirled. "I just happened to be looking at it. It doesn't mean anything."

"You should stay away from her." Chase's voice was surprisingly stern.

"I know." She gave Chase a hurried squeeze on the arm. "Look, go visit your mom. I'll get you razors and come by your house in an hour, okay?"

Chase still looked so uneasy, but eventually, he backed away. "Okay . . ."

He'd barely said goodbye when Fiona spun around and sprinted toward the store. She rewound the video Scarlet just made. In the vlog, Scarlet climbed out of her Range Rover. She walked into the drugstore. The sales clerk asked her if she needed anything . . . and the video went dead. The end.

That was it? Fiona ran all this way—and lied to her boyfriend—for nothing?

Cool air-conditioning smacked Fiona's face as she stepped through CVS's automatic doors. A sales clerk, probably the same one who'd greeted Scarlet moments ago, smiled from the register. "Help you find anything?"

Fiona paused. Should she ask if the woman saw Scarlet? But Fiona didn't want to give herself away. She shook her head and made a beeline for the aisles. Beauty products. Hair stuff. She poked her head down row after row, but Scarlet wasn't in any of them. She checked the front register again, thinking that Scarlet might be up there now, making a purchase. The sales clerk leaned against shelves of cigarette boxes, reading an *Us Weekly.*

She tried the paper products aisle next. The headache medications. Vitamins. Stomach remedies. No Scarlet. She swept to the back, where a few people were waiting on orange chairs for their prescriptions. Scarlet wasn't there, either. What the hell? Was it possible she *wasn't* at this CVS? Perhaps the spa was through a back door or something, an über-secret, celebrity-only entrance so as not to alert the paparazzi. It was actually kind of a genius idea, putting a secret entrance in an unassuming drugstore. . . .

But then a sign snagged Fiona's attention: *Restrooms.* A large green arrow pointed around a corner. Fiona peered down a corridor. It was quiet. A drinking fountain quietly hummed. Inside the women's room came the telltale *whoosh* of an industrial toilet flushing. In moments, the door swung open. Fiona caught sight of Scarlet a split second before Scarlet looked up—and Fiona ducked behind a display for shoe inserts, her heart thundering.

Scarlet emerged from the hallway. Her eyes were red. Her face was pale. As she pulled the strap of her handbag higher onto her shoulder, her fingers trembled. She drifted to the front of the store, but she didn't go to the register to purchase anything. Was she only in here to use the bathroom? Perhaps it was an emergency? Except why wouldn't she just go straight to the spa she'd mentioned in her video and use the bathroom there? Surely their bathrooms were nicer. . . .

Then a warning bell clanged in Fiona's brain. She could think of a few reasons why girls might need to use less-than-great bathrooms. An eating disorder might be the answer . . . but Fiona was pretty sure Scarlet didn't have that issue. But what if . . . ?

She tiptoed to the women's bathroom, feeling a tug of dread. The two stall doors stood wide open, unoccupied. Fiona stepped into the smaller stall, and then into the handicapped one, trying to figure out what she was looking for. In the handicapped stall, she noticed that the small silver trash bin built into the wall for discarded feminine products was propped open. It seemed like someone had jammed something big in there. *Germs, germs, germs,* the Voice hammered, but Fiona lifted the lid higher anyway. Wedged in there was a large cardboard box with bright pink printing on the side.

Pregnancy test.

Fiona peered into the box, heart lurching. Stuffed inside was an unwrapped test, the plastic pink cap facing outward. She pulled out the test and turned it over, checking the results. Unbelievable. *Unbelievable.*

Practically hyperventilating, she wrapped the test in toilet paper and tucked it into her purse. This still didn't mean anything, necessarily—just because Scarlet used the same bathroom where someone took a positive pregnancy test didn't prove that *she* was pregnant. But deep in her gut, Fiona was pretty sure Scarlet was. She could tell by Scarlet's weird detour on her way to the spa. And by Scarlet feeling sick in one recent vlog, and suddenly fainting in another. And by Scarlet's expression when she came out of the bathroom—like her world was crumbling.

And now you have to take advantage of that, the Voice told Fiona. *Here's how you get your life back.*

DELILAH

"Chin up. Just like that. Gorgeous, gorgeous!"

Delilah posed in front of a crushed-velvet curtain in chunky white platform sneakers and a short red lace dress. The floor was covered in so many red, pink, silver, and white balloons that it was difficult to move around. For the last hour, she'd been asked to throw the balloons into the air, kick them wildly, and even kiss one of them, all while Patrick and his team photographed, adjusted the lighting, switched songs on the Spotify playlist, fluffed her hair, and plied her with some sort of pressed juice called "Serenity," which came in a space-age bottle and tasted like raspberries.

And it was thrilling.

"I can't believe this is your first shoot," Patrick said as they took a break to switch lenses. "You're a natural, girl."

"Aw, thanks." Delilah ducked her head, kind of wishing her mom were here to witness this. But Bethany had been so cool earlier, agreeing to run some errands with Ava and Faith, who'd of course tagged along. Naturally, that was *after* Bethany thoroughly vetted the scene, even making two of the female PAs swear up and down that they would never let anything "sketchy" happen to Delilah—that they wouldn't pose her in a way that made her uncomfortable, and that she wouldn't be left alone with any men. Thankfully, the women had looked at Delilah's mother in horror and said, "Oh good heavens, no!"

After another half hour of shooting, Delilah was finally done. Kandace, one of the PAs, brought her a pair of slippers, a clipboard, and a gift card for the Olympic Korean spa, which was down the street. "Just as a thank-you," Kandace said. "We're really excited to be working together."

"You don't have to do this!" Delilah cried. "You're doing *me* the favor!"

"C'mon, you have to try a Korean body scrub," Kandace urged. "It'll be great for Gratitude Prom. You are going tonight, aren't you?"

A streak of nerves invaded Delilah's stomach. *Gratitude Prom.* Yesterday, she'd received several DMs from Jack; he'd laid out a foolproof plan that would break him and Scarlet up at Gratitude. *I'm going to put York in her path,* Jack wrote. *You know who that is, right?*

Of course Delilah did—York, known only by his first name, was one of the hottest influencers around. He'd recently put out a record that went platinum. He was in an upcoming Marvel movie. He was starting a menswear line with Neiman Marcus. *Everyone* had a crush on York—apparently, including Scarlet.

York owes me a favor, Jack continued. *I'm going to ask him to hook up with Scarlet. Right where everyone can see . . . and snap pictures. Then I'll pretend it upsets me . . . and I'll act betrayed . . . and Scar and I will have a discussion . . . and Jacklet will be done. The fans can't be angry about that.*

You think it'll be that easy? Delilah typed, feeling incredulous. *What if Scarlet begs for your forgiveness? What if she doesn't want to break up? What if it doesn't work?*

Yeah, but York's kind of into her, too. Maybe they'll hit it off. Maybe I'm setting up a successful ship! I'll bring you as my date to their wedding. . . .

Kandace cleared her throat. Delilah realized that she hadn't answered her question.

"I am going to Gratitude Prom," she said. "Maybe I will get the body scrub, thanks."

"You'll love it. Going with anyone special?" Kandace's eyes glimmered.

"Oh, I shouldn't say," Delilah mumbled, coyly casting her eyes down.

Kandace cocked her head, then made a zipping motion at her lips as if to say, *I'm a vault.* "You have that look like you really, *really* want to tell someone. . . ."

Delilah's eyes darted. *Could* she spill? She was really dying to. And Kandace was, what, twenty-six, twenty-seven? She probably didn't even know who Jack Dono *was.* "Okay, I'm meeting this guy Jack," she whispered, feeling a whoosh of relief to finally get the secret out there. "It's kind of complicated—he's breaking up with his girlfriend tonight, and they've been together forever. But when we met, it was like, *fireworks.*" She smiled nervously. "I'm so excited. But please don't tell anyone, okay?"

"I won't tell a soul." Then Kandace tapped a few papers on the clipboard. "Now, do you mind signing these for me? I already had your mom look them over."

Delilah looked down, surprised at the change of gears after her big confession. That was probably good, though. Kandace couldn't care less.

Fresh from that Korean body scrub Kandace had recommended—which *was* wonderful—Delilah dressed, got her hair and makeup done, and met Jasmine at the Dove, where they were going to ride together to Gratitude Prom. Fiona was arriving separately with Chase, though she promised to find them as soon as she was at the venue.

Delilah hadn't made the same underdressing mistake as she had at the Snapchat TV party. Ava, Faith, and even Bethany—even her dad—got into the fun of dressing her for the event, parsing through the designers who offered to dress Delilah, considering gown after gown and whether any of them were worth pairing with and linking to on her official Gratitude Prom post. In the end, they chose a navy, one-shouldered dress by Alice + Olivia with a slit down the leg that was sexy without being too revealing and giving her father a heart attack. She paired it with strappy wedges and some funky jewelry from Adina's Jewels, the woman who'd approached Delilah at the Real Real party.

"You look incredible," Ava and Faith had chirped to Delilah as she left. They reminded Delilah of the little mice in Cinderella who helped the princess get ready for the ball. "Take a million pictures, okay?" Ava cried. "Please tell all the celebrities I say hi!" Then Faith tapped Ava and did the old whisper-in-Ava's-ear trick she still sometimes reverted to. Ava's expression clouded, and she looked at Delilah guiltily. "Also, be careful," she'd added.

For some reason, it had given Delilah a small frisson of fear. Ava had promised not to tell anyone about her and Jack—not even Faith. Delilah hoped she'd kept her word.

"Whoa," Delilah said when Jasmine opened the door. "You look . . . different."

Jasmine's face fell. "Different bad?"

"No! Different good." Jasmine was in a wine-colored strapless dress that was slinky, sexy, and sophisticated, showing off a little more cleavage than her typical Lulu C numbers. Her normally blown-out hair was slicked back into an artful bun, and her makeup was dark, smoky, and dramatic. She wasn't wearing white heels but sharp black stilettos with red soles. She looked at least five years older than when Delilah had seen her last.

"Wh-what are your sponsors going to say?" Delilah blurted out.

Jasmine shrugged. "Oh, now that I don't have my sister breathing down my neck, I want to have more of a personal style, you know?"

Delilah blinked. "Are things . . . okay?"

"Oh, not in the slightest." Jasmine's voice was breezy, but her expression told a different story. "She did something that pushed me over the edge. That girl I kissed? Apparently, she was looking for me, too. But Ruby shut her down. Even though I was dying to find out who she was."

"Oh, Jasmine," Delilah moaned. "I'm so sorry."

Jasmine leaned into a large round mirror in her foyer to touch up her lipstick. "Ruby didn't have my best interest at heart, I guess. Just my brand."

Delilah felt her throat close. Jasmine's words were eerily similar to what Jack had said about his family's involvement. How could a family member's motivations become so warped?

"So what are you going to do?" Delilah asked.

"Oh, I don't know." Jasmine's voice was shaky. "Ruby and I aren't speaking. But things are okay with Lemonade. As for that lady in the mask, I guess it's a lost cause." A regretful look crossed her face. It was clear this was weighing on her. "Anyway," she said, wrapping the chain of her quilted evening bag around her wrist. "Tonight's about fun. Not about Jasmine's problems."

"You can always come to me with your problems," Delilah said.

Jasmine hugged her gratefully. "Thanks, babe."

It gave Delilah a euphoric little lift. Things felt so right—good friends, a great career, that awesome photo shoot, even her family on board. In a few hours, she hoped, once everything was cleared up with Jack, once she and Jack could be together, things would get even better.

She couldn't wait.

Transcript of Scarlet Leigh's personal vlog, 6/27 (for her YouTube channel)

Camera on Scarlet. She's riding in the back of a limo, wearing a gorgeous emerald gown. Hair is loose around her shoulders. She has dramatic rosy smoky eyes, contoured cheekbones, vampy red lips. She sits next to Jack Dono, who's in a tux. But as she turns on the camera, he's looking out the window. Distracted.

SCARLET

Hey, guys! It's Scar, and we're on our way to . . . (nudges Jack) Tell them where we're going, baby.

Jack turns. Grimaces slightly at the camera, but then says . . .

JACK

Grat Prom, what!

SCARLET

Gratitude Prom! That's right! And oh my God, we are so excited. It's going to be amazing. Isn't it going to be amazing, babe?

Nudges Jack again. He jumps. Looks a million miles away.

JACK

What?

Scarlet giggles.

SCARLET

Clearly someone hasn't had his Starbucks Cold Brew. But we are PSYCHED. Now, let me tell you about my outfit. Cory and I PORED over designers and chose Valentino. It just felt . . . *right*. You like?

She pans down the dress, shows a bit of leg. We also catch her kicking Jack. Hard. He turns away from the window once more.

SCARLET

And my love Jack's in a tux by Armani. Which he spent a *lot* of time admiring in the mirror once it was on, I might add.

JACK

I did not.

SCARLET

You did too, cutie! But it's okay. I know you want to look good for me.

The car pulls up to the curb. Out the window, we can see a red carpet, photographers, flashing lights, fans.

SCARLET

Here we go! You ready?

She reaches for Jack's hand, the camera still rolling. Together, they get out of the limo. The fans erupt into screams. People are calling, "Jacklet, Jacklet!" Scarlet pans over the bleachers of onlookers, and we see someone familiar—is that the über-fan from the restaurant the other day who stalked Scarlet? She's wearing a long T-shirt with #JACKLET printed on the front.

Scarlet turns the camera on herself.

SCARLET

So we're at the red carpet. Isn't it pretty? I see a lot of my friends. . . .

We see influencers talking to the press, posing for pictures. The camera pans over some of Scarlet's friends. There's Jasmine Walters-Diaz in an elegant wine-colored dress. There's Fiona Jacobs, Scarlet's nemesis. Cory runs over and shakes Jack's hand and pecks Scarlet on the cheek.

Then Scarlet gasps. Turns the camera on herself again.

SCARLET

Oh my God, guys. Do you know who's here? *York.* Yes, *that* York. (to Cory) Did anyone know he was coming? I thought he was in Milan. . . .

CORY

Scar! He's coming *over*!

Camera swings again. We get a look at YORK: strapping, devastatingly handsome African American hottie. Literally a *star:* everyone is staring. He saunters up to Scarlet. . . .

YORK

Scarlet Leigh.

SCARLET

What's up, honey?

YORK

Girl, *you* are what's up. You look amazing. I can't believe I haven't seen you around.

SCARLET

Oh, well. I mean, I didn't know you were *looking*. . . .

Camera swings onto Cory, who is silently freaking out.

YORK

(leaning in seductively)

I mean, can I walk you in? You wanna . . . (sexy pause) . . . you wanna be my date?

He puts a hand on the small of her back—almost on her butt. It looks like Scarlet is considering it. But then she smiles awkwardly. Removes his hand.

SCARLET

York . . . you know Jack and I are still together, right?

YORK

Wait, what?

SCARLET

We're still together. I can't be your date. I'm sorry.

York's smile dims. His gaze flicks from Scarlet to Jack, who's standing nearby, as if to say, *Uh, dude, what now?*

Scarlet catches on. She glances at Jack, too.

SCARLET

What's going on?

YORK

(to Jack)

Sorry, man. I tried.

SCARLET

(to Jack)

He . . . tried? Did you put him up to . . . something?

Jack looks pained.

JACK

Scarlet, I . . .

Scarlet grabs his arm and storms off. As she goes, the camera pans the crowd again. Most people haven't noticed what's happened. York is now talking to someone else.

Scarlet marches into the party, ignoring the cascade of balloons and event planners trying to steer her into fun Gratitude activities. She drags Jack into an empty back room. Strangely, the camera is still rolling.

SCARLET

What the hell?

JACK

Scarlet...

SCARLET

Were you trying to break us up? Is this because of *her*?

JACK

Let's just calm down....

SCARLET

You really think I'd fall for your little York plan? That guy hits on *everyone*.

Jack squeezes his eyes shut. Takes a breath.

JACK

Scar, why are we still together?

SCARLET

You're really going to do this right now? Who is she, Jack? You know I'll kill her, right?

JACK

Jesus. Don't say that. Look—you don't want this. I know you don't. And I don't want it, either. We should honor those feelings.

Scarlet doesn't move.

JACK (CONT'D)

I want you to be happy. *Really* happy... but I know that's not with me.

A tear rolls down Scarlet's cheek. She quickly pushes it away.

Jack reaches out to touch her. Scarlet stiffens, like she isn't sure she wants him to.

SCARLET

Jack... I can't.

JACK

Why? Tell me what you're thinking.

SCARLET

I...

(takes a deep breath)

I... I think I'm pregnant.

Comments: (8,872)

@ChanelGoddess7623: First!

@LeighIsMe99IO: OH MY GOD WHAT?? WHAT JUST HAPPENED

@MultiFanScarlet: Is this REAL? Tell me it ISN'T REAL.

@ScarLeighJackletHeart: I knew it! I knew it all along! The nausea... the fainting... CVS... Holy crap holy crap

@Jacklet4Ever: JACKLET CANNOT BREAK UP THEY ARE KILLING ME THEY HAVE TO BE LYING WHEN THEY SAID THEY WEREN'T INTO EACH OTHER ANYMORE.

@TheEndMyFriend99: There's literally NO WAY they are gonna break up @Jacklet4Ever—didn't you hear? They're going to be PARENTS.

@VvroomColin887: OMG this vid took so long to load it's breaking the internet but it's freaking WORTH it except I feel kinda sorry for Jack man who wants to be a dad at 17?

@uwuscarletleigh: THIS IS SOME KARDASHIAN LEVEL DRAMA but lowkey I would totally watch a scarlet reality show

@AndyCandy: That's gonna be one adorable bambino! #ScarBunInTheOven

FIONA

"Something bugging you, babe?" Chase asked for the thirtieth time.

They were at Gratitude Prom, and Fiona had just finished interviews on the red carpet, most of which involved reporters asking her why she turned down the Kate role despite her manager saying that was an off-the-table topic for the evening. Inside the ballroom, big balloons spelled out "No bullying beyond this point!"—which required a *lot* of balloons. Tons of people were taking photos in front of it, but Fiona rolled her eyes. Didn't they know that no matter how hard you tried, no matter how many hashtags you used or how many celebrities you got behind the cause, bullies wouldn't just dry up and vanish? The world just didn't work that way.

Her phone pinged, and she glanced down. *Here's some images from Getty*, her publicist wrote. *Please do an in-feed post and tag Zimmerman. They were so sweet to gift you the dress.*

Oh, the pull of work. Still, Fiona scrolled through the pictures of herself, trying to find a good one to post. Her publicist sent over fifty to choose from, but by the end of Fiona's cutthroat analysis, only a single picture remained. She performed her usual routine of smoothing out her imperfections, adding a filter, and coming up with a witty caption. By the time she hit *Post*, she felt exhausted.

Chase held her hand as they walked to the dance floor. Some of the dancers were famous people, and they were having an actual dance battle. Everyone was filming, of course. Chase cheered for them wildly; at least *one* of them was having fun, anyway. Fiona plastered on a smile, but she just couldn't get in the mood. The secret she knew about Scarlet was at the forefront of her mind, blocking out all other thoughts. She needed to find Scarlet tonight. She needed to tell her what she knew so they could cut a deal. The sooner she got it over with, the sooner she could relax.

"Fiona?"

She looked up and saw Kylie, one of the organizers of the event, beaming. "Hey! Would you mind having your fortune told? It would make a great photo for our branded page. I would so appreciate it."

Fiona followed Kylie's gaze. At the back of the space was indeed a fortune-teller's booth. It was the typical setup—a table festooned with glowing red candles, a stack of tarot cards, and a woman who looked appropriately spooky with a head scarf and a drawn-on beauty mark and a lot of bead necklaces.

"Uh," Fiona said. Seeing a fortune-teller was just about the *last* thing she wanted to do. But to Fiona's horror, Kylie was already leading her over, saying that it would be *so* huge if they could get a picture of her for their Story.

Fiona sat down in the chair across from the woman, then felt a hand on her shoulder. Chase stood above her, his head cocked in surprise. "I thought you weren't into fortune-tellers."

"Um," Fiona said, but then Kylie told her to turn to the left and smile. The moment Kylie was finished, Fiona readied herself to stand—it wasn't like she had to go through with a reading. But then the fortune-teller grabbed her hands tightly and said in a commanding voice, "Let's start."

The woman was peering at her with such a fixed, haunted gaze that a chill zoomed through Fiona's bones. The woman's fingers were dry, and she spent a lot of time caressing Fiona's fingers and the creases in her palms.

"Getting quite the hand massage," Fiona choked to Chase over her shoulder, forcing a smile.

A very strange expression settled over the fortune-teller's features. When she opened her mouth, her voice was deep and full of warning. "You're troubled, my dear. Something looks over you, something . . . something that's breaking you." She peered up at Chase, too. "It's going to tear you apart."

"What?" Chase cried. "You've got that all wrong. We're great."

Fiona's face was suddenly on fire. "Yeah." She yanked her palm away from the woman's thin, bony fingers and grabbed Chase's hand. "He and I are perfect."

The woman's bright blue eyes narrowed. "*Are* you? You two need to tell each other the truth. Or do you want *me* to spell it out for you?"

This wasn't happening. Fiona leaped up, knocking the chair over. "Thanks!" she cried. "Very informative!"

Then she staggered away. She could feel everyone else in the line, including Kylie, staring at her in shock as she lunged for the other side of the room. And even though the music was deafening, she swore she could hear the fortune-teller making a *tsk* sound, disappointed that Fiona had been too cowardly to hear her truth.

When she reached a set of doors that led to a huge patio, Chase was behind her. "Fiona?" He spun her around to look her in the eye. "You're not actually worried about what she said, are you? You know those people are scammers."

Fiona licked her lips. "Of course not. Totally. I just . . . I can't quite . . ."

But she couldn't finish. She was breathing too hard. Panic was filling her. How did the fortune-teller *know*? What if she told everyone?

By this time, she was hyperventilating. Chase put a hand on her heart. "Fiona. It's okay, it's okay, angel. Just breathe, in and out. What are you panicking about?"

"I . . . ," Fiona started. "It's just . . ." This was a mess. The way she was freaking out, Chase was going to know something was up. She was overreacting. She needed to breathe. *In and out. Don't faint. Get a grip.*

Finally, her breathing began to slow. "Thanks, babe," she said to Chase. "I don't know what I got so worked up about. I don't deserve you."

The relief seemed to drip down Chase's face like rain. "Are you kidding? I don't deserve *you.*"

"No, I really . . ."

But then something caught Fiona's attention. There was a burst of blond hair in the corner. Was that . . . *Scarlet*? It *was.*

She jumped up. "I'll be back."

"What?" Chase frowned. "W-where are you going?"

Her gaze remained fixed on the blonde in the corner. She needed to do this, *now.* "BRB. Grab us a couch, 'kay?"

She moved through the crowd, desperate and frantic, and . . . *there.* Scarlet had moved through a curtained archway that led onto yet another dance floor. Now she was talking to Cory, her smile frozen and fake. Fiona marched toward them. She was going to get this over with.

But then she felt someone pull her backward. When she whirled around, Chase's brow was creased in annoyance. "What's going on?" His tone was both concerned and kind of impatient.

"Huh?" Fiona spluttered. She glanced over her shoulder again. Scarlet was leaving. . . .

"I don't understand you," Chase demanded. "You have a panic attack, and then you're running off. . . ."

"It's nothing," Fiona moaned, her eyes zinging to the other side of the room once more. She couldn't lose track of Scarlet. "I just have to take care of something, okay?"

"What is it?"

"It's not worth getting into. It's dumb."

His eyes searched her face. "Dumb . . . how?"

Fiona tried to channel her actress abilities and pretend that this was just a normal social media gaffe she needed to fix. She could say that one of her friends was angry because she accidentally posed for a picture with an ex. She could say one of her less-important sponsors was here and she needed to show them she still cared about them.

But it felt unfair to lie. She also was pretty sure her boyfriend would see through it. And this annoyed her. *Badly.* "Just . . . I'll explain later, okay?" she muttered peevishly. "I'll be back in a sec, and then you can have me all to yourself."

A muscle tightened in Chase's jaw. "Is something up with Scarlet?"

Fiona's heart plummeted. "No!"

"Then are you cheating on me?"

"What?" Fiona barked out a laugh. "No! Why in the world would you think *that*?"

"Because when we're apart, you never text or Snapchat. You haven't returned my calls. And you barely pay attention to me when we're together. You're a million miles away."

"You're being paranoid. I would never cheat on you."

"But you obviously don't want to be here with me."

"What are you talking about?" Fiona couldn't believe what she was hearing. Then she peered into the crowd once more. *Shit.* Scarlet was gone.

"See? You're doing it right now!" Chase's body was tense. "Your eyes have been roaming this party, like you're looking for someone else. *Are* you? Am I not good enough anymore? Is it because I'm not an influencer? Not an actor?"

Fiona wanted to groan. "Don't be the jealous boyfriend. That's not what we are."

Chase gave her a long, sad look. "I'm starting to think I actually don't *know* what we are."

Was this really happening? The music was too loud. Fiona's

dress was too constricting—and the Voice had a lot to say about that. She didn't want to fight with Chase.

"Let me just clear something up. Then we'll talk, okay?"

And then she flew across the room, hoping she could figure out where Scarlet had gone. "Fiona!" Chase roared. He was pushing through the crowd, trying to catch her. *Why*? She needed to lose him. He couldn't witness the conversation she was about to have.

She turned right, then left. The crowd was thick, and when she peeked behind her again, Chase was gone. A hallway led to a set of bathrooms. The other way opened into a courtyard. Fiona's instincts tugged her toward the outdoors. Her heels clicked against the hard marble. She walked through an archway and was suddenly in the teeming, unexpected humidity of Los Angeles in mid-July. The courtyard was empty—she presumed kids hadn't discovered it yet, since most people were still on the red carpet or getting acquainted with the space.

But then she noticed a figure standing behind a large topiary, her chin down. Her stomach tied itself into dozens of knots.

Scarlet.

Fiona started toward her. Her mouth had gone bone-dry. Scarlet looked up just as Fiona approached, but she didn't seem particularly surprised. Her eyes were dark and foreboding. And . . . was that a *juul* in her hand?

"Juuling can't be good for the baby," Fiona blurted out, unable to help herself. She might as well dive right in.

A muscle next to Scarlet's temple twitched. Fiona felt a rush of triumph, because until this moment, she wasn't entirely sure what she had on Scarlet was real.

"That's right," Fiona went on. "I know about you. Just like you know something about me. But I'm hoping we can come to some kind of agreement."

For a second, Scarlet's face was pliable and open, and she looked almost childlike. Fiona put herself in Scarlet's position: she was still a teenager, at the height of her career, but now pregnant. What would *she* do? How would *she* handle it? It wouldn't be easy.

Then the corners of Scarlet's mouth twisted. She set the vape pen on the edge of the teak planter. "You think it matters that you know about the pregnancy?"

Fiona flinched. *This* wasn't a question she expected. "Well, yeah."

Scarlet sighed. "Nah. The whole world knows. There's something going on with my phone—at first I thought *I* was making the mistake, but after tonight . . . I think I've been cloned."

Fiona's eyes widened. "Oh, shit." Cloning was everyone's worst nightmare. "All of your stuff was stolen? *Everything*?"

"Don't pretend to feel bad." Scarlet rolled her eyes. "Anyway, I told Jack the big news a few minutes ago, and whoever's cloning me posted it everywhere. So actually, you're behind on the gossip, Fiona."

Fiona's heart felt like it was suddenly weighted down with stones. *Everyone* knew?

Scarlet leaned her hips against the planter. "And also? Blackmail isn't very nice. What would your fans think?"

Fiona felt the hairs on the back of her neck rise. "Like *you're* one to talk?"

Scarlet narrowed her eyes. "Huh?"

"*You* know."

There was confusion in Scarlet's gaze. *Lies, though. All lies.* She was just trying to mess with Fiona's mind, just like Lana used to. Fiona balled up her fists. *Hurt her,* the Voice whispered. *Do it now. You know you want to.* It was the same pulsing need that had come over Fiona that last night with Lana, on the roof. She felt her hand lift and her body shift forward. She grabbed Scarlet's arm hard. And it felt . . . *good.*

"Ow!" Scarlet screeched, rearing back. "What's wrong with you?"

Lightning crackled in her veins. She could hurt Scarlet more. She could ruin her.

But then she let out a horrible groan and wilted against the planter. Of *course* she couldn't hurt Scarlet. She wasn't that person.

Scarlet stood opposite her, cradling her wounded arm. "You need serious help, girl."

And then she turned and walked calmly away. Fiona didn't have the nerve to follow her.

A strange, muffled sound emerged from the hallway. When Fiona lifted her head, she realized that she wasn't alone. Behind her, a group of people—some of them minor influencers, but some of them fans—had gathered in the corridor. *Staring.* And by the looks on their faces, they'd heard—and *seen*—everything.

JASMINE

After an evening of dancing, Jasmine and Delilah stood on a raised white stage, speaking in a late interview to a rep from *Tiger Beat*. From this vantage, Jasmine could see exactly how the giant warehouse had been transformed: the walls were covered in red velvet, and the bar was decorated with an intricate flower design. Lavish couches were placed in all corners of the room, and balloons and beaded curtains dotted the giant dance floor. She looked up at the DJ booth, which had a neon sign above it that read GRATITUDE. It seemed like wherever she looked, internet stars were eyeing up one another, reuniting, posing, and sometimes ignoring. Which, c'mon, wasn't the evening about being *inclusive*?

"So, ladies, tonight's been all about gratitude." The reporter, a perky, petite girl in clear-framed glasses and a long, layered dress, held her cell phone, which she was using to record the interview, outstretched. "As you know, Instagram is launching the 'gratitude' feature—when you're beyond grateful for whatever—someone's account, a like, a comment, anything—you can click on the gratitude function and send anyone a truly dreamy montage of exploding prayer hands. *And* it stays up on a page forever—meaning your gratitude is there for all the world to see. So I'm wondering how you guys feel about that?"

The reporter looked at Jasmine first for an answer, but Jasmine didn't feel like taking this one. Old Jasmine, under Ruby's thumb, would be obligated, but New Jasmine didn't kowtow to reporters. She gestured to Delilah. "Delilah? What do you think?"

"Oh." Delilah straightened. "So, yes. It's a fantastic app. I plan to use the feature all the time, for every single one of my fans. For me, who's just starting out in this world—my whole *existence* is about gratitude. That I get to communicate with amazing people and talk about what I love. That I get to speak with interesting designers and jewelry makers and pet-store owners and workout gurus. That I get to have awesome new friends like Jasmine, who is *amazing*, no matter what."

"Aw," Jasmine said, slinging an arm around her.

"So you're just brimming with gratitude!" the reporter crowed.

"I'm a gratitude smoothie," Delilah joked.

The reporter's eyes lit up. "Great sound byte!"

Then she dismissed them, even though she'd forgotten to get Jasmine's take. Normally, Jasmine would consider this a monster gaffe—and Ruby would freak. But today, it felt like a win.

"You did amazing up there," Jasmine told Delilah as they stepped off the stage.

"Are you sure?" Delilah looked worried. "I didn't talk too much?"

"Nope." It was surprising how good Jasmine felt—both inside and out. People had whispered all night that Jasmine was sure to get on the night's "best dressed" list, which seemed huge considering *she* had styled herself. It made her feel empowered. She was out in the world, not dressed like Lulu C, and people still liked her. It gave her hope.

But Ruby? *That* was a mess. Jasmine was gutted over her sister's absence. She hadn't heard from her since the California Adventure appearance—no pleas to take her back, no check-ins to see how Jasmine was doing, *nothing*. Sure, Jasmine had fired her, but Ruby was still her sister. Wasn't she going to apologize for what she did? Did Ruby honestly think she'd been *right*?

The evening was beginning to wind down. A coordinator stood at the front of the party space telling everyone that an after-party was planned at the Dove condos, and that if people didn't have transportation, party limos were available at the curb. "What do you think about a little after-party?" Jasmine asked Delilah. "There won't be any media there, just us. Should be fun."

But Delilah looked stricken. "Wait, you mean prom is *over*?"

Jasmine laughed. "You want to take *more* pictures with people? There will be plenty of them at the after-party. *And* probably better food—Buca di Beppo is catering it."

"But . . ." Delilah peered around the room nervously. "I mean, I *guess*. . . ."

"Are you looking for someone?" Jasmine asked, slowly smiling.

Delilah's cheeks turned red. She bit a thumbnail in lieu of an answer.

Jasmine grabbed her hands. "Oh my God, girl! Are you holding out on me? Are you *into* someone?"

Delilah hid a cautious smile. "I mean . . . someone was supposed to meet me here. I'm guessing he got held up." She glanced at her phone, a wrinkle in her brow.

"Spill it. *Who?*"

"I can't." Delilah shook her head vehemently. "It's kind of . . . complicated."

Jasmine wracked her brain for who Delilah's mystery person could be. "And you're supposed to meet him here? If it *is* a him?"

"It's a him." Delilah nodded, looking miserable.

"Well. Text him and tell him to come to the after-party. It'll be way more laid-back for you two." Her eyes gleamed. "I can't *wait* to find out who it is!"

They stepped out onto the busy street. A bunch of people were waiting in line for the party limos, but Jasmine called her driver, and soon enough, she and Delilah were in the backseat, heading to the Dove. Delilah was unusually quiet. Jasmine touched her knee. "You worried because he didn't show up?"

"Kind of," Delilah admitted. "Last we talked, it was a done deal. There was a promposal and everything."

"He gave you a promposal?" Jasmine whistled. "Then he wasn't messing around, girl. Are you sure you can't tell me who it is?"

Delilah pressed her arms tightly to her chest. "I just want to keep it personal for now . . . but soon. I promise."

It felt like only minutes passed before they were stepping out

of the limo at the Dove's front entrance. Velvet ropes had been set up outside the atrium, and a bouncer was checking wristbands—anyone who'd attended Gratitude Prom could come. The pool area had been transformed into a sexy, slinky fete. A DJ spun records in the corner, and squeaky-clean influencers Jasmine had known forever were grinding provocatively on the dance floor—apparently, *they* didn't have morality clauses. A fitness YouTuber, notorious for her "eat clean" posts, was at the bar, a martini in hand. By her flamboyant arm gestures, Jasmine suspected it wasn't her first drink of the night.

"Total hedonism," she murmured, leading Delilah to some comfy couches in a private alcove near the pool. "Everyone seems super drunk already."

"People do seem kind of . . . wild," Delilah mused. She still had that wounded puppy expression. Jasmine wished she could somehow fix it. But then Delilah turned to Jasmine. "You have any idea where I can find a bathroom?"

"Oh, anywhere." Jasmine gestured to the condo doors on the pool's perimeter. Many of them were thrown open, inviting the partygoers into the different apartments. "Practically everyone who lives here is invited to this thing, and they open their doors so we can come and go as we please. *I'm* not letting anyone in my place—it's a huge pain to clean afterward—but you can go through any of the open doors. But I'll warn you." She raised an eyebrow. "Don't go into the bedrooms. Last year, they were prime real estate for makeout spots."

"Got it," Delilah said, shooting Jasmine a sad smile before she left.

Jasmine lounged on the couch for a few moments, letting the

heady, electronic music rock in her ears. She felt good, mostly . . . if a little sad. If only Ruby had handled things differently. If only Ruby had quietly brought the girl's Tumblr post to Jasmine's attention . . . and let *Jasmine* decide what to do with it.

Snap.

A shadow moved around the bushes. Jasmine sat up straighter. "Hello?"

A beautiful girl in a long emerald dress stepped backward, looking caught. Her face was pale. Her mouth was drawn. But when she noticed Jasmine, her face opened.

Jasmine blinked. "Oh. Hey, Scarlet."

Scarlet tentatively stepped into the little cabana. Jasmine tensed. She'd nearly forgotten about Scarlet's spying presence over the past few weeks. It was Scarlet's incognito appearance at California Adventure that had kicked off World War III with Ruby, actually.

"Hey." Scarlet's voice trembled. She almost sounded afraid. "I—I was looking for you."

Jasmine wanted to roll her eyes, but she was surprised by Scarlet's gentle, unsure tone. "Why?"

Scarlet's eyes shifted. Jasmine could only see the shadows on her face and not the definition of her features.

"I saw you," Jasmine said. "At that tattoo place. And my sister saw you at California Adventure. For someone as busy as you, I don't know why you care so much about what I'm up to." She shifted her weight. "You already took my friend's role on that show. If you're hoping to take me down, too, go ahead. I don't really care."

Scarlet blinked. "Wait, no . . . it's not what you think. That

TV role—and what I was doing, following you—you've got it all wrong."

"Right. So you didn't threaten my friend to give up her role so you could have it?"

Scarlet shook her head, looking very sad. *Such an act.*

"You really think you're fooling anyone?" Jasmine leaned against the couch cushions, her feet suddenly aching in her tight shoes. Maybe she should just go to bed. She was over this night.

Scarlet dipped her head down, and Jasmine could see the jagged part in her hair. "I didn't . . . it wasn't . . . I see how Fiona *thinks* it was me. But never mind. It's not worth explaining, because it's over now, and who knows if *I'm* even going to take the role. So maybe Fiona will get it back in the end."

"Huh?" Jasmine frowned. "What are you talking about?"

"I want to explain why I followed you. Except . . . well, except I don't want to say too much. Those threats your sister made. I don't want lawyers involved."

A cool breeze swirled. People laughed in the distance. Scarlet's words scrambled in Jasmine's mind. *Those threats your sister made?*

One answer bubbled to the top. Except . . . *no.* It couldn't be. *Could* it?

Scarlet's face softened. She clasped her hands at her waist like a little girl. When she peeked at Jasmine, she looked like she was afraid Jasmine might send her away. And then, as the wind kicked up once more, a familiar smell wafted into Jasmine's nostrils. A smell of caramel—the very same smell from the night at that masked party. But this was impossible. *Preposterous.*

"That was . . . *you*?" Jasmine croaked. "At that party?"

Scarlet's nod was nearly imperceptible. They both sat down.

Jasmine blinked hard. "And you tried to find me? You wrote something on an anonymous Tumblr?"

Scarlet stared at her palms. "Your sister figured out that I was talking about you, considering there was already that picture of you at a party with masks. Good save saying you were doing a movie, by the way."

Jasmine's heart thumped. This couldn't be happening. The girl she was searching for, *dreaming* about—it couldn't be Scarlet freaking Leigh. Obviously this was a joke, right? Because the girl she danced with, the girl she kissed—that girl was different. That girl was soft, and open, and giving, and sweet. Scarlet was none of those things.

Except that now as she was looking at Scarlet, sitting next to her, wringing her hands in her lap, she seemed like an entirely different person.

"Ruby contacted me through the dummy email I used to put up that post," Scarlet continued. "And said—well, I guess you know what she said. She said you weren't interested. She said you'd sue if I bothered you ever again. She said you guys talked about it; you were in complete agreement. Except I just . . . I don't know, I didn't quite believe her. That kiss we shared . . . it felt *real.* To me, anyway."

To me, too, Jasmine wanted to say. Except . . . no. *No.* She had to get out of here. Her dream girl—it *couldn't* be Scarlet. This was *insane.*

"It's why I started following you. I wanted to talk to you—wanted to see . . ." Scarlet arched her neck, staring into the starry sky. "But I couldn't get up the guts to ask. But then, at Disneyland . . . I heard what you and Ruby were talking about. I heard how shocked you were at what she'd done. So I thought—wait, maybe Ruby was lying. Maybe you had no idea that Ruby reached out. Maybe you're as controlled in your career as I am in mine."

That last bit caught Jasmine off guard, and she wanted to ask Scarlet what she meant, but Scarlet kept talking. "I get it if you think this is a prank. I know I have a reputation for being . . . ruthless. But everything isn't how it seems. It's complicated, but I'm not as terrible as you think I am. I went to that masked party, too. I wanted something that my current life can't give me. And when I was there, I found you. And I don't regret that."

The music thumped loud. The air crackled with . . . danger, maybe, but also possibility. All Jasmine could see were Scarlet's bright red lips and the luminous paleness of her hair. Jasmine's heart was beating crazily, like a Super Ball that had been dropped off a balcony. And though she didn't want Scarlet's words to affect her, they did anyway. Was Scarlet Leigh's persona just as crafted and artificial as Jasmine's? She considered all the vlogs Scarlet posted—and all the rumors of the ways she ruined people's careers. Was it possible that wasn't true? The way Scarlet denied being the one to threaten Fiona to drop the Kate role—*could* that have been someone else's doing?

Jasmine cleared her throat. "You're . . . right. Ruby spoke for me without my permission." It was hard to get the words out. "She doesn't understand that I've grown beyond my role on a kids' show. I have desires. Wants. And that I want to change—as a human, and in my career, too."

Scarlet's eyes were full of empathy. "You should be given that opportunity. We *all* should be."

Jasmine nodded. "So . . . that thing you wrote on Tumblr—I never got to read it. But I would have liked to."

A tiny smile danced across Scarlet's lips. "I would have liked that, too."

Jasmine's brain spun in too many directions. She shifted closer to Scarlet, her pulse racing. Scarlet leaned forward, too. Their lips connected hurriedly and desperately, and warm, whooshing feelings zoomed through Jasmine's body. It felt exactly the same! How she'd *longed* for this! How she was so afraid she'd never feel this again!

Their kisses were messy—too much lipstick, random hairs in mouths, a snagged earring—but they were delicious and fulfilling and worth the wait. Jasmine's heart exploded with gratitude. *Here,* she thought, was what she was grateful for. It only seemed appropriate that she was given such a beautiful gift at Gratitude Prom. Already, Jasmine could imagine a future she and Scarlet might have. It could involve messy complications, but it would also be joyful and sexy and full of love.

"Scarlet?"

A voice pierced through the music. Scarlet flew off Jasmine, her eyes wide.

"Scarlet?" the voice cried again. "Are you back there?"

Scarlet straightened her dress just as her friend Cory peeked around the corner. "Uh, hello?" he asked in a snarky voice. When he looked harder at Scarlet and Jasmine—with their mussed hair and guilty glances, it must have been obvious what just went down—his face hardened. "Your mom's been tearing apart this place looking for you. She wants to talk."

To Jasmine's horror, a weird, inscrutable expression crossed

Scarlet's face, and she stood. Like a zombie, she walked to the edge of the cabana. Jasmine wanted to reach out and pull her back . . . but she felt powerless. Was Scarlet really going to pretend this hadn't happened?

"Scarlet," Jasmine called.

But Scarlet didn't turn. Cory fixed Jasmine with a level, knowing glare. He raised one eyebrow as if to say, *You'd better watch yourself.* And then he turned and followed his best friend into the party.

DELILAH

Delilah's mind was a laundry list of worst-case scenarios. Maybe Jack was sick. Maybe Jack was in the *hospital.* Maybe Jack had been in a car accident. Maybe Jack's house was burning and he needed to stay home and put out the fire. Maybe Jack's father had figured out the plan and put the kibosh on it. Whenever she shut her eyes, she envisioned how violently Jack's father had barged into that hotel room. Should she tell someone? Should she worry?

She checked and checked his accounts. YouTube. Instagram. Snapchat. Jack hadn't posted all night. Where *was* he? What was happening?

Jasmine said it would be fine, she reassured herself as she peered at her reflection in the bathroom mirror of the Photo Studio Condo. *She said a promposal was a big deal. Just give him time. He's probably still trying to make the York thing happen.* Or, heck, maybe Scarlet didn't even *come* tonight. It wasn't like Delilah had seen her around.

When Delilah returned to the couch she and Jasmine had been sitting on, Jasmine was gone. Delilah stared at the messed-up throw pillows, considering sitting . . . but maybe it would be lame to sit all on her own. She checked her phone for the millionth time, eager for a DM from Jack's Finsta. But there was still nothing. Uneasiness roiled in her gut. Then a text from her sister popped up: *Have you seen it? Are you okay?*

Delilah frowned. Okay? Okay about *what*?

"*There* you are. I've been looking for you all night."

Fiona strode toward her, looking gorgeous in a customized floral gown. Delilah had seen her friend at the beginning of the night, but had lost track of her since. They quickly embraced, but then Fiona pulled back. Her mouth was drawn, and she looked bedraggled and sweaty . . . but not in an exhilarated way, like she'd been dancing. More like she'd been running from a ghost.

"What's going on?" Delilah asked. "Where's Chase?"

"We . . . had a fight." Fiona's voice was tense. "I guess he went home. You haven't seen Scarlet pass by, have you?"

"What?" Delilah's nerves prickled. "Scarlet's . . . here?"

"Of course she's here. She lives here." Fiona's throat bobbed as she swallowed. "She was at Gratitude, too."

"She *was*?" Delilah's mind stalled. How did she not see her?

"We had a strange conversation . . . but she ran out before we could finish. Now I can't find her. I even banged on her door—nothing."

"She's probably figuring things out with Jack," someone

piped up. The girls turned: the person who spoke was a girl whose videos were popular on TikTok. Delilah couldn't remember her name—Amity? Emory? "I'm sure they have *tons* to talk about," Amity-Emory added with a wink.

"Wait, what?" Delilah's heart sped up. "Jack and Scarlet? Why?"

Amity-Emory and Fiona exchanged a loaded glance. "There's kind of a scandal going on about Jack and Scarlet right now. People are just beginning to gossip about it," Emory said.

Fiona leaned in closer. "It's gossip *I* figured out, too, but it leaked on her account before I could actually use it to my . . . you know. Advantage."

"Scandal?" Delilah tried to keep her voice neutral. Her brain zinged in so many directions. Did Scarlet and Jack break up? Did Jack *tell* Scarlet about Delilah? Oh God, she hoped he didn't. Or maybe she hoped he did. But what if Scarlet was now going to ruin her?

"Scarlet . . . is pregnant," Fiona whispered. "She told Jack tonight . . . at Gratitude . . . and it somehow leaked on video."

Delilah's vision tunneled. Sound fell away until she felt like she was listening to her friend from the bottom of a deep, deep well. *Take a breath.* There was no way she could faint.

"Anyway, Scarlet's here," Fiona said. "I need to talk to her. Wanna help me look?"

"S-sure," Delilah stammered, though this was the absolute last thing she wanted to do. Still, she needed to be moving, because otherwise, she might spontaneously combust. A single refrain thundered in her head: *Scarlet is pregnant. Scarlet is pregnant.* Even worse, Scarlet was at Gratitude . . . and apparently, she'd *told* Jack this news at Gratitude . . . meaning Jack had been there, too. Perhaps only rooms away from Delilah. And he hadn't even said hi. All those York plans, all those promises that they'd be together, that promposal . . . was it just a joke?

He'd probably never intended to break things off with Scarlet. Delilah's chin started to tremble. *Oh no.* She steeled herself. *You won't cry in front of all these cameras. Don't you dare.*

"Are you okay?"

Fiona was peering at her as they walked along the concrete path that led to the condos. "Fine," Delilah managed to squeak.

"You sure?" Fiona looked worried. "You seem really pale. You didn't smoke anything, did you? Who knows what sort of stuff is being passed around."

"I'm good," Delilah said faintly. But then she remembered something. She touched the edge of her bag, feeling for her insulin supplies. She glanced at Fiona guiltily. "Actually, I probably need to check my sugar."

Fiona nodded. "Of course. Let me help you."

She guided Delilah into her own condo and showed her the hall bathroom, and Delilah sorted herself out. Within a few minutes, she was feeling steadier and more level. "That's intense," Fiona said as they waited for the elevator back downstairs, glancing at Delilah's small travel pack of syringes and insulin vials. "I mean, in your Instagram, you make it out like it isn't a big deal. But do you have to carry that around everywhere?"

"Yep, and people think I'm on drugs," Delilah joked wearily—though the Scarlet joke now made her doubly miserable, because it had come from Scarlet and Scarlet was pregnant and Jack would never be hers. "But this stuff isn't for partying, that's for sure. Too much insulin to a normal person would *not* be fun."

They emerged into the party again. Delilah tried to smile at everyone passing, but her mind was galloping. She kept returning to the worst of what she now knew about the Jack-Scarlet scandal: that it happened at Gratitude Prom, *right under her nose.* There she was, giving interviews about how thankful she felt, feeling giddy that tonight, she'd finally get her prince . . . and clearly, Jack had no intention of making that happen. Something even more terrifying hit her: if Jack never cared about her, what if he *did* tell Scarlet who she was? Maybe she was in store for something awful.

A waitress with a tray passed, and Delilah, feeling reckless, grabbed a drink off the tray. She took a greedy sip, some of the liquid dribbling down her chin. Fiona gazed at her worriedly. "Are you allowed to drink with diabetes?"

It wasn't advised, but this felt like an emergency. "I'll be fine," Delilah answered.

She felt unhinged, a loose rope flapping in the wind. The first sip of the drink went down well—the liquid was sour without being too sour, sweet without hurting her teeth, and she could barely taste the vodka. Good, because she wanted more.

She swallowed most of the cocktail before coming up for air. When she set the empty glass down on a passing tray, she felt emboldened. Spiky. *Angry.* She thought of that line from Shakespeare her mother quoted a lot: *Hell hath no fury like a woman scorned.* That certainly applied to Delilah tonight.

But she needed to calm down. Because otherwise, she might do something she'd regret.

Transcript of video found on Scarlet Leigh's phone: 6/27, 12:13 p.m.

Official police evidence. Never posted.

Camera on Scarlet. She's in a dark room. Her makeup is smudged. Heavy bass thuds from somewhere nearby. But she's hiding.

SCARLET

Hey, guys. You're probably surprised to hear from me, but I thought I might as well be real with you. Isn't that what social is about? Trying to be as real as possible? Or, oops, maybe it's the other way around. But you've been seeing a lot of the real me lately anyway, so I might as well keep going with that.

Camera cuts out for a moment. Cuts to Scarlet at a slightly different angle. This video isn't live.

SCARLET

I'm at the Gratitude Prom after-party, which also happens to be the condo building where I live. So basically, I'm in my apartment, hiding. . . .

(takes a breath)

Some really serious stuff happened tonight. Like, things I can't even explain. Maybe you saw some of it. I know you can't believe it—I can barely believe it myself. I gave him a shock. I regret it, but I didn't know how else to tell him. But I guess we'll have to roll with it, you know?

(shifts her weight. There's a knock on the door.)

SCARLET

Uh, hello? This is a private residence!

GARBLED VOICE THROUGH THE DOOR

Oh! Sorry. I'm so sorry. I'll leave you alone. I was just—I'd love to talk to you, when you're done.

SCARLET

(uneasy)

Uh... yeah... whatever.

Looks at the camera again.

SCARLET

So Jack's upset. I get it. I've made some other people upset, too. Some for reasons I have control over. Others because I acted impulsively. I'm not good at owning my mistakes. But now I've made my bed, and I'm gonna have to lie in it.

Looks determined. Stands.

This might be the last you hear from me. This might be the end of Scarlet Leigh as you know her. So say a prayer for me, guys. Tonight feels weird. Tensions are high. Emotions are spiky. But let's get our gratitude on. And maybe our forgiveness, too.

Turns from the camera, but then turns back.

Jasmine, I'm talking to you.

BLACK.

DELILAH

Delilah jolted awake to vibrations against her cheek. Neon light shone through her eyelids, and when she made the slightest movement, explosions went off in her brain. Everything hurt. Her head, her body, her *soul.*

The buzzing stopped, but then started up again. Where was she? The mattress she was lying on felt like a cloud. There was also a strange, unfamiliar hum in the air, like an air filter or some sort of high-powered fan.

The night before came back to her in quick, disjointed snaps. Gratitude Prom. Delilah's blind optimism that Jack was going to come. And then heading to the after-party at the Dove. And Fiona breaking the horrible news about *Scarlet's baby.*

Then . . . what? She downed drinks. A *lot* of drinks. First the pink one in the martini glass. Then a lemony shot. After that, Fiona went to look for Scarlet some more—but Delilah didn't follow. She wandered through the open door to another condo and sat down next to two influencers passionately making out, feeling too woozy and numb to move. She felt foolish for drinking; it was hitting her hard. She felt foolish for believing in Jack and his stupid promposal, too. What an idiot she was.

Faces from last night flashed before her eyes: Jasmine, slipping behind a door. *Her* door?

Fiona's boyfriend, but he was alone, his hands in his pockets, looking around for someone. Fiona?

Ali, another girl who lived at the Dove, gently taking a drink from her hands, saying, "I think you've had enough, honey."

And then someone else coming up: "Can I just tell you I love you more than life itself?" And then an arm slinging around her waist. Someone told her she needed to lie down. And she plopped here, on this bed, to sleep it off.

Experimentally, she opened her eyes. She was in a white, gorgeous bedroom, presumably somewhere in the Dove. In the corner next to the closet—the farthest she could look around without having to turn her head—was a pile of clothes, a huge vase of flowers, a stack of brightly colored books, and a tall oil painting of a gorgeous young woman Delilah recognized on sight: she had long blond hair, crystal-blue eyes, a vampy gaze.

Scarlet Leigh.

Why was she looking at a painting of Scarlet Leigh?

She sat up, despite the sharp pain in her head. The rest of the room wobbled into view—a beautiful, antique vanity, and next to it, a gilded chair that looked like an honest-to-goodness throne. This was Scarlet's bedroom—she recognized it from Scarlet's vlog. Had she seriously passed out in *Scarlet's bedroom*?

Then she felt a weight on the other side of the mattress. Delilah turned with a start. "Hello?" she croaked. "S-Scarlet?"

The figure didn't answer. Didn't even move. They were passed out cold.

"Hello?" Delilah said again, giving the figure a poke. She pulled at the covers uneasily. When she saw the pale, curled fingers of the left hand, she let out a little yelp. Next she saw an arm, a shoulder, and long, fanned-out blond hair. *Scarlet's* hair.

She scuttled back, nearly falling off the bed. *"Scarlet?"*

Scarlet didn't respond. Her hand was so pale, almost bloodless. Delilah's heart pounded. This had to be some kind of trick—something Scarlet was going to use to her advantage. *Think. Did something happen with Scarlet last night? Did I speak to her?* A blurry memory swam back: Scarlet emerging from a doorway, seeing Delilah, and making a face: *What are* you *doing here?*

Get out! a voice in her brain exclaimed. *Get out now!*

Delilah struggled to her feet. Her party dress was half-undone, and she had no idea where her shoes were, but it wasn't worth looking for them. She located her purse, staggered out of the room, hurried through the living room to the front door.

The outside air was refreshing. She stood on the walkway that overlooked the atrium and took deep breaths. The hall was trashed from the night before. A girl in a hot pink dress was passed out on the concrete fifty feet away. Some of the condo doors were still wide open from yesterday, everyone too messed up to remember to lock up tight. Then a figure emerged from the stairwell. Delilah recognized Scarlet's mother's coiffed long bob from the vlog.

Gasping, Delilah ducked behind a pillar.

Mrs. Leigh walked up to Scarlet's door and knocked. "Honey? Will you please, *please* open up?" Then she tried the knob. It wasn't locked—Delilah hadn't known how. This seemed to surprise Mrs. Leigh, but she let herself inside. "Scarlet?" she called, shutting the door behind her.

Delilah darted from the pillar to the stairwell. She just needed to get out of here. This felt really wrong.

As she was heading to the ground floor, her phone buzzed. *Busy,* flashed the screen. Delilah wanted to ignore the call, but she hadn't heard from her best friend in weeks, and maybe Busy could offer some perspective. She was good at talking Delilah off the ledge.

"Hey." Delilah's voice cracked. "Aren't you in Paris?"

"I'm on a train, actually. I'm calling from my mom's phone, which apparently, *she* didn't have to leave behind. She's letting me, just this once." In the background, Delilah heard a rushing sound, perhaps a train moving down the tracks.

"Oh. Cool." Delilah made it down one flight of stairs. The pavement was chilly against her bare feet. Her head throbbed with hangover and fear. "Well, I'm glad you did. I've had a really weird night."

Busy laughs uncertainly. "Uh, *yeah.* It popped up on my *mom's* Instagram, even. I can't believe you didn't tell me your . . . news."

"Huh?" Delilah asked. "News?" Had she posted something? All she remembered was taking some shots of Gratitude Prom. She'd posed with some people. Done some interviews. Normal things. She didn't remember looking at her phone once she started drinking. A terrible thought stabbed her: Did she still have her insulin?

She pawed through her bag. The caddy was there, but two vials were missing, not one. There was no way she'd injected more than once last night. But before she could dwell on this, Busy started speaking again.

"Dee? Are you there?" There was a crackling sound on the line. "Oh man. We're going into a tunnel, and I'm going to lose you—but we need to talk. I'll call you back in a little, okay?"

Then the line went dead. Delilah stared at her phone. What was Busy talking about? What *news*?

She tapped the Instagram app, quickly pulling up her account. She pressed on her profile picture, and her story loaded. It was the expected stuff she'd posted last night: a panoramic party shot, a picture with Jasmine, a pose in the photo booth.

Then her fingers trembled as she navigated elsewhere on the screen to Breaking News. And there, the second story down, was a piece that broke at about midnight: There was a picture of Delilah's smiling face . . . and Jack's frowning one . . . and a caption. *Jacklet Mystery Homewrecker Revealed!*

"Oh my God," Delilah whispered, feeling her knees turn to Jell-O. She made herself keep reading. *A source close to Miss Rollins, a fairly new influencer, says that Delilah and Jack are planning a secret rendezvous at Gratitude Prom tonight—"but it's complicated," Rollins adds. "He has to break up with his girlfriend first." That girlfriend, of course, is über-famous Scarlet Leigh. And their ship? It's none other than Jacklet, one of the most posted-about ships on the internet.*

"No, no, *no*," Delilah whispered. The wording. The way this story was told. It was exactly what she'd told *Kandace*, the photographer's PA. Kandace must have called this website and reported what she'd learned verbatim. Of course she knew who Jack was. Of course she'd figured it out. Her disinterest was just a ruse.

A shrill, terrified scream echoed through the courtyard. For a split second, Delilah was afraid it was *her*, but then she looked up and noticed Scarlet's mother rushing out of the condo, her face strangely pale. "Someone!" she cried. "Help! Please!"

Delilah's heart started to pound. She looked down at her phone again. Jack's face. Her face. That story. Delilah's rage. *Scarlet.* And waking up in Scarlet's bed. And that missing insulin.

Oh God. What happened? Did they argue? Did she *do* something?

She heard the frantic roar of sirens drawing near. And then Mrs. Leigh screamed, over and over again, just in case anyone in the Dove missed it: "It's my daughter! She's *dead*!"

FIONA

Someone pounded on Fiona's door, waking her from a sound sleep. She opened her eyes a crack, her head wailing in protest at the beams of sunlight sneaking through the blinds. She checked the bedside clock—10:02 a.m. How had she slept so long? The Ambien she'd popped before bed must have really done its job. She didn't like taking sleep aids, but after the stress of last night—and the unfinished business of Scarlet—she knew it would be the only thing that would help her get through the night.

The pounding continued. Fiona heaved out of bed and peeked at her phone. She had dozens of missed calls and more Notifications than she could count. The night snapped back in a grotesque collage, including how she'd confronted Scarlet . . . *grabbed* Scarlet. . . .

Oh God, oh God. Had Scarlet posted something? Is *that* why her phone was buzzing relentlessly? Vengeful, vindictive Scarlet. Of course she'd retaliated with Fiona's secret. How could Fiona be so *stupid*?

Two bulky shapes were visible through the little window in the door. Fiona's chest seized. Police officers. Her worst nightmares were coming true. Scarlet had posted what she knew, and now they were coming to arrest her.

Her throat went dry. No rituals could stave off the crushing anxiety that was flooding in. Should she run away? Hide? Slip out a back window? But they'd probably already heard her footsteps. They could likely sense she was on the other side of the door, listening.

This is what you get, laughed the Voice. Chase popped into her mind, too—their stupid fight last night. She wasn't even going to get to say goodbye to him before she was hauled off to prison. She wasn't even going to get to *explain.*

"Miss?" a voice called. "Can you please open up? It's LAPD."

Tears built behind her eyes. Her legs were wobbly as she turned the knob. Two officers with massive shoulders and biceps bore down on her. Maybe she should just fall to her knees and beg forgiveness. Maybe she shouldn't even fight.

"Are you Fiona Jacobs?" the taller one asked.

"Yes," Fiona could barely whisper.

"I'm Detective Carlson, and this is Detective Rodriguez." He gestured to a stocky Latinx guy with pretty eyes and a jagged scar on his chin. "We're wondering if you have a few moments to speak with us about the crime."

A few moments? Fiona blinked.

"We've been told you knew the victim," Detective Samuels added. "There was a little trouble between you two."

Knew the victim? *Trouble?* "Um, yeah, there was trouble between Lana and me," Fiona squeaked.

"Lana?" Detective Rodriguez frowned. "Who's Lana?"

"I . . . ," Fiona started. The men were looking at her like they had no idea what she was talking about. "Wait. What's going on?"

Then something outside caught her attention. Police tape was strewn all over the pool area. Kids were milling about. Some were taking pictures. Some were crying.

She turned back to the men, her heart suddenly pounding. "What happened?"

Carlson crossed his arms. "There was an accident. A girl's body was found in one of the condos. You didn't know?"

"A . . . girl?" Fiona could barely choke out the words. "*Who?*"

The men exchanged a look. Carlson peeked over his shoulder at the onlookers, the ambulances, the mayhem, as if to say, *You really slept through all this?*

"I-I'm a deep sleeper," Fiona said ludicrously. She didn't have to tell them about the Ambien, did she? Could that get her in trouble? "What happened? Who was it?" *Oh God, please don't let it be Jasmine,* she thought. *Or Delilah.*

"Scarlet Leigh," said Rodriguez. "They found her in her bed. It looks like some sort of poisoning—or an overdose. We're wondering if you can give us some details of what happened."

Fiona's brain went blank. "Wait, Scarlet was poisoned?" she barked. "That's . . . impossible."

"I'm sorry?" Carlson asked. He looked startled. "Why?"

"Because . . ." And then Fiona did something ridiculous. She *laughed.* She didn't mean to, but the whole thing was so preposterous. Scarlet, *dead*? She always seemed like one of those mythical creatures who would *never* die. And then something else occurred to her, a thought she felt a little bad for considering: now that Scarlet was gone, her secret was gone. She was free. Maybe she could even get her part on *Like Me* back.

But then Samuels jumped in. "You know where her apartment is, don't you, Miss Jacobs?"

"I . . ." Fiona felt woozy. "Sure. She lives downstairs."

"Do you have a key to get in?"

"What? No." Her skin started to crawl. "Do you think *I* did something to her?"

Carlson tapped at something on his cell phone. "Do you recall having an argument with Miss Leigh yesterday?"

Fiona's mouth opened. "Uh . . ."

"Someone sent us a video this morning, even before we found the body." Carlson showed Fiona his phone screen, and she saw her argument with Scarlet at Gratitude. Fiona grabbing Scarlet's arm, Scarlet yanking away.

"Want to explain?" Carlson asked, eyebrow raised.

Don't say anything, Fiona thought. *Get a lawyer.* "I didn't hurt her," she squeaked. The cops studied her for a long beat like they didn't believe her. "I *didn't.*"

"You know what? We can talk at the station." Rodriguez jingled his keys. "How about it?"

"B-but I didn't even *see* Scarlet last night after that discussion!" Fiona cried.

"We have evidence that you were *looking* for her. Quite a few people we've spoken to confirmed it. Clearly the fight wasn't over, was it?"

"That's true, but . . ." Fiona's stomach sank to the floor. "Who sent you that video?"

"Our internet security team is looking into it. It's from an encrypted account."

"Isn't it possible *that* person is the person you should be looking for? Maybe they're framing me—especially if you got it even *before* you found Scarlet's body."

Rodriguez offered a wan smile. "Anything's possible, miss."

The cops suggested going to the station again. Fiona accepted, knowing from the many police shows she watched that if she resisted, she'd look even guiltier. She could feel the prying eyes on her as she walked through the courtyard with the officers. She could only guess what the people milling around were thinking. *It was totally Fiona. There's been bad blood between those two for years.*

She cleared her throat as they stepped into the parking structure. "You should question Scarlet's boyfriend, Jack. And her friends—that Cory guy. People who actually spent time with her last night."

"We're speaking to all of them," Carlson said in a neutral tone.

A crowd had gathered outside the gates, too, which made Fiona wonder if Scarlet's story had broken far and wide. Two cops were putting up roadblocks to keep the paparazzi at bay. And there was an ambulance pulling away from the curb, sirens off. *Jesus.* Was Scarlet in there? Fiona felt sick. She recalled the ambulances coming for Lana, too. The sight of her body on that stretcher after they pulled her off the rocks was imprinted in her brain for all eternity.

Rodriguez opened the back door for Fiona, and she climbed inside. "We're also meeting your friend Jasmine there," he added.

"Jasmine?" Fiona frowned. "What does *she* have to do with this?"

"She was mentioned in a video Miss Leigh posted before she died." Rodriguez swung into the front seat. "And we're in touch with another one of your friends, too—Delilah Rollins."

"Delilah?" Fiona's voice crackled with even more uncertainty. "But Delilah's new in town. She doesn't even *know* Scarlet."

Carlson started the engine, meeting her gaze in the rearview mirror. There was a weird, smug look on his face. "According to social media, Miss Jacobs, you girls were all the best of friends."

JASMINE

Scarlet is dead.

The horrible fact stabbed at Jasmine's mind like a blade. With every breath, with every blink, she wished it wasn't true. And yet as the moments passed, nothing changed. Something had happened to Scarlet last night. Someone had killed her. And now the cops wanted to question . . . *Jasmine.*

The same officer who broke the news at Jasmine's door—though she'd already wondered what was going on, having heard the screams in the hallway—now walked her into a waiting room at the central police station in downtown LA. "We're interviewing a few other people first," he explained. "Just wait here."

He pointed to a room. Jasmine turned in the direction of the officer's gaze. To her shock, Fiona and Delilah were sitting on plastic chairs, their faces ashen, their cheeks streaked with tears.

"What's going on?" she cried. "Why are *you* here?"

"I was about to ask you the same thing," Fiona said in a haunted voice. "I guess you're here because of the vlog?"

Jasmine frowned. "What vlog?" The officers hadn't explained why they wanted to talk to her. They'd just knocked on her door, said they had some questions at the station, and they weren't taking no for an answer. Thankfully, Jasmine had negotiated with them to exit through a private passage so she wouldn't have to pass all the rubberneckers in the courtyard. She might have been stunned, but she'd still had the good sense to preserve her reputation.

"Scarlet posted a vlog last night," Fiona explained. "She mentions your name. I watched it on the way over. It's . . . weird."

Jasmine blinked hard. Scarlet mentioned her in a video? How did she not know? And was that good . . . or bad?

She quickly pulled it up on her screen. It was heartbreaking to see Scarlet in her ball gown and gorgeous updo. She sat on the couch in her apartment and talked soberly to the screen. The video was time-stamped at 11:45 p.m.—so after Scarlet and Jasmine had kissed.

The content of the vlog *was* weird. Jasmine's chest tightened. Why was Scarlet seemingly saying goodbye to her fans? Did she somehow know she was going to die? Was she getting threats? Or did she *want* to die?

And then Scarlet said Jasmine's name. Jasmine pressed her hand to her mouth. Just seeing Scarlet's mouth form the words, just knowing she was on Scarlet's mind . . . it broke her heart in a zillion pieces. She pressed pause, feeling overwhelmed. She could sense her friends watching her, but she couldn't meet their gaze.

"Why'd she mention you?" Fiona asked. "Were you guys in a fight?"

Jasmine wanted to explain, but the words felt stuck in her throat. "It's complicated." She glanced at Fiona. "Were *you* in a fight? Because of what she had on you?"

Fiona nodded miserably. "I confronted her last night. And apparently, someone got our argument on video . . . and sent it to the cops." She shook her head vehemently. "But I didn't hurt her. I couldn't even find her for the rest of the night, at the after-party."

Jasmine nodded. She'd looked for Scarlet, too. It hadn't occurred to her that Scarlet was simply in her condo, not talking to anyone. "But why would the cops bring you down here?" She cocked her head. "So you had a fight. Who cares?"

"Yeah, but . . ." Fiona heaved a breath. "The video shows me grabbing her. Hard. I was angry." Her expression was riddled with shame.

Jasmine tapped her phone again. The story about Fiona popped up right away. *What were these two fighting about last night?* screamed a clickbait link. *Developing Story: Fiona Jacobs in feud with Scarlet Leigh. Did she take things too far?*

The video began. The picture was blurry, but Fiona indeed rushed at Scarlet, grabbing her hard. Then Scarlet left. Okay, it didn't look *great* for Fiona . . . but it didn't prove anything. Then Jasmine noticed the comments. Yikes.

Fiona totally did it. I heard she murdered a girl once.

I heard that, too. She's got a killer instinct. She totally killed Scarlet, too.

"Fiona, people are saying some seriously messed-up stuff about you," Jasmine murmured. "Like—that you killed someone? Where do they even *get* this nonsense?"

Silence. When Jasmine looked up, her friend had turned white. Her eyes welled with guilty tears. A strange feeling settled over Jasmine. "Wait. *Wait.*"

"It was an accident," Fiona whispered. "A long time ago."

Delilah's head swiveled from girl to girl. "Wait, *what* was an accident?"

"Are you saying it's true?" Jasmine cried. "Is this what Scarlet has on you?"

Fiona covered her face with her hands. "It's the biggest regret of my life."

Jasmine's neck prickled with cold sweat. The lobby suddenly smelled overwhelmingly like road tar, which turned her stomach. "What happened?" she finally asked.

Fiona glanced guiltily around the room, her eyes huge and scared. "I can't talk about it here. People might be . . . listening. But I didn't mean to do it. I would never . . . but Scarlet figured it out. I don't know how, but she did. Though when I asked her about it, she pretended likc shc had no idea what I was talking about. But she clearly knew. *Clearly.*"

Jasmine rubbed her temples. "Okay. Okay." But this was too much to process at once. She didn't know whether to be supportive or angry or what.

"But I didn't do anything to Scarlet," Fiona added. "I swear."

"Okay." Jasmine wanted to believe Fiona, though she still felt too stunned to really process anything. She looked wearily at Delilah. "So why are *you* here?"

Delilah chewed on her bottom lip. "I guess you didn't see *my* story, then."

"What story?" Once again, she consulted her phone. Delilah's name auto-filled after typing in just a few letters. *Breaking News! New Influencer to the Scene: Jack Dono's Mystery Girl!* Beneath it was a Delilah profile picture . . . and then a blown-up viral image of Jack and the Mystery Girl at the restaurant.

Jasmine almost dropped her phone. "*That's* who you were waiting for last night?"

Fiona looked shocked, too. "Why didn't you say anything?"

"It's not what it looks like," Delilah protested. "And, Jazz, I'm so sorry, I know Scarlet suspected *you* were with him, and I should have said something sooner. . . ."

Jasmine waved her hand. That was the least of her problems. "I just wish you would have told us," Jasmine murmured. "We could have helped you."

"We would have told you not to touch Jack Dono with a ten-foot pole," Fiona added.

"I'm so stupid," Delilah blubbered. "I didn't even realize who he was at first. And then . . . well, I thought I was keeping it under the radar. I was terrified to tell you guys. I thought you'd hate me. People like me don't break up ships."

Fiona's eyes softened. "We wouldn't have hated you. Things happen."

Jasmine nodded. "But how did people find out?"

Delilah winced. "That's the worst part—it's my fault. I told someone at this photo shoot I did yesterday. But I didn't say Jack's last name—I didn't even think she was listening!"

"This was an Instagram photographer?" Jasmine cried.

"Yeah," Delilah admitted guiltily. "One of his assistants."

"Delilah, you never tell those people *anything*. Of course they

turned around and told the whole world what you were up to." She shook her head. "So Scarlet knew?"

"I'm not sure. The story broke when everything went down—I didn't even know about it until this morning. So Scarlet might have already been . . ." Delilah trailed off before she could say the last word. "I guess that's why the cops want to talk to me. Because technically, I'm an enemy."

Jasmine felt stunned. How could they be capable of such secrets? Also, with this new information, they had motive. Not that she thought they'd killed Scarlet, but she didn't want them to be in any trouble.

"But what about you, Jasmine?" Fiona asked. "Scarlet mentioned you in that video. Were *you* guys fighting? Does this have to do with her following you around?"

Jasmine's throat felt tight. "Not really. And I would have never hurt her."

"Yeah, but you didn't like her," Fiona said worriedly. "A lot of people could vouch for that."

"I *used* to not like her," Jasmine corrected. "But that was before . . ." She shut her mouth and turned away.

"Before what?" Delilah goaded.

Jasmine wrapped her arms tightly around her waist. "Before I found out she was the person I kissed at that party," she said, feeling a dam inside her break. She glanced at her friends, registering the shock. Jasmine could sympathize. She'd been just as surprised last night.

"So I never would have killed her," she went on. "I was falling in love with her."

DELILAH

As the midday sun hung languidly overhead, washing out all the shadows, Delilah slipped back into her house. The rooms were still and quiet. In a back room, she heard someone exhale, and then there were footsteps.

"Honey?" Bethany rushed for her. "Thank God! I've been calling you all morning!"

"Hey," Delilah croaked, lowering her chin. Her head spun, her mouth tasted like bile, and she was on the verge of sobbing. She wanted to throw herself on her bed and never get up again.

Bethany took Delilah's hands. "I was so worried, especially after I heard the news. Why didn't you pick up your phone? I was about to call the police!"

"My phone died," Delilah mumbled. "I'm sorry."

"That girl—at your event. Scarlet something? It was at the same condo where you were staying last night. . . ."

"I know." Delilah knew that if she looked her mother in the

eye, she'd blurt out everything. Preemptively, she'd told Bethany that she would be staying at Fiona's last night—because, well, that was where she thought she *would* be. She'd sort of lied and said Fiona's mom would be there, too, though she was pretty sure Mrs. Jacobs had no plans to come over.

But it was all supposed to go fine. There wasn't supposed to be any disaster or scandal or, God forbid, murder. And how she'd wound up in Scarlet Leigh's bed was beyond her. Which was something she could never, *ever* tell a soul.

"I'm just glad you're okay." Bethany pulled her into a hug. "I heard it was an accident? An . . . overdose or something?"

Delilah nodded. *Say nothing. Say nothing.*

Bethany peered at Delilah suspiciously, sniffing her hair. "Were you drinking?"

"Of course not," Delilah said automatically. But she'd told too many lies today already—they literally felt like bricks on her back. She sighed. "Maybe just a tiny taste. I'm so sorry—it was a mixed drink, and I didn't enjoy it at all."

Bethany crossed her arms and gave Delilah a long, disapproving look. "I appreciate you being honest. But what is *wrong* with you?"

"I'm sorry. . . ."

"And why are you so late getting home?" Bethany continued. "Even if your phone was dead, you should have called."

"I . . ." Delilah shut her eyes. Here came the awful part. But it wasn't something she could hide—the cops said they'd check in with her mom shortly. "I had to answer some questions with the police," she admitted.

"The *police*?"

"It's no big deal. Everyone who was at the party had to." Or everyone *would,* she assumed. "This is embarrassing, but there was some internet confusion about me and . . . that Scarlet girl's boyfriend."

Bethany blinked. "What do you mean, *internet confusion*?"

"He and I kind of . . . liked each other." Delilah felt her cheeks go red. "We were talking online. It's a long story. But anyway, he and Scarlet are this famous Instagram couple, and some gossip about him and me broke, so the cops wanted my take on Scarlet's death. But, I mean, I have no take. We're not officially a couple . . . and I have no idea what happened to Scarlet."

Lies. All lies.

Some cops had noticed Delilah just outside the Dove after Scarlet's mom screamed bloody murder and a team ran in to ID Scarlet's body. Maybe Delilah had guilt written all over her face, because an officer stepped toward her, saying, "Is everything all right, miss?"

Delilah had frozen. She wanted to run, but she knew how guilty that would make her look. And so she'd blurted out, "I knew that girl who died. I was fooling around with her boyfriend."

It seemed counterintuitive, serving up her motive when they hadn't asked, but she'd rather the cops get their interview with her out of the way instead of her stewing around at home for days, waiting for them to show up. And the interview wasn't even bad. The cops had very little information to go on about Scarlet's death, so all Delilah did was share what happened between her and Jack, that she wasn't sure if Scarlet knew, and that she had no idea who could have hurt Scarlet. After she was done, the cop who was interviewing her leaned back and said, confidentially, that cases like these often ended up being suicides. "An overdose, probably," he said sadly. "But we can't rule anything out quite yet. Not until we have all the facts."

Delilah nodded and said she wanted to help. But as she was leaving, that same garbled memory suddenly assaulted her: Plopping onto Scarlet's bed. And then Scarlet emerging from a doorway, glowering at a very drunk Delilah: *What are* you *doing here?* But Scarlet didn't seem suicidal. Actually, she seemed wary . . . maybe even afraid. Of Delilah, though . . . or someone else?

She'd frozen in the police station hallway, wondering if she should go back and tell the cops this. Except . . . that would put her in Scarlet's bedroom. She'd instantly become a suspect. But saying nothing made her feel even worse—it was probably a huge crime to lie to a police officer, right?

Delilah wished she knew a little more about forensics, too. On the drive home—Jasmine had dropped her off—she'd surreptitiously studied her phone, googling what sort of DNA cops could dig up in a crime scene. It seemed like any tiny speck you left behind could be evidence: a hair follicle, a fingernail, some sort of identifying cell. It made her sick with panic. How careful were they going to be when they combed Scarlet's bed for clues? Should Delilah be quaking with fear, certain the cops were going to ring the bell any moment to arrest her? And where the hell were her shoes?

The worst part? She didn't even have anyone to talk to about this. She didn't dare tell Jasmine and Fiona she'd woken up in Scarlet's room—they'd freak. Actually, *nobody* would understand—not her sister, not Busy, and definitely not her mom. Everyone would panic.

"Let me see this gossip about this boy," Bethany demanded now, holding out her palm.

Delilah handed over the phone, humiliated. She'd read the Jacklet article too many times to be deemed sane, but she couldn't stop staring at the words.

Her mother's brow furrowed. All kinds of shocked and fearful expressions crossed her face. "People are saying awful things about you."

Delilah ducked her head. "They're just trolls."

"We should go to the police." Bethany clucked her tongue. "People can't send you death threats because of some *guy*."

"He's really famous," Ava piped up.

Delilah looked over. Ava, dressed in white overalls and Vans, had slipped into the room without her knowing. She glanced at Delilah with a mix of fear and pity. "A lot of my friends have crushes on him," she added.

"*So?*" Bethany looked enraged. "There are tons of other non-famous boys around here that you could be interested in instead! Since when have you become so celebrity-obsessed? Is it since we moved here? Has this place already warped your brain?"

"Mom, it's not like that," Delilah protested. "It's not a big deal. It's awful that the girl is dead, but . . . I don't know. It was a freak accident." *Hopefully. Except if it was, how did you get in her bed, next to her?*

Bethany rubbed her temples furiously. "Okay. Okay." Then

she pointed up the stairs. "Go take a shower, Delilah. You smell like someone puked on you."

Delilah slunk into the bathroom. The moment she slammed the door, the tears started to flow. How could she keep up these lies? How could she live with this secret? And how bad a secret was it? Was she guilty of something?

There was a soft knock on the door. "Dee?" Ava called.

Delilah opened the door a crack. Ava's hands were wedged in her pockets. "You okay?"

Delilah turned back to the sink. "No."

"I'm really sorry." Ava shifted uncomfortably. "About Jack, too. I, um, saw the video. About Scarlet . . . being pregnant . . . and everything else."

Delilah shrugged. Jack felt like small potatoes compared to what else had happened, though she did wonder how he was dealing with Scarlet's death.

Ava held out her phone. "I've been reading a lot of the comments."

Delilah eyed her warningly. "Don't."

"The world is losing its mind about Scarlet."

"Seriously, Ava. Get offline."

Ava shrugged. "People are freaking out about the Jack stuff. But there are a bunch of fans who support you—*and* Jack. There are also fans who aren't even sure the news about you and Jack is true. Like, they think you made it all up."

Gee, thanks, fans, Delilah thought bitterly.

"It was a weird night, wasn't it?" Ava murmured. "I mean, first everyone's hysterical posts when they got to Gratitude

Prom. Then that live video of Scarlet's where this guy York tries to hit on her, but she realizes it's some kind of setup—and Jack tries to break up with her, but she tells Jack she's pregnant. . . ."

"Wait." Delilah collapsed against the wall. *"York?"*

"Yeah." Ava searched her face. "You didn't watch it?"

Delilah shook her head. In the confusion of last night, she'd only heard about Scarlet's pregnancy live. So York had carried through with Jack's plan . . . but Scarlet had figured it out. Was that why Jack had never gotten in touch with her?

"Can I ask you something?" Ava said, shifting from foot to foot. "Are you even a little happy about this?"

"Happy?" Delilah spluttered. "About someone being dead? Are you serious?"

Ava bit her lip, looking wrong-footed. "It's awful she's dead, obviously. But . . . Scarlet was *scary*. And her fans are even scarier. Every time I saw a creepy comment from one of them about how they were going to kill Jack's Mystery Girl . . . I mean, didn't that freak you out?"

"You can't take those comments seriously. It's just . . . the internet. And also? Those comments are still there, Scarlet or no."

"I know." Ava looked like she might burst into tears. "It sucks."

Delilah glanced at her harried expression in the bathroom mirror. Maybe her family was right to be worried. Fans were crazed. They seemed to care more about the influencers and brands and ships than they did things in their real lives. She remembered the hordes of screaming people on the bleachers outside Gratitude Prom. Most of them were in T-shirts bearing the names and images of their favorite Instagram or YouTube star. Some of them had signs, flowers, even gifts for the influencers. And their eyes—so many of them were full of longing and hope. *Notice me,* their expressions said. *It'll make my whole world.*

"Do you think Scarlet knew?" Ava asked quietly. "About you and Jack? And she, like, hurt herself?"

Delilah swallowed hard. "I'm not sure." Scarlet had kissed Jasmine last night, after all. Why would she care if Delilah was with Jack?

"So she didn't confront you about it, or anything?"

Delilah had no memory, but that tiny moment of Scarlet coming out of the bathroom and glaring at her pulsed in her mind. Why had she remained in Scarlet's room? *Had* they said more to each other? Why had she still been in Scarlet's bed in the morning?

Then a line from Scarlet's vlog popped into her mind: *We see what we want you to see. Nothing more.* It was a bizarre coincidence that she'd woken up next to Scarlet's body just hours after Scarlet said she was pregnant *and* the story about Delilah as the Mystery Girl broke. Almost too convenient, actually—like Delilah was an easy scapegoat, an obvious target. Was it possible someone *put* Delilah in that bed, next to Scarlet—to frame her? Except Delilah had woken up too early and escaped—before anyone found Scarlet's body and put her at the scene?

Her heart started to pound. Maybe someone had seen the opportunity for the perfect murder. Perhaps it was the same person who sent the cops that video of Fiona, too—to throw them off their scent. Someone was framing them. Someone wanted them to go down. And Delilah needed to figure out who it was.

Before someone blamed *her.*

FIONA

Back when she was a dorky middle-schooler, Fiona used to be an expert on celebrity funerals. She studied them like she was studying for an algebra test. People who wanted to attend Michael Jackson's funeral, for instance, which was held at the LA Staples Center, had to enter a lottery, and tickets sold for upwards of ten thousand dollars on eBay. Princess Diana's memorial was a four-mile march through London, her casket passing over a million mourners and touching hundreds of million more viewers on TV. Long ago, the old film star Rudolph Valentino's death caused a few crazed, distraught fans to commit suicide—and over a hundred thousand people went to see his open casket.

Scarlet Leigh's memorial wasn't much different.

Her funeral was being held at Milk Studios, a giant space usually reserved for massive parties and benefits. Outside, on the clear morning four days after Scarlet's strange death, dozens of photographers snapped pictures of the invited guests heading inside. Grief-stricken fans clamored behind police sawhorses—it was the same sort of mob scene as the Oscars, except there was no red carpet.

Fiona pulled a black straw sun hat low on her face, but it didn't stop people from spotting her. "Fiona!" fans and reporters called. "Were you and Scarlet in a massive fight before she died?" "Was it about *Like Me*?" "Did you poison her?" And even: "Did you know she was pregnant? Did you honestly willingly poison a *baby*?"

"Jesus," Fiona whispered to Jasmine and Delilah as they hurried inside. Like everyone else here, they were in black dresses, high heels, dark sunglasses, and dark hats. As they walked into the room, every black dress was more exquisite than the last—Fiona was almost certain she spotted a few couture frocks among the crowd. Leave it to Scarlet to throw a funeral that was posher than Gratitude Prom.

The lobby was packed. Delilah looked around. "How many people were *invited* to this thing?"

Fiona shrugged. "All of LA, it seems."

She'd been surprised when she'd gotten an invitation—she'd almost thought the Paperless Post she'd received a few days ago, sharing the details, was a hoax. Because why would Scarlet want *her* at the funeral? The internet had exploded with Fiona/Scarlet snark, after all. *Did that shove lead to a second argument where Fiona killed her? Did that argument contribute to Scarlet's suicide? Is Fiona secretly happy because Scarlet took away her part in* Like Me? It was relentless. Fiona almost wanted to tell her trolls that the police weren't considering her a suspect anymore. There was no evidence she had ever been in Scarlet's condo. There was no evidence she had even *seen* Scarlet at the after-party.

But the fans didn't care about facts. They loved conspiracy theories, behind-the-scenes tales, clear-cut sides of wrong and right. In this case, Fiona was the bad guy, and Scarlet the victim.

Anyway. Fiona hadn't intended to come—her mother had said that maybe she should stay away, considering "the mix-up" about her being involved with Scarlet's death. But then Delilah had called. "If we don't go, everyone will assume we have something to hide," she'd said. "This is all about optics. So we go, and we all stand together." Delilah had shared the theory that because of their issues with Scarlet, Scarlet's *real* killer might have been trying to nudge the police to consider them suspects. "If we go, maybe we can figure out who that killer is," Delilah added.

So now here they were. The most-talked-about girls on the planet. Everyone was speculating about Delilah and Jack, too, and memes, articles, and posts had cropped up about why Jasmine's name was mentioned in Scarlet's last vlog, ranging from the girls were in a cult together to the girls had a suicide pact to—accurately—they were in love. But so far, Jasmine had stayed quiet on how she felt about Scarlet in her final moments alive. Fiona didn't blame her.

"And how did they pull this together so fast?" Delilah murmured.

"I guess everyone in LA was dying to decorate," Fiona said sarcastically.

But it was true: no detail had been spared. So many flowers had been trucked into the space where the memorial was to be held that the air teemed with humidity, like the mourners were in a giant greenhouse. There were beautiful, life-size paintings of Scarlet on every wall. It was standing room only. There was no casket, however, because Scarlet's body was still being investigated. The coroner was still trying to figure out the exact drug that killed her . . . *and* whether it was suicide or murder.

The girls found a spot at the back of the large room. Fiona leaned against the wall, gazing around at the spectacle. She nudged Jasmine. "Okay, so who among the people looks like they secretly had it in for Scarlet . . . and used *us* as scapegoats?"

Jasmine stared blankly back, her eyes welling with tears. "Never mind," Fiona said quickly. Jasmine had barely said a word since they got there. Fiona still couldn't believe that Jasmine had fallen for *Scarlet,* of all people. It was such a weird notion, but Jasmine claimed she'd seen a different side of her. Truth was stranger than fiction.

"I'm not sure," Delilah said out of the corner of her mouth. "What should we look for, exactly?"

Fiona scanned the crowd. At the front of the room was a pew saved for Scarlet's V-VIPs—her BFF Cory, that dog nanny who appeared in a lot of her videos, and a bunch of bitchy friends who hung on her every move. Scarlet's manager sobbed uncontrollably, clinging to the arm of Jack Dono, who stood straight and stone-faced next to a huge vase of flowers. Fiona wondered if Delilah had noticed Jack, too. She didn't dare point him out.

But those who weren't VIPs were chatting like this was just another party. Fiona was surprised to see ChloeDIY—the influencer Scarlet had all but shut down last year after she badmouthed Scarlet online—slumped in a back row. Could *she* be behind this? But Fiona didn't remember her at Gratitude or the after-party. . . . Basically, Chloe *hated* social media now. And she didn't seem like a particularly murderous person.

There was also a small section for some of Scarlet's über-fans—Fiona recognized a few of them from their pages. For a reason she couldn't understand, they were all *dressed* like Scarlet today. All had either dyed their hair blond or were wearing blond wigs. They wore a version of the signature mega-short, leopard-print dress Scarlet had worn to the Teen Choice Awards a few months ago and Scarlet's must-have ultra-red lipstick—the color she'd created for her makeup line at Sephora, *Scarlet A Scarlet.* Did Scarlet have some sort of end-of-life directive that she wanted people to dress like her at her memorial service? It was three parts strange, one part twistedly fabulous . . . but maybe one of those fans was a little *too* twisted and had done something terrible? Had any of *them* been at the after-party? Fiona wasn't sure.

Tons of people tapped on their phones, too. They were probably scrolling through the Scarlet memorials that were clogging Instagram feeds. New accounts had even cropped up that dealt specifically with Scarlet's murder. People who lived in Canada or India or a little town in Arkansas spoke of Scarlet as though they'd been real-life friends.

Suddenly, heads swiveled, and what felt like millions of pairs of eyes clapped on Fiona, Jasmine, and Delilah. The whispers began. Sky Matty, an up-and-coming influencer who was obsessed with sneakers, actually gasped. Everyone glowered at Delilah, the evil Mystery Girl, in particular.

Fiona pulled down the brim of her hat to hide her face, not that it really helped. "What do we do now?" she murmured to Delilah.

"Nothing," Delilah answered, though she was cowering, too. "We have a right to be here. We were invited. We have nothing to hide."

Speak for yourself, Fiona thought, just as Delilah seemed to register what she'd just said. She placed a hand over Fiona's. "*You* know what I mean. We didn't do anything to Scarlet."

Fiona nodded. She hated that her friends had found out what she'd done to Lana, but they hadn't judged her. She'd gotten to explain what happened. A weight had lifted from her . . . though perhaps that was for reasons beyond her friends' finally knowing the truth.

Scarlet was dead, after all. Fiona's threat was gone. Those online comments about Fiona being a murderer were just mean rumors—and they weren't very specific. Fiona scoured Scarlet's online tracks from the night of her death, but she couldn't find any evidence that Scarlet had told Fiona's secret. Sure, she might have DMed someone privately . . . but it wasn't like the cops could arrest Fiona because of a Snapchat message.

So she should be grateful, right? It was the same sort of reprieve she'd gotten with Lana. But she still felt uneasy. It was difficult to explain why. . . . It just felt like something was nagging at the back of her brain, deeply wrong. If only she could put her finger on what it was.

A man leading the service approached the altar, breaking Fiona from her thoughts. The room quieted. People lowered their phones. In a laborious, droning tone, the funeral director said a few words. Then he ceded the floor to Scarlet's mother, who rose from the front row.

Mrs. Leigh walked slowly to the podium, a squashed-up ball

of Kleenex in her fist. Fiona's mouth dropped when the woman faced the crowd. Mrs. Leigh looked like she'd lost fifteen pounds. The skin on her face sagged. There were dark circles under her eyes. Her hands trembled as she clutched the sides of the podium, but when she spoke, her voice was clear and loud. "My daughter was a beacon of light. She inspired so many—including me. She had so much promise. Such a bright future. To have that snuffed out—and for what? Jealousy? A feud? Don't you people realize there's more to life than social media?"

To Fiona's horror, Mrs. Leigh peered through the audience . . . and located Fiona, Jasmine, and Delilah at the back. Her mouth shrank to the size of a button. Everyone swiveled around and stared once again, and new whispers rippled through the crowd. The Voice snickered in Fiona's head. *You deserve this!*

"Head held high, head held high," Delilah chanted in a whisper, though she sounded on the verge of tears. And so, even though Fiona badly wanted to bolt, she remained where she was, listening as everyone said their final goodbyes to Scarlet Leigh.

Maybe even Scarlet's murderer, somewhere in the crowd.

If Fiona thought the funeral was insane, the reception was even worse: it was on a *yacht*, which was sailing toward Catalina Island. Mrs. Leigh must have spent hundreds of thousands of dollars, and though it was closed to the public and the press, a few people managed to sneak on. Lesser-known influencers were using the party as a means to gain notoriety and followers. A quick glance at Instagram told Fiona that a hashtag was trending:

#RIPScarletLeigh. All the posts tied to the hashtag were selfies of people at the reception. Their expressions were slightly less joyful than usual . . . but only slightly.

Fiona's friends weren't boarding the boat—Jasmine was too distraught to attend, and Delilah was only allowed out for the funeral. Fiona weaved through the crowd alone, head down, ignoring the stares and whispers. She was only there because Chase had mentioned in a very terse text that though he couldn't make the funeral, he was coming to this. They'd been talking sporadically since Gratitude. But sporadic, for them, *wasn't normal.*

She spotted Chase's tall frame in a corner of the ballroom. His back was turned, and he was talking to an older guy she didn't recognize. They were murmuring about something—the man's expression was grave.

Fiona walked over and tapped Chase's shoulder. "Hey."

Chase whirled at the sound of her voice, and a bloom of red appeared on his neck and cheeks. "Uh, hey. Fiona." He said her name like it was synonymous with *ebola virus.* Nerves swirled in Fiona's gut. Could he really *still* be mad at her?

She studied him. They had to put that stupid argument aside. It had gone on too long. She touched his arm. "Wanna go somewhere private? I hear the upper deck's nice."

Chase pulled away, his expression cold. "I'm actually heading out."

"Wait, what?" She frowned. "But didn't you just get here?"

Abruptly, Chase walked to a quieter corner, and Fiona, feeling even more jittered, followed. He stopped and looked at her, swallowing hard.

“What is it, babe?” Fiona whimpered. She felt on the verge of tears. “Gratitude—let’s talk about it. I’m sorry.”

“What were you arguing with Scarlet about that night?” Chase blurted out.

“I . . .” Fiona’s mouth was suddenly too dry. “Just . . . stupid stuff.” He’d seen the video of their fight, then. Of course he had. Then something else hit her: Did Chase think she’d *done* something to Scarlet?

“I didn’t hurt her, Chase,” she whispered. “You believe me, right?”

Relief seemed to flood his face. “Yeah, I do. . . . It just looks so bad, Fiona. You got so mad at her. You . . . *grabbed* her.”

Fiona shut her eyes. It did look bad . . . and there was no way she could explain why she’d been so angry. She wondered if reporters had been calling Chase, wanting to know if he had any insight on his girlfriend’s bizarre behavior—or even if he knew what Scarlet had on her. What an embarrassment. What if he wanted to break up with her because of it?

“Chase?” she cried, her voice stretching thin. “Can we get past this?”

“I have to go.” He started to walk away. “I’ll call you later, okay?”

“Chase?” she said weakly, but he didn’t turn. Fiona watched him weave through the crowd, her index finger systematically picking off the skin on her thumb. Had that really just happened?

She straightened her shoulders, watching Chase as he walked to the exit. Where was he going, anyway? Perhaps she should follow him. She started to push through the crowd. There was no way she was staying on this ludicrous yacht now that Chase was gone.

But the room was so packed, it was difficult to move. In a corner, she spied Mrs. Leigh on a leather couch with Scarlet's agent. Both looked brain-dead. *No wonder,* Fiona thought. Mrs. Leigh had way too many things to wrap her mind around—not only that Scarlet was dead, but also that she'd been pregnant. How could a mother handle all that?

Not far away, Scarlet's friend Cory was whispering to that stylist who was always showing up in Scarlet's videos . . . though when he noticed Fiona staring, he frowned and gave her a sharp *What are* you *looking at?* glare. And there was Jack Dono, talking to a couple of comedy YouTubers near the bar. Fiona considered approaching him about Delilah. She didn't know Jack very well, and she had no idea whether he was leading Delilah on, but Delilah's career might be ruined now, and that was partly Jack's fault. It was unfair that Delilah was getting all the hate while the Jacklet fans bombarded Jack with sympathy messages. The last thing people remembered about Jacklet was the vlog where Scarlet admitted she was pregnant, and they'd chosen to see him as a grieving father-to-be, not a cheater.

Thankfully, the yacht hadn't pulled away from the dock yet, but by the time Fiona reached the gangplank, she didn't see Chase anywhere. The only people she noticed were the paparazzi, ready to snap pictures. "Fiona!" they cried. "Why are you leaving? What happened?"

Ducking her head, Fiona hurried off the ship and headed down the dock toward the pier. She looked right and left, but still no Chase. Maybe inland? Maybe in a parking lot? She needed to move.

One, two, three, four, her mind automatically counted, noting each step. Her crossbody bag slapped rhythmically against the small of her back. Or she *thought* it was her crossbody bag . . . but half a block up the street, she realized it was footsteps behind her. Her body stiffened. There was someone following her, just visible out of the corner of her eye.

Her heart picked up pace. The side street she was on was desolate and bathed in eerie, late-afternoon shadows; if something happened to her here, no one would know. She started to run . . . but so did the person behind her. She glanced over her shoulder, letting out a wail. The shadows played tricks with her eyes—it was difficult to see who was after her, but all of a sudden, she knew they were dangerous.

She turned a corner, and her ankle hit a lip in the sidewalk and buckled. "Ugh!" she cried, half falling. She recovered quickly and kept going.

"Fiona! Stop!"

A hand clamped on her shoulder. Fiona spun around and took in a young woman standing behind her, and her brain went still. It was . . . *Lana.* Lana's face, her pretty Cupid's-bow lips, her bright blue eyes looking right at her.

The world went white. Fiona let out a bloodcurdling scream.

Lana lurched back at Fiona's shock. "I'm so sorry! I didn't mean to scare you. . . ."

Fiona had fallen to her knees. She gasped for breath. The woman—*Lana*—crouched down next to her. She had long, sinewy, devilish hands. "Are you all right?" she cried, touching Fiona's shoulder. "I am *so* sorry!"

Fiona recoiled, confused. Why was Lana being so nice? And also . . . *how* was Lana alive? Fiona remembered Lana's funeral in startling detail. There was a casket. There was a *body.*

"I—I need to go," she cried in a tremulous voice, scrambling from Lana's grasp.

Lana looked chagrined. "Please. Don't. Oh God, this isn't how I wanted to approach you. I saw you leave the funeral, and I wanted to catch you . . . but now I've screwed everything up." She inhaled deeply. "Please let me start over. You're Fiona Jacobs, right?"

Fiona gaped. Lana *knew* this. Was she asking just to mess with her?

"And you're looking for an assistant?" Lana went on.

The mica in the sidewalk sparkled too brightly. Fiona's heart banged so hard she felt her pulse in her gums. "Yeah," she heard herself say. "Wh-why?"

"Well, *I* want to be your assistant," Lana—*was* it Lana?—blurted out. "Please?"

"Wait, what?" Fiona asked.

"I'm a huge admirer. And I want to break into this business, but my mom says I have three months to find a job—otherwise I have to go home to Orange County. And I heard you need a new assistant. I'm sure you've been inundated with applicants, but I swear I'll be amazing. And also, we know someone in common. You knew my sister."

"Your sister," Fiona repeated. And suddenly, she knew what this girl was going to say before she said it. It chilled her to her core.

"You knew Lana Hedges, right?" The young woman smiled. "I'm her younger sister, Camille."

DELILAH

Delilah peered back and forth down the sketchy street in downtown LA. It was quiet here—*too* quiet. Across the street were shops full of ugly clothes and accessories. A bodega on the corner looked like it sold absolutely nothing healthy. Even the air here smelled different—smoggier, grittier, like she was in an old noir film.

Her nerves jumped. Every tick of the clock, every passing hour, she felt like time was running out. *Someone* was going to figure out she'd been in Scarlet's bed when Scarlet had died. She needed to figure out what had really happened before someone made the connection . . . and told the cops. The pressure was killing her. She'd only been in LA for a month, and *this* was the mess she was in? Last night, she'd scrolled through ancient posts on her Instagram from her life in Minnesota, yearning for the simplicity. Back then, her biggest worry was that she'd spent too much time on her phone and not enough on her history report.

She was barely sixteen. She wasn't ready to handle such scary stuff. She almost wished she could blink and return to that life, in all its innocence.

More memories snapped back to her from the night Scarlet died. She kept hearing a gentle voice telling her *She won't mind if you lie here.* She felt someone's hand on her arm, guiding her to Scarlet's bed. She couldn't remember a face, only something glinting near the person's head—gold jewelry, maybe. She sank into the soft pillow, the room spinning. But then she rolled over and noticed Scarlet emerging from a doorway—the bathroom, maybe. Scarlet made a face at Delilah and said, *What are* you *doing here?* And then . . . nothing.

But why hadn't the person who put Delilah in Scarlet's bed told on Delilah by now? *They'd* seen Scarlet last . . . alive . . . and they could place Delilah at the scene of her death. Delilah's only conclusion: the person who helped Delilah into Scarlet's bed was the murderer. He or she wouldn't want to put themselves anywhere near Scarlet's bedroom, and so they hadn't reported their little Delilah tidbit to the police. But it still felt like a clock was ticking. That person—they *knew.* Perhaps they had some sort of ammo to use against Delilah if she got too close to the truth. She needed to figure out who they were before that happened.

But who'd wanted to kill Scarlet that night? Delilah tried to think of all the bombshells Scarlet had dropped. A huge one: her pregnancy. That must have rocked a lot of worlds. Including . . . *Jack's.*

Was it Jack who had helped Delilah into Scarlet's bed? Delilah didn't want to believe it . . . but anything was possible. And that was why she was at his office, waiting for him.

Finally, after almost forty-five minutes of waiting, the side door to a modern, low-slung office building opened, and Jack stepped out, pulling his hat low on his forehead. Delilah had had to do some pretty serious internet stalking to figure out where his studio was located—she guessed he kept it über-private so fans wouldn't mob him—but she'd come today on a hunch that he was here, trying to escape the Scarlet mess. So far, he'd released no comments about Scarlet—actually, he'd released no content at *all.* Delilah wondered what the police had asked him and what he knew. If only there was actual news about Scarlet's death . . . but almost no details had come out besides the fact that cops suspected she died by some sort of drug or medication. They were still waiting on official autopsy results.

She stepped toward Jack, her heart pounding. Was she really going to do this? They hadn't spoken since before Gratitude. Since then, she'd watched the vlog of Jack and Scarlet arguing over and over again, trying to make sense of it, reading way too much into Jack's halfhearted attempts to break up with her—and trying to gauge Jack's reaction once Scarlet dropped the bomb that she was pregnant. Was he happy? Scared? *Angry*? But the camera didn't register Jack's expression. According to Jasmine, Scarlet hadn't even meant for the video to be rolling.

"Hey," she called. "Jack."

Jack whirled around, halfway down the access ramp. When he saw it was her, he looked startled . . . and then relieved . . . and then unnerved. "Delilah," he said. "What are you doing here?"

"I—I wanted to talk to you."

Jack's hands fidgeted at his waist. "I've been meaning to get in touch with you. But things have been . . . hectic."

"It's okay," Delilah answered robotically. She hated Jack's trite excuse . . . but she also understood. Sort of.

"This is all nuts." He squeezed his eyes shut. "That story—about you and me? I didn't tell Scarlet. I have no idea how someone found out."

"Oh," Delilah said quietly. "That's my fault, actually. I was excited about seeing you at Gratitude . . . and I accidentally told someone I shouldn't have."

"Really?" He gave Delilah a strange look that she couldn't decipher. "Okay . . ."

"I feel like an idiot. I wasn't trying to stir up trouble."

"I know." Jack looked surprised. "You'd never do that."

Now she felt like a squished bug on the sidewalk. *I wouldn't?* The memory of waking up next to Scarlet flashed like a strobe light. *Scarlet's unmoving hand. Scarlet's eerily pale skin.* And then Delilah running out . . . saying *nothing.*

Should she tell him? What if he turned her in?

"Is there anything I can do to make things better for you?" Jack asked. "Do you want me to put out a video or something? Say you're a nice person? Tell the Jacklet fans to leave you alone?"

The idea was tempting, but Delilah shrugged. "I don't want your very first video about this to be about me. That doesn't seem appropriate."

"Yeah, but I don't want people hating you for something that isn't all your fault." Jack crossed his arms. "I'm a guilty party, too. And I told Scarlet I wanted to break up. I don't know why the shippers aren't hearing that part."

Probably because she dropped a bomb that she was pregnant right after that, Delilah thought. Why would the shippers care about anything else in that video when they found out Jack and Scarlet were going to be parents?

"And . . . about Gratitude . . . ," Jack went on. "I wanted to find you, but . . ."

Delilah held up her hand. "It doesn't matter." She didn't want to rehash that awful night.

"No, it *does* matter. You know I tried to do the York thing, right?"

"Yeah, but Scarlet was going to have your baby. You couldn't have broken up with her after she told you that."

"That's the thing. It couldn't have been my baby. There's no freaking way. And Scarlet—she *knew* that."

Delilah straightened her spine. "Wait, what?"

"Scarlet and I hadn't . . . *done things* . . . in a long, long time." A blotch of red crept up Jack's neck. "So when she said that—it was for the camera. For her *audience*. There's no way it was true. Or, well, there's no way it was *mine*."

A car alarm sounded, making Delilah jump. Was that possible? If it *was* true—and part of her really *did* want it to be true, for Jack's sake—then what was Scarlet hoping to achieve by telling him? There was only one answer. "She's having someone else's baby . . . but she wants people to believe it's yours?" she said slowly.

"I guess. Though I'm baffled why she'd admit any of that on a live stream."

"She said her phone was cloned," Delilah said. "She didn't *know* it was a live stream."

"Yeah, but if she was really worried, wouldn't she say *less* at all times instead of *more*?" Jack blinked. "You know what I mean?"

"So . . . you think maybe she *wanted* her fans to know?" Then she had a thought. "Now that you mention it, some of her vlogs hint she might be pregnant. She faints in one. Gets nauseated in another."

"I watched those, too." Jack sighed. "Maybe some fans were already on to her. And maybe she was scared of what was going to happen next and wanted to control the story."

"So she comes to you. Makes it a Jacklet baby, even though it isn't true. Who *is* the father, do you think?"

"I have no idea." Jack lifted his palms to the air. "Scarlet was a little . . . wild. Her and Cory? They were out all the time. I wouldn't be surprised if she's hooked up with other people."

Delilah nodded. She *knew* Scarlet hooked up with other people—Jasmine being one of them. But that wasn't her gossip to spread.

Jack's skin was gray. The harsh sunlight accentuated the dark circles under his eyes. He looked like he hadn't slept since Gratitude. "Are you okay?" Delilah asked.

"Not really." He heaved a sigh. "I have no idea what to think. And even though Scarlet and I weren't together, she was still a big part of my life. And now she's just . . . *gone*? It's so weird."

Delilah chose her words carefully. "Did you . . . *see* her, after your conversation at Gratitude?"

Jack shook his head. "I ran after her after she dropped the pregnancy bomb, but she vanished. And then my phone started blowing up—my team was reacting to Scarlet's video, luckily before most people saw it. My manager wanted to hold an emergency meeting. A driver came to get me. I was put in hiding for the rest of the night so we could figure out how to handle it.

I wasn't even allowed to have my phone. Wasn't allowed any way to contact the outside world—including to tell you I wasn't coming." He peeked at her guiltily. "I feel so bad about that, by the way."

Delilah hid a sad, relieved smile. It was nice to hear an apology. She was also glad to know that Jack had an alibi—he wasn't even at the after-party. Which meant he didn't drag Delilah into that bed with Scarlet. Which meant she didn't have to be afraid of him.

Jack studied the '50s-style sign for the women's lingerie shop across the street. "My dad was so pissed. And Scarlet's mom—man, she was breathing fire."

"Why didn't they have an emergency meeting with Scarlet, too?"

"They tried to track her down. Her mom called Scarlet's friends, even went down to Gratitude—but I guess Scarlet dodged her."

"Scarlet's mom was at Gratitude?" Delilah asked, surprised. She didn't remember seeing Mrs. Leigh there.

"And the after-party." Jack rubbed the top of his head, making his hair stand in spikes. "She was looking all over for her. We were worried Scarlet had gone off the rails." He glanced at her hopelessly. "She could have done this to herself, you know. If she was pregnant . . . and afraid . . ."

Delilah nodded. It *could* be true. Maybe Scarlet was more damaged than she let on.

They were quiet for a while. On the street, cars jammed up behind the light. "If Scarlet didn't kill herself, who do you think did it?" Delilah asked.

Jack's eyes darkened. He opened his mouth a few times without speaking, but then finally said, "If I were to put my money on someone? Cory."

"Her best friend?" Delilah was shocked.

"More like her frenemy. That guy was jealous of everything she did. Always has been."

"*Really?*" Delilah thought of Cory in Scarlet's videos, always offering his support, always cheerfully by her side. "Are you sure?"

"Check this out." Jack reached into his pocket for his phone and showed her a screenshot dated a few months before. "This is a picture of Scarlet and Cory's texts. I snapped it once, when she left her phone out. It just seemed . . . creepy. I wanted to talk to her about him—be like, hey, this guy is kind of toxic for you, maybe you should drop him. But I never had the chance. We were always being so carefully *posed* together, at the end."

Delilah leaned in for a closer look. *You're mine, bitch,* Cory wrote in one. And *Don't you ever act that way again.* And *I've had just about enough of you, and you know what* that *means.*

A chill rippled through her. "But why would Cory kill her?"

"Maybe he was furious that she was pregnant."

"Because . . . why, exactly?"

Jack slipped his phone back into his pocket. "Scarlet was a huge part of Cory's life. If she shifted gears and became a mom . . . that's a big change. He had this hold on her. He might not have wanted to lose that control."

Delilah rolled the possibility in her mind. It didn't entirely make sense . . . but then, nothing did. And she remembered Cory at the after-party—in fact, she'd fixated on Cory's glinting, almost pirate-like hoop earring as he'd passed. Suddenly, it glowed in her memory like a beacon. That same memory flared once more: Delilah stumbling, dead-drunk, down a corridor, and someone's hand touching her shoulder. "You should lie down," someone said as they opened the door to Scarlet's condo. "Come in here." And there was that flash of gold again. Was it Cory? His earring?

Jack coughed. When she looked up, he'd moved closer to her. "I know this is bad timing, but I still can't stop thinking about you. Do you think, after all this dies down, we could maybe . . . ?"

Delilah's chin wobbled. Carefully, she entwined her fingers with his . . . and squeezed. But then a prickly sense of paranoia smacked her. Was someone watching?

She pulled away from Jack and looked around. Was that a shadow ducking behind a car? A pair of eyes clapped on her from across the street in this beaten-down part of town?

She turned back to Jack, shaky and sweaty. "I have to go."

"Wait," he said. "Please."

"I'm sorry." She weaved around a few parked cars to a side street. The anxious feeling still dogged her. Her fingers clamped around her phone. To her surprise, at that moment, it started buzzing in her palm.

An Instagram DM had come in. It was from an account that was a bunch of letters and underscores. A hater, probably?

Delilah read the message, then read it again, confused. Her heart started to pound. She clicked on the account, but it seemed to be a bot—no posts, no followers, and it was only following one account: hers.

But the message wasn't bot-like in the slightest.

Stop digging, Lila D. For your own good.

FIONA

Fiona sat on her bed at her parents' house—with all the paparazzi and reporters and forensics dogs, the Dove was just too insane to go back there—reading a list of questions from a gossip website. They wanted an exclusive interview with Fiona to get her take on Scarlet's death. The questions were tacky and crass, things like *Did you ever see this coming from Scarlet?* And *Describe your best and worst moments with Scarlet* and *Did Scarlet have some deep, dark secrets we don't know about? Besides the preggo thing, of course!* Did they honestly think Fiona was going to respond?

Then again, the world was gripped with Scarlet Fever. It had even become a hashtag. Scarlet's picture was on the cover of every tabloid. Fiona's feeds were filled with whodunit theories and fake news about what the police had discovered, outlandish things ranging from Scarlet's killer being a jealous producer to Scarlet's cleaning lady to Kyle Charlie, Scarlet's cohost at Gratitude. News alerts popped up every fifteen minutes saying the cops had arrested someone, or that someone had posted a new memorial message in Scarlet's honor. But most of it was bogus.

Fiona navigated away from the questions and tapped Chase's name in her contacts list. His phone rang once, then went to voice mail. Fiona groaned. Had Chase just ignored her? He'd never done that. But he seemed to want nothing to do with her.

She heard a rustle behind her and turned. Camille was suddenly standing right next to her, so close that their bodies almost touched.

"Oh my God!" Fiona screamed, whipping out her arm to push Camille away. Her skin connected with hot liquid instead. She leaped up. "What the hell?" And then everything came into focus: Camille was backing up, her hands held high. Scalding liquid was all over Fiona's legs and dripping onto her sheepskin rug. The stainless steel coffee carafe clattered to the floor.

"Oh no!" Camille cried, rushing for the spilled carafe. "I'm so sorry! I was trying to bring you some coffee, and . . ."

Fiona scrambled into her en suite bathroom for a towel. Her nerves were twitching. Camille had come in so stealthily, like a burglar. "How did you even get in the house?" Fiona shrieked. Her parents had left hours ago. Freaked out at all the Scarlet news, Fiona had made sure the door was locked.

Camille smiled innocently. "Your mom gave me the security code. I thought she told you."

Fiona blinked. Did her mom do that? But what was Camille doing with a pot of hot coffee just inches from Fiona's face?

She blotted her skin until the pain began to subside. Camille looked devastated. "God, my third day on the job, and I give you second-degree burns? What is wrong with me?"

"It's okay," Fiona said begrudgingly, trying to calm down. Camille wasn't Lana. It was unfair of Fiona to transfer all her feelings about Lana to Camille. And yet, how could she not? Camille was Lana's eerie younger twin. Even her voice was the same. It all felt too diabolically apropos to be a coincidence.

A few days ago, once Fiona had gotten over the initial shock of Camille chasing her down on that spooky, deserted street near the docks, she and Camille had gone to a nearby café and talked about the personal assistant position.

"So why do you want to be a PA, exactly?" Fiona had asked, trying to wrap her mind around what was happening. "This isn't the only route to break into the entertainment world. You could work on a set. Intern somewhere."

"Yes, but I want to be an influencer." Camille grinned. "Just like you."

Fiona wasn't sure if Camille had a crazed look in her eye . . . or if she was just eager. "And . . . have you interviewed for a lot of positions?"

"Nope!" Camille smiled. "I mapped out my favorite influencers and was going to systematically apply for PA jobs one by one. As luck would have it, I heard you were looking."

"Heard . . . how?" Fiona felt beads of sweat on her neck. A wild theory hit her: Had Scarlet told Camille her secret before she died? Was this a continuation of Scarlet's blackmail?

Camille ducked her head. "I know someone who works with your manager. She passed the information along. It made my mom more comfortable, too, that I was going to apply to work for someone we knew from the old days. She always thought you were really nice."

Oh God, it was like salt in a wound. Fiona had to struggle to keep from choking on her sparkling water. "That's . . . great," she managed to say.

She had to hire Camille. It felt like terrible karma to turn her away, like Scarlet would retaliate from beyond the grave.

"But speaking of work." Camille now picked up the binder she'd created yesterday, which was divided up into various parts of Fiona's life: influencer deals, movies/TV, appointments, goals, miscellaneous. "I hope you won't be mad, but I scrolled through your missed calls from the past few days, and I returned a few of them. Most of them were just from places like the dry cleaner—I picked up your dresses—and the facial place—I rescheduled you because you didn't go to your appointment the day after the Gratitude event—and some reporters because of, you know. Scarlet. Obviously I didn't call them."

"Oh." Fiona was surprised—and impressed—and weirded out. Then again, she had given Camille phone access. It was pretty standard, for PAs. "Thanks."

"It was nothing!" Camille beamed. "But the last message? It was from someone at ABC. Mona."

"Mona Greenblatt?" Fiona spluttered. "What did she want?"

"I called back to check. I hope that's okay. Mona was saying something about a role in a sitcom. They'd love for you to reconsider."

Fiona blinked. "For Kate?"

"Yes, Kate! I looped in your agent and manager. They had a long talk with Mona, though, and they really, really want you back, Fiona. This is way over my pay grade, but apparently, their offer is even better than it was before. You should call your agent.

She said something about you being a hot commodity now that you're notorious."

Fiona felt dizzy. She didn't want to be notorious. She peeked at Camille, too, to check if Camille had any inkling that some of Fiona's notoriety might have to do with what she'd done to Lana. So far, Camille hadn't mentioned her sister much, but even the most estranged sibling would have strong feelings if she found out she was in the presence of her sister's killer.

Then what Camille had just told her sank in. "Wait a second. *Like Me* wants me back?"

Camille nodded. "Badly." Her brow furrowed. "It's okay that I opened that can of worms, isn't it? I don't know the backstory.... Hopefully I didn't make trouble."

"It's fine," Fiona said faintly. Did she dare take the network up on the offer? Scarlet was dead, and the threat of Fiona's secret had receded. Or had it, considering Fiona's secret's little sister was standing right here, a constant reminder?

She shut her eyes to listen to what the Voice thought, but the Voice was eerily silent. Ironic, considering Fiona wouldn't mind a second opinion.

She took a breath. "I'd love to talk to them," she admitted. "And thank you, Camille. I really appreciate you reaching out."

"It's no problem!" Camille crowed, settling closer to her on Fiona's bed. It gave Fiona a tiny, ironic pang—after all, this sort of girl-talk pose was what she always dreamed of Lana doing with her, back in middle school. "They sent over a new pilot script for you to read." Camille reached into her messenger bag. "Mona said they want to make some changes if you're back on board—she wants your approval."

Fiona started to flip through the pages, delighted to be reading the *Like Me* pilot again. The teaser was just as she remembered, but then she got to the part about Kate's entrance. There were some new character traits to describe Kate's personality.

In walks Kate (19), her phone outstretched. She's doing a live video. Counts her steps as she walks into the room. Kate is major OCD—the cleaning kind, the counting kind, the germs kind. She's working on it.

Fiona's head whipped up. "Why have they made Kate OCD?"

Camille looked worried. "Oh. I—I thought that was the reason you didn't want to do the show. Your symptoms . . . they're kind of obvious." She lowered her eyes respectfully. Fiona felt her face flush. "I mentioned to Mona and your agent that maybe we'd just work it into your character. Mona loved the idea. Maybe you could even talk about it in interviews."

"I'm not talking about OCD in interviews!" Fiona's heart was in her throat now.

Camille blinked. "Did I do something wrong? This isn't what you wanted?"

Fiona let the pages of the script flop closed. She didn't know what to say . . . but all of a sudden, she wondered if her instincts about Camille were right. Because this kind of trick. Like a Scarlet move from beyond the grave. *Ha, ha, bitch, if you're going to be Kate, I'm going to make the role unflattering for you.* Come to think of it, it kind of felt like a Lana move, too.

"Um, can I have some time alone to absorb all of this?" she asked Camille, her voice wobbling.

"Oh! Of course! I'll just be in the other room, okay?"

Fiona opened her mouth to protest but shut it again. She'd rather Camille just leave . . . but she also didn't want to upset her. "Okay," she croaked weakly. "Thanks."

Camille smiled sweetly and picked up the binder and coffee tray. But as she turned to leave, she tilted her head just so, shooting Fiona a new expression. It wasn't sweet at all. It looked victorious. Satisfied. *Vindictive.*

JASMINE

The next day, Jasmine parked in the underground garage at the Dove and put on the hat and sunglasses she'd been wearing nonstop. The moment she stepped off the elevator in the atrium, she spied a couple of paparazzi. They'd been following her constantly ever since Scarlet's death, fascinated that Jasmine was somehow mysteriously linked to Scarlet Leigh's last few hours on earth.

When their backs were turned, she made a run for her condo, feeling safe only when she'd double-latched the door. She collapsed on the couch, gathering her dog in her arms.

Her feelings were so ambivalent. A week had gone by, and she was still so shocked that Scarlet was the person in the mask. She was still trying to process why Scarlet had come to her at the Gratitude after-party, unveiling herself . . . only to leave with Cory without saying goodbye. It was like as soon as Scarlet had heard Cory mention her mother, she'd panicked.

And all those things Scarlet had said to her—*everyone thinks I'm one thing, but I'm other things, too; I'm behind a curtain; I'm living a lie*—swirled in Jasmine's mind on auto-repeat. It was strange that Scarlet would finally have the guts to admit her feelings and then wind up dead hours later. Did the two connect? Had someone been listening in on their conversation in the cabana? Did someone disapprove of the path Scarlet wanted to choose?

But then . . . the pregnancy admission. That made no sense at all. Jasmine hadn't known that rumor when Scarlet had found her, and she hadn't gotten a pregnancy vibe from Scarlet at all.

And why did Scarlet's vlog seem like a suicide note? Jasmine couldn't help but take it personally. Was the prospect of being in love with a woman that bleak . . . or did that have nothing to do with it? Jasmine really had no idea what Scarlet had been going through. She'd probably had a whole host of struggles going on. Maybe, for whatever reason, Gratitude had been the straw that broke the camel's back.

Her phone beeped, and her mother's name popped onto the screen. *So worried about you all alone in that condo with a killer on the loose, baby. Dad, too. He's at the ER, by the way. Just some breathing troubles.*

Jasmine gasped. *Want me to come down there?* she typed.

No, he'll be fine. I'm sure you have work to do. Ruby is here. Just keep him in your thoughts, okay?

Her mother added a line of kissing emojis. Jasmine let her phone drop. She hoped her father didn't develop new breathing problems because of all this Scarlet stuff. So far, it hadn't gone public that Jasmine had been questioned by the police, nor was she an official suspect in Scarlet's murder—to her knowledge, it didn't seem like anyone was a suspect, which made her wonder if either the cops were completely incompetent or they'd found a critical clue that proved Scarlet killed herself.

Still, living alone in a building where someone had died was eerie. Every creak at night, every footstep in the hall, made Jasmine cringe. She'd taken to sleeping with the lights on. Double- and triple-checking the security system.

Or perhaps Ruby had broken the news to her parents that Jasmine had fired her—and that was why Jasmine's dad had fallen ill. What had Ruby said? And why was Ruby still not speaking to her? Scarlet Leigh had died a few doors down from where Jasmine lived, and Ruby hadn't reached out to see if she was okay. Jasmine would have thought Ruby would at least have commented on the post she put up commenting on the Scarlet scandal: last night, she'd recorded a live stream on Instagram that addressed Scarlet's vlog and murder, telling the world she was heartbroken that Scarlet was gone. She explained that before Scarlet recorded the vlog, the two of them had had a deep conversation about things like being real on social media, and how life was more than just Instagram. She said that the two of them were closer than they seemed on social because their condos were right next to each other's at the Dove. It wasn't the whole truth, but it wasn't a lie. She really wanted to tell the world everything . . . but maybe Scarlet wouldn't want her to share that they hooked up. Jasmine didn't want to exploit what happened just to soothe her feelings.

Jasmine was tired of waiting for Ruby to come around. She opened a new text. *Hey, Rue. Would love to talk. Hope Dad's okay. Please call me.*

She hit Send. Olive branch delivered. In moments, the little icon appeared indicating that the text had been delivered. Jasmine was positive that even in the ER, her sister was likely glued to her device . . . but Jasmine's phone didn't ring. She stared at it hard, willing the little bubbles to appear in the text window to show Ruby was writing a reply . . . but nothing happened.

Her heart sank. Truthfully? She missed her sister. She wanted Ruby's take on all this—not as a personal assistant, but simply as a family member and friend.

When her phone rang a few seconds later, Jasmine's heart leaped—Ruby had come to her senses! But then she noticed a Beverly Hills area code. WME Agency, read the caller ID. She shut her eyes. She was so not in the mood to speak with her agent.

"Hello?" she answered tentatively. Surely this was a call about the Scarlet mess. Everyone wanted to gossip.

"Jazz? It's Kim!"

"Uh, hi . . ." Jasmine wriggled with uneasiness. Kim sounded unexpectedly chipper.

"Hey, girl! Listen, I have some news for you."

Jasmine covered her eyes. "I'm so sorry, Kim. The Scarlet thing—Lemonade's pissed, right? They hate that I'm in the middle of it?"

"Wait, what?" Kim shuffled some papers. "No, honey. I haven't heard from Lemonade about that Scarlet thing. They saw that you handled it."

"So . . . what's up, then?"

"Well, I got a call from a producer who's interested in you," Kim went on. "He loved your look at Gratitude. Very Jasmine 2.0.

It's Pete Kong—he's involved with the DC franchises, and a new one is in production. He'd like you to read for it."

"Me?" Jasmine jumped to her feet. She'd always wanted to do a superhero movie. "B-but DC isn't Lemonade." Not by a long shot.

"I know. But I talked to them about it. Worked my magic. And they're okay. They understand you need to grow, honey. You can't be rainbows and butterflies Lulu C forever."

Jasmine blinked. "Is there a catch?"

"No catch, honey. You still have your contract with Lemonade. This doesn't bump up against your noncompete because it's a totally different genre. I cleared everything—trust me! Now, do you want to do the audition or not?"

Five minutes later, Jasmine was off the phone, grinning with bewilderment. That had been a surprise. She almost picked up the phone to call Ruby . . . until she remembered Ruby didn't care. Still. Lemonade was letting her audition for other things. Could the worst week of her life really have given rise to something so . . . positive?

Kim's words echoed back. *You need to grow. You need to change.* Hadn't Jasmine just said that very same thing to someone? With a flash, she realized who it was.

Scarlet. Just before they kissed.

The wind whistled, pressing up against the windowpanes. Jasmine peered through the blinds into the atrium. She could see down to the spot by the pool where she and Scarlet last spoke. She remembered Scarlet's sage expression when Jasmine bemoaned how trapped she felt. How she'd said, *Yes, we need to do something about that.* And now something had been done, all right.

There was no way Scarlet had sent the producer that picture. Was there?

Jasmine swallowed hard. She'd love to know what Scarlet had thought of her before she died. If only they'd had more time to talk.

She peered into the atrium again. Normally, at this time of the evening, when the humidity broke and the sun wasn't so punishing, she liked to stand out on her deck or even pop up to the rooftop pool. She wondered if anyone was there now or if they all felt like she did . . . a little lost, a little freaked, and not in the mood for partying.

Suddenly, she noticed a tiny yellow light on in Scarlet's condo.

Her heart jolted. She moved closer to the window. If Scarlet's apartment was set up like Jasmine's, the light was coming from her bedroom. But Jasmine hadn't noticed any lights in Scarlet's condo since the day after Gratitude. Was it possible the forensics workers just left something on? Maybe Scarlet's mom was in there, cleaning up?

Then a shape passed in front of the window. It looked like a person with long limbs, long hair, and an angular face. Jasmine clapped her hand over her mouth. No. Could it be?

She snatched her keys from the console table near the door and sprinted through the corridor and down the stairs. When she reached Scarlet's door, she was trembling with a mix of fear and anticipation and excitement and dread.

She pressed Scarlet's bell. Her heart thudded so hard she

could barely hear the chime. When no one answered, she rang it again. She waited another minute before knocking.

"Scarlet?" she whispered. "Scarlet, are you in there?"

Behind her, she heard a faint giggle. She whirled around just as someone slipped around a corner. A fan, probably. Or a paparazzo. Or a spy, probably reflecting on how Jasmine Walters-Diaz was seeing ghosts, slowly losing her mind.

DELILAH

On Wednesday, Delilah delved into the world of Instagram again. She put out her first post since everything went down, and it was crafted to perfection.

She sat on her bed in a simple navy tee and black jeans. She'd originally planned to do the video somewhere else more professional, but Jasmine told her to keep it authentic. "Remind the audience of *why* they fell in love with Lila D. You're sweet, not showy. Just like every other girl." And so, she sat in front of a wall plastered with stickers and trendy band posters. She even plopped her stuffed bunny, Marmalade, whom she'd had since she was two years old, by her side.

The little red light flickered on, and she took a deep breath before starting. She and Jasmine had rehearsed this speech for hours, but she still wasn't sure she'd be able to get the words out. *Breathe.* She inhaled. Exhaled. Looked straight into the lens.

"First off, I want to say that I'm sorry. To anyone I hurt or upset, that was never my intention." She peeked at Jasmine in the corner, who gave her an encouraging thumbs-up. "This might be hard for some of you to believe, but when I first met Jack, I didn't know who he was. And I know, I know, this sounds like a poorly crafted excuse, because seriously . . . how could you not recognize Jack *freaking* Dono? But I was new to this world, and I was clueless and stupid. Once I found out that he was with Scarlet, I ended it. I never wanted to be the person to break up Jacklet, and I never in a million years wanted it to end like this. Scarlet . . . she didn't deserve this. No one does."

And with that, she clicked off the button, and the recording stopped.

Jasmine applauded. "Bravo!"

"You think?" Delilah asked uncertainly. "I didn't sound too cheesy?"

"You sounded really heartfelt. Your fans are going to love it."

Delilah guzzled a bottle of water, feeling oddly drained. "If I even have fans *left*." That week, she'd lost almost fifty thousand followers. None of the sponsors who'd reached out before, eager to work with her, followed up. She hadn't heard from Kerri at Digi, whom she'd met at Instagram Roll. Patrick's people hadn't sent her the edited photos from the shoot . . . but then again, Delilah was furious at Patrick's people for leaking the Jack thing, so she didn't really care.

But even worse than that, the fear of being caught still dogged her. She couldn't stop thinking about that strange DM she received after visiting Jack—the one that said, *Stop digging*. Who had sent it? Someone who saw her talking to Jack? A jealous fan? Or someone who actually . . . *knew* something?

"Follower counts go up and down all the time," Jasmine was saying. "And sure, this might be a setback, but all you can do is rebuild. Plus, people know that I was on good terms with Scarlet, so if you and I show a united front, I'm sure people will get over this Jacklet drama faster. I'll also comment on and re-share your video just so people know that we stand together, and that I'm with you."

Delilah hugged her. "Thanks." She felt so lucky that Jasmine was pushing through her grief to help her with this.

There was a rustle behind them. Delilah turned as Ava and Faith quickly ducked out of the doorway. Was her sister listening? "Ava!" Delilah called out. "Private conversation! Please don't make me tell you again!"

"Sorry!" came Ava's small, sheepish voice.

Delilah shot Jasmine an apologetic smile. "Ava can't believe you're here."

Jasmine nodded, though she seemed to wait a while to speak again, as though she was waiting for Ava and Faith to truly leave. Then she settled on Delilah's bed and cleared her throat. "So I need to talk to you about something . . . *weird*."

Delilah studied her friend. It was astonishing that despite everything, Jasmine looked as polished as ever. She'd been keeping up her social media brand throughout all that had been happening—even in the face of tragedy, the influencer show went on.

Jasmine glanced back and forth. "What would you say if I told you I'm not sure Scarlet is dead?"

Delilah blinked. "Wait, what?"

"This whole thing seems fishy, you know? Almost . . . *controlled*. Don't you think?"

"How so?"

"Well, isn't it weird that the police haven't called with any more questions? I've asked a few other people, and they haven't asked them anything, either."

"I mean, I guess. . . ." Though in truth, Delilah was thrilled the police hadn't called her again. She'd heard that the forensics teams were no longer at Scarlet's apartment—which meant they'd collected all their data. They must not have found any of Delilah's DNA. A total godsend.

"Maybe they're ruling it a suicide?" Delilah suggested. She hated the idea of Scarlet taking her own life—especially if it had *anything* to do with her and Jack. It didn't explain why whoever settled Delilah in Scarlet's room didn't come forward to tell the cops, either. . . .

Jasmine picked at a loose string on Delilah's comforter. "I swear I *saw* her, yesterday."

"What?" Delilah's jaw dropped. "Where?"

"In her apartment. It was her silhouette . . . in the window."

"Are you *sure*?"

"No." Jasmine looked chagrined. "I rang her bell, and no one answered. But it was *her*. In the window. I *saw*."

Delilah felt dizzy. "Whoa. Okay." Maybe Scarlet and whoever put Delilah to bed were in on it together? Maybe Scarlet had *faked* her death? *That* was a weird thought.

"And also, some really good stuff has happened to me lately—stuff I confided in Scarlet about. It's like she's been my fairy godmother, making it all come true."

"Yeah, but maybe those good things are because of *your* efforts," Delilah said slowly. "I mean, can someone honestly fake their death? There were tons of people around. Someone must have, like, *seen* her dead."

"Yeah? Who?"

A car passed outside, its rumbling motor interrupting their conversation. Delilah couldn't admit that she'd woken up next to Scarlet. Too much time had passed—telling Jasmine now would seem suspicious. And anyway, it wasn't like she'd gotten a good look at Scarlet in the bed that morning. She'd seen a delicate hand, some blond hair—that was all. Maybe it hadn't even been Scarlet's body.

Except Mrs. Leigh had run outside saying her daughter was dead. So what was *that* about?

Delilah rolled her ankles until they cracked. "Is it possible you want it to be true because of what happened between you guys?"

Jasmine shrugged. "Maybe. I mean, all those ambulances, all those detectives . . . it's unlikely to think that Scarlet could have been able to stage all of that."

"It would be a pretty impressive accomplishment," Delilah agreed. "And why would Scarlet want to stage her own death?"

"Attention?" Jasmine suggested. "Fame?"

But they stared at one another blankly, not sure that theory made sense.

"Who do you think the father is?" Delilah asked, switching tacks. "Unless that's too hard to talk about."

Jasmine flopped against the headboard. "To be honest, I can't wrap my mind around the pregnant thing. I didn't get a pregnant vibe from her at *all* when we were together. The partying stuff that's come out about her? Sure. But being pregnant? I just can't believe it."

"Maybe Cory has an idea?" Delilah suggested, thinking about what Jack told her.

Jasmine made a face. "That guy gives me the creeps. You should have seen his face when he interrupted Scarlet and me on the couches. He looked murderous."

"So maybe Cory *did* it?" Maybe it was true that Cory didn't have Scarlet's best interests at heart. Delilah had also researched his Stories from Gratitude—he was at the after-party for hours. He'd posted a ton. Though when she looked at Jasmine again, her friend seemed circumspect. "*If* Scarlet's dead, I mean. And I'm not saying she is."

Jasmine's phone buzzed. She groaned. "It's my agent. I have to head over to her office to meet this person who wants to talk to me about a movie role."

"That's great!" Delilah cried.

"It's terrible timing." Jasmine rose to leave, then eyed Delilah worriedly. "You're going to talk to Cory, aren't you?"

"Maybe." Delilah looked away. "Any idea where he might be?"

Jasmine thought for a beat. "I kind of recall Cory's gotten into dance." She tapped on her phone, and sure enough, she located a post Cory took of himself at a dance studio on the west side. *About to go to a hip-hop class! #SweatItOut!* "The beauty of the internet," she deadpanned. "People are never really lost for long. But, Delilah?" She moved closer. "Please be careful."

Delilah nodded, the weird DM she'd received weighing heavily on her mind. She was thinking the same thing.

Jasmine's driver agreed to drop Delilah in West Hollywood, though when he pulled up to the dance studio, Delilah looked around, certain she was at the wrong place. The storefront was named *1-2-3 Dance!* and the windows were covered with pictures of little kids in leotards. She'd been expecting a studio like Millennium Dance Center, where Jasmine had trained—the classes were taught by bona fide dance stars. This looked, in comparison, like the setup they had going at the YMCA down the street from Delilah's house in Minneapolis.

Delilah pushed inside anyway. She was greeted by a thundering mass of four-year-olds with tight buns and in pink tutus or with little-boy haircuts and in gray sweats. Everyone was screaming, and Delilah's head instantly ached. Parents swarmed, pulling off dance slippers, handing over water bottles, ushering kids out into the street. Delilah threaded through the mess to a reception desk, though there was no one in the chair. She spied a schedule of classes on a laminated sheet of paper. The classes were broken down into tap, ballet, and jazz. No hip-hop, as Cory claimed.

Then she noticed a tall figure coming out of one of the studios. Cory was in a black shorty leotard and covered in sweat. He was speaking to a little boy of about six, and the kid was rolling his eyes. The sight was so disconcerting and incongruous—Cory just didn't seem like the kid *type*—that Delilah burst out laughing.

Cory looked up and noticed her. He excused himself from the kid and stormed over, his eyebrows low and angry.

"What do *you* want?" he demanded.

"What is this place?" Delilah asked, looking around.

Cory raised his chin haughtily. "What does it look like? Dance class."

"Do you . . . *teach*?"

Cory gritted his teeth. Once again, Delilah eyed the sweat on his back and forehead. "Are you *in* the class?" she guessed.

Cory tightened his jaw. "Look, this is LA," he said under his breath. "Dance is competitive. I should have gotten in when I was young, but I didn't, and I have to start at the beginning."

"But don't they have *adult* classes? My mom took ballet when she was twenty something, and she didn't have to take it with a bunch of kids!"

"All the adult classes were full," Cory snapped. "And to be honest? I enjoy the kids. They don't judge."

"But you tell all your fans you're going to hip-hop at a *normal* studio because *you* don't want to be judged," Delilah figured out. Cory shot her a look. "Hey, more power to you," she added, kind of liking Cory. Until she remembered that she was supposed to suspect him.

Cory sank into one hip. "I'm surprised you aren't with Jack right now. Transgressing or whatever." He made a face.

Delilah licked her lips. "Jack and I aren't together. I feel terrible that that news got out."

"*I* felt terrible you even dared to do such a thing," Cory spat. "In fact, you being here is wrong. Scarlet was my best friend. I'm lost without her. You're like salt in a wound."

Delilah crossed her arms. Was Cory being melodramatic . . . or honest? "First of all, I didn't *do* anything to Scarlet," she protested. "And I want to ask you some questions. About Scarlet."

Her heart was pounding. Part of her was terrified to be standing so close to Cory . . . especially if he'd been the one who dragged her into Scarlet's bed.

Cory studied her coolly. "What kind of questions?"

Delilah swallowed hard. She needed to start at the beginning. She couldn't just go in, guns blazing, making accusations. "How did you really feel about Scarlet being pregnant?"

Cory looked unnerved by the question. "I didn't have much time to process it. I only found out after that vlog where she told the whole world." Then he corrected himself. "Well, when whoever *cloned* her told the whole world."

"Are you sure? You seem perceptive. And you were with Scarlet in her vlogs where she showed symptoms. You never had a conversation about it with her—off camera?"

Cory's eyelid twitched. "Why does this matter?"

"Well, because then you *would* have had some time to process it. I mean, you and Scarlet party a lot, right? That would come to an end. And also, Scarlet's your bread and butter, as a stylist. If she got pregnant—dropped out of being an influencer—where would that leave you? Do you have other clients?"

Cory leaned against the concrete-block wall. Behind them, in the lobby, all of the kids had cleared out, and the studio was suddenly empty and dark. "Scarlet would have never stopped being an influencer. Her mother wouldn't have allowed it. And second, you're giving Scarlet way too much credit. I'm not, like, *chained* to her. I work with other people."

"Okay, okay." Delilah raised her palms in apology. She should have known Cory would be touchy. "But can you at least admit that you suspected what was going on before she told Jack? I mean, come on—looking back at those vlogs, it seems pretty obvious."

Cory pressed his lips into a line. "Fine. And I might have said something to her about it. Mostly just that it was a terrible idea."

"What did she say?"

"She blew me off. Said she had everything under control. Which was a lie."

"Do you have any idea who the father is?"

"Nope," he said in a clipped voice, but something told Delilah it wasn't a lie.

"What did you think about that vlog with Jack?" she asked.

"Uh, I thought it was completely insane," Cory explained. "Scarlet was worried she was being cloned before that video happened. I have no idea why she even *did* a vlog that night, all things considered. I would have locked up my phone in a bulletproof box if I thought someone was listening in on me."

"Yeah, but Scarlet would have *never* locked up her phone," Delilah said. "So, after that first vlog, the one where she talks about being pregnant—did you talk about it?"

"Yeah, sure. I found her at Gratitude. And I was like, girl, you just torpedoed your career. But she blew me off—*again.* Just walked away." Cory waved his hand. "Said she had something to do."

"And then what?"

"Then I left. Got the hell out pretty soon after that. Truth be told? I hate those big events."

Delilah narrowed her eyes. "Your Instagram Stories show you were at the after-party until the end. They're time-stamped."

A slow smile spread across Cory's face. "Do you think *I* did something to her?"

Delilah's heart pumped a little faster. "I just . . ."

Cory was beaming. "Oh my God! You are just the cutest little Nancy Drew." He pulled his phone from his canvas gym bag and tapped the screen. "You don't know that you can time posts? I snapped a bunch of things at Gratitude—and the after-party, all ten minutes I was there—and then I just doled them out every half hour or so to make it look like I was by Scarlet's side, blah blah blah." He rolled his eyes. "I wasn't around to poison Scarlet. Sorry."

Delilah studied his face. He looked assured. Relaxed, even. But she still felt skeptical. "Prove it." And then, mustering all her gumption, she showed him the screen shot. His abusive tweets to Scarlet were preloaded. "Or I show the police this."

Cory's expression shifted only a hair. "So Scar and I had a love-hate relationship. Lots of friends do."

"The police might not read it that way."

Cory chewed on his lip. Finally, he sighed. "You're not the only person around here having a secret affair, okay? That's where *I* was."

Delilah frowned. "But . . . don't you already have a boyfriend? Cooper, right?"

Cory's eyebrows lifted a hair. "Aren't *you* a student of Scarlet's vlogs? *Yes,* Cooper is my boyfriend, which is technically why my other thing is a *secret affair.*" He put his hands on his hips. “Cooper got sick at the last minute and couldn’t be my date to Gratitude. So I called my guy on the side. But I didn’t want Cooper to be suspicious—and *voilà*, timed posts. If you look carefully, those pictures of me could be anywhere. I took them just outside coat check.”

Delilah narrowed her eyes. “But why don’t you just break up with Cooper instead of going through all that?”

“Like it’s that easy? And also, like taking ballet with first graders, he’s not exactly . . . *on-brand*.” Then he muttered something else Delilah didn’t hear.

“What was that?” she asked, leaning forward.

“I said, *he’s in high school*.” There was a splotch of red on his neck. He swiped on his phone. “You want proof?” He turned the screen to her: on it was a close-up of Cory and a cute, fresh-faced boy. “Here’s your time stamp. I took this at ten-oh-three p.m. There are dozens more like it stretching for the rest of the night. But I’d appreciate if you didn’t mention this to anyone.”

The fluorescent light flickered. Delilah studied Cory’s intense gaze, the sweat on his brow, the tension in his shoulders. He had not, she realized, added *or else* to his request. He had not said that if Delilah blabbed, he’d tell everyone that *she’d* woken up in Scarlet’s bed.

Perhaps he didn’t know. Perhaps he wasn’t there.

“Okay,” she said softly. “So . . . who do you think killed her?”

Cory studied her carefully before answering. “Maybe you should stop right there.”

“Why?” His voice unnerved her.

“Scarlet’s whole life . . . Some things aren’t exactly what you think.”

A chill shot through Delilah. "What do you mean?" *Was* Scarlet still alive?

"We play a role on her vlog, but that isn't who we are in real life. Well. Except for me." He looked at her carefully. "I was always trying to protect her. Sure, we fought, but I cared about her."

"But someone else . . . didn't?"

Cory didn't answer. Delilah flipped through the possibilities. "Who? Her agent? That dog nanny? Her mom?" Cory's expression wavered a little at that last one. "Her mom?" Delilah repeated. She recalled Scarlet's mother slipping into the condo just after Delilah left that morning. Were those screams that her daughter was dead an act? Maybe she'd already known Scarlet was there.

"But Mrs. Leigh seems so *supportive*," Delilah said quietly.

Cory sniffed. "Yeah, well, too much of a good thing can be poison."

"What does that mean?" When Cory didn't answer, she stepped closer. "*Please.* Don't say stuff like that and then not explain."

Cory lowered his shoulders. "Okay, Nancy. I wasn't going to show anybody this, because I don't know what to make of it, but . . ."

He pulled up something else on his phone. A video started, a hazy, around-the-corner shot of two women arguing in a living room. It was Scarlet and her mother. Scarlet was wearing the beautiful emerald dress she'd had on at Gratitude. Scarlet's mother was in a tight black gown.

"You never supported me!" Scarlet screamed, the veins in her neck popping out. "You've always been toxic. You've always been ruthless. You're pulling shit I don't even know about. You're making me clean up messes I don't even know I've made."

"Get ahold of yourself!" Mrs. Leigh screeched. "You're acting like a lunatic!"

"Am I?" Scarlet's eyes flashed. "You've never cared about me in your life—it's all about *you.*"

"How dare you!" Mrs. Leigh hissed. She made a grab for Scarlet's arm, but Scarlet jerked back just in time. "Come back here!" she yelped.

"Leave," Scarlet said over her shoulder. "I never want to see you again."

"You don't mean that," Mrs. Leigh warned, her voice suddenly taut.

"I do." Scarlet held out her hand. "Give me your key."

The camera zoomed in. After a beat, Mrs. Leigh handed over her key.

Cory raised his gaze to meet Delilah's. "Whoa," Delilah whispered. "Is this real?"

"I think so. It's time-stamped the night of the party."

"How did you get this?"

"Someone sent it to me. I have no idea who."

Delilah tried to think. Was it the same person who'd sent the cops that video of Fiona? Or the person who'd sent her that eerie DM? Or someone else?

"Are you going to send it to the police?" she asked.

Cory's smile was cautious. "You must not know Mrs. Leigh. You really don't want to get on that woman's bad side. If she found out *I* turned her in, she'd come after me, even in prison."

A memory snapped into Delilah's brain: the same blurry

image of someone leading her into Scarlet's bed and lying her down—but maybe it *wasn't* a guy. Maybe the person had feminine, shapely eyebrows. And her voice was higher, sweeter. And yet again, there was that glint of gold. . . .

Delilah looked again at the last frame of the video paused on the screen. There, blatantly obvious, was a delicate hoop of white gold around Gina's neck, winking in the bright overhead light in Scarlet's living room.

Maybe it wasn't Cory's earring she remembered. Maybe it was Mrs. Leigh's necklace.

Delilah stared at Cory in horror. "You think Scarlet's mother killed her?"

Cory pulled his hoodie tighter around his face. "I don't know," he said quietly. "But if you're going to question her, I'm coming, too."

FIONA

"This is *something*." Fiona's mother looked around Fiona's dressing room. It was Fiona's first day on the set of *Like Me*, and the brand-new trailer smelled like roses. An Edible Arrangement sat on the table with a note that read "Happy first day!" The trailer's interior was top-of-the-line, with marble countertops and a full shower and tub and a pretty leather couch. It was the best dressing room in the hierarchy of actors—a clear sign that the producers had jumped through all sorts of hoops to get Fiona back on the show. Fiona was also at the top of the call sheet for the day's shoot, which seemed arbitrary but was apparently a *big* deal. Actors viewed their position on the call sheet as an indication of how important they were to the producers. Fiona's name was even above Julie Robins, who'd been in the acting business for a long, long time.

"Everything okay?" Dr. Jacobs asked, turning back to her daughter. "Want to run lines?"

Fiona snickered. "You've never run lines with me before, Mom."

Her mom's face drooped. "If you're sure. You just look so nervous. . . ."

Fiona stared down at the blush-pink manicure she'd gotten yesterday for her first day on set—the wardrobe person had asked her to get "clean, pretty" nails to match Kate's efficient, perfectionist personality. She wasn't nervous because of the acting she was about to do. It would be a relief to escape from herself. No, it felt like the other shoe was going to drop. She wasn't sure why she felt this way, exactly—just an eerie hunch. Or like someone was watching her. Someone who didn't have her best interests at heart.

A knock sounded on the door, and Fiona sat up straighter. Camille poked her head into the trailer. "Hey!" She brightened when she noticed Fiona. "How are you?"

"Fine," Fiona mumbled. She didn't want Camille here, but the superstitious part of her was afraid that if she sent Camille away, Camille would grow upset, and . . . *what*?

But maybe her fears were insane. Camille was just doing her job, obsequious as she might be. "What's up?" Fiona made herself ask.

"I brought a guest," Camille said as she stepped inside. To Fiona's surprise, Chase followed behind.

"Oh my God!" Fiona leaped up. "H-hey!"

Chase offered Fiona a lopsided smile. Dr. Jacobs cleared her throat. "I need to answer an email," she said loudly, quickly excusing herself. To Fiona's relief, Camille did, too.

Once they were alone, Fiona stepped closer to Chase. "Thanks for coming," she said slowly. She wanted to say she missed him, too, but she suddenly felt shy.

"Yeah." Chase looked cowed. "I had to see your big debut. Though, I'm so sorry—my sister is in town with her kids, and my mom's making me go to Disneyland with them this afternoon." He looked apologetic. "Is that okay?"

"Of course it is. I'm just glad you came at all." A lump formed in Fiona's throat. She'd burst into tears if she didn't think that would make her face puffy. "Chase," she started. "I'm really sorry."

"No, *I'm* sorry," Chase said. "I shouldn't have gotten so mad at you. And I should have been supporting you through this Scarlet stuff. I know you had nothing to do with hurting her. I should have never doubted you."

"It's okay," Fiona breathed out. "Everything is okay. I *was* being sketchy."

"You were just dealing with your typical social things. I get it."

He pulled her in for a delicious hug. Fiona missed his clean, healthy smell, the way his arms wrapped fully around her body, making her feel contained.

"But there's nothing else going on with you?" she asked into his neck. She had to word this part carefully. She thought about how Chase had looked at her at Scarlet's funeral reception—like she was the worst person on earth. And the fact that he hadn't reached out to her at *all* this week. Just as she was worried that Scarlet had somehow contacted Camille before she died, she feared that Scarlet had told Chase, too. It could explain why he'd stayed away from her.

Chase pulled back and drew in a breath. "Actually, now that

you mention it," he started, his voice sober. "There's something I need to . . ."

The door swung open again, and a PA popped her head inside. "Fiona? We're ready for you in hair and makeup." She pressed a hand to her chest. "We're on a tight schedule, so I need you right now, if that's okay."

Fiona swung her gaze from the PA back to Chase. "Now that I mention . . . *what*? What were you going to say, babe?"

Chase rubbed his head, looking uncomfortable. "Let's just talk about it later." He gave her a kiss on the cheek. "See you out there!"

Fiona walked on wobbly legs to the hair and makeup trailer. *Three steps, four steps, five steps.* Maybe it was a good thing that Kate was now plagued with OCD, because Fiona could feel her compulsions needling her. What did Chase mean? Why didn't he just spit out what he wanted to say?

The hairstylist gave her big, soft waves, though Fiona was trembling so badly, she nearly got charred with the curling iron. The makeup artist asked her to stop blinking so much so she could apply fake eyelashes. When Fiona was finished getting coiffed, she walked onto the soundstage, found a quiet, dark corner, and practiced her lines over and over in her head. Chase wouldn't cavalierly say he and Fiona could talk about Lana's murder later, would he? He *couldn't* know.

"Fiona?"

Camille was by her side, as obedient as a golden retriever. "Can I get you something from Craft Services? You're looking pale."

"Uh . . ." Fiona licked her lips. "Water, maybe?"

Camille skipped off. Fiona collapsed in a director's chair and stared at the blank TV screens, where eventually the producers and directors and writers would watch how the shoots were going. She felt scattered and nervous, but then she realized how silly that was. Chase didn't know a thing. Scarlet wasn't tormenting her from beyond the grave. She needed an attitude readjustment.

She hopped off the chair. From now on, she was Kate, not Fiona. Her problems weren't Kate's problems.

And it worked—like a charm. As long as Fiona was in Kate mode, the twitches were gone, and the fire in her chest was extinguished. She breezed through her first scene, nailing her jokes. She accentuated her tics and compulsions in a way that was both funny and compassionate, drawing from her own experience to really make them authentic. She heard chuckles from the director once he yelled cut, and he gave her a thumbs-up from the sidelines, telling her she was doing great. She gelled with Andy, an actor she'd done a few chemistry reads with over the past few days, and the dialogue-heavy mental sparring of the scene kept her brain occupied for over an hour.

By the completion of her first scene, she was totally relaxed. It felt like an enormous victory to have overcome such a mountain of panic. She spied her parents and Chase watching and gave them a thumbs-up. They beamed back. But when she glanced at Camille, her assistant wasn't even paying attention to the shoot. Her gaze was on her phone, her brow furrowed.

Fiona nailed a few more scenes. Some of her takes were so hilarious they had to stop the camera because everyone was laughing. While the camera operator adjusted the lighting, Fiona stepped away and posted a few Instagram story videos, bashfully admitting that her first day on the set was going awesome. Margot Labouche, a comedy veteran who was playing Fiona's mom, brushed by and squeezed her arm. "You are a *natural,* honey. I'm so glad you reconsidered. That other girl who was going to play Kate? God rest her soul, but she was god-awful."

After a delightful few hours, the director called lunch. Fiona was almost bummed to go back to her trailer—she wanted to stay on this fantasy set forever, being Kate. But the other actors quickly gathered their things and hightailed off the soundstage, so Fiona reluctantly followed. She searched for her family and Chase, but they were no longer in the cavernous building. Maybe Chase had left for Disney already. Maybe her mom needed to go back to work.

The sun assaulted her when she stepped outside. Fiona noted that it was the "Golden Hour," aka the most flattering lighting of the day. *Score.* She whipped out her phone and started snapping. The first three pictures she took, she was happy with. *That* was a first. She didn't even open Facetune; she just added her filter and posted it with the caption: "Not sure if it's the lighting or the amazing first day on set I've had, but I could get used to this glow."

She bounced to her trailer, trying to preserve her high. She was grateful that her trailer was empty—she needed a few moments alone to process everything. There was a bottle of pressed juice waiting for her on the little table, and she twisted off the top, flopped onto the couch, and closed her eyes. She had to admit it: she loved acting. She was made for this.

Buzz.

She scanned the room. That wasn't her phone making noise—she'd put it on silent when they started the shoot.

Buzz.

She rose from the couch. In the corner was a tiny closet where some of her wardrobe options hung—polished shirts, crisp skirts, and structured blazers, all fitting with Kate's personality. To the left was a familiar messenger bag—*Camille's* messenger bag. The buzzing was coming from there.

Fiona undid the Velcro fastener. *I'm just going to shut it off,* she rationalized. She had no interest in looking at Camille's phone. But when she saw the name of the person who'd just called on Camille's locked screen, the blood drained to her toes.

Scarlet: How's it working out with Fiona?

The phone slipped from her fingers. When she came to, seconds later, she was lying on the floor, taking elephant-wheezing breaths. Her fingers fumbled for her own phone. *Jasmine. Jasmine will know what to do.*

Fiona pounded out a text. *My new assistant just got a text from Scarlet Leigh. What the hell is going on?*

A cough sounded just as she sent it off. Fiona whirled around. Camille stood over her, a look of concern on her face.

"Fiona?" Camille placed a hand on her shoulder. "Are you okay?"

Fiona scrambled away. "Don't touch me."

Camille's eyes widened. Her gaze flicked to her phone on the floor. Hurriedly, her arm shot out to scoop it up. She lifted her gaze to Fiona's and held it for a long beat.

"You know her," Fiona whispered shakily. "Did she send you here? Are you guys working together?"

Camille blinked hard. "*Who?*"

"Don't play dumb!" Fiona cried. "She's *texting* you! Is she still alive? Did she send you here? Did she tell you about Lana?"

"Lana who?" said a voice.

Fiona's mother stood in the doorway. Chase's head poked behind her. Dr. Jacobs's head swiveled from Fiona to Camille. "What's going on in here?"

Camille turned back to Fiona. "What about Lana?"

Fiona licked her lips. This was ridiculous. Camille already *knew*. She was playing dumb because Chase and her mom were there. Scarlet had told her. Scarlet, who was maybe *alive*.

"What about my sister?" Camille repeated. "You mean what happened to her?"

"*No!*" Fiona cried. It was a knee-jerk reaction. "I mean . . . I don't know anything. I swear."

Camille blinked hard. Realization slowly flooded her features. "You *do*. Oh my God. It's all over your face. *Tell* me."

"No!" Fiona screamed.

"Fiona?" Fiona's mother took a cautious step forward. "What is she talking about?"

You need to salvage this! Fiona's brain screamed. *You need to put the cap back on the bottle.* "She sent you," she roared to Camille. "Are you going to kill me? Is that your goal?"

"Fiona!" Fiona's mother cried. "Honey, stop!"

Camille turned to Dr. Jacobs desperately. "I don't know what she's talking about!"

"Yes, you do!" Fiona said. "Whatever you're planning—you need to stop!"

Suddenly, there were more people in the trailer: Mona, fellow actors, the director, PAs. Everyone was talking at once. And then Fiona realized—*she* was talking, too. It was like a dam had broken inside her. "She's trying to kill me!" she said over and over again, stabbing a finger at Camille.

"Miss," a gruff voice growled in her ear. Fiona's gaze slid to the right. One of the security guards she'd noticed outside the soundstage clutched her arm, tugging her toward the trailer's steps. "If you can't calm down, we're going to have to remove you from the lot."

"She should see a doctor, maybe?" Mona added, sounding dismayed.

"No doctors!" Fiona couldn't see a doctor. A doctor would ask what had just happened. A doctor would force her to spill the truth. And then what? She'd be arrested. She'd spend her life in jail.

She wheeled backward—away, away, away. As she stepped out of her trailer, past the guard, she spied a line of rubber-neckers watching this unfold. They were guests, here on a studio tour. Phones were raised and aimed at her face.

This is how I'm going to be remembered, she half realized. But she didn't care. She just needed out of there. And so she turned . . . and ran.

JASMINE

"Pick up, pick up, pick *up*," Jasmine muttered, dialing Fiona again. Her friend still didn't answer. She navigated to the text window and stared once more at the shocking text Fiona had sent: *My new assistant just got a text from Scarlet Leigh.*

From Scarlet.

FROM SCARLET.

Jasmine paced the length of the Nike office, where she'd been meeting with the head of the design team to review the rainbow line. What if Fiona was in danger? What if she needed Jasmine's help? She checked Fiona's Instagram Story. It appeared that Fiona was on set right now, shooting her first day of *Like Me*. She'd posted an update about forty-five minutes ago, saying all was going really well. So what had happened?

And could Scarlet be alive?

Elation filled her, followed by something more discomfiting—because what did that *mean*? And where *was* Scarlet? Jasmine had been gazing obsessively into Scarlet's windows from her penthouse nonstop. She'd even positioned one of her home monitoring cameras at the very spot where she'd seen Scarlet's silhouette so Jasmine wouldn't miss anything when she went out. So far, she hadn't seen anything more.

And also—Scarlet wanted to *hurt* Fiona? *Why*?

Her phone buzzed in her hand. "Fiona!" Jasmine cried. "What's going on?"

Fiona breathed heavily. "I . . . I don't know, Jazz. There was a text on my assistant's phone . . . *from* Scarlet. How can that be? Is she still alive?"

Jasmine swallowed hard. "I . . . I might have seen her."

"Oh my God." Fiona's voice wobbled. "Oh my God, *how*?"

But then, abruptly, the call dropped out. "Fiona?" Jasmine called. "Fiona?"

Jasmine tried Fiona one more time, but the phone went straight to voice mail. It was hard to know what to do. What about this assistant . . . and Scarlet?

Jasmine wanted to believe Scarlet had planned her alleged death. Maybe she wanted to escape the life she was living. Maybe it was a matter of uncovering and interpreting all the clues. But if Scarlet wasn't in her condo, then where would she be hiding? A luxury suite? That seemed too public. Had she fled the country? But someone would have noticed her at the border. She had fans everywhere.

Or maybe it was much simpler than that. If Jasmine were to fake her death, she knew where *she* would go.

Home.

Two years ago, Scarlet had thrown a birthday party for herself. She'd wanted it to be "low-key," she'd said, and held it at her mom's house in Beverly Hills. "Low-key" was a bit of a joke, because there'd been not one, not two, but *three* different photo booths, and Travis Scott had performed.

Jasmine had been invited. Not because she and Scarlet were close, but because they were Instagram friends . . . *and* Jasmine's star power was an added bonus at any event. Ruby had made her go, which had annoyed her at the time, but now Jasmine was grateful. Because otherwise, she'd have no idea where Scarlet's mother lived.

Still, she had to drive around the Beverly Hills Flats a few times before she found the right street—they all sort of looked the same, with their enormous houses and pristine lawns and gardening trucks parked at the curbs. Finally, she came to a stop on Alpine, at a large estate with a stone walkway and a fountain. She was almost positive this was the place where they filmed *Clueless,* something Scarlet had bragged about at her party.

She texted Fiona the address. Thankfully, Fiona wrote back quickly. *In an Uber. I'm scared.*

Be strong, Jasmine replied. *You want answers. You want to know what's going on.* And that included Scarlet blackmailing Fiona—*could* she be doing that? It was difficult for Jasmine to reconcile the sensitive young woman she'd been with the night of Gratitude and the conniving blackmailer intent on ruining Fiona's life . . . but then again, that *was* Scarlet's reputation. And maybe there was some sort of explanation.

A heavy oak door separated Jasmine from the inside of Scarlet's house. It was quiet on the front porch—Jasmine was happy that there were no news vans at the curb, hoping to get dirt about Scarlet's murder. Still, Jasmine couldn't help but feel that she was being watched. She spied a surveillance camera discreetly mounted in the eaves. Who was watching the monitor? Scarlet?

"Where are you?" she muttered, scanning the road for Fiona. The street was calm and still.

There was a *click,* and she turned halfway. A glint flashed at the corner of her eye, and someone exhaled sharply. All at once, a face appeared in the doorway. Jasmine's heart leaped—*Scarlet!* Because there she was, those eyes, that hair, that smile. Except everything seemed a little . . . off.

The figure stepped back into the house and glowered at Jasmine disapprovingly. "What do *you* want?" Mrs. Leigh growled.

Jasmine's mouth felt gummy and useless. "I . . . I want to see her. Is she here?"

Mrs. Leigh's eyes narrowed. Then, ever so slightly, she peered past Jasmine, focusing on something on the street. Jasmine didn't have time to turn because all at once, she was falling forward, over the threshold of the Leighs' doorway, her chin knocking heavily against the tiled floor. Blood filled her mouth. Pain throbbed in her head. And somewhere, far away, she heard the sound of twisted, satisfied laughter.

And then she felt nothing.

FIONA

"Excuse me?" Fiona leaned forward toward the Uber driver. "Is there any way you can go a little faster?"

"The speed limit's twenty-five, miss," the driver answered.

Fiona gritted her teeth. Of all the times for an Uber driver to obey traffic laws! She peered down the residential streets, pretty sure that Scarlet's road was only a few turns away.

Her phone vibrated. It had been blowing up ever since her meltdown. *Chase. Mom. Dad.* The texts cycled in waves. One from Mona Greenblatt even popped up—probably to tell Fiona that she was fired. What kind of person freaked out on set? Fiona was already generating negative gossip about the show, probably. The studio wouldn't like that a bit.

And her mom. And *Chase.* Were they still with Camille? What did they think about what had happened? And what was Fiona supposed to believe—that Camille really knew *nothing*? It had to be a lie. Why else was there a text from Scarlet on her phone?

Still, her stricken expression when Fiona mentioned Lana's name haunted her. Camille had looked so blindsided. So stunned.

Finally, the driver pulled up to the curb in front of a pretty, enormous stone house. Fiona's heart pounded as she jumped out of the car and headed up the walkway. Things were quiet and desolate out front. But didn't Jasmine say she was here?

"Fiona?"

She whipped around. Delilah—and of all people, Scarlet's friend Cory—were cutting across the grass. Fiona gaped. "W-what are you doing here?" she cried. "Did Jasmine call you, too?"

"No . . ." Delilah looked around. "Jasmine's also coming?"

"I thought Jasmine was already here." Fiona faced the door again. Where had Jasmine gone? Then she glanced at Cory suspiciously. "Why did *you* come?"

Cory put his hands on his hips. "I loved Scarlet. I want to be part of your mystery team. But I have to warn you, we have to watch ourselves with Mrs. Leigh. She's slippery. And dangerous. We need to talk this through before we go in guns blazing."

"First of all, we're not a mystery team," Fiona snapped. "And how do I know you're not in on it?"

"He's not," Delilah answered quickly. "He didn't kill her—he wasn't even at Gratitude. He has proof."

"I don't mean *killing* her. How do we know he isn't helping Scarlet fake her death?"

"Wait, what?" Cory and Delilah blurted out in unison.

But before Fiona could explain, a scream sounded from inside. Delilah's eyes went wide. "What was that?"

"I—I don't know." Fiona took a small step back toward the street. Maybe it was a bad idea to come.

Inside, a thump. And then the sound of shattering glass. Fiona swallowed hard and hurried onto the porch. "Do you think Jasmine's in there?"

Something flashed in the tiny sidelight window to the left of the door: A shimmer of dark hair. Two wide violet eyes. The realization hit Fiona instantly: Jasmine *was* in there. *Screaming.*

The girls stared at each other in horror. Delilah started pounding on the door. "Let us in! Don't hurt her!"

"Please!" Fiona echoed.

Surprisingly, just a moment later, the door whipped open. Mrs. Leigh looked exasperated. "What the hell?" she grumbled, glancing around at the group.

Fiona peered behind the woman. Jasmine was standing at the back of the foyer, rubbing a spot on her head. She seemed okay. "What's going on?" Fiona demanded.

Mrs. Leigh grabbed Fiona and yanked her forward. "For God's sake, get inside. Don't you know photographers are hiding in the trees? They're like ninjas. What are you thinking, standing where everyone can see you?"

Fiona stumbled across the threshold. Mrs. Leigh swung around and pulled Delilah and Cory in, too. Fiona rushed to Jasmine, who was leaning against a curved, stucco wall. "Are you okay?" she whispered. "What's going on? We heard you scream!"

Jasmine nodded. "I know. I tripped when I came in—it knocked me out for a minute," she whispered. "She was trying to keep me from the photographers. She's *really* paranoid."

"What do you people want?" Mrs. Leigh interrupted. "Haven't you caused enough problems?" Then she turned to Cory. "And where have *you* been?"

“Sorry,” Cory said in a small, feeble voice. He sounded so cowed, Fiona almost wanted to laugh.

No one else spoke. Finally, Fiona stepped forward. “Where is she?”

Mrs. Leigh’s expression didn’t waver. “Where’s *who*?”

“You know. Scarlet’s been threatening me. She sent someone to *hurt* me. Are you hiding her?”

“Wait, what?” Delilah cried. “Scarlet’s *alive*?”

Cory raised his hands submissively. “I have no idea what she’s talking about, Gina.”

Fiona held up her phone, undeterred. “I’m going to call the police about you—about all of this. That Scarlet’s hiding here . . . that she’s out to get me. All because—what? I stole her role? I stole her boyfriend?”

“Hold on a minute,” Delilah interrupted. “Scarlet wouldn’t be here. She and Gina hate each other. Had a big showdown the night of Gratitude. Isn’t that right, Gina?”

“Delilah,” Cory said uneasily, cowering a little. “Maybe we shouldn’t . . . I thought we were going to . . .”

Gina looked like she was about to speak, but then Delilah grabbed Cory’s phone, which he was holding limply in his hand, and pressed Play on a video. Fiona leaned in to peer at a grainy video of Scarlet and Mrs. Leigh in the middle of a vicious argument. Was this from . . . *Gratitude*? Fiona recognized Scarlet’s dress. At the end, Scarlet declared she never wanted to see her mom again. Mrs. Leigh protested, but Scarlet didn’t back down. Scarlet’s mother looked murderous. Vengeful.

Fiona listened to the words carefully, some of the things Scarlet was saying catching in her mind. *You’re pulling shit I don’t even know about. You're making me clean up messes I don't even know I've made.*

What did *that* mean?

Mrs. Leigh looked shaken when thc video ended. "Where did you get that, Cory? Were you spying on us? After all I've done for you, this is how you treat me?"

Cory lowered his head, looking like he was going to shatter. Delilah stepped forward. "He wasn't spying. He wasn't even at Gratitude. Someone must have sent this to him because they were worried. So do you want to explain what this is all about?" Then she stepped back, arms crossed. Fiona was impressed. *Go, Delilah.*

"First of all, you're barking up the wrong tree," Mrs. Leigh said through gritted teeth. "That argument with Scarlet—you're taking it out of context."

"Am I?" Delilah put her hands on her hips. "Or was she telling you what you needed to hear? And maybe you didn't want to hear it?"

"Yes, I was shocked that she chose *then* to say all of that." Mrs. Leigh kept her voice even. "And . . . okay, that video isn't particularly flattering. But I just wanted my daughter to come out on top, always. We were arguing over the vlog. About her being pregnant. I thought she'd lost her mind. But I didn't kill her! She made me forfeit my key to the apartment after that—I couldn't even get into the condo until the next morning! I couldn't believe it when I tried the door the next day and it was open. Then again, the murderer must have left it unlocked. . . ." Her expression wavered at the word *murderer.*

Fiona and Jasmine exchanged a spooked, skeptical glance.

"I already told the police this, anyway," Mrs. Leigh continued. "I said we argued. I said I didn't have a key. So can you please get out of my house? Or I'll call the police on all of *you*."

"Wait a minute." Fiona's mind was whirling. She was still trying to process Scarlet and Mrs. Leigh's showdown. And what Mrs. Leigh had just said: *I just wanted my daughter to come out on top, always.* Fiona kept thinking of Scarlet's expression when she'd asked her about Scarlet's blackmail, too—that Scarlet knew about Lana. Scarlet had seemed, well . . . *confused.* Fiona had thought Scarlet was just putting on an act, but perhaps something else was at play here.

"Who threatened me to give up my role as Kate?" Fiona demanded, turning to Mrs. Leigh. "Was it Scarlet . . . or was it you?"

Mrs. Leigh seemed startled by the switch of gears. "Does it matter?"

"*Kind* of. It's why I confronted your daughter at Gratitude. I thought *she* was threatening me. But was it you instead?"

Mrs. Leigh walked to the sweeping double staircase, sat on the first riser, and rubbed her temples. "Look. My daughter got what she wanted because I made sure she got what she wanted. And when she didn't, I figured out loopholes. I was her biggest supporter."

The color drained from Fiona's face. "So that means . . ." *Mrs. Leigh* had sent that threat? *Mrs. Leigh* knew her secret?

But . . . Mrs. Leigh was still alive. Meaning Fiona's threat was still out there.

Mrs. Leigh smiled sinisterly as if this had just occurred to her, too. "The most incredible thing, Fiona? I didn't even know what you were hiding—I just guessed. I saw you around. I noticed your OCD. I knew you fled from Orange County without much explanation—shortly after a classmate died. I make it my business to understand my daughter's friends and adversaries—but I took a gamble with you. A gamble, I guess, that paid off."

Fiona felt like she'd been sucker punched. "I-it was all a bluff?" Mrs. Leigh smiled mysteriously. "And you contacted Camille, too? Did you pose as Scarlet in her texts? Because she just got one . . . *from* Scarlet."

Mrs. Leigh shrugged. "I reached out to her as Scarlet because I knew she'd respond to someone of Scarlet's level of fame, though later on I confessed I was Scarlet's mother. Perhaps she still had my information in her contacts as Scarlet, I don't know. But that assistant doesn't know a thing. I just sent her to you to mess with you. I had no idea it would work so well."

Fiona's mouth opened, but no sound came out.

Delilah scoffed. "You could be arrested for what you did, Mrs. Leigh. Blackmail is a crime."

Mrs. Leigh sniffed. "No one's arresting *me*." She pointed at Fiona. "Or I'll spill that this one is hiding something, too."

Fiona glanced at the others, then lowered her head. She'd ruined things for everyone.

Jasmine cleared her throat. "So wait. A-all the blackmailing Scarlet's responsible for . . . that's all you?"

"Don't make me out to be the criminal. I was just being a good mother. A good manager. My daughter worked hard for her image. She sacrificed. *I* sacrificed. And I was going to make sure our efforts paid off."

"But then she got pregnant," Delilah croaked. "What did you think of that?"

A strange, startled expression crossed Mrs. Leigh's lips. "You honestly think she was pregnant? Even *you,* Cory?"

Fiona glanced at Delilah, then Jasmine, and then Cory. ". . . Wasn't she?" Cory asked tremulously.

"I'm stunned *you* don't know." Mrs. Leigh looked at everyone. "My daughter had a condition called PCOS—it made her ovaries very cystic, and she was more or less infertile. We've gone to appointment after appointment for it. I took her to an appointment just days before Gratitude, in fact—for a sonogram. And at that appointment, she had to take a pregnancy test because of the radiation."

"Wait, *what?*" Jasmine cried. Fiona felt the same bolt of shock.

Mrs. Leigh held out her iPhone. "Call the clinic up if you want. They'll tell you. The pregnancy test was negative. So what Scarlet has been telling everyone—it's a lie."

DELILAH

A few minutes later, Delilah and the others were tucked inside Jasmine's car. Shortly after Mrs. Leigh dropped her Scarlet's-not-pregnant bomb, she kicked them out . . . though she'd kindly let them out through a side door to avoid the photographers she was certain were hiding, ninja-like, in the trees.

"Do you think she's telling the truth?" Delilah's mind thrummed over what they'd just learned. "About Scarlet not being pregnant, I mean?"

"We *could* call the clinic and make sure." Jasmine glanced at Cory. "You really knew nothing about her condition?"

Cory looked bewildered. "Not a thing. I've never even heard of PCOS—"

"Hold on a second," Fiona interrupted. "Why would Scarlet stage a pregnancy? I mean, this was definitely premeditated on her part."

"Was it, though?" Fiona asked. "Scarlet's vlogs—she said her phone was cloned. It's not like she realized the footage was recording before it posted."

"Or *did* she?" Delilah asked. "If Scarlet wanted everyone to think she was pregnant, maybe *she* was letting those vlogs run on longer than intended? Maybe the cloning is a lie . . . and she wasn't being cloned at all."

Everyone fell silent for a moment, their minds blown. "Huh," Jasmine mumbled.

"So this was all her doing?" Cory echoed. "And we were all just being manipulated?" He scoffed. "That makes me feel sort of violated."

"But it makes sense," Delilah said. "Scarlet knows her fans obsessively watch her vlogs. They analyze her every move. She dropped in little clues about being pregnant in the videos. The sickness. The fainting."

"And then finding that pregnancy test in CVS . . ." Fiona was thoughtful. "She stuffed the test into a trash can. She ran out of there like the place was on fire. Her acting skills were amazing."

"How do you even fake a pregnancy test?" Cory asked.

Jasmine steered onto Doheny. "You can buy HCG in liquid form. People take it when they do IVF. I saw it on *Dr. Oz* once."

"But . . . *why*?" Cory said quietly.

They passed a few stoplights. High-rises twinkled in the midday sun. Jasmine tapped her mouth. "The only thing I can think of is that Scarlet wanted to escape her life. When she and I talked at the after-party, we both said the same thing—that our images were getting to be too much for us to handle. That we just wanted to be *ourselves*. Maybe this was her attempt to break away."

"But then someone killed her?" Delilah asked aloud. "It seems like a lot of effort for nothing."

Jasmine glanced at Fiona, who was taking a halting breath. "Unless that's a ruse . . ."

Delilah opened her mouth but didn't reply. Did they honestly still believe Scarlet wasn't dead? Mrs. Leigh seemed so convinced she was gone. . . .

Fiona noticed her skeptical expression. "Look, Scarlet's become an even bigger star now that she's dead. Have you looked at her account lately? *So* many followers. And that record she cut last year? It didn't do much when it came out, but now it's on the charts."

"So she did it just to get famous?" Delilah frowned.

"Or her mother *killed* her to make her famous," Fiona said. "I mean, that woman has as much to gain as Scarlet." She chewed a thumbnail. "Clearly she's more ruthless. *She* was the person who made me drop Kate. A role I probably won't have, after today."

"But then why did someone send the cops the argument between you guys, Fiona?" Cory asked. "And why did someone send *me* that fight between Scarlet and her mom?"

"Maybe just to stir up trouble," Jasmine suggested.

"*Or* to put the heat on someone else, if it's the killer who's sending that stuff around," Fiona added.

Cory thought this over. "But if Scar's still alive, would she really not tell me where she is?"

Fiona glanced at him sympathetically. "If she wanted to cut all ties, maybe."

Delilah felt more confused than ever. Was Scarlet lurking

somewhere, laughing at them? Or was Mrs. Leigh laughing behind the door of her Beverly Hills mansion, having tricked all of them into believing she didn't hurt her daughter? Was Delilah a pawn in this game, too? Was someone gaslighting her, making her think she killed someone and woke up next to a dead body . . . when that wasn't the case at all?

It felt like the answer was locked in her memory, but she couldn't access it.

She was so lost in thought that the whoop of the siren behind them jolted through her system. She whirled around. A cop car had its lights on and was signaling for them to pull over.

Jasmine groaned. "Are you kidding me?"

"Gina had better not have called the police on us," Cory muttered.

"Would she do that?" Fiona cried nervously. "We didn't do anything wrong!"

Jasmine pulled to the side of the road, rolled down her window, and gave the approaching officer an innocent smile. The officer, a tall, rangy man with pockmarked skin, poked his head in, frowning at the group in the backseat.

"Here's my license." Jasmine flashed the card. "And my registration's here somewhere. . . ." She reached over to open the glove box.

"That won't be necessary," the cop cut her off. He lowered his sunglasses a half inch. "I'm looking for Delilah Rollins."

Delilah's stomach plummeted. "M-me?" she asked, her voice dry.

The officer eyed her coldly. "Miss, I'm going to need you to step out of the vehicle."

"What? Why?" Jasmine cried. "Delilah didn't do anything."

But Delilah knew why they wanted her. *Stop digging,* warned that DM. And yet she'd kept at it. She didn't listen.

The officer's jaw was taut. "Out of the vehicle, please."

Jasmine squared her shoulders. "Look. Whatever Gina Leigh told you about Delilah, it's not true. Gina is a vindictive psychopath. She's been blackmailing people, impersonating her daughter, for years."

The cop gave Jasmine an exasperated look. "This has nothing to do with Gina Leigh. But it *is* because of some details we've uncovered about Scarlet Leigh's death."

Delilah's heart went still. Everyone turned to stare at her in shock and confusion.

"We received an image from the Dove's surveillance system," the cop went on. "It was malfunctioning the night of the party, but our team was able to recover some footage regardless. We have images of someone coming out of Miss Leigh's apartment very early on the morning after she died." His eyes slid darkly to Delilah. "*You.*"

JASMINE

Several minutes later, after the police car pulled away, Jasmine's car was still parked on the shoulder. While the traffic zoomed past, Jasmine, Fiona, and Cory sat comatose inside, staring at the traffic.

"*Her?*" Cory finally said. "She's the one who did it?"

"M-maybe they got the details wrong," Fiona said in a dazed voice. "I mean, are they sure it was Delilah on that surveillance video?"

Cory scoffed. "Did you see Delilah's face just now? She didn't look surprised. She looked . . . relieved. Like she was dying keeping it a secret."

"But why wouldn't she have told us this?" Jasmine whispered.

Cory shrugged. "Uh, because you guys would turn her in?"

Jasmine tipped her water bottle to her lips. Her heart felt smashed. Delilah had kept such a horrifying secret from all of them. Was that why she was scrambling around, trying to find another suspect? But why had she done it—because of Jack?

And there was another terrible truth she had to come to terms with. Jasmine had prayed that the reason the news had been spotty with details of a police investigation about Scarlet's murder was secretly because there was no police investigation to speak of—that maybe Scarlet was paying off the cops so she could fake her death. But that officer who arrested Delilah seemed very invested in Scarlet's case. Which meant that maybe there was actually a girl's body in the morgue. Which meant Scarlet probably wasn't alive after all.

Tears pricked her eyes. She didn't know if she should cry or throw up.

Cory kept talking. "Anybody who's that obsessed with solving someone's murder obviously has something to hide. Clearly Delilah is way more nefarious than we imagined. I mean, look, the girl is ballsy enough to run into a burning building to rescue a puppy. I guess she's tough enough to poison Scarlet, too."

"But . . . ," Fiona said weakly, then trailed off.

Jasmine's phone buzzed in her purse, and she gazed blearily at the screen. Jack Dono's number was on the caller ID. "Uh, hello?" she answered tentatively. She didn't realize Jack even had her number. She put the call on speaker.

"Jasmine. It's Jack. I just read the news about Delilah."

"Yeah . . ." Jasmine swallowed hard. "Did you . . . know?"

"No. Of course not. But something seems weird. Delilah couldn't have done this."

"But they have surveillance of her," Jasmine answered miserably. "She was coming out of Scarlet's apartment."

"Cops told me that Scarlet's estimated time of death was sometime in the middle of the night. But the video shows Delilah coming out of the apartment in the morning. What sort of murderer hangs out after they've committed the crime? That makes no sense."

"She was really drunk," Fiona said. "I mean, maybe she had no idea what she was doing. She must have just passed out."

"Okay, maybe, but it's still unlikely. And also, Delilah just randomly had access to some sort of medication that killed Scarlet?" Jack scoffed. "She doesn't do drugs."

"She's diabetic," Fiona said quietly. "She carries insulin with her—I saw it. A shot of insulin to a healthy person is dangerous."

"Oh," Jack said softly. "Oh. Huh."

No one said anything for a while. Traffic swished noisily past. Jasmine could feel her chin wobbling again. "I'm sorry, Jack," she said. "This just doesn't look good."

Jack cleared his throat. "Talk to her anyway. I'm begging you. Something doesn't feel right."

Jasmine squeezed the steering wheel. She wanted to believe Jack . . . and maybe there wasn't any harm in getting Delilah's side of the story. "Okay. Innocent until proven guilty." She glanced at the others. "What do you guys think?"

Fiona cleared her throat. "Something is strange about all of this. I can't buy that it was Delilah who sent that video of Scarlet and me fighting to the cops. Or that she was the person who sent the video of Scarlet and her mom fighting to you, Cory." She started to nod. "That's who we should look for. The person trying to frame everyone."

Jasmine placed her hands back on the steering wheel. "Well,

I want to find out for myself," she said. "We go to Delilah. And we get the truth."

One good thing about being an influencer and having a fat bank account: when a friend needed to post bail, you could come up with the money pretty easily. Another good thing: the press hounded you so much, you knew how to avoid them. On the way to the police station, Jasmine called Marianne Winslow, a crisis PR specialist best known for her work with Miley Cyrus during her "breakdown" days, and Marianne managed to get them into the building without the lurking photographers having a clue.

Inside the station, Jasmine filled out the bail paperwork, and Delilah was released. She looked wrecked when she came out of the holding cell: her makeup smeared, her posture bent, and her arms held to her chest like a shield. When she saw that Jasmine and the others had bailed her out, her eyes widened in confusion. "I thought you were my parents."

"Yeah, well, we're worried about you, too," Jasmine said. "And we'll wait here with you until they come." She gestured to a few uncomfortable-looking chairs in the lobby. "We want to talk."

"I'm so sorry I didn't say anything," Delilah blurted out, tears welling in her eyes. "I don't remember what happened that night, and I was too afraid to tell you guys that I woke up in her bed. I don't think I did anything, but my memory's a blank, and—"

"Slow down." Jasmine sat Delilah down. "Why don't you just tell us everything you *do* remember?"

Delilah wiped her eyes and took a breath. Then she launched

into the story about how she got drunk after finding out Scarlet was pregnant with Jack's baby. "The alcohol hit me hard," she explained. "It was stupid to drink. I remember talking to lots of people—influencers I didn't know, random guests, even fans." She winced. "And then I was just . . . staggering. I thought I might throw up. Someone put their hand on my shoulder and was like, 'You should lie down.'"

"Who was it?" Fiona asked.

"I don't know. Someone I know—but maybe not that well. I just remember white gold glinting above me—jewelry of some sort. I thought it was you, Cory, because of your earring. And then I thought it was Scarlet's mom—I guess it *still* could be Scarlet's mom. Except . . . whoever it was had access to Scarlet's apartment. If Scarlet's mom really forfeited her keys, how could she have gotten inside?"

Jasmine nodded. "So what happened next?"

Delilah explained how whoever it was had led her into Scarlet's bedroom, saying that Delilah had better not throw up on the sheets. "I didn't realize it was Scarlet's condo—I just wanted to lie down. But then Scarlet came out of the bathroom and stopped at the sight of me. She was like, *What are* you *doing here?* She looked angry—I mean, obviously. I was a drunk girl lying in her bed. *And* I was cheating with her boyfriend."

"What did she say to the person who brought you in there?" Jasmine asked.

Delilah shrugged. "I don't recall. . . ."

"Did they leave?"

"I'm not sure. But I remember Scarlet having this weird look on her face. She seemed sort of . . . uneasy. Maybe even afraid."

Delilah took a deep breath. "But maybe she was afraid of *me*. I was a mess that night. Angry at Jack for lying to me . . . angry at Scarlet for being a bitch . . . but next thing I knew, I woke up, and it was morning. And Scarlet was next to me. . . ."

"You *saw* her?" Fiona cried.

Delilah ran her tongue over her teeth. "I saw her hand. Part of her hair. She wasn't moving. I didn't realize she was dead at the time—I ran out of there because I didn't want her to wake up. I didn't want to face her."

Delilah paused for a breath. Jasmine felt a stab of sympathy deep in her bones. How scary that must have been for Delilah to have found herself in that position.

"So when you ran out, you saw no one around?" Fiona asked.

"Just her mom. She came up the stairs, walked to Scarlet's door. Knocked at first, but then twisted the knob and found it open." She looked at the group. "Remember, at her house, how she said she was glad the door was open because who knows how long it would have been before someone found Scarlet's body? I don't think she was lying. She really *did* seem surprised that the door wasn't locked."

Fiona crossed her arms. "Here's what doesn't make sense. Why would someone put you in bed next to Scarlet . . . but then not come forward to ID you on the scene?"

"It's obvious," a voice said. "Because they don't want to put themselves at the scene, either."

Jack stood in the doorway, his hands in his pockets. Delilah let out a small squeak, then covered her face.

Jack stepped forward. "Someone led Delilah into that condo. There were a million other beds where she *could* have crashed—

why Scarlet's? Unless this person was planning to kill Scarlet . . . and frame Delilah. Use her insulin, even, to kill Scarlet." He looked at Delilah, who was still covering her eyes, probably both embarrassed and grateful that Jack was there. "You being diabetic isn't a secret. I reread your Instagram posts on the way over—you've posted about it a lot. Someone could have known you carried around supplies."

Delilah gulped. "I only used one dose over the course of the night. Not two."

"But who would do that?" Fiona asked. "We've ruled out so many people. Unless it's someone random. Like that Chloe girl Scarlet ruined. Or like someone else she blew off. Or maybe an über-fan who was furious that she was pregnant?"

"Not just anyone can get into Scarlet's condo, though," Jack said. "Scarlet never left her door open when there were parties at the Dove, like some people do. She was protective of her sacred space. It had to be someone who had a key."

"So who had a key?" Jasmine asked aloud. She turned to Cory. "You?"

Cory nodded. "Yeah, but I wasn't there. And I didn't give a copy to anyone."

"And Jack." Jasmine turned to him. "You had one."

"But Jack wasn't at the after-party, either," Delilah piped up.

"That's true," Jack said. "And I never let my key out of my sight."

"So who else?" Jasmine looked around. "Another friend, maybe?"

"Are you kidding?" Cory scoffed. "Scar didn't trust any of her friends except for me—not even that dog nanny. She had to buzz him in every time he came over. She only gave the key to her mom, me, and boyfriends."

Jasmine looked around. "There has to be someone else we're not thinking of."

Fiona drew in a breath. Her face had gone pale, and when she noticed everyone had turned to her, she clamped her mouth shut. "*What?*" Jasmine cried.

"I . . . I think I know someone else," Fiona said in a whisper. She was trembling suddenly. "He said he had a key. He joked about breaking into her condo since we live in the same building. . . ."

At the same time, Cory's phone bleated. He glanced at the screen, and then his mouth dropped open. "*Whoa.*"

He turned the screen to show a new video of a dark club, flashing lights, deafening techno music. A banner overhead that read *Happy Memorial Day*. Two people pressed together, their mouths close, their hands searching each other's bodies. Jasmine's heart cracked in two when she saw that one of them was definitely Scarlet. But the other—the guy. Wait, was that . . . ?

Jasmine looked up and registered the disbelief on Fiona's face. Then she stared at the video again. There, on the screen, feverishly making out with Scarlet Leigh, was Fiona's boyfriend.

Chase.

FIONA

This can't be happening. This can't be happening.

You deserve this. For what you did to Lana. You deserve a terrible boyfriend. One who cheats on you. One who murders.

Fiona sat in the back of Jasmine's car in a full-on panic attack. Every so often, the others glanced at her, making sure she was still breathing. They wanted to just take her home, but she insisted on coming with them to Disneyland's California Adventure, where Chase was spending the rest of the day with his family. She couldn't let them confront him on their own.

But Fiona had no idea what she was going to say to Chase when she saw him. How could it be possible that Chase, her sweet Chase, had done such a thing?

But some of the pieces fit. Scarlet's mother had purchased the Dove condo for Scarlet back when she was in high school—right around when Fiona met her, in fact. Scarlet used to brag about how she had her own place to shoot videos, hang with friends, and have alone time with her boyfriend—*Chase*. And then, after Fiona and Chase got together, Chase had mentioned that Scarlet had given him a key, though he'd only gone to the condo once. For whatever reason, Scarlet had never asked for the key back. Chase figured she'd forgotten.

So Chase had the means to get in.

Why, *why* had Chase made out with Scarlet? All this time, he talked about what a bitch Scarlet was, so high-maintenance, and that she made him feel so low. Was he actually pining for her? Was *he* the one who got her pregnant . . . or, well, he *thought* he got her pregnant? And then, what, he killed her so that would never come true?

And also—and this was the most infuriating part—Chase had made *Fiona* feel guilty this past week. Asking about her fight with Scarlet, implying that he knew Fiona's secret, even implying that Fiona might have killed her. Maybe he was really worried that Fiona had found out about Chase and Scarlet and *that* was why she was confronting her. It all felt so manipulative. She thought about how grateful she'd felt when he'd showed up to the set earlier today. In truth, she should have been furious.

It took an hour and a half to get to Anaheim. No one said a word as they pulled into one of the massive Disney parking lots. It was weird Delilah wasn't with them for this part of the journey. Her parents had picked her up shortly after their talk at the police station, and though Jasmine had begged them to let Delilah join, they'd said absolutely not.

Fiona's stomach turned, and she hunched over, feeling a wave of nausea. Jasmine placed her hand on her back just as the tram rolled up. "Sure you don't want to stay behind? We can handle this."

"I know you can," Fiona mustered. "But no. Actually, I want to question him myself."

Jack looked horrified. "What do you mean, *alone*?"

"This is Chase. I know him best." Fiona's mind zoomed back to the psychic at the party, when she'd said there was something terrible looming between her and Chase. Was this what she was hinting at? Yet Chase had let her think otherwise. And Fiona had felt so guilty, figuring Chase would dump her if he found out about Lana. She'd been so consumed by and ashamed of her lies, but as it turned out, Chase was lying, too.

Jasmine, who had a permanent all-access pass, had alerted the staff beforehand, and a worker waved the group in through a special entrance. Fiona wondered what they must look like, their eyes haunted, the corners of their mouths turned down. The park was crowded with happy people; Disney characters marched by, waving and clowning around. A few noticed Jasmine as she passed, and several girls squealed at Jack. "We'll be back!" Jasmine said in a surprisingly smooth, placating voice. "We just have to do some business first, but then we'll come back to pose for pictures!" It was astonishing that she could think about appeasing her fans at a time like this.

Fiona checked her phone again. She'd texted Chase that she was coming—and that they needed to talk. She knew he probably presumed she wanted to talk about what had happened this morning with Camille. He'd even cheerfully replied that he was waiting in line for the California Adventure Ferris wheel ride. *See u soon,* he added, punctuating it with a kissing-face emoji. Fiona's heart twisted; he had no idea what was coming. She almost hated to ambush him until she remembered . . . he was the one who'd ambushed her trust.

The Ferris wheel ride was just ahead. Fiona's legs trembled as she approached the FastPass line and spied Chase's tall head behind a set of ropes. Jasmine touched her shoulder, sensing her nervousness. "You don't have to do this."

"No." Fiona set her jaw. "I *do.*"

When she tapped Chase on the shoulder, he spun and broke into a happy—if concerned—smile. "Babe. You made it." And then his eyes searched her face, which must have been a death mask of terror. "A-are you okay?"

Fiona wished she could burst into tears right then and there, but too many people were watching, so she forced a smile. "I need to talk to you," she said under her breath.

Chase frowned. "What's going on?"

The tenderness in his voice was too much. Fiona desperately wanted to fall into Chase's outstretched arms like always and pretend this nightmare wasn't happening. But there was no way. She couldn't unsee that video of him with Scarlet. She couldn't unlearn the facts about what he might have done to her.

Say it! her brain screamed. *You need to say it. Get this over with.*

"You're next!" a worker called.

They were at the front of the line. Before she knew what was happening, a Disney employee was escorting Fiona and Chase into a car and shutting the gate. "Keep your seat belt fastened at all times!" he chirped, and just like that, the car lifted into the air. Fiona felt paralyzed. She hadn't actually planned on *getting on the ride*. She stared down at the ground as it receded from view. Soon enough, she could see the tops of the trees and everyone else still in line, including Jasmine, Jack, and Cory. They were staring up at her in horror. This was the worst possible scenario: she was trapped in a tiny car with a guy who might be a murderer.

Fiona sat frozen for a few beats, trying to control her breathing. Her body was pressed up against the opposite side of the car. If Chase tried to touch her, she might scream. "Babe," Chase said, his voice laced with concern. "Whatever it is, tell me."

And then, for some reason, a horrible screech sounded, and the car halted. Fiona looked around. Did the Ferris wheel always stop like this? Maybe she should wait to tell Chase when this awful ride was over.

No. She needed to tell him *now*. Before she lost her nerve.

She cleared her throat, her tear-streaked gaze fixed on the horizon. "You can't let an innocent girl go to jail, Chase. You just *can't*."

"What?" Chase's voice cracked. "What are you talking about? What innocent girl?"

Fiona's fingers fumbled for the video on her phone. She couldn't quite look at it again—seeing Chase kissing Scarlet once was enough. "What's this?" she asked coldly.

Chase's eyes went wide, and then he made a strange, gurgling noise. There was something so tense about his body suddenly, like a wire about to snap.

"I didn't . . . ," he managed to say. "How did you *get* this?"

"Does it matter?" Fiona asked, her heart cracking into a million pieces. Chase wasn't denying it. This was really him. "*Why*, Chase?"

"Look." He sounded angry now. "She was all over me. Totally into it. I didn't . . ." He held up his hands innocently, but she looked away. She wasn't going to let his I'm-the-victim act sway her.

"And then, afterward, she got this weird smile on her face and was like, *Oh, by the way, I'm not on birth control anymore. I hope I'm not pregnant, for Fiona's sake!*" He squeezed his eyes shut. "I just thought it was her being . . . *Scarlet.* She was always like that. Always hitting me where it hurt. But then, when I saw that video . . ."

"The vlog?" Fiona asked. ". . . Of her telling Jack?"

"Yeah." Chase looked away. "I watched it after you and I fought."

"You thought *I* was cheating." She laughed bitterly. "You were so worried about me cheating when it was really *you* who'd been unfaithful."

Chase set his jaw, not answering.

"You made *me* feel guilty this week," she went on. "Like I was worthless. A bad person."

"I'm sorry, Fiona." His face softened then. He looked shattered. Almost like he was going to cry. But then it hardened again. "You don't understand the kind of pressure I was under at the end of school. All those exams . . . college applications are coming up . . . and it's not like *you're* around."

"What are you talking about?" Fiona cried. "Of course I'm around!" She couldn't believe he was twisting the blame to her.

"No, you're really not," Chase said in a pouty voice. "You're always on your phone. You're always putting up content. It's all about auditions and sponsors and being photographed with the right people—you had no time for me anymore. You've changed. A lot."

Fiona gaped. Who *was* this guy? This was the first she was hearing of any of this. It made her hate him suddenly. Instead of confronting her to talk about his issues like a normal person, he'd gone behind her back and made out with a devious, triggering ex-girlfriend. It wasn't Fiona who'd changed—it was *Chase.*

The Ferris wheel was eerily silent and still. Far below, she could still see Jasmine and the others, but she couldn't make out their expressions. Cory seemed to be talking to an authoritative-looking adult. Security? What were *they* going to do, if the ride was stuck?

Then she turned back to Chase. She was all in now. She had to keep going. "What did you do to Scarlet?" she asked in a low voice.

Chase flinched. "I didn't *do* anything."

"Yes, you did." Her voice trembled. She could feel the angry tears about to cascade down her cheeks. "That wasn't the end. Tell me the truth. What did you do the night of Gratitude?"

A long silence passed. Fiona's heart was pounding. Chase didn't answer, so she decided to fill in the blanks for him. "You saw Scarlet's vlog, right? And that got you *really* scared. You couldn't have Scarlet pregnant with your baby. Not with *college applications.*" She stretched the words out nastily, throwing them back in his face. "So what did you do, Chase? Did you find her? Kill her?"

"No!" Chase's eyes flashed. "I just wanted . . . I just wanted to end it. I knew that's what she wanted, too. So I went to my mom's practice. Down the street from the Dove. I had my key."

"What did you want *there*?" Fiona asked, momentarily confused.

"I wanted . . . Plan B." He lowered his eyes. "I thought I was doing Scarlet a favor." He swallowed nervously. "I was *trying* to help."

Fiona sucked in a breath. "What did you do?"

"I went back to the party. And ran into Scarlet in the hallway. She seemed really impatient. Kept saying she needed to find someone." He ran a hand through his hair. "She was looking for Jasmine—she said so. But I forced her to stop. I made her look at me. I asked if the pregnancy thing was true. She just brushed me off, being like, *We're done here, Chase.* And then . . . I felt desperate. I thrust the water bottle at her—I'd crushed up a couple of Plan B pills in there. And I was like, *You look thirsty.* She seemed grateful. Said thanks. She drank it all. After, she looked at me and was wondering why I was watching so intently, and . . . then, well, it all sort of spilled out."

"You told her?" Fiona asked, her mind spinning. Did she know Chase at *all*?

Someone in a car above them banged on the metal grate with their hand. "Uh, hello?" a voice screamed. And someone else cried: "Are we really *stuck*?" A nearby car swung wildly, like it might snap.

"I felt bad, so it all just came tumbling out," Chase admitted under his breath. "And Scarlet freaked. She was like, *Holy shit, I'm not actually pregnant, you asshole, what is this stuff going to do to me?* So then, of course, I panicked, too. I told her to try to throw up the water. Scarlet headed toward her condo, saying that if she was going to have some sort of reaction, she wanted to do it in private. I still had her key on my ring. I opened the door for her. Walked her to her bed."

Fiona's heart pounded. "A-and then what?"

"She made me leave. She was furious. Kept saying that with her hormonal problems, this might kill her." Suddenly, his features crumbled. "And it *did*."

He pressed his hands into his face and let out a tormented sob. Fiona felt the natural, automatic pull of wanting to comfort him—hours ago, it would have been second nature. But she stayed rooted to her spot in the car, vibrating with confusion and shock and fury.

"I'm going to have to tell the police, Chase," she said after a moment.

"No." His head whipped up. "You can't. It was an accident. I—I was only telling you because I *trust* you. But . . . but you have no proof except what I told you. I mean . . ." His eyes searched hers. He sat back, a look of realization washing over his face. "You *do* have proof, don't you. You recorded this."

Fiona's fingers curled around the second phone in her pocket—Cory's. He'd slipped it to her just before she'd run for Chase on the ground. On it, a video was running. "I—I had to," she admitted, her eyes clouding with tears.

Before she knew what was happening, Chase lunged for her. "Give me the recording."

"No!" Fiona cried, twisting her body away.

He pressed hard against her chest, using it as leverage. "*Give* it to me. You don't *understand*."

Fiona elbowed his chest. Swatted his hands. "Get away from me. Get *off*."

"You can't tell anyone about this," he pleaded. "My life will be over."

"You should have thought about that before!" Fiona screamed.

Her voice echoed. She could tell that the other people around her were listening in. "Yo!" a voice called out. "Are you okay down there?"

"No!" Fiona wailed, kicking Chase off her. "Help!"

But what was there to do? The ride was stuck. She had nowhere to go. Chase had a deadly look in his eye—maybe the same look he had when he gave Scarlet the cocktail that killed her. Was Fiona next? Was this how she was going to die, suspended in this tiny car at California Adventure?

He advanced toward her again, and she shoved him back. He slammed against the side of the car, but rebounded quickly, throwing himself on top of her.

"Are you really going to be like this?" he asked. "Just give me the phone."

Fiona shut her eyes. It hit her: this was how she felt when she was on that roof with Lana. And suddenly, a new memory snapped into place, a blank she'd skipped over in her recollection of that horrible evening. She envisioned Lana standing opposite her on the roof. Taunting Fiona. Telling her she was a loser. And she saw herself, telling Lana that she knew Lana hurt Zoey. *I know because I gave you the idea,* she said. *I'm going to tell everyone.*

No, you won't, Lana said, snickering. *Because that'll get you in trouble, too.*

I don't care, Fiona said. *I just want the truth to come out. For people to understand what a witch you are.*

Lana charged at her with a look like she wanted to destroy her. The sudden, unexpected memory took Fiona's breath away. She shoved Lana back—shoved her over the edge—but it wasn't out of pure hatred and murderousness. It was in defense. Fiona was afraid Lana was going to do to her what she'd done to Zoey. That was all.

Chase pressed against her, holding her arms still. Panic radiated from his pores. "Please," Fiona whispered. "Please, Chase. It's me. It's still me."

"And I'm still me. Give me the phone."

But suddenly, there was a loud *clank,* and the car jerked downward. The force threw them both backward hard, and Chase's head hit the metal cage with a loud *thud.* His body crumpled. Fiona scrambled to her side, eyeing him cautiously. Someone must have reported her peril, because their car went express all the way to the exit point. As soon as it stopped, Disney employees, including a few burly-looking guards, rushed over and lifted up the safety bar. Fiona spilled out, climbing over Chase's limp, dazed body, desperate to be away from him.

Jasmine pushed through the onlookers to find her. "Are you okay?" she cried, holding her tightly.

Fiona nodded, but she could feel the tears spilling down her cheeks. "I got it," she whispered. "He told me everything."

Jasmine's face broke. "I'm so sorry."

"I know. Me too." She remembered what else had happened up there, amid the fear and heartbreak and shock of it all—that missing Lana memory. Could it be? Was what happened to Lana not entirely her fault? All these years, had she felt guilty about a crime she didn't really commit?

She wiped the tears from her face as she staggered toward the exit. Behind them, the Disney security and EMTs dragged Chase from the Ferris wheel car. Fiona was certain that on the other side of the park gates, police officers would be waiting, wanting to talk to her. She was ready. Maybe she'd even tell them about Lana. She could start over completely, with a clear conscience.

It was only then that she noticed the line of people gawking at her from the sidelines. "Fiona!" they screamed. "Jasmine!" "Can we take a selfie?"

Jasmine glanced at the crowd, smiling tensely. "Now isn't a good time, guys. Sorry."

"Actually, it's okay." Fiona ran her finger under her bottom eyelid to catch any smudged mascara. "Maybe just one, Jasmine."

And so she, Jasmine, Cory, and Jack, who'd fallen into step with them, posed next to the fans. Fiona tried her best to smile. And suddenly, she realized: someday—not soon, but someday—things might be okay again. Because if she could take a selfie *now*, she must not be that far gone.

DELILAH

"Wow," Delilah said to Jasmine on the phone as she paced her bedroom. All day, she hadn't been permitted her phone, but her parents had allowed this one exception. "Chase gave Scarlet an overdose of Plan B. That's kind of . . . insane."

"He told Fiona everything. She has it all on video. The police have him in custody. Which means they'll probably be calling you soon. You're off the hook."

"That's great," Delilah murmured. There was a lump in her throat as she sat down on her bed. "Th-thank you, Jazz. For believing in me." Seeing Jasmine and the others at the police station was the last thing Delilah expected. But then they'd gone all the way to Disneyland and Fiona had risked her life to clear Delilah's name? *Those* were true friends.

She hung up and sat quietly for a moment. Soon enough, she'd go out and tell her worried, stressed, probably-preparing-to-move-back-to-Minnesota parents the news, but she wanted to process it first. So it was Chase who walked her into Scarlet's apartment, then. So it was Chase who had access to Scarlet's place. Chase had hooked up with Scarlet recently, which gave him motive to want to get rid of Scarlet's baby. He was worried Scarlet's pregnancy vlog was true. He was worried he was the father. But he needed to frame someone for what he was about to do, so he laid Delilah—who *also* had a motive—in Scarlet's bed, knowing she'd pass out and wake up next to a dead body. He was banking on someone seeing. And *telling*. And he'd be off the hook.

It was a neatly tied-up story. The only problem was that it didn't feel quite right. In those blurry memories, Delilah kept seeing a glint of metal. Over and over again, that white gold winked at her, the most striking detail in the whole scene. She didn't recall Chase wearing any jewelry—not even a watch. It bothered her.

That doesn't matter, Delilah told herself. That night was so fuzzy. It was a wonder she remembered anything at all. Who cared if a detail didn't match up? People remembered things incorrectly all the time. Chase had confessed. And who cared that his story didn't account for that second vial of insulin that had gone missing? Delilah had probably just dropped it somewhere. Did this also mean Chase was the person sending those videos to people, trying to divert the attention from himself? Had he sent her that DM, too? It was heartbreaking that this was Fiona's boyfriend.

She wriggled off the bed and opened the door. In the living room, she was startled to see two police officers sitting on the wing chairs, speaking to her parents. "Oh," she said, stopping short. "Uh, hi."

Her mom rose. "Honey. These detectives stopped by to tell us about that boy's confession."

Delilah nodded. "Yeah. I just heard, too."

One of the officers, a short, stocky man with kind eyes, turned to her, his hands clasped at his waist. "You remember Chase McGeehan walking you into Scarlet's bedroom? This all fits in your recollection of the evening?"

Delilah nodded woodenly. But *did* it? If only her brain could give her a clear yes or no.

She glanced at her parents. "Can I get a drink of water? I'll be right back."

Bethany frowned at the officers, but they nodded. "Of course," said the second one, a woman. "Take your time."

Delilah's legs felt like noodles as she stepped into the kitchen and turned on the tap. Her head was spinning. She almost felt on the verge of panic. What was *wrong* with her? Why couldn't she just be okay with the answer everyone wanted?

She filled a glass to the very top. The liquid was cold as it streamed down her throat, and she shut her eyes, trying to settle. But it felt like there were insects crawling along her skin. Her heart was on fire.

And then she heard a scuffling sound by the table.

She whipped around. Ava and Faith were sitting quietly in the corner, staring at Delilah with wide, scared eyes. "Jeez!" Delilah cried, nearly dropping her glass. "W-what are you guys doing?"

Ava's gaze slid to the door that led to the living room. "Because the police," she whispered. "There's never been police in our house before. Is it because of you?"

"Actually, no," Delilah said. "I'm fine. This other person, he . . ."

But then a crack formed in her brain. She stared hard at Faith, sitting so mouselike and still on the other chair. Something bright glinted at her sister's friend's throat. A white-gold cross, as shiny as the sun. It obliterated all thoughts in Delilah's head. She fixated on the gold until her eyes crossed. And then she saw a flash from the after-party: *Can I just tell you I love you so much?* It was a voice. A *girl's* voice.

What are you doing here? Delilah remembered slurring. The world wobbled. The light was too bright. The music was too loud. An open, eager face stared at her, seemingly appearing from out of nowhere. *What are you . . . ?* Delilah asked, startled. But then she lost her balance. Leaned against a wall that wasn't there, started giggling.

Oops! The person reached out and grabbed Delilah's arm. *Here, let me help you up.*

"Lila?" Ava's voice cut through the jagged memory. "What's the matter?"

Delilah snapped back to earth. Faith was now staring at her, her skin even paler than usual, her freckles in startling relief. "Oh my God," Delilah whispered, pointing a shaky finger at her.

"What?" Ava's head swiveled from Delilah to Faith. "Oh my God, *what?*"

That voice echoed back. *I just love you so much. I just hate what people say about you. And especially this Jacklet thing, it's so cruel, you know?*

But Delilah was so drunk. She could hardly track the

conversation, much less answer. *I don't feel so good,* her own voice wafted back, suddenly clear.

And then that second voice again: *Maybe you should lie down.* Ahead of them: a blurry condo door, slightly ajar. A peal of laughter in the distance. Thumping bass. *Here,* the voice said, leading her inside.

The door opened. Delilah's head lolled. The carpets were white. Furniture, too. "Beautiful," she heard herself say. She felt pulled along, her feet useless beneath her. *Aha,* the voice said. *Just don't puke on her sheets, okay?*

Just like that, Delilah was horizontal. Her head spun. She couldn't figure out if it felt better to be lying down or worse, but it did feel good to close her eyes.

Then a gasp forced her back to consciousness. A figure stood in the doorway. Scarlet Leigh.

Scarlet glared, astonished. *What are* you *doing here?*

Delilah moaned in answer. Scarlet looked at the person who'd walked Delilah in. Her expression warped. She looked afraid. *Who are you?* she asked.

But the person just smiled. *Faith* just smiled.

A sharp *crack* jolted Delilah back to the present once more. She breathed in, about to say what she'd realized, but then Faith was on her feet, moving to Delilah so quickly that Delilah didn't even have time to get away. Faith clapped a hand over Delilah's mouth. "Don't say a word," she whispered, her palm clammy, her breath hot in Delilah's ear.

"Faith!" Ava leaped up, too. "What are you doing?"

"*Shhh!*" Faith said. She made swishing motions with her

hands, gesturing for Ava to sit back down. Then she turned back to Delilah. "We were just trying to *help* you, Delilah. We didn't want her to hurt you anymore."

"Wait, what?" Ava looked confused—and afraid. "*We* were trying to help her—how?"

Faith glared at Ava. "You're the one who was worried first. All those angry anti-Delilah fans. All those horrible Jacklet people who said they wanted Scarlet dead. How can people be like that? They should be ashamed!"

Ava's gaze darted from Faith to Delilah. "I don't . . . ," she cried, then sank back into a chair. "Faith. What did you do?"

Delilah turned back to Faith. *What are you doing here?* she'd asked her at the party. She wriggled from Faith's grasp so she could speak. "H-how did you get into the after-party?" she whispered. "How did you know where to find us?"

Faith shrugged. "The security wasn't that tight. And anyway, I was determined. After that video—I was afraid for you." She raised an eyebrow at Ava. "We were *both* afraid, weren't we?"

But Ava shook her head. "I—I have no idea what she's talking about!"

"We talked about getting rid of Scarlet." Faith said this part so quietly, her gaze sliding toward the cops in the next room. "She was going to hurt Delilah. We *both* agreed."

"You used my insulin?" Delilah guessed. "That's what killed her—not the Plan B?"

Faith's eyes flashed. She clapped her hand over Delilah's mouth again, then set her jaw. "I didn't mean for you to stay there overnight. I tried to get you out of there after it was done.

But you wouldn't budge. So I planned to get you the next day. Early. But you woke up before me. Ran out. And then it all just went downhill."

"Wait a minute." Ava had her hands pressed to the sides of her head. "What is *happening*?"

Faith gave her a sharp look, then turned back to Delilah. "Don't punish me for caring about you. The world is a better place without Scarlet. You have to believe that."

At the table, Ava broke down into silent, stunned, breathy sobs. Delilah stood stock-still, Faith pulsating close, her palm clapped over Delilah's mouth once more. The memories kept rushing back, stronger now: Faith's slender form darting through the party, heading right for her. Faith nudging the door to Scarlet's apartment open with her hip, saying, "Huh! Here's one that's unlocked!" Faith's eyes widening when she realized she'd taken Delilah to *Scarlet's* apartment—so maybe that part wasn't planned, or maybe Faith was only pretending. Faith rounding on Scarlet when Scarlet emerged from the bathroom, Faith's fists balled, her shoulders squared, ready for battle.

This memory felt right. Delilah shut her eyes, starting to tremble. Slowly, carefully, she unwound Faith's thin fingers from her mouth and turned to the girl, mustering up all her courage. "I am so, so grateful I have such faithful fans like you," she said sadly. "But I still have to turn you in."

Two weeks later

JASMINE

Jasmine's hands shook as she switched her phone back on. She'd turned it off after she'd made the post—the most important post of her life—and for three hours, she hadn't been ready to see the comments. But she'd done a lot of deep breathing. A lot of meditating on the belief that whatever people said, it wouldn't change who she was. She was scared, but she was ready.

The week before, after Scarlet's autopsy results reported that she'd been poisoned by a fatal dose of insulin; after Faith was taken into custody; after Chase was let go but then subsequently arrested because Scarlet's mother was so outraged he'd given her daughter Plan B that she'd decided to press criminal charges; after Delilah was cleared; and after Scarlet's case was closed, Jasmine had decided she was done with all the hiding, lying, and deception. She wanted people to know her, *all* of her. When she'd talked to her agents about it, they'd warned her that not everyone was going to be supportive, and that it was inevitable that some hate would flood her comments and DMs. That she might even lose sponsorships and opportunities.

But she'd countered with the fact that she'd be helping people, showing them that they're not weird or different, but most importantly, she'd be showing them that they're not alone.

The post she'd made before shutting off her phone and going into panic mode was a simple selfie of Jasmine with no makeup, wearing a plain black tank top. The caption read: *Recent events have shown that there is no good in hiding who we are on social media. Yes, I'm Lulu C, rainbows and lace and all that. But I'm also Jasmine Walters-Diaz. I love curling up with a good book, my favorite color is maroon, I'm god-awful at math, horror is my favorite genre, and I'm gay. Influencer or not, we're all just people. People who need to embrace who we are, and not hide our identities behind a screen. Scarlet Leigh taught me that, and now I pass her advice on to you. Embrace who you are, not who the internet wants you to be.*

Now, her phone back on, she watched as her home page popped up. Notifications rolled in. Nervously, she tapped Instagram. Time to face the music.

Whoa.

In just three hours, the post had over seven million likes, two million comments, and more re-shares than she could count. "Oh my God," Jasmine whispered, feeling a combination of relief, disbelief, and faith in the goodness of humanity. Different celebrities were tweeting at her, showing their support. News outlets had written a story about it. Her publicist just texted: Cosmo *wants you to be their next cover star!* There was even a hashtag, #Embrace, and others were posting their most natural selfies and telling their followers unknown facts about themselves. And sure, there were some hateful comments, but they didn't sting as bad as she thought they would.

Because now she was free. Free to be Jasmine 2.0, no longer pigeonholed, no longer silenced, no longer trapped.

The doorbell chimed. Jasmine opened it to find Delilah's and Fiona's smiling faces. Before she could get a word out, they wrapped her in a hug. "We're so proud of you," Fiona gushed.

Delilah's hand slipped into Jasmine's. "Agreed."

Jasmine hugged back. "I don't know what I'd do without you two. Seriously. I have no idea where I'd be if I didn't have your support."

The girls migrated to a coffee shop called Alfred's. Jasmine liked the place because every month, the proprietors got interesting artists to design new coffee sleeves that were aesthetic and mega-postable. This month, the coffee sleeve read, in a comic strip font, *Girl Power.* At first, Jasmine took a picture of it for her Story. Then she studied it for a long time, feeling a pull of sadness. It kind of reminded her of Scarlet.

Over the past few weeks, she'd had to revise her idea of Scarlet Leigh so many times. A jealous rival. An enigma. Her future. A pregnant teen. A tragedy. A con artist. A victim. Scarlet had become larger than life in Jasmine's mind, but that distanced Jasmine from what happened between them on that magical night at the party. Maybe she also felt distanced because there was no *after* for them. There were no last words. There was no *Wait, what did you* mean *by that?* Jasmine never got an answer as to why Scarlet left her when Cory came looking. She presumed it was because Cory mentioned that Scarlet's mother was there—Scarlet clearly felt beholden to her. And Jasmine did have it confirmed—

from Chase, of all people—that when he intercepted Scarlet—a thought that made Jasmine cringe—she'd told him, tersely, to leave her alone. "I'm looking for Jasmine," she'd explained.

But Scarlet never found Jasmine again that night. And though Jasmine held out hope that Scarlet's death was a ruse—she never did get to the bottom of who was in Scarlet's apartment, though Scarlet's mother said it may have been a cleaning person, or the real estate agent, assessing the property for sale—Scarlet had a burial plot now. There was somewhere Jasmine could physically go to *see* her, on a pretty slope of grass not far from the ocean. So now, she had to let her go.

But this didn't fill her with the same sort of despair as it did just a few weeks ago. Maybe because of the post she'd just made. She'd finally climbed that mountain, and now she was on the other side. She loved kissing Scarlet, and she loved the doors Scarlet had opened in her heart and mind, but it wasn't as if she actually *knew* Scarlet. Maybe no one really did.

But there would be someone new that Jasmine *would* know—completely. She could feel it coming. It was like how, at the beginning of her time on TV, when she'd do press in New York City, and she'd insist on taking the subway because she didn't want to be a fancy diva, you could tell when the train was coming before it appeared in the tunnel just by a shift in the air. Great things were coming, and her life was going to be anything she wanted it to be, because now it was really and truly up to her.

Her phone chirped as she walked to the little table Fiona had chosen. To Jasmine's astonishment, Ruby's name popped up on the caller ID. "H-hey," she stammered, nearly dropping her latte. This was the first time she'd heard from Ruby in months. "H-how are you?"

"I saw your post." Ruby's tone was neutral, giving nothing away.

"Oh," Jasmine answered. There was a ball in her throat. She felt nervous about the long silence on the other end of the line. Was Ruby judging her? Was Ruby *mad*?

But then Ruby said, "Actually, I'm, um, outside the coffee shop. I kind of stalked your Story and tracked you down. Can we talk?"

Startled, Jasmine peered out the plate-glass windows. Sure enough, Ruby was standing on the sidewalk, her cell phone pressed to her ear. "Sure," Jasmine spluttered. "Come on in."

She watched, chest jumping, as Ruby opened the door and wove through the crowd toward her. Her sister looked mostly the same as when Jasmine had seen her last. She was in her usual athleisure uniform, and her hair was pulled back from her face, and she was wearing too much ChapStick—but there was also a rested quality about her that was new. She looked . . . unstressed, actually. Chill.

"Hi," Jasmine said shakily as Ruby reached their table.

"Hey." Ruby's mouth twitched. But then, suddenly, she reached down and gave Jasmine a huge hug. "I'm proud of you."

Jasmine was so shocked, at first she just sat there. "You are?"

Ruby pulled away and looked at her. "You tried to tell me. I didn't listen. But I'm glad you figured out what to write on your own without a team telling you what to do. It's good that you didn't have a million people in your ear. That's probably why you got so much of a response. People can tell that it was all you."

"I wasn't doing it to get a zillion responses," Jasmine explained. "Not everything I do is for the public."

"I know." Ruby picked up her phone and started tapping the screen. Suddenly, Jasmine felt the old, stressful knot in her stomach—business, *now*? Sure enough, she showed Jasmine an email. Jasmine turned away.

"Oh, don't be like that." There was a hint of amusement in her voice. "I think this is an email you're going to want to see."

Jasmine peeked at the screen. The email was from someone called Jane Sullivan—which sounded familiar. Wasn't that the head of DC Films? *Haven't heard from you, but we have a part in mind for Jasmine in our latest Catwoman remake,* it read. *She'll have to do a screen test, but it's really just protocol. She's who we really want, especially in light of her latest Instagram post, so consider this a semi-formal offer.*

"*Catwoman?*" Jasmine blurted out.

Ruby grinned. "I got this twenty minutes ago. The part sounds awesome—you'd be a badass villain. And you *seduce* Catwoman. I guess they figured I was still your manager, which is why they sent this to me." She ducks her head. "I also may have put your name in the hat."

Jasmine blinked. That call she'd had with Kim a little while ago, talking about new parts. The one she thought *Scarlet* had arranged. That was Ruby's doing?

Of course it was. Ruby wasn't working for her then, Ruby wasn't even *speaking* to her, but she still had her back. Jasmine thought she might cry.

She gaped at Ruby. "D-do you think I should do it?"

"Well, it's a total one-eighty from Lulu C, so from that perspective, it's a no-brainer, considering how much you've complained lately," Ruby said with a smirk. "However, it shoots in Berlin. For three months. It starts in two weeks."

Jasmine turned to her best friends. *Three months*? She still felt so fragile after everything that had happened. Was she really ready to be in a strange city, alone?

"I got them to sweeten the deal," Ruby added, pulling something out of her pocket. She handed two plane tickets to Fiona and Delilah. The girls stared at them, puzzled.

Ruby looked at Jasmine. "I figured you'd need your friends with you for at least the first two weeks. The studio paid for everything—flights, accommodations. You'll have a great time."

Delilah and Fiona squealed. Jasmine was so overwhelmed she needed to sit down. "B-but what about Mom and Dad?" she said. "If I start doing movies that aren't on-brand with Lulu, the company will probably phase out my merch deals. All that money went to our parents."

Ruby shrugged. "I explained it to them. They get that you need to grow. So don't worry. They have money invested, and also—I think they can live a little more simply, if it comes to that. They'd rather do that than for you to be miserable." Then she paused. "Well. Abuela probably wouldn't care. Her life revolves around that stupid dog." She rolled her eyes.

"Don't throw shade at Snuffy!" Jasmine cried. "It's not *his* fault his owner is a cranky old lady!"

They dissolved into giggles. And suddenly, Jasmine could picture it: the next time she and Ruby went out to visit their parents, they'd go together. They'd make the same old bets they used to. They'd nudge each other behind their parents' backs. They would be a team again.

"Ruby." She felt grateful tears come to her eyes. "*Thank* you."

Ruby shrugged in that flinty way that was so characteristically *her*. "Well, you're going to have to confirm with your agent yourself." She flipped her hand. "As I'm not your manager."

"Oh Ruby," Jasmine said, flinging her arms around her sister's bony shoulders. Ruby had her same smells—cocoa butter, new-car leather, the sweet, minty gum from the organic store she [illegible]ed with—and it filled Jasmine with such nostalgia and love and *rightness*, she dropped to her knees on the dirty coffee shop floor. "Please come back and work for me. Work *with* me. I miss you so much."

Ruby laughed. "But look. I wouldn't be able to control your every move anymore. I can't handle that."

"That's wonderful!" Jasmine said. "I would *prefer* that! So please? *Please?*"

Ruby pretended to think about it, then rolled her eyes. "Fine," she said, mock-exasperated. "Now, get up off your knees before you get e. coli!"

The whole store had turned to look at Jasmine kneeling in front of her sister, but Jasmine didn't care. She felt blissed out, totally at peace. And she realized: right here, in this little coffee shop, she felt like *herself*. Not Lulu C. Not "Instagram Jasmine." Not "Lemonade Jasmine" or even "*Catwoman* Jasmine." Just . . . Jasmine.

And that felt like more than enough.

FIONA

The following morning, Fiona plopped into the driver's seat of her car and started to type an address into GPS. *One hour, thirty-four minutes,* read the display. She swallowed hard. She really dreaded this trip . . . but it was one she needed to make.

She peered into the rearview mirror, but it was only after a few moments that she realized who she was looking for, out of force of habit. But of course Chase wasn't coming. Chase was on house arrest. Chase was trying to put his life back together, something Fiona couldn't be part of because, well, he'd hurt her too badly.

And, well, she was working through that. It was probably better that she was going alone, anyway. First, she was going to the Hedges family house to talk to Lana's parents. The Hedgeses had insisted Fiona didn't have to come all the way out here—she'd already spoken to them about Lana over the phone, telling them about that night on the roof, and though at first they'd been shocked—and a little upset that Fiona hadn't confessed sooner—they'd assured her that it wasn't her fault, that they fully acknowledged that their daughter, though they loved her, was cruel. They brought up Fiona's busy schedule, too—miraculously, she hadn't been fired from *Like Me*, and her outburst even earned the show a cheeky, meta sort of notoriety that gave them a big bump in advertisers and pre-premiere chatter online. The Hedgeses didn't want to overburden her. But at the same time, Fiona heard longing in Mrs. Hedges's voice. "Of course, if you *do* want to visit, we'll make you dinner. It's not often we have a celebrity come over."

So that was what she was doing now. Driving to Orange County, where she was going to have dinner with the family of the girl Fiona was convinced she'd murdered. *And* Camille, too—who'd come home after Fiona practically attacked her at the studio. Fiona didn't expect it would be a relaxing event, but it would put her mind at ease and her guilt to rest.

And it didn't stop there, either: after talking to the Hedgeses, she was going to have coffee with Zoey Marx. Fiona had finally gotten up the courage to look up Zoey on social media the other day after years of avoiding it, certain that Zoey would either have no presence or a page so sad and despondent that it would fill her with shame. To her surprise, Zoey was . . . okay. She was in her second year at Stanford, having graduated high school two years early. Tech companies were already grooming her. It didn't seem to matter that she could no longer play the cello—she'd bounced back and found a new path. In fact, her presence online was impressive—she took a lot of interesting shots of graffiti, and it seemed like every night, she was out to dinner with friends.

Unlike the Hedgeses, Fiona hadn't told Zoey the nature of their coffee date yet—she bet Zoey was a little weirded out that Fiona had pushed to meet. At first, Fiona had composed a variety of texts, trying to explain it, but none sounded right. She just needed to do it in person. But she dreaded Zoey's reaction. Zoey could freak. It could trigger something in Zoey that would send her into a downward spiral of PTSD. Fiona wouldn't admit the part she played in Zoey's bullying if it was going to ruin Zoey. She'd have to gauge what she said and didn't say at game time, probably. But again, she had to try.

"Turn right," instructed the GPS, and Fiona did. A text pinged through from her mom, then her dad. They were probably just *drive safe* messages. Her parents thought she was nuts for driving all the way to Orange County just to revisit her past. They also thought she was nuts for keeping what she had inside for so long. "If you'd explored that night with a psychologist, you would have come to the conclusion much sooner that it wasn't your fault," her mother bemoaned. "I just hate that you've wasted so much time feeling guilty and ashamed."

But it wasn't like they'd been in Fiona's position. The secret was so big and scary, of course it destroyed her, and the longer she kept quiet, the worse it became. Funny, though: since Fiona had that breakthrough memory—of Lana pushing her first, of Lana lashing out with all of her venom and fire—the Voice had withered away. Fiona still had compulsions, but she was starting to understand that those things could be managed, especially with therapy and medication. Mona and the other producers and execs on *Like Me* had been extremely understanding, too. "Oh my God, I had a bully," Mona sighed the day she brought Fiona into her office to chat after Fiona's meltdown. "Her name was Carla Wiggins. I still think of that bitch after forty years."

They were, more or less, shooting around Fiona's schedule—so she could leave for psych appointments, and she had a massage therapist on call, and they were making sure not to give her any über-late nights, so she could rest. It felt like an embarrassment of riches. An undeserved gift. But then, maybe that sort of thinking was the *old* Fiona—the one ruled by the Voice. And this Fiona? She was trying to see that she was worth it.

Out of habit, when she passed the turnoff to Camarosa Drive, where Chase lived, she glanced to the right toward Chase's house, as if Chase was going to be standing on the sidewalk, waiting for her. Of course he wasn't. She bit her lip hard, once again grappling with what had happened. It was hard to accept that Chase had had a private, complicated world that Fiona had no knowledge of. And also, he'd been so *angry* with Fiona. Resentful of her time away. Bitter about all the time she spent on social and auditioning. She'd had absolutely no inkling—it was eerie, how well Chase had stuffed that down inside him. Until, well, it had all come exploding out.

Eventually, the 101 highway turned into the 5. As she changed lanes, the traffic moving at a glacial pace, she suddenly had the urge to make a post. Fiona hadn't posted quite as much lately—she'd been so busy with *Like Me*, and she hadn't felt the urge. But today, she wanted to let her fans know she was okay. *Fans.* It was such a silly term, wasn't it? It wasn't like they knew her. Did they look at Fiona and see . . . what? A pretty girl? A girl who had it all? A girl whose life was aspirational? It was how Fiona used to view her Instagram idols. But was that a healthy way to live? Was that a realistic ideal to aspire to?

With traffic at a standstill, she turned the camera on herself. The sun glare was in her eyes, and she was wearing very little makeup, and normally, if she saw this version of herself on the screen, she would delete it—or, at the very least, run it through a filter that washed out all her imperfections. But she was driving—she couldn't take her eyes off the road. And also? Who cared if she had imperfections? Who cared if this post wasn't filtered within an inch of its life? It was *okay.*

Stuck in traffic, along with 2 million other Angelinos! Fiona dictated into the phone, and the caption appeared under her picture. Glancing at the screen at a dead stop at a merge point, she pressed POST. And suddenly, the image was up. Squinty Fiona. With a zit on her chin. And pale eyelashes. And slightly greasy hair. And a terrible angle. And a little bit of red-eye.

Totally, totally what she was going for.

Late August

DELILAH

"Welcome, incoming class of Ventura Heights High School!" a petite, peppy woman with pink streaks in her hair boomed as she walked backward across a pristine green lawn. "My name is Marjorie, and I can't wait to show you around our beautiful campus!"

Delilah glanced at Ava, who was wearing a yellow name tag with her name and the letter *F*, which indicated she was an incoming freshman. Similarly, Delilah's yellow name tag had a swirly *J* at the bottom—junior. It was unthinkable that she was only two years away from college. It was unfathomable that she was going to full-time high school, considering what she *thought* she'd be doing in September.

Just then, she heard whispers. Three girls also on the tour snuck peeks in Delilah's direction. As they walked across the grounds, Marjorie blathering about how the turf on the lawn wasn't actually grass but some sort of eco-friendly, biodegradable product made out of recycled water bottles, one of the girls got the courage to come up to Delilah's side. "Excuse me?" she whispered. She was athletic and Korean; her name tag read *Katie*. "But you aren't Lila D, are you?"

"I am," Delilah said, a little sheepishly—and under her breath, so she didn't cause a scene.

The girls' eyes boggled. "You're *going* here?" a second girl, whose name tag read *Olive*, gasped. Delilah noticed they both had *F*s on their name tags, like Ava. "I thought you were in Berlin with Jasmine Walters-Diaz!"

"I was," Delilah admitted. "And it was amazing. But I have school now."

Acquiescing to full-time high school wasn't really a choice for Delilah—it was more of a decision she'd had to make in order to keep her family from spontaneously combusting. There was no way, after everything went down with Scarlet and the police and, worst of all, Faith, that Delilah's parents would allow her to do online school and go whole-hog down the influencer path.

Her parents really had tried to hear both sides, though. They'd spoken to Faith's parents and understood that Faith had always been overly anxious, and that she sometimes had trouble differentiating between fact and fiction—though they'd *never* expected she'd do something like what she'd done to Scarlet. Delilah's parents had also read articles and Congressional testimony about online bullying and how social networks needed to make better efforts to protect their users. Conversely, they'd spoken to several managers and lawyers and other parents who had children in the influencing game—and asked how they stayed sane and grounded, and how they prepared for the future, and how they kept some semblance of privacy. But in the end, what had happened with Scarlet had scarred them badly. There really was no choice.

And to be honest? Delilah hadn't fought that hard for online school, either. Her parents' decision stung, sure, and she didn't relish the idea of regular school hours, but she was shaken by what had happened this summer, too. She still couldn't quite wrap her mind around the fact that Faith, who was more or less a stranger—but also someone that her little sister had come to trust—had obsessed over Delilah so intensely, she'd *killed* for her. And that Faith had also gathered damning evidence against a whole bunch of other people, including Delilah's friends, to throw the cops off the scent of herself *and* Delilah, her biggest fan. And finally? That Faith had even threatened *Delilah* in that DM, telling her to stop digging. Faith must have done that because she was beginning to realize Delilah was getting closer to the truth. She was running out of options.

A month ago, Delilah and Ava had visited Faith at the children's psychiatric hospital where she was being treated. Delilah hadn't wanted to go, but Ava needed closure with Faith, and it was clear she didn't feel strong enough to go by herself, so she'd mustered up the courage. Most of the time, Delilah had stood in the back of Faith's little room, arms crossed over her chest. But she had managed to ask one question: *Why*? Why would she sacrifice her life for something so silly? And Faith, bewildered, had answered, "Because it just isn't *fair*, the things people say about people online. Scarlet needed to go away." What if Faith's alliances had been elsewhere? What if it had been Scarlet she loved . . . and Delilah she hated? Would Delilah be dead now instead? And did Delilah want to live in a world where she regularly feared that happening?

She didn't think so. She didn't want her dumb mistakes to create seismic shifts in the universe. Or her flirtations with boys to cause a domino effect felt around the planet. She wanted to accidentally flirt with other people's boyfriends without it becoming something shippers considered committing murder over. In fact, she'd rather people didn't track her flirtations at all.

She did want to keep her account active, though—she still liked posting about animals, diabetes, and anti-bullying. And, crazily enough, in the wake of the Scarlet stuff and after the Jacklet hate died down, she was kind of a hot commodity. So her parents offered her a deal: if she went to regular school, they'd get her a part-time manager. They found a normal person named Gloria, who promised she wasn't going to push Delilah into intense commitments or send her on auditions or force her to be a brand and only a brand. Gloria was a mom, too, and she was willing to work around Delilah's schedule, and the opportunities she'd found for Delilah so far were age-appropriate, scandal-free, and refreshingly low-key.

It was all going okay. Certainly better than the roller coaster she'd *been* on.

Another girl moved closer. She was tall, with honey-blond hair styled to perfection, and her name tag read *Romy*. "So have you seen that post?" she asked Delilah.

Delilah licked her lips, then nodded. There was no question which *post* this girl meant. "What do you think of it?" Romy whispered.

Delilah inhaled sharply. The other day, on Instagram, a new

photo had popped up on Scarlet Leigh's official account. It had stopped the whole world in its tracks. It was a blurry, unreleased shot of Scarlet at Gratitude Prom—Delilah knew Scarlet's gown instantly. And the caption read: *What happened at Gratitude was not in my plans. You see, in my world, we planned things very carefully. Everything we did, every move, every smile, every word out of our mouths—it was crafted. We showed you only what we wanted you to see. And, okay, a few things leaked recently that surprised you. But it was fine. I don't know about everyone else, but I had my life under control.*

Or did I?

Scarlet went on for a while, talking about Gratitude, and how she felt worried at the end of the night, though she didn't explain why. Instagram exploded, naturally. *What is this?* fans raged. *How dare you hack her account!* But there were also the believers that Scarlet wrote the post—and Scarlet was still alive. After all, Scarlet's Instagram had been "memorialized"—Scarlet's mother had told E! that she'd done so herself. When an account was memorialized, nothing could be changed on it—no new posts, no edits in the profile information. The only way to *un*memorialize the account was to fill out a form for Instagram and prove that you were the account holder. *Maybe* a hacker could do that, but . . .

Delilah called her new friends as soon as the post dropped. Fiona said it was a skilled hack, nothing more. Jasmine, in Berlin, tried to sound unaffected, but Delilah could tell she was shaken. Cory, whom she'd grown kind of close to, swore up and down that he absolutely did *not* break into Scarlet's account—that was bad karma. And Busy, who'd flown out to hang with Delilah after the Scarlet stuff went down, cutting her trip to France short, thought it was downright disrespectful—but also said, nervously, "I mean, *could* it be Scarlet?"

As for Delilah's take . . . well, she looked at the new girls now. "If you're asking me if I think she's still alive . . . I don't know."

The girls looked intrigued. "So you believe those sightings of her in, like, vacation spots?" Olive asked.

Romy nodded. "I heard someone just saw her in Hong Kong."

"It's hard to say." Delilah thought of the pale, still hand she'd seen the morning she'd woken up in Scarlet's bed. Whoever was in that bed wasn't breathing. But *was* it Scarlet? It wasn't like Delilah had pulled back the comforter to see for sure. Scarlet's mom seemed to think it had been her daughter, but maybe she was part of the ruse.

Then again, if Scarlet hadn't been next to Delilah, who had? Was that who was in the grave with Scarlet's name on it? One pulled string created a tangle of questions. It all seemed so far-fetched. It was enticing to consider that Scarlet's death could be a hoax, of course. But Delilah understood why everyone was so shaken up with this new post. It was delicious to think that Scarlet was a cat with nine lives, quick to spring back, gloriously eternal. And maybe that was the aim of this mystery post that had appeared on Scarlet's page—someone, not Scarlet, wanted to keep Scarlet's spirit alive forever. After all, just because someone was gone didn't mean a fandom had to die.

Suddenly, Katie's eyes widened, and she clutched Romy's arm. "Oh my God."

Romy followed her gaze and let out a similar squeal. "Is that . . . ?"

Delilah shaded her eyes to see what they were freaking out over. A figure strode across the green toward them. It was a tall guy with floppy chestnut hair. He was wearing a T-shirt and jeans and looked unassuming enough—the kind of guy one might pass on the street and think nothing of, only to turn back and be like, *Wait, that guy was gorgeous.*

"Jack," Ava whispered, squeezing Delilah's hand.

Delilah's heart thudded hard. She hadn't seen Jack since he showed up at the police station months before. Not long after that, in an attempt to cut ties with his dad, he'd moved out of his family home and spent a few months camping in the Pacific Northwest. He'd posted a few videos here and there, but mostly, he'd been off the grid. And while he'd kept in touch with Delilah—sending her beautiful images of mountain vistas and enormous Oregon pine trees and the blue-gray Pacific Ocean from a brand-new, unknown-number phone—she had no idea when he was coming back. Or even *if* he was coming back. Scarlet's fate had rattled him, too.

But now here he was. Walking toward her with a shaky smile. Everything else dissolved. Delilah stepped forward tentatively, feeling nervous. This was the first time, she realized, that she and Jack were talking together in public . . . and not trying to hide.

"H-how did you find me here?" she babbled when he got close.

"I went by your house," Jack admitted. "Said you were getting a school tour." He looked around appreciatively. "This place is sick. Kinda makes me miss high school . . . though not entirely."

Then he turned back to her. "I got back this morning. I wanted to see you."

Delilah blinked. "You did?" she said stupidly. The words felt gummed up in her mouth. "I'm glad."

There was a thoughtful, almost distracted look on Jack's face. "I've done a lot of thinking. About me. My career. Where things are going."

"Me too." Then Delilah chuckled and gestured at the school grounds. "Hence me doing school instead of delving headfirst into the void of influencers."

"I think it's a good decision," Jack said. "I mean, you should be an influencer, if you want. But . . . you can be a lot of other things, too. Keep your options open." Then his green eyes sharpened a little. "I thought a lot about you while I was gone."

Delilah's heart skipped. She stared down at the recycled-bottle grass. "Same."

"And . . . I owe you an apology. We met in such terrible circumstances . . . but that doesn't mean I wanted to keep things secret. Had I been braver, I would have broken things off with Scarlet the day we met."

Delilah scoffed. "Oh, I would have never wanted you to do *that.*"

"But that's how strongly I felt about you." Jack's brow furrowed. "I hate how I behaved. Making you feel like we had to sneak around, not condemning those fans more when they gossiped about you being the Mystery Girl. I shouldn't have hidden you. You're way better than that. I should have stood up to my dad, Scarlet, those fans—everyone."

Delilah smiled, touched. Still, she thought he was being too hard on himself. "I tried to hide as much as you did. And no offense, but your dad is *brutal*."

"I know." Jack sighed. "But I talked to him. *Really* talked to him. Scarlet's death has knocked some sense into him, anyway. We're parting ways, professionally. Gonna just try and be dad and kid again. I'm not really sure how that's going to go—probably terribly—but I need him out of my business."

"Oh. Wow." Delilah rocked on her heels. "That's great."

Then he stepped a little closer. She could smell creamy sunscreen wafting from his skin. "But even if I was still working with my dad, I would have put my foot down about you. This is my life. I'm dating who I want." He bit his lip. "If you're still interested."

Delilah blinked, letting this sink in. Here it was: the opportunity to date Jack Dono, without complications. Could she do that? Could she dive into his arms?

But she took a breath. "I've been thinking." She noticed Jack's face fall and waved a hand. "No, I *do* want to be with you. I just . . . I'm not sure I want to be, you know . . . a *ship*."

Jack blinked. "You mean on Instagram? With fans?" He chuckled. "Oh God, we *absolutely* don't have to be Instagram official. We can be as private or as public as you want."

Delilah nodded, a giddy feeling rising in her chest. That was what she wanted: some control. They'd probably end up being a ship anyway, especially if they both maintained some sort of presence online. People would snap photos of them the first time they walked a red carpet together, or when they canoodled at a restaurant, or in matching sunglasses, hiking in the canyons. (All of those fantasy dates sounded amazing.) She just didn't want any of it to be contrived. *Staged.*

"Promise me we'll never do apology videos," she said. "Or present-swapping vlogs. Or exploit our relationship in any way."

"I am totally on board." Jack's smile was broad and real. "Well. Unless . . ."

"Unless *what*?"

He leaned in close, his lips touching her ear, which sent tingles down her spine. "Unless our videos are about Tide Pods. Or My Little Pony."

Delilah's eyes lit up, and she erupted into giggles. The alter egos they made up when they met: he remembered. And suddenly, she knew this was going to work. Ship fans or no ship fans, ups and downs, apologies and complications and fan gossip and sightings and photobombs, what she was going to have with Jack wasn't going to be something just for people to aspire to.

It was going to be real.

ACKNOWLEDGMENTS

LILIA

First and foremost, I want to thank the incredibly talented Sara Shepard. For a woman with her success, she is so humble and willing to take chances on the people and stories she believes in. A year ago, I came to Sara with this little idea, nervous and intimidated and, well . . . fangirling. But she welcomed me and my little idea with open arms, and I could not be more grateful for that. Sara, thank you for helping me bring this fantasy to life. I'm lucky to have you as a mentor and partner but most importantly as a friend.

Thank you to Wendy and the hardworking team at Random House who loved our story as much as we did. Without you guys, none of this would be possible!

To my wonderful team, Nick, Tim, and Andy. Thank you for having faith in me and constantly supporting me through it all. Having people behind you who truly care about your well-being is a blessing, and somehow, I got lucky enough to have all of you. You've all made this possible for me, so here's to many more creative endeavors with this dream team!

And to all of my amazing friends who validated my ideas and listened as I read them one hundred variations of the same sentence because I wasn't sure which one sounded best. You guys have been with me through it all, and I thank you for sticking by my side no matter what. I love you all.

Lastly, thank you to my followers and supporters. Words cannot describe the impact all you beautiful people have made on my life. Your words of love and support keep me going, and my world would be a much darker place if it weren't for your sweet comments, edits, and accounts. You guys make it possible for me to live my dreams every day, and for that, I am eternally grateful.

SARA

Just as Lilia thanked me first, I want to thank her first. The world of influencers is mostly a mystery to me (though it's certainly something I'm obsessed with), and to have Lilia as real-life inspiration was just incredible. I remember Lilia sending me the idea for this story in the summer of 2018—I was at an amusement park—and literally getting so excited I stepped out of a line for a roller coaster to write back that I wanted to work on it, much to my kids' chagrin. The characters on these pages are Lilia's creation; the scenarios and scenes are from things she regularly experiences. (Well. Except for the murder.) It was fantastic to sit down with Lilia and map out what these characters were going through and how their lives would end up. Lilia, thank you for all the creativity and thoughtfulness and, most importantly, the *content* you've brought to this project. It's been so much fun to work with you.

Next, thank you to Wendy Loggia, Audrey Ingerson, and the amazing team at Delacorte Press. I've wanted to work with you guys again for years and I'm so happy that we're finally together again! I'm so happy you championed this project, and your insights about the plotting and the manuscript were so vital. I hope we do many more books together!

Thank you also to Andy McNicol, Althea Schenck, and Jill Gillett at WME for also believing in this project. Thanks to Jane, Lilia's mom, for connecting Lilia and me, throwing great parties, and being one of the smartest, savviest people I know—and raising a great daughter. Thanks also to my family—Michael, Kristian, and Henry—for your endless support. And thanks, too, to Lilia's fans—and my own. Your support is amazing! I wish there were actually a Gratitude function on Instagram that could issue exploding praying-hands emojis, because that's what I'd extend to all of you.

That said, I also want to say one more thing about the content of this book. *Influence* includes a lot of bullying and nastiness, and I want to make it clear that it's something I don't condone. I truly hope that the internet becomes a kinder, more accepting place, not a more hateful one. So please, think before you post a comment. Consider that on the other end of an account, there's a living, breathing person with feelings. Be good to one another. And sometimes? Even step away from your phone altogether. It'll be okay, I promise!

ABOUT THE AUTHORS

SARA SHEPARD is the #1 *New York Times* bestselling author of the Pretty Little Liars series, The Perfectionists series, and many more novels for teens and adults. She lives with her family in Pittsburgh.

saracshepard.com

LILIA BUCKINGHAM is a seventeen-year-old writer, actress, dancer, and student. With a strong social media presence, Lilia hates the term "influencer" but loved writing *Influence.* She lives in Los Angeles with her mother, brother, and two dogs.

liliabuckingham.com